BLACK EASTER

BLACK EASTER

Dario Ciriello

Panverse Publishing

Cover by Janice Hardy

Published by Panverse Publishing
Altadena, CA 91001

Visit Panverse Publishing online at www.panversepublishing.com

First edition December 2015

Printed in the United States of America

ISBN 978-1-940581-85-9

ACKNOWLEDGMENTS

No book is written in a vacuum, and I have many people to thank for their support, assistance, and invaluable insights without which this novel wouldn't have been possible. I think I have all of you, but if I forgot anyone please accept my sincerest apologies.

Among the many who contributed in one way or another (and sometimes without realizing it!) are Griffin Barber, who, along with Rick Martinez, took an early interest and said the right words at the right time; Chuck Cherry, who answered all my questions on the inner workings and protocols of the Greek Orthodox Church and whose recommendations I followed faithfully with a single exception, which sin I hope Chuck will forgive me; and Steven F. Murphy, who put me in touch me with Chuck in the first place.

Among those who gave early input are Jon DelArroz, Angela Estes, Aidan Fritz, Herma Lichtenstein, and Setsu Uzume—thanks and hugs to all of you for being kind over an early partial.

Pre-final draft readers whose critiques and encouragement were of enormous help include Aliette de Bodard, Ken Liu, Bonnie Randall, and my wife Linda—all of you went above and beyond, and your laser-like insights exceeded all my expectations: I can't thank you enough.

To Janice Hardy, as always, my thanks for your wonderful graphic skills in designing the book's cover, and for graciously accommodating all my picky requests.

Finally, I want to express boundless gratitude to my loving wife Linda, without whose incredible patience, support, and encouragement throughout, I would long ago have thrown in the towel.

for Tony

my dear friend
who was always there for me,
even in the darkest days

PART ONE

CHAPTER ONE

January, 2014

"Anástasi," said Elléni, the realtor, as she dropped the little Fiat down into first and pulled it around a hairpin turn. "You look for *anástasi.*"

Paul turned. "I'm sorry?" He'd been gazing out at the rain-dimmed landscape below, hoping but failing to catch a glimpse of the sea. Rags of cloud, wind-shredded as the sails of any haunted wreck, shrouded the olive groves to merge seamlessly into a leaden sky. The Fiat picked up speed.

"To be born again. You want the new life."

Paul made an involuntary sound, a chuff of surprised amusement. Resurrection. Damn if she wasn't right. "I suppose I do," he said, and smiled despite himself.

"Eh, you see. And I think you have come to the right place."

A sudden squall hit them, drumbeat tattoo on the car's roof. Elléni slowed again, flipping the little Fiat's wipers to high. The clouds pressed down, and a runnel of muddy water thick as a man's thigh poured along the middle of the road beneath them. A muttered curse from the woman made him grin.

"So why have you choose Vóunos, Mister Hátzis?" she asked. "Your name I think is from Peloponnese?"

"My father's family. And call me Paul." He turned back to the window as they bounced along past one of the island's innumerable tiny churches and chapels. This one was a little larger than most, and immaculately kept, with bright-glazed plates randomly inset in the stucco walls and a low wall separating it from the road. Just beyond, a dirt road forked away into thinning woods to the right. Elléni steered them onto it, slowing the car to walking pace.

"Most people they choose the tourist islands like Mykonos and Santorini. There is very little to do here, especially in winter. You will not be bored?"

Paul smiled. "I don't bore easily. I found Vóunos in 1978 and loved it. I'd just finished my studies and was bumming around Europe. Then in 1996 my ex and I were on a sailing tour of the Northern Aegean with some friends. We anchored here for three days, exploring and swimming, eating and drinking." It would have been just an overnight if Karen and the others had had their way, but he'd insisted, and been dubbed Robinson Crusoe for the rest of the voyage.

"Can you see the sea?" he added. "From the house, I mean?"

"Oh, yes! Of course, today you will not. But it is very nice view." She twitched the wheel to the right to avoid a football-sized rock on the track. "Also as you see, we are only three kilometers from town." She pushed the gearshift back into first to negotiate another tight bend. An outcrop of broken rock loomed close and sudden at Paul's right, and woody green scrub brushed his window as if to rake dark fingers across his cheek. They crested a small rise and the track dead-ended in a patch of grass.

Elléni yanked on the handbrake. "And so, we have arrived." She pushed back a hank of wavy chestnut hair that had fallen across her face, dislodging in the process the silver-on black crucifix hanging from the rearview on its silver chain. Paul felt it brush his thigh as it fell. He released his seat belt and dipped to retrieve it, feeling around on the mat in the gloom by his feet. The woman leaned over, looking down.

"Hold on…" He opened his door to let in more light. Rain like cold scattershot hit him, borne on a wild gust. "It must have gone under the seat," he said.

They palmed about on the floor mats and under the front seats as best they could, probed inside the narrow space between seat and handbrake. The woman made a dismissive gesture. "I will find it after. Come."

The wind rose to a moan as they closed the car doors. Paul had donned his old Barbour jacket, veteran of many climes, and was glad for it. An umbrella would have been useless with these wild gusts. He took a floppy fisherman's hat from his pocket, pushed it down on his head, and turned his collar up against the storm. Elléni, wrapped in a bright red raincoat, covered her head with a woolen scarf. Strands of free hair whipping in the wet wind, she seemed unperturbed by the weather.

She was a tall woman and attractively built, with generous curves and warm brown eyes under accurately waxed brows. Her makeup was restricted to eyeliner and eyeshadow: her skin didn't need it. The essence of the Greek woman, rich and openly sensual.

He took a deep breath, forcing his mind back to the place. The heavy air smelt of wet earth, of the sea, of ancient memory. It was important to him, the sea, isolating and calming, with a deeper intimation of the unifying, the eternal. And if one wanted a sea, what better than the wine-dark Aegean, with its myths and heroes?

The house stood before them, as though it had always been. Elléni gestured as if introducing a person. "'The stone house,' they call it. It is from before the war."

The war. Seventy years past, and yet here they still spoke as if it were a recent event. Even this young rental agent, who probably wasn't even forty. But Greeks had especially long memories for these things, and the islands, even the small ones, hadn't escaped German or Italian occupation.

The stone house. No mystery about its name. The place was a sizeable two-story built in the traditional fashion from rough blocks of common brown fieldstone and accented by blue-shuttered windows. Water streamed from downspouts at each corner. The walls looked in a good state of repair, the red-tiled roof less so in places. Elléni caught his gaze. "Yes, a few tiles are broken. We can get a man to replace. But I think you will not have water inside."

Remnants of a low stone wall were visible off to the left beyond a small orchard. On the right side of the house, the direction from which they had come, a cobbled patio extended a half-dozen yards to where the land dropped away. Anything beyond was lost in the murk.

"As you see, you have apricots and plum trees," said Elléni. "And at the back, some lotus fruit."

"Lotus...." His mind went immediately to mythology, and long, dreamless sleeps. Then, "Oh, persimmons? With the creamy yellow insides?"

"Exactly! They are my favourite, very good to eat. Come," she said, and gestured towards the faded blue door.

It was dark inside—the electricity was off—and Paul peered about while Elléni circled the room, opening windows and shutters for light.

The ground floor was a single, huge room. There was a large traditional fireplace fronted by a rounded hearth in the far left corner of the spacious living area; a pine-framed sofa and a blue-upholstered wingback chair, both well-used but comfortable–looking, faced it. To the left of that, along the entry wall below the stair, was a raised platform with a wide communal bed of the sort loved by the Greeks. A scarred pine table with six of the little wicker-seat chairs found at every taverna throughout Greece, and a long, low credenza defined the dining area. The bare walls looked as though they'd been freshly whitewashed.

Against the wall to the immediate right of the front door was an old but well-kept wood-burning stove. Beyond that, the kitchen that occupied the near right corner of the ground floor was small but adequate, with white-painted cabinets and drawers below an L-shaped counter that served as both room divider and breakfast bar. There was a modern, four-burner propane stove by the sink.

Paul liked the feel of the place immediately. Chill and damp as the air inside was, there was something safe, welcoming about the house, like a sanctuary.

"If it is very cold, you can use this wood stove also for extra heat," said Elléni. "The fireplace is good, but with only this you can heat the whole house."

"And for wood…?"

"There is one small building to keep this, and already it is full of dry wood. Also you have a cellar where you can keep wine."

He nodded. Eighteen-inch stone walls, hardwood floor beneath colourful scatter rugs. The house would stay cool in the island's hot summers.

"Who owns it?"

"Ah. It is strange story. They say one English family has owned it for many years, but we have instructions from one lawyer in Athens. As you see they keep it in good condition. It has been empty for some time, but they pay one old couple to come every week to keep clean and open the windows for fresh air, and to heat it every few days in the winter. I have permission to hire people to make any repairs. Also this old couple makes a little work in the garden and orchard."

Upstairs were three bedrooms and a single bath with a magnificent claw-foot tub; the enamel on the rim was chipped in two places to reveal the cast iron beneath, but the interior was pristine and free of scale. There was no shower. The largest of the three bedrooms overlooked the stone patio.

As Paul stood at the open window, the mist magically parted to give a brief, rain-blurred view down the low valley to the village and its semicircular harbor, where heavy seas exploded against the breakwater. A moment later, the mist was back, the view gone.

"I'll take it," he said.

‡

He signed the papers the next morning, a two-year lease, and paid the first three months' rent, eighteen hundred Euros, in advance. Paul's spoken Greek, picked up from his father in childhood and during the family's infrequent pilgrimages to visit family, was barely serviceable; his written language was worse. Nonetheless, he insisted on slogging through every document, frequently asking a patient Elléni to translate unfamiliar words or phrases, before the customary sign-countersign-rubber-stamp-and-notarize ritual. Greek professionals of every stripe loved their rubber stamps.

Elléni handed him three copies of the lease. "You will need these for the electricity and telephone companies." She opened a drawer, fished around, and handed him a pair of shiny new keys. "I will send a man to do the roof work as we said, but you can move in when you like."

She had other business to conduct, and left with him. Paul didn't have a car and the rain had started up again, so she offered him a ride back to the little cottage he'd rented.

"Actually, I'm going to the internet café," he said. "It's not far."

"You will be very wet," she said. The car bipped as she thumbed the door remote. She held open the passenger door for him and gestured with her head. "Come."

"Did you find your crucifix?" he said, indicating the unadorned rearview.

Elléni laughed. "Yes. All the time it was on your seat, but we did not see." She put the little car in gear and set off down the narrow lane. "Do you have furnitures coming from San Francisco?"

He shook his head. "I sold most of what I had and put the rest in storage. There isn't much." Actually, beyond a dozen of his mother's best watercolours, there was quite little. Some books and papers, music and a player, a couple of photo albums, some family keepsakes. Antique dealers came in two sorts, those who accumulated possessions and those who didn't. He was in the latter category.

"You will need a car, also," she said, waving to someone as they passed the post office. "You can buy a used one from the rental company, I know the man who owns it. They always have for sale."

"Thanks." Paul pursed his lips. "I'm thinking a motorcycle, too."

"Yes, this is good for the summer. You can buy one small Honda also here on Vóunos."

He grinned. "I want something larger, a real motorcycle. It's been a long time since I had one."

A veritable pond had formed where the road dipped, and Elléni slowed to navigate it. She gave him a veiled smile, as though he'd revealed a small secret. "A big motorcycle. For your *anástasi,* eh?"

For his rebirth. He nodded.

Maybe.

‡

At the internet café he ordered a frappé and sent two emails. The first was to Charly, his sister, telling her about the house and confirming he'd be able to accommodate her and Alex, his niece, if they cared to visit in the summer. He was glad to not have to include Wayne, Charly's recently-ejected and soon-to-be second ex-husband of four years. A self-centered, macho son-of-a-bitch whom Paul had mistrusted from the beginning, though he'd made every effort to get along and conceal his feelings for Charly's sake. Of course, she'd seen through him almost at once.

"You don't like him, do you?" she said, with typical directness.

"I don't *dis*like him," he lied, "I just don't think we have much—"

"Is it the sports thing?" Wayne was a sports reporter for the *San Francisco Chronicle.* "That's just his job, you know. It's not who he is."

Sport was the dividing line between them, had been since Charly was a kid. In that regard, she was fully their father's daughter. Dad had expected only two things of his kids: that they have children and share his passion for sports. Despite being the successful one, Paul had failed him in both regards.

And sports was *totally* who Wayne was. So when the scandal blew up last fall, Paul was vindicated. But he felt his sister's pain as though it were his own, and never crowed.

The second email was to Alison at the property management agency, confirming that he'd decided to stay at least a year or so and instructing her to go ahead and lease out the house. The income would comfortably cover his expenses here. Not that money was a problem; with a hair over a million in various investments and his mortgage paid off, it never should be. It was everything *else* that ground at his soul.

He felt his thoughts starting to tread old, shadowed alleys. *No. Not going there, time to go, get into the sunlight.* He went to the counter and settled the bill for his frappé and the internet time. As he left, he noticed one of the village priests—they'd passed more than once in the street—sitting at one of the two outdoor tables nursing a lemonade. The priest, a big man with huge hands, and young, grinned at him. A big, well-worn leather satchel hung from the back of his chair.

"*Kaliméra*," said the priest. And still in Greek, "You're new."

Paul nodded. "I am," he replied in his halting Greek. "I just moved here."

The man waved him into the chair across the table. Paul hesitated—his first instinct was always to make an excuse—but the priest casually extended a leg under the table and pushed the chair out. "Come," he said. "The first rule here is never to hurry." His grin broadened, and Paul caught a glint of gold in his mouth. Cleric or not, there was something raffish, almost piratical about the man that he liked immediately.

The priest introduced himself as *o Pápas* Tákis. "Of course you can drop the 'Father', but since we are always on duty…" He pointed to his robes and chuckled.

Paul extended a hand and they shook. "I'm Paul. *Pávlos.* I just moved here from the US. San Francisco, actually."

The priest nodded. "San Francisco. You know," he said, leaning forward and looking theatrically around as though someone might overhear, "I'm rather an admirer of St. Francis."

Paul's mouth may have opened slightly. One thing he really didn't need was religion. He wondered if sitting down might have been a mistake.

"Yes," said Father Tákis, probably mistaking his silence for interest. "Although he's not recognized in the Orthodox church, he was really the first environmentalist. Are you fond of nature, Pávlos?"

Paul relaxed as the subject veered away from religion. "I really am. And it's something I've..." he struggled to find the Greek word for *neglected*, and failed, "not been doing. Getting outdoors and just walking. I want to do a lot of that here, spend time in the woods and hills."

"It's good for the soul. I'm from Tríkkala, off in the northwest. It's a big town, but surrounded by great, wild mountains. I used to love to walk in them. And nearby is Meteora, where the monks live hundreds of meters up in the monasteries on top of the tall rocks." He shuddered. "Not for me! One earthquake and..." He made a falling-down motion with his hands. "They're all mad, you know. Not one of them can fly!"

Paul started to laugh. *Well, well, an irreverent priest.* He was liking Vóunos more by the day.

‡

Much as Paul loved walking, he needed to get transport, and quickly. He lived three kilometers from town and he'd been lucky not to get caught in a heavy rain yet. Elléni had given him the home number for the owner of the car rental agency—the business was closed for the winter—and a few days later Paul bought one of the ubiquitous little Pandas, a three-year-old model in slightly sun-faded red with forty thousand kilometers on it. It was basic transport, but the engine was strong and the tires had plenty of tread on them. It would serve him perfectly well.

CHAPTER TWO

Friday March, 14, 2014

It was, he supposed, a date. No: it was *definitely* a date.

In the six weeks since Paul's arrival, Elléni had gone out of her way to help him get services connected—the internet had been especially challenging—and most of all to walk him through the bureaucratic thickets of buying the big KTM dirt bike and getting it insured. He could have bought a house in the States with less trouble and paperwork, not to mention the two trips to Thessaloniki. But in the end it was done. He'd found her both intelligent and thoughtful from the beginning, but he'd suspected for some weeks now that her solicitude towards him went beyond simple professional courtesy. And his interest in her was undeniable.

The day was sunny, with a breath of spring in the air. Paul was just leaving the post office when he saw the familiar little blue Fiat pull up. Elléni beckoned him over and rolled down the window. After a little small talk, she said, "Do you have a plan tomorrow night?"

The question caught him off-balance. She meant, of course, was he doing anything. He shook his head. "No. My social calendar is quite empty." He kept it to a wry smile. Other than a few chats with Nikos, the hardware store owner, and a beer in the store with him last week when things were slow, the only other person he'd spoken to at any length was Father Tákis. Beyond that, Paul had kept pretty much to himself. "Why do you ask?"

Elléni pushed her lustrous hair off her face. The action made him think of Stacy, his ex; he pushed the image away. Old tape.

"The Poseidon café is opening early this year. It is very nice place. I am meeting some friends there and I thought you will enjoy this."

"Ah. Well, I…." He was still enjoying his time alone, and really didn't want to deal with a gaggle of strangers—too much work, and he'd never been big on socializing in groups. But caught off guard, he couldn't think of any reason to refuse that wouldn't be seen as rude, and after all she'd done for him he didn't want to offend her. Especially when her warm brown eyes had him trapped like that. He nodded. "I'd be delighted."

That brought a smile. She placed a hand on his where it rested on the windowsill. Her hand was warm, and the unexpected touch a strange thrill. "Wonderful! Then you will come at ten. We shall have drinks and good food and you will meet very nice people."

‡

The Poseidon café was a warm cave in a narrow lane off the paralía, or seafront—the *strand*, he supposed would be the most accurate term, except nobody who didn't read nineteenth-century literature would ever use the word. Heat from the open kitchen and a big woodburning stove kept the dozen or so locals in the place cozy.

The *very nice people*, whom Elléni introduced as her best friends, were named Anna and Stávros. They ran a tour agency. He'd passed their office several times. Anna was both lean and petite, with a shock of short black hair in a severely contemporary cut; Stávros was a six-foot slab of a man who could have been a wrestler. Both looked in their late forties.

Paul's visceral discomfort at being cornered into a group social situation started to dissolve over ouzo and plates of mezés, small appetizers which could be anything from feta and olives to bites of spicy sausage to tiny grilled fish. In two months of full immersion his Greek had improved enormously, and once the other couple realized his relative fluency, the conversation switched entirely to Greek.

His desire to keep a distance and not form close bonds wasn't the only thing that seemed to be dissolving with exposure to the natural beauty and close community of the island. The cloud of negativity which had been his companion for the last three years, though he hardly dared believe it, appeared to be lifting. Some would call it depression; as a stoic, he hated the concept. He didn't have time for counselors, happy pills, and self-pity. His brain chemistry was just fine—he just needed to find a new purpose, to reorient after the chaos of the last years.

But in just a few weeks on Vóunos, with its sheltering isolation and absence of crime, its lack of artifice and crowds, he was starting, tortoise-like, to peek out of his shell. Perhaps Elléni had been right when she spoke of his *anástasi*.

By the second round of drinks, with the introductory casual banter out of the way, Anna asked, "So did you come here to retire?"

Paul wiped his mouth. "Perhaps. I'm not really sure."

Stávros tilted his head. "A year or two is a long break. Did you leave a job, Pávlo? A family?"

He was aware of Elléni watching him. "Just one sister, and my niece, Alex. They'll come to visit in the summer. As for work, I'm in the antiques business. *Was,* really. I sold my share of the business to my partner." He wasn't going to go into the other stuff with strangers.

"You must have done well," said Stávros. "I wish it were the same for us. But even with the slowdown in tourism, life is good here." He called for another round.

"Elléni tells me you rented the stone house," said Anna.

Paul speared a piece of sausage. "I did. And I love it."

"It was empty for many years," said Stávros.

Anna snorted. "Many years? It's been empty ever since the war!"

Paul smiled, just a bit puzzled. Elléni hadn't mentioned that. "My luck, then."

The drinks arrived, another four tiny individual bottles of ouzo, with a plate of olives and feta; Anna, who'd passed on the sausage in observance of Lent, served herself at once. Everyone refreshed their own glasses and Stávros raised his for a toast. "Yamas! Perhaps you'll also bring our island luck. Obviously you're not superstitious, eh?"

The ouzo was good, warming. "No. Why?"

Stávros glanced at Elléni, seemed to hesitate. "Well…there are some stories about the stone house."

"Oh?" Paul felt a chill settle on the table. Where was this going? He plucked an olive from his plate, chewed on it. "Elléni said it was owned by an English family. Do you know them?"

Stávros tilted his head backwards, eyebrows raised, in the silent Greek *no.*

Paul chuckled. "All right, so are you trying to tell me it's haunted or something?"

Anna leaned forward, palms on the table. "I must tell you that your house has a very bad history. They say it was used for devil worship. Satanism!"

His mind slipped a gear. *Oh fuck, not cults again.* But after a second

11

the sheer, unexpected melodrama cracked him up. "I'm sorry," he said. "Satanism?"

Anna looked offended. "It is true!" She turned to her husband. "Stávro, tell him!"

Stávros gave a half-shrug. "They say that during the war it was owned by a black magician, a sorcerer. That some bad things happened there. Of course, these are just stories."

"Sacrifices!" hissed Anna. "*Human* sacrifices!"

"Understand, Pávlo," Stávros's upright index finger invoked reason over superstition, "we islanders have wild imaginations. Over decades small stories and minor events grow into crazy legends. Every island in the Aegean has a story about someone being chased by *o Diávolos.*"

Anna looked a bit put out at her husband's light dismissal of a matter she obviously considered serious, but she left it at that.

Paul turned to Elléni for comment. She just raised her palms and made a "whatever" face, disowning the entire conversation.

"Ahh. So you rented me a haunted house," he said, teasing. "Do I get a discount?"

Straight-faced, she replied, "If you're woken by devils, we'll discuss it then. Yamas!" She raised her glass, clinked it against his. Both of them laughed, and Stávros signaled the waiter for another round of drinks.

Talk turned to Easter, which that year fell on April 20th—unusually, the same date as Easter in the West. As everywhere in Greece, it was the highlight of the year. There would be processions all through the island and celebrations with family and friends.

Lanced by an odd pang of loneliness, Paul had the sudden, crazy notion of inviting Alex for Easter. Charly wouldn't be able to come, but Alex would be on spring break. He could meet her in Thessaloniki and she could still come with her mother in the summer, as he'd promised. With Easter still over a month away, there was plenty of time to buy a ticket and make arrangements.

It was gone one o'clock when they called it a night. Despite the many drinks, the steady flow of oily mezés had cushioned the alcohol so that Paul just had a pleasant buzz. The party shrugged on jackets and coats and, as Stávros and Anna led the way to the door, Paul found Elléni's arm had wound into his. He half-turned; she smiled at him and upped the ante by slipping her hand into his and giving it a brief squeeze. Well, now.

It had begun to drizzle. Stávros and Anna's home was just a brief walk away; Elléni's was further, and Paul asked if he could give her a ride. She assented, favouring him with a huge smile.

"So did you enjoy the evening?" she asked, as he buckled his seat belt. In typical Greek fashion, Elléni ignored hers.

"Very much. Good people." After a moment, he added, "Anna seemed very serious about the stone house. Its history, I mean."

"You seemed quite shocked when she mentioned it. You went very pale."

He shrugged it off. "I thought I was back in California for a moment. Old tapes," he said, touching his temple. "Dead and gone."

Her laugh was a chime. "Don't let it worry you. As Stávros said, we islanders love our ghost stories. Anything mysterious or unexplained is like a magnet for our imagination. In a tiny community cut off from the world by dozens of kilometers of sea in every direction, reality is more plastic than in a large city. Take the next left."

He nodded. The rain-slick cobbled lanes were narrow, and of course Greeks parked everywhere, so that he had to thread his way along at not much more than walking pace.

Imagination and legend, yes, he got that. But, human sacrifice? That was pushing the boundaries of all imagining. "I'd certainly be interested to know more about the place, though. Any suggestions how to go about it?"

"I can ask my yayá," said Elléni. Her grandmother. "She's lived all her life on Vóunos, and her memory's all there, even at eighty-six."

"Does she live with you?"

A shake of the head, hair a molten cascade in the dashboard light. "No, with my parents in Mikró Kástro."

Mikró Kástro, the island's second village, was a sleepy fishing harbour on the east of the island, about a thirty-minute drive. He'd spent a cold, blowy day there just after buying the car, poking around on the pebbled shore among the wrack of the winter storms. At the far end of the beach, on a sudden crag that leaned over the restless blue, was an immaculate little monastery. The tourist sign proclaimed that it had once been a Venetian fort. The village itself was a somnolent place, with a single café open and a strong sense of everyone hiding indoors. Wandering the streets, he saw several houses which had clearly been abandoned and left to rot.

Elléni's raised hand brought him back to the now. They'd reached her house, a narrow, nineteenth-century building. The windows had peaked pediments. The shutters—blue, of course—looked freshly-painted.

She turned to him. "Would you like to come in for a drink? A coffee?"

His heart thumped. Was that an invitation to stay? He wasn't yet sure what customs and mores held on the island. Still, Elléni was an independent professional woman. He didn't imagine sex on a first date was a no-no, especially as she was the one who'd opened the door to the possibility..

It had been almost a year since he'd slept with anyone and his blood raced at the thought. But this wasn't San Francisco. This was a small, a *tiny,* island, a pressure cooker community in which everyone knew everyone. And he was an outsider, a *xénos.* One good error of judgment would make him the subject of gossip and possibly get him ostracized, and heaven knew what the fallout for Elléni might be. A casual lay, though increasingly attractive as he hesitated in the grip of those lambent eyes, was probably a really bad idea. He doubted that *friends with benefits* operated here. Plus he liked her, liked her a lot. Much as he craved warmth and intimacy, he wanted to keep her friendship.

"I, ah…. You know, I'm still not used to keeping such late hours," he improvised, though it was also true. "I'm pretty well fading. In the 'States we eat dinner at six and go to bed by ten. But maybe we can go out again soon?" *Idiot. In an hour you'll regret this.*

She made it easy. "I'd like that." It came out softly, almost a breath, the settling of a gossamer net. As he unbuckled his seat belt, she leaned in towards him in the dark, one hand going to his shoulder, and brushed her lips against his. The kiss was precise, her lips velvet-soft. His heart definitely stopped.

"Well," she said, pulling back with a smile, gaze lowered; in someone else he'd have interpreted that as modesty or mild regret, but neither was her style.

And then he was hurrying around to her side of the car, opening the door for her. She took his arm for the four steps to her front door and he hovered as she opened it—it was unlocked, as was normal here.

"Thanks again," he said. "I'll call you during the week."

Which got a big smile.

This time he was the one who leaned in. Their lips met again, current arced, and each withdrew as if by mutual agreement—this could easily escalate out of control, passion trumping reason. Two singles on a cold night, each perhaps needing love, each unmistakably interested in the other. Her lips were still slightly parted, her cheeks distinctly flushed.

He held up a palm, retreated a step, then two. "Well, goodnight."

CHAPTER THREE

May 1934

The wind came off the Sahara and seared its way north, leaving a thin reddish dust everywhere and painting the waxing moon the colour of blood. It blew hot and hard, ruffling the sea and making the passage lively.

Dafyd spent a good deal of time on deck, watching the shimmering, limpid-eyed undines gambol in the salt spray with the wind-quick zephyrs. Twice the ferry passed near an ancient wreck, and Dafyd, eyes half-lidded and defenses down, touched the unquiet ghosts of long-drowned Greeks and Phoenicians fallen to the treacherous Levant gales that shrieked between the Pillars of Hercules.

He drank it all in thirstily. Two years in the North African desert had left him dry and parched of blue and wet, as if he had himself become a creature of the desert, some orange-brown chitinous thing that scurried from rock to rock under the hammer of the pitiless sun.

Orange-brown, like the ruddy glow in the desert night as he and Magda had run from the pyre that was the Lodge. The image of Maurice, ablaze and screaming as the damned fool—now truly damned—lurched about the room before collapsing in a final burst of purifying flame, was impossible to dispel. Magda had lunged forward to help him, and only Dafyd's own magical defenses and the hysterical strength of the moment saved her life. You couldn't help a man burning from within, and you couldn't fight the thing the fool had allowed in—you could only run.

Run they had, down the narrow alleys in the still Moroccan night, while others ran *towards* the blaze, the fools. The fire, they could contain; the demon, Crane…it would be recalled, but only after it had taken a few more souls. Thankfully, it was one of the weaker of its kind.

They'd snatched up their coats along with Dafyd's wallet and Magda's handbag, and fled before the echoes of Maurice's screams even faded. Found a taxi to the port and paid a fisherman who was just setting out for the night to take them across to Gibraltar and safety. It was only once they were at sea that she'd begun to tremble from the shock.

There'd been a week-long business in Gibraltar over passports and all that nonsense. But if the Moroccan police, who had records on him and the others, had notified the authorities in Gibraltar of the suspicious fire and death, it had come too late. The *quartier* would have been in uproar for a few days and the police, anxious to pin the blame on someone, would probably arrest and convict some local they had it in for. Sentencing and imprisonment, possibly execution, would be swift, and the case closed. And even if he, the vanished foreigner, were held responsible, shoulders would simply be shrugged. The judiciary in these countries was generally more concerned with expediency than justice.

From Gibraltar they crossed to La Linea in Spain, and thence set off by train from Algeciras in a great arc around to Genoa, and the boat for Piraeus in Greece.

The time in Spain had been tense, and both of them—at his insistence—had avoided reflecting on what had happened. Better not to feed the mishap with more energy. Instead, they passed the week largely in meditation, forcing themselves into the present rather than focusing on the unpleasantness they'd left behind in the burning Lodge. He hoped she was over the shock of Maurice's death, but he needed to be sure.

They shared a first-class sleeper compartment for the train journey, glad to be leaving Spain. They dressed for dinner—they had replaced their wardrobe essentials in Algeciras—in their little compartment, Dafyd going first while Magda arranged her mane of red hair in the minuscule *toilette;* when her turn came, he sat on the upper bunk so as to allow her room to move. Her nudity was of no concern to him, nor his to her: each had seen the other naked several times. Though she had a fine figure, the sight left him unstimulated. Years of self-discipline and the practice of conserving his sexual energy for higher uses had made him proof to the unwilled reactions ordinary men suffered.

The dining car was paneled in rich wood, with tables set for two on one side of the aisle and four on the other. The tablecloths were of fine linen, the place settings silver and crystal. As they made their way past other diners to one of the smaller tables, Dafyd was amused to note how each man's eyes settled—openly or covertly—on Magda. She had curled her hair, and the contrast of fiery tresses against the clinging ultramarine cocktail dress was evidently irresistible. Nor was she unaware of the fact—quite the opposite: a practitioner of the Art needed every ounce of energy they could acquire, whether stolen or freely given, and missed no opportunity to increase their store. That need, not any weak vanity, was why she took the trouble. And though he, with his pudgy and unremarkable build, gained far less from the effort, his own evening clothes gained him at least modest respect and attention. Every iota of others' regard made them stronger.

They sat facing one another, the small electric table lamp casting a warm pool in the car's subdued light. She ordered a Vichyssoise followed by lobster, he, a terrine and roast duck; which, put together, meant champagne. The waiter nodded appreciatively at his choice of the Pol Roger 1921 and floated elegantly away, an accomplished feat on a moving train.

"Five days and we'll be in Greece," said Dafyd.

Magda, gazing out at the twinkling lights of small villages in the deep black, nodded absently. She was on the fence, he could feel it. And he couldn't lose her.

He offered her a cigarette, a rare indulgence for both of them; she accepted. A moment later, the waiter returned with a glistening ice bucket.

As they sipped their champagne, he said, "So. Now Maurice is gone, will we find a new Third there?"

"I've scried it out. Everything tells me he'll find us."

He cocked her head. "He?" He'd have preferred a woman. Men were so prone to arrogance and over-confidence, and after Maurice…

"I'm certain of it. But it will be some years."

Magda's Sight was unerring. So their Third would again be a man. A trio was a necessity for higher-order summonings, and it had to comprise both genders. The lower entities and transitionals could be handled by one alone or a duo, but without the third leg of the tripod more ambitious work was too risky. Risky enough *with* a Third, should that Third prove unreliable. As Maurice had discovered.

When their first course arrived, the waiter reached for the champagne to top up their glasses. Dafyd held up a hand. "We'll serve ourselves, thank you." He wanted her to talk, to re-engage free of interruptions. He feared she might balk once he explained what he was really working towards.

She'd come to him just three months ago on the recommendation of a mutual friend, an Irish clairvoyant to whom Magda had confided her desire to study the Art. Unlike Maurice, who'd spent time in the Golden Dawn and already had some experience of magic, Magda brought only her phenomenal native talents as a seer. And that very innocence, the fact that she'd come to him as a *tabula rasa,* her powerful mind uncluttered by archaic models and wrong-headed notions, was a huge asset. He hoped that the new Third, when he appeared, would be equally inexperienced, ready to be shaped by Dafyd's teaching.

As they ate, the miles unspooling between them and the recent shock, Magda began to visibly relax. "Greece," she murmured. She sipped her champagne and turned again to the window as though she might see it out there somewhere. "I always thought I'd end up there."

He let out a breath. "So you'll stay on, work with me?"

Moss-green eyes settled on him. "What really went wrong in Morocco, Dafyd?"

And there, matter-of-fact, the question he'd known he would eventually have to answer. Though there was nobody at the tables immediately adjacent to them, he spoke in low tones. "I mostly blame Maurice, but I have to take some responsibility. I suspected that he still had doubts, that some part of him still clung to Aleister Crowley's Thelema teachings. But Crane was too severe a test for him—and, consequently, almost for us. Demons see all the way through the operator. The power was too much for a circuit that was weak and defective."

She continued to eat her soup. When he didn't elaborate, she cocked an eyebrow. "And?"

Dafyd smiled. She didn't miss a thing. "And I think we have to go back to the beginning," he said.

"By which you mean…?"

"A new approach. An entirely new system of magic. I've been considering this for some time, and the accident of the other week convinced me. With your agreement, I'd like us to approach it together."

She set her spoon facing precisely twelve o'clock in her empty bowl and leaned back in her chair, attentive.

He took a breath and began. "Every practitioner of the Art working today is using techniques and craft based on Dee and Kelley's work of the 1500s. My personal conviction is that much of Dee's knowledge is lost to us, and without that, we risk building increasingly flawed structures on poorly-understood foundations. Without ironclad technique and a fully-developed, internally consistent system of magic, the operator risks destruction when working with higher-order entities. We were lucky to get away at all."

"But then, Crowley and his colleagues, how did they survive? What stopped him and the entire Thelema Lodge going up in flames like…"

"Like Maurice? Simply put, they never dealt with any entity beyond the transitional orders—sprites, elementals, and the like. The idea that by intoning ancient so-called angelic names, silly words of power, and all the old Hebraic nonsense, not to mention Aleister's occasional perverted sexual acts at the altar—" acts which Dafyd had witnessed during his short time there, and found hard not to laugh at "—the idea that by these actions he became powerful is ridiculous. Aleister never achieved a single result that had repercussions in the real world. Real magic is a deadly dangerous business. And when things go wrong—as they sometimes will—you always look after yourself first, dear." He gave her a pointed look, which she acknowledged with lowered eyes and a small movement of her head.

He continued. "But Thelema? He snorted a laugh. "If they'd tapped into the real demonic sphere in their workings and encountered something like Crane, they'd have died on the spot, the lot of them. As it was, Mussolini got to them first and closed the Abbey in '23."

He sipped his champagne and went on. "Now, any magical system is just a vessel to contain and shape the power. Native witch doctor or Vodun priest, it doesn't matter. Even some of the Christian mystics could wield power. All that matters is internal consistency and the degree of alignment between system and operator." He paused to let his words sink in.

"So you're saying all magical systems are equal?"

"Yes, providing they're well-designed and consistent. It's no coincidence that the three greatest magicians in history—the Egyptian, Nakhte; John Dee in England; and the Paduan, Pio Gemelli—all developed their own systems. So while any well-designed framework can be effective, it will work best of all for its creator, since it's mapped directly to his psychic architecture."

She pursed her lips. "So, an entirely new system of magic. Intriguing. Where does one even begin?"

"Mathematics," he replied at once. "Mathematics and Geometry. From the Greek and Arab scholars on through Newton and our own Einstein, we learn that the cosmos entire is founded on numbers and their relationships. Whereas language is a mere human edifice, numbers are the foundation stones of the cosmos, divinity itself. Although, " he added, "I would keep the elemental correspondences as well as the cardinal points, the four quarters."

She looked puzzled. "Why?"

"Because unlike the medieval inventions, the Enochian Keys and all the rest, the elemental correspondences of Fire, Water, Air, and Earth go back millennia, possibly scores of millennia, to the very dawn of human thought. They're inextricably bound with consciousness."

"I see.. Yes, I suppose they are." She was silent a moment. "Where in Greece, Dafyd? Arcadia?"

It was a natural conclusion. The wild mountain province, legendary home of Dionysus. But he shook his head. "An island, where the elements are more balanced, would serve better. Tangiers was all Fire and Earth. I don't think that was helping us."

She seemed to contemplate her empty bowl. Then, "What was he really like?" she said. "Crowley, I mean?"

Dafyd refilled her glass, then his own. "Aleister, the Great Beast? Arrogant, brilliant, and ultimately deluded. Like all the rest of them—MacGregor Mathers, Waite, Regardie—his prime sin was that of laziness. What they were practicing was closer to Freemasonry than magic. I see it now, and yet I made the mistake of treading the same path. No more."

Her eyebrows went up. "Laziness? From what I've heard, I would have thought that the last thing that group would be guilty of."

"Oh, they worked hard enough, don't get me wrong. Obsessively, even. But their laziness was that of the Romans who, instead of inventing their own pantheon of Gods, simply adopted that of the Greeks and changed the names. Similarly, the Golden Dawn and its various offshoots just took Dee's work and built on it, instead of questioning its foundations and doing the hard work of starting from scratch." He paused as the waiter took their plates, then continued. "Aleister had the will, no doubt about that. But despite his blathering about religion as science he was still, for all his protestations, a Christian at his core. And for all his will and discipline with regard to the Art, he never saw the need to apply it to his own weaknesses and lusts. It was just lip service."

She frowned. "But haven't we been working in essentially the same tradition? And only now you come to see what all of them missed? At the fundamental level, I mean?"

Fair question. "I didn't see it until Tangiers, and Maurice. In the decade after leaving Thelema, all I did was build on those same tired old foundations. I'd learned everything of value which Aleister had to teach in my eighteen months there, and I tired of his arrogance and excesses. But although my doubts had been growing, I kept refining the old methods. I was blind. It took the accident in Tangiers to make me see my error." He leaned forward, dropping his voice further still. "At the same time, over these last years, I've finally begun to understand what demons really *are*."

"You've alluded to that."

He nodded, and popped the last point of toast spread with terrine in his mouth, savouring it slowly. They'd come to it: the moment of truth, the knowledge which would be the test of her true ambition. He went on. "Curiously, it was a writer of popular tales, macabre fictions, who pointed me onto the correct track. Once I took that first step, I studied alone until, by degrees, I uncovered the central truth: that what we historically see as demons are actually the *protectors* of the human sphere, not its oppressors. And if we want to survive we had better learn to communicate and work with them. Because what lies beyond is an abyssal, soul-consuming chaos that cares nothing about us. To the entities which rule that chaos, we're just food… because, in truth, humanity, far from being special, is an insignificant manifestation of the rampant life common in the universe."

Their entrees arrived, and they waited while the waiter split the lobster and cracked its claws, then deftly carved Dafyd's bird.

When he had served them both and retired, Magda said, "How pervasive are mankind's myths."

"Indeed. And how comforting to believe in Good and Evil, those two mutually dependent poles. Though he professed not to be, Aleister was as tainted by Christian thought as his predecessors. Yeats, though…. Reading him, I sometimes think he might have caught just a glimpse of the truth and, wisely, decided to restrict his efforts to the literary rather than the practical sphere." Dafyd took a sip of wine. "And finally, of course, there was the mathematics."

Magda cocked her head.

"Cambridge. My doctorate. Numbers always fascinated me, though I had no idea I'd use them to pursue the occult." He popped a bite of duck in his mouth, waiting as Magda absorbed it all.

She rubbed her brow. "But if we dispense with tradition…if the reality—a fragile human world beset by horrors from beyond this plane, with demons somehow our only defenders…if this reality leaves us without purpose or place, a random happenstance, just food to something beyond comprehension…then what's the point in attempting anything? Why not just give in to the base instincts, as you imply Crowley did?"

The question was crucial, the oldest fear that shored up or shattered each man's faith. How many of the most devout Rabbis and Jesuits had foundered on these very shoals? "Where there's no meaning, we must find one, but not by lying to ourselves. Aleister spoke of awakening, but what he wanted was power."

She looked dubious. "Whereas we strive for knowledge? I'm not sure I see the difference."

"The difference is one of *intent*." He tapped the table to underscore his point. "Aleister wanted power, to control and subjugate demons, but his true goals—which he was too arrogant to see or admit—were worldly power and self-aggrandizement in the eyes of others."

"But aren't we trying for those very things? Controlling and subjugating demons?"

He shook his head. "Yes and no. There's a huge difference. Aleister saw them as servants. When I understood what the demon sphere actually *was* and what its true relationship to humanity, everything began to fall into place. Demons—of which Crane is one of the lowest sort—by their very existence are already doing their part for us. They're essential to our survival, and though they do exact a small price on humanity, without them all life on Earth would be quickly consumed and our souls would spend all eternity in unimaginable torment. To use theological language, Crane and his kind are our guardian angels and our metaphysical teachers. It behooves us to learn to communicate with them. Even, perhaps, to love them"

CHAPTER FOUR

Monday March 17, 2014

The Skype connection was phenomenally clear. "It sounds as though you're next door," said Charly. How're you doing, bro? Met any sexy Greek girls yet?"

Paul laughed. "Not really. But I did go out with one this weekend, just for drinks. The woman who found me the house, actually."

"Yeah? How're you liking the place?"

"Oh, I love it. I can't wait for you to see it."

"Well, I've let my boss know that I want to take my whole two weeks at once this summer. It's going to have to be late, though, like mid-August…will that work for you?"

"Anytime works for me. Actually, I was wondering…how would you feel about Alex coming out for Easter?"

"For Easter? On her own?" He heard the concern in her voice, could see her eyebrows clench the way they did when someone threw her a curve ball.

"She *is* eighteen," he reminded her gently. "And I'd meet her off the plane at Thessaloniki. Of course, I'd pay for the ticket. I know you can't take time then, but she has spring break, and since the Easter dates coincide this year…. Of course, I wanted to run it by you before asking her."

"Yeah, no, I get it. And I don't think she has plans. But spring break at Cornell is only four days. I don't want her to miss classes, at least not more than a day or two. How long are you thinking?"

"Maybe five or six days here, and add two or three days for travel? So figure eight days total."

A moment's quiet. Then, "Oh, hell, why not. She can make up three or four days. Go for it. I'm sure she'll jump at the chance, you know how she adores you. Are you already set up for visitors?"

"If you mean, do I have space and beds, yeah, absolutely. The place is fully furnished. There's three bedrooms and a big sleeping platform downstairs as well. I bought a pile of linens and towels, pots and pans—everything. I might have a ghost, too," he added.

"A what?"

He grinned. "A ghost."

"A *ghost?*" Charly chuckled. "She'll love that. But come on, get outta here! You never even believed in Santa Claus when we were kids!"

"Well, it's what they tell me. Not a ghost, maybe. But there's stories about the house, that it was used for some kind of black magic during the war. I keep expecting the old ladies in the village to cross themselves when they see me."

"And you believe this hooey?"

"Not for a moment. But every old house should have a scandalous history. So anyway, if you're okay with the idea, I'll give Alex a call and see if she'd like to come. It's just over a month, so I'll need to book flights pretty fast."

"You're the best uncle any girl ever had. And brother, too. We could never have managed to keep her at Cornell without you." Her voice dropped from its upbeat register to a more sober tone. "So seriously, how are you doing? Are you getting out of your funk?"

"You know, I really think I am." The daily rhythms of island life, the constant views of the violet sea, the surprise and promise of last night's kiss, even the house itself…all these things seemed to be lifting the darkness which had surrounded him for so long. "The island is very…*healing*. You know I hate the word, but in this instance it's the only one that fits."

"Amen to that. I was worried about you, bro. I know how much you keep below the waterline. Even with me."

"Yeah." And he'd known she was. If she'd known just how dark it had really got she'd have been panicked.

"I think I'm having an *anástasi*," he said.

"A *what?*" Three years younger, Charly had been raised with a sibling already fluent in English, and his parents spoke far less Greek around her than they had to him. Pity.

"A rebirth. That's what Elléni called it." *You look for anástasi.*

"Elléni? Is that your girlfriend?"

"My friend, who happens to be a woman," he corrected her.

"Oh. Well, I'm glad we got *that* straight."

He laughed. Then, "How about you? Are you doing okay on your own?"

"I'm loving it," she said. "Not just having the sonofabitch out of my life, but not being asked dumb questions by cops and reporters every hour of the day. I'm just glad Alex was already away at college when it blew up. But, yeah, I got my job, I got my friends, I got my softball league, I have the best brother and daughter in the world. Life is good."

He found himself smiling as she spoke. Charly had always seen the glass half-full. Her resilience amazed him. "You're a star, sis. Listen, I'm going to ring off and email Alex. I love you. Can't wait till you get out here this summer."

"Same. I love you too, bro. And don't let the ghost get you!"

25

"Promise," he said.

Paul tried Alex's number next but his call went straight into voicemail. Ten-thirty P.M. on the East Coast, so, yeah, it was possible she was in bed. Unlike the kids who slept with their cell by their ear in case they might miss a text, Alex was smart enough to take care of herself. He left her a brief message then emailed her with the invitation. *Just let me know if you want to come,* he wrote. *I'll take care of all the bookings, and make sure the flight dates work with the ferries. Hope you can make it.*

With that done, he spent a while online browsing books. He was interrupted by a call from Fadakis, the island's small trucking business, to let him know that his stuff from the US had arrived and that they'd be delivering tomorrow. He thanked them and went back to his book shopping. By the time he'd found and purchased some fresh reading for his e-reader the room had grown gloomy around him.

He felt the chill the moment he rose, as though he'd been cocooned in a static pocket of air warmed by his own body heat until he stood up.

He fired up the woodstove and warmed himself up by bringing in more firewood while the iron mass heated up. It was mild outside, but the living room felt as cold as it had been back in January when he'd first arrived. Colder, even. How was that possible? He'd been sitting too long; that, or he was getting a chill.

He went upstairs, took a scalding bath, put on flannel pajamas and his winter robe, and set about preparing dinner.

‡

Alex giggled to herself as she read Paul's email for the second time. She was in the college's so-called Harry Potter library prepping for her Religious Studies class when it came in, and in an instant she'd forgotten all about her notes.

OMG, she typed, *are you kidding? Of course I want to come! And what do you mean, "it's just five days"? It's five days on a Greek island!! I love the snow but I'm so ready for some sunshine. This is just so awesome of you, Unc. What can I bring you? Anything you want from here? Let me know just as soon as you book the flights. I can't wait!!*

She hit *send* and had a mental image of her uncle lying on a beach reading her reply. Of course, he probably wasn't lying on a beach, but it was the first thing that came to mind. She looked about, bursting with the desire to tell someone, but there was nobody around that she knew. Which was just as well because she'd probably have yelled it out loud.

But holy crap! She was going to *Greece!*

‡

Paul's belongings arrived mid-afternoon the following day, delivered on a flatbed truck and covered by a green tarp against the steady rain that had begun in the small hours. He donned his Barbour jacket and hat to help the driver bring in the load. There were six boxes of books—he'd got rid of almost all the paperbacks—and several more containing assorted clothes, shoes, music, light tools, and sundry possessions; last were two large wardrobe boxes and two sturdy crates of well-packed paintings.

The driver, an older man, paused for several seconds at the threshold, peering around the doorway in all directions before first entering. He was serious and disinclined to chat. The moment they'd set the final crate down, he produced his paperwork and stood, frowning, while Paul signed. The ten-Euro tip brought a fleeting smile to his lips, and he was out of there in a moment with muttered thanks and wishes for a good evening.

Was the man's odd behaviour related to the house's reputation as revealed by Anna? It was curious that neither Nikos at the hardware store nor *o Pápas* Tákis, the priest, had spoken of it. But both were young, and *o Pápas* was from the mainland.

Paul was halfway through opening boxes and the day was starting to dim when there was a knock on the door. He had music playing—he'd plugged in his Bose as soon as he'd unpacked it, and found a station playing *Rembétiko*, the so-called Greek Blues—and hadn't heard a vehicle pull up. Maybe the driver had forgotten something.

To his surprise, he found not the surly driver but Elléni on his doorstep.

"Hi," she said. "Sorry I didn't call, but I was passing by and—"

He stood aside and ushered her in. "No, no. Come in. I'm glad to see you." The fact that she felt comfortable just stopping by without first calling, something that would have annoyed him a good deal in his old city life, kindled an unaccustomed glow in him.

"It's not a bad time?" she said, as he closed the door behind her. She was wearing her red raincoat, and perfectly round raindrops sparkled in her chestnut hair.

"Not at all! Here, let me take your coat." He moved to help her.

She saw the boxes. "Oh! Your things arrived," she said, easing first one arm, then another out of the coat.

"Yes, I was just unpacking. Can I get you a drink? A coffee?"

"Wonderful. And yes, please. A drink would be lovely."

"A glass of wine? Or something stronger?"

"Wine is perfect, thanks."

She looked terrific in a white cashmere sweater and well-cut jeans tucked into boots. The snug fit of the sweater emphasized the twin swell of her breasts.

As he went to the kitchen she crossed to where he'd been unpacking stuff. "I had a day off and was on my back from Mikró Kástro."

"Your parents' house?" He got out two glasses and uncorked the two-thirds full bottle of Kir-Yianni *Xinomavro* he'd opened last night.

"Yes. I went last night and stayed for lunch today. It was long enough. I love them very much, but you know how it is with family sometimes."

"I don't have much family, but yeah."

"You mentioned a sister and niece," she said. She was sitting cross-legged on the floor, sifting through a stack of books, looking entirely at home.

"Yes." He poured for her and himself, crossed back to her.

" You're close?"

"Yes. And I'm especially fond of my niece." That was understating it: he adored Alex.

"Thank you," she said, taking the glass. "You like poetry and plays, I see."

"Very much."

"Me too. Though I don't know many of these. Yamas!" she said, raising her glass slightly before taking a sip.

"They're mostly British. Except for Frost and Tennessee Williams, of course." He sat on the floor beside her and extracted a slim volume from the bottom of the pile, handing it to her. "You know Euripides, though, I think?"

"*The Bacchae*. It's my favourite play." She took it from his hand. "Of course, I've never read it in English."

"Nor I in Greek. Though I think I'm ready now."

"And like Euripides, you have abandoned the city for the wild places." Her gaze flicked to his eyes. God, intelligent and beautiful all at once.

"True," he acknowledged. *Are you like them, the Bacchae? Do you periodically abandon reason and run wild in the hills, tearing animals and even men limb from limb?*

But Elléni had moved on. Holding up his *Judaism for Dummies*, she teased him, "I don't think you're a dummy, so I'm guessing you're Jewish?"

"Correct. My father's family escaped Greece in 1941, just after the Germans invaded."

Smiling, she put the book back on the pile. "And those?" she said, pointing to the crates.

"Paintings. My mother's mostly. She was a good artist."

Her eyes widened. "Really? I shall enjoy seeing them."

"You can help me unpack them if you like." And then, remembering Greek custom, "But sorry, how rude of me! Let me get us something to nibble on."

She followed him to the kitchen, bringing her wine glass. Leaning on the counter while he assembled snacks, she said, "You don't have a television?"

"No," he said, setting out two bowls. "I hate the things." He pulled out a container of olives and a package of sliced salami.

"Why? Everyone watches television."

He shook his head. Would she even understand? "I'm a city boy. I don't like to be reminded of how unpleasant we are to one another, especially when packed together like rats."

"Ah. You don't like the violence on television."

"I don't like to see conflict, even verbal, constantly rewarded. But mostly I don't like banality. I can't even *begin* to understand why

29

people take any interest in celebrities, or why we make heroes out of sports players." He slid a hunk of feta onto a plate and glanced up expecting to see dismay, or at least puzzlement, on her face. But she seemed to be taking him seriously. He smiled. "Sorry. Shall we?" he said, indicating the living room with a motion of his head.

"No, it's interesting," she said. They set the snacks on the coffee table, and she sat herself on the sofa. "But do you really think this banality is so bad? People need to escape from their everyday lives." She took an olive and a bite of feta.

He took a chair facing her. "I do think it's bad. I think that when we worship media and sports personalities, or make false prophets out of glib, flashy, politicians…when we value looks and power over heart and soul…. Yes, I think this is the true evil in this world. And unlike black magic, it's real."

She took a sip of wine, was silent for a long moment. Then, "So I asked my yayá about the history of your house."

"Oh, you did?" Change of subject. Damn, he really hadn't meant to rant. But she'd seemed to get it, or at least take it in her stride rather than think him weird. "And…?"

"At first she didn't want to talk about it. She said there were many things that the village tried hard to forget about and bury after the war, and that the stories about the stone house were at the center of them."

"Uh-oh. That sounds ominous."

She nodded, then looked around, gesturing at the walls, the stair, the warm pine furniture, the woodstove with the merry flames dancing beyond the flameproof glass inset in the door. "And yet, to sit here, it seems so peaceful."

"Maybe you're not superstitious," he said, reaching for a slice of salami. *Like me.*

"I'm not. But the story's an odd one. Would you like to hear it?"

CHAPTER FIVE

September 21, 1943

The rowboat nosed up as it ran aground on the harbour beach with a growl of displaced pebbles. The two sailors shipped their oars and Otto, Klaus's aide, was first ashore, hand extended to help him disembark. Klaus, still deeply nauseous from the sea voyage, stood unsteadily and allowed himself to be assisted. It was cool, and the thickening clouds promised rain.

There were two men there to meet them, the exiting Hauptsturmführer and his unteroffizier. They were tanned, disgustingly healthy. Klaus, all too aware of his own sick pallor, gave the Hauptsturmführer a curt nod and introduced himself.

"Klaus Maule. You are Hauptsturmführer Bergl?"

"At your service, Standartenführer." The soldiers saluted. Klaus responded. *For God's sake, get on with it.*

The sailors handed Otto Klaus's bags as well as his own. The unteroffizier moved to help Otto as the sailors stepped ashore and pulled the boat higher onto the beach.

"I trust your journey was a good one?" said Bergl.

"Tolerable." Klaus glanced back at the Kriegsmarine cutter anchored a hundred metres out in the bay. The sea alone he might have tolerated, but the all-pervading diesel fumes had been too much for both his stomach and his psyche. It was Kharkov and Kursk and Orel all over again.

Bergl nodded. "One hour," he said to the sailors. He gestured inland, towards the white houses of the village. "If you please, Standartenführer, I can take you to your residence."

Otto and the unteroffizier picked up the luggage, the unteroffizier taking three of Klaus's four bags, as Otto was already burdened with his own pack and rifle. The sailors sat on the beach and lit cigarettes.

It was a short walk in the quiet of the autumn noon. They passed a small taverna and a few dingy little *werkstatten,* though the name seemed too grand for the gloomy hovels with their clutter of nets and fishermans' gear, wicker and wood, hammers and saws. Fish and cooking scents greased the morning air. Several of the islanders, the usual small, weathered specimens of these places, stared openly at the new arrivals as Bergl steered him towards the townhouse that was the island kommandant's home. Otto and the unteroffizier trailed them, chatting quietly.

"You have come from the East, I hear," said Bergl.

Klaus felt his teeth clench, took a breath. *He heard.* Exactly what, he wondered, had Hauptsturmführer Bergl heard? And from whom? "The East. That is correct."

They had come to the door of a house. Bergl stopped, turned to him. "Is it as bad as they say?" he asked, in low tones.

"As bad. Yes." Klaus closed his eyes—*the door visualize the door strong and shod with iron close it bolt it fast fast*—and reopened them. They'd given him the affirmation in the clinic for these moments, which were still many. He drew himself upright, took a deep breath.

Did he notice? Do I care? He met the Hauptsturmführer's curiosity directly. "So. This is it? The residence?"

Bergl's heels clicked. With a quick nod, he turned the handle and ushered Klaus inside.

‡

"It is an easy command," said Bergl, as he prepared to leave. His own aide and the unteroffizier stood by with his bags, ready to walk back down to the rowboat and the waiting sailors. "I think you will find it pleasant."

"I am sure, Hauptsturmführer." And wished the man would just go and leave him to settle in. Though his nausea had mostly gone, Klaus still felt himself at sea. Nor could he dispel the stench of diesel: it had saturated his clothes, his thoughts, everything. The house would do, but the small talk had eroded his thin reserve of patience, and he could feel his irritability growing. He wanted his injection.

"The locals will give you no trouble," Bergl was saying. "They suffer rather than like us, but they are essentially decent. Ah—I must tell you, there is one man on the island you may find especially interesting. An Englishman by—"

"An Englishman? *Here?*"

"Well, not truly English—he is a Celt. From Wales." Bergl's words fell over themselves. "I know, I had the same reaction at first. But there is a difference."

Klaus stared at the man. "Hauptsturmführer, I have been in the Waffen SS since its founding, and in the SS for eleven years before that. I *know* the difference."

A wave of fear rolled off Bergl; the two soldiers behind him stood wide-eyed and silent.

"Did you report his presence?" said Klaus.

"Standartenführer, the man is extremely well-educated and the best company you will—"

Klaus repeated his question, louder than he'd have liked.

Bergl swallowed. Beads of sweat had begun to form just below the peak of his cap. "No, sir."

"And it has not occurred to you this man could be a spy?"

"Standartenführer, I can promise you he is no spy. The man has lived here many years, almost from before the Reich. Jones is his name, Dafyd Jones. He lives quietly with a young woman. Unteroffizier Kretchmar can take you to his villa, it is just three kilometers. You will decide for yourself."

"Indeed I shall, do not doubt it. Well." He gave a curt nod. "Thank you, Hauptsturmführer. A good voyage to you."

They exchanged salutes, and Bergl was on his way, doubtless filled with relief, trailed by his aide and the unteroffizier.

Otto—good, faithful Otto, his rock—appeared at Klaus's side. "Standartenführer," he said softly, "I have unpacked your bags and prepared your medicine. Shall I draw you a hot bath?"

‡

Twenty minutes later, reclining in his bath with a cigarette and a glass of cold Moselle, Klaus found himself again at peace with the world. The morphia and the deliciously hot, clean water had relaxed him and restored his clarity of mind enough that he could consider his situation with poise and equanimity.

Vóunos had less than two thousand inhabitants. The island was tiny, remote, and strategically insignificant, hardly the place a spy would choose for a base. Still, to allow an enemy national to remain in residence was an unforgivable lapse. What Bergl had been thinking, he could not imagine, but Klaus would quickly rectify the situation. He would not directly accuse Bergl of dereliction of duty: that would involve paperwork and unpleasantness, and he was not here for that. Higher command would take care of Bergl when Klaus had dealt with the Englishman—or Celt, there *was* a racial distinction, but he was still an enemy national—and made his report to Thessaloniki.

But tonight, Klaus would relax, enjoy a good meal, and sleep peacefully, finally removed from the fray. Once he had rested and properly settled in he would arrest the Englishman and have him removed. There was no great hurry

He sipped his Moselle.

Except that sending the Englishman to the mainland would mean recalling the Kriegsmarine. Now he was finally here, Klaus was not anxious to deal with anyone beyond the half-dozen Wermacht soldiers of his small command. And, really, why make trouble for Bergl, a court martial, perhaps the firing squad? Enough good Germans had died. The man might be a fool, but, unlike himself, he probably had not wanted this command, would have regarded it as unjust exile to a primitive backwater. It was understandable that he would find educated company and conversation seductive, even to the extent of ignoring rules. It happened all the time in these places far from the main theatres of the war.

So. Easier perhaps to just eliminate the Englishman and be done with it. Klaus wanted nothing more than quiet and simplicity, and for his own war to be over. He would deal with the problem when he had rested and recuperated.

CHAPTER SIX

"Of course I'd like to hear the story," said Paul.

Elléni gave that tiny sideways nod of the head, the Greek gesture of agreement, which he had more than once found himself using in the last weeks. "Good. Then I shall tell you exactly as Yaya told me."

She took a notebook from her purse.

He smiled. "You took notes?"

"Eh. I didn't want to forget the details." She set the pad on her knees and began without opening it.

"There were two foreigners on Vóunos, an Englishman and a woman. They came here in the 1930s, well before the war. They weren't married—everyone knew this from the policeman—but they caused no trouble and kept mostly to themselves, just coming to the village for shopping. The policeman, who had of course seen their passports, told people that the man was a writer and that the woman was his secretary and companion. Of course, everyone knew she was his lover.

"At first they lived in a small house on the edge of the village. But soon the Englishman—everyone was convinced he was very rich—bought a piece of land on the hill three kilometers from the village and began to build a house. A stone house, in the traditional fashion." She paused, one eyebrow raised as if inviting him to comment.

He obliged her. "This house?"

"Exactly. They lived there quietly for many years, and the locals came to accept them. They kept to themselves, were polite to everyone, even learned our language. The only people who ever went into the house were the occasional workman, when something needed fixing or changing. They kept chickens and a few sheep.

"Early in the occupation a German *kommandant* was installed on the island with a small garrison, just a handful of men. His name was Bergl and he was tolerated, if not actually liked. The population gave him no problems, and he treated them well. Yaya was a teenager, and she remembers secretly thinking he was rather nice. He ate in the tavernas, his men went to the bars and even made friendships. Bergl himself was on good terms with both *o Pápas* and, of course, the local policeman—at the time there was only one. And before long he became friends with the English couple, and often visited them."

"Wait, wait. A German officer in command of an occupied island, fraternising with the enemy?" It sounded too fantastic. Maybe Yaya's memory wasn't as reliable as Elléni thought.

"I know, it seems strange. But many strange things happen in wartime, especially in remote places."

"Hm. I guess they do. Anyway, sorry, please go on."

Elléni glanced down at her notes. "So in 1943, a new German *kommandant* replaced Bergl. This new man, an SS colonel called Maule, was very different. A hard, thin man, the islanders came to call him 'Colonel Lunatic'. Anyway, one of the soldiers in the garrison, a good-looking young man who had fallen in love with a village girl named Fotini, had told her there was a rumour Maule was coming from the Russian front and that he was not right in the head.

"Just two days after arriving, Maule, who had apparently found out about this liaison, called the mayor to the house where he was headquartered and warned him that any social contacts between the islanders and his soldiers would not be tolerated, and that the punishment would be quick and harsh. The soldier never visited Fotini again, and whenever they passed one another in the village, he always looked away." She finished her wine and held out her glass.

"They were lucky to get off with a warning," said Paul, leaning forward to refill it. "But what does this have to do with the house?"

"Ah, we're coming to that part. So..."

CHAPTER SEVEN

September 25, 1943

The Englishman's villa was a two-floor stone structure set on the edge of an orchard. The plum trees were heavy with fruit, the apricots less so; the remaining fruit was well past its prime. To the right, a short stone walk led to a bench on the edge of the hill where the land dropped steeply away, leading the eye to where the distant village and harbour glowed in the bright morning sunlight. Yesterday's rain had polished the air to brilliance and the day, already warm, promised to be hot, as though autumn had been canceled in favour of more summer.

Klaus, flanked by Unteroffizier Kretchmar and one of the privates, rapped sharply on the door. It was opened almost at once.

The man before him was short and carried a good bit of fat around the middle. He had a wavy head of coarse black hair, dense eyebrows, and eyes of the most startling colour Klaus had even seen on a human being, like peering into fog.

For his twelfth birthday, Klaus's grandfather had given him a grey mare, Freyja. The moment Klaus's eyes met the Englishman's, he was *there,* seeing Freyja's silvery coat for the first time. The handful of summers he'd spent on her strong back, exploring the fields and gently rolling hills around his grandparents' farm in Wiesenbach, had been the happiest time of his life. When, on his first tour of duty at the age of nineteen, he received the letter telling him Freyja had been sold off to the knacker's yard, his world collapsed. He never spoke to either of his grandparents again.

The man extended a pale, chubby hand, and Klaus, caught off-guard, found himself shaking it. The man's grip was warm and unexpectedly strong. To Klaus's further surprise, the man greeted him in German. His accent was execrable, his voice higher than expected. Klaus, proud of his own language skills, gave a tiny nod and replied in his crispest English.

"Standartenführer Klaus Maule of the Waffen SS. Your name?"

"Jones. Dafyd Jones. And your English is excellent! Do come in, please. And your men, of course."

Klaus had crossed the threshold into the living area without realizing it. He glanced back to see a puzzled-looking Unteroffizier close behind him, and the private stooping to clear the doorway with his slung rifle.

Klaus frowned. He was about to ask for the man's papers when a woman appeared on the stair to the left of the entry. The air in the room seemed to thicken; he caught a quick hiss of indrawn breath from one of his men.

She was small and simply dressed. A loose white cotton dress, belted at the waist, suggested a very fine figure. Something—perhaps the smooth slope of her breasts, the way the dress rode at the flare of her hips—made him certain she wore nothing beneath. Her long hair was a hot carrot red, her complexion very fair. She descended the stair and moved towards them with poise and assurance, her steps silent on bare feet. The room became impossibly still.

The Englishman's eyes twinkled. "Ah, Magda. Allow me to

present Standartenführer Maule and his men. Standartenführer, Miss O'Whelan, my companion."

Companion. Extraordinary. Klaus's first impression of the Englishman had been that the man might be a homosexual, an impression conveyed perhaps by the high voice and his overly friendly manner. But something in the man's eyes and that handshake had contradicted that notion. And now…

"A pleasure, sir." The woman inclined her head but did not extend her hand. Gravity and respect in just the right measure but without submissiveness, and not a hint of fear in those green eyes. Her accent was unusual.

"Madame." Klaus acknowledged her with a tight little bow and a click of the heels.

Jones said, "Hauptsturmführer Bergl told us you'd be coming. He—"

"Herr Jones," said Klaus, "Frau O'Whelan. Our nations are at war with each other. I must ask that you produce immediately your documents and account for your presence on Vóunos."

The Englishman chuckled. "But Miss O'Whelan is not an enemy national."

"Oh? Klaus's eyes flicked to the girl. "You are not English?"

"I am a Citizen of the Irish Free State, sir."

Another Celt. That explained her appearance, then. Jones was another matter, his dark complexion suspect. "So. I will examine both your papers."

Jones said, "Of course, of course. But won't you take some refreshment while I fetch them? Magda will do the honours. There's a fresh pot of tea in the kitchen, and scones just out of the oven. The apricot jam is our own, you know. And the goat butter, contrary to what one might expect, provides just the right degree of tart contrast." He indicated the sofa and the two nearby armchairs. Please do take a seat. We are on quite a different time here on the island, and haste seems so ill-suited."

Klaus wanted to protest, but something—perhaps the couple's graciousness, which seemed wholly sincere, and certainly the outstanding beauty of the woman—gave him pause. Of course, the morning's morphia had soothed his disposition. But either way there was, after all, no hurry. He had not experienced much by way of refinement and civility in recent years, and he was fond of tea. And also, he remembered with the dazed wonder of a man waking from a long sleep to a sunny and comfortable room, of beautiful women.

He glanced around at his men. Unteroffizier Kretchmar looked uncertainly at him, clearly expecting an order. The private was staring at the woman with the slack-jawed aspect of a village idiot. With a quick motion of his head towards the door, Klaus indicated to Kretchmar and the private to wait outside. Acknowledging him with a crisp salute, the Unteroffizier tapped the other on the shoulder and more or less pushed him out of the door, following him out with what Klaus thought was a distinct air of relief.

A few moments later, comfortably ensconced in one of the two green velvet armchairs beside the small table upon which the girl had set his tea and what indeed proved an excellent scone, Klaus flicked through the couple's passports.

"So. You have been here many years, I see. And before that, Morocco. Your passport says you are a writer, and I see you live comfortably." He leaned forward in his chair. "What are you doing in Greece, Herr Jones?"

"You have to put something on passports. I'm really more of a student, as is Miss O'Whelan."

The answer was so unexpected that Klaus actually laughed. "A student? Here, in this—" he groped for the English word, couldn't find it—"*abgelegen* place? And what is it you study, Herr Jones? Fish?"

"The occult arts, Standartenführer. Magic, if you prefer the popular term."

Klaus stared at the man. The lie, spoken so simply and without artifice, was an audacious one. Perhaps the man was mad and actually believed his claim. Perhaps both were mad. Klaus would find out, and quickly.

"So. A magician. *Eine zauberer.*" Klaus sipped at his tea, keeping his expression neutral. "And you, *meine Frau?* Do you claim to be the same?"

The woman gave a grave nod. The room was so silent that Klaus could hear his own breathing. *Like a church.* It had been so long…

Klaus took a deep breath, forced himself to remember why he was here. It was certainly not to discuss fables. He took out his cigarette case, extracted one, and lit it. The woman produced an ashtray from somewhere and set it on the coffee table.

"Very well. Then you will satisfy my curiosity with a demonstration, Herr Jones. Some trick of your art, a proof of your powers." He thought a moment, let his hand stray to the butt of his pistol. "If I were to have you shot, for example, would you live or die?"

"Passing so severe a test would require considerable time and effort in the preparation, Standartenführer," Jones replied, perfectly calm. His eyes dropped to Klaus's holster.

As Klaus watched, all the blood drained from the man's face, turning his formerly ruddy complexion deathly pale in a matter of seconds. The coward had realized the magnitude of his stupidity in making such a crazy claim. Pathetic fool.

But now the charlatan found his voice again. Clearing his throat, he said, "Still, I think I can offer another proof that might satisfy you, Standartenführer." He indicated Klaus's holster. "Please be so kind as to carefully examine the weapon you are so eager to employ."

His patience eroding, Klaus took a deep drag on his cigarette and rested it on the rim of the ashtray. He unlatched the holster one-handed, anxious to end this charade. As his fingers curled around the grips and he withdrew the pistol, he experienced a moment of shock so jarring that the world around him seemed to shudder and stop, reality suspended.

His pistol was *cold*. Not just cold, but ice-cold. In a frozen heartbeat he was back at Kharkov, fumbling with numbed fingers at his holster, fear-slicked hands sticking to the pistol's icy slide. Fighting down the instinct to scream, he brought the weapon before him and saw, with mounting dread, that every metal surface was rimed with frost.

Aware of the intense scrutiny of the strange couple sitting on the sofa opposite him, Klaus struggled to control his emotions. He ejected the magazine into his shaking hand.

The bullets—not only the topmost, but also that immediately below it—had corroded. The corrosion was so advanced that the contours of the rounds had become indistinguishable from one another. Klaus pushed down on the cold, grey-green crust coating the topmost round to free it from the magazine. It did not budge.

The entire stack had become a single, ruined mass, the heavy layer of pitted material filling the magazine, perhaps down to the spring mechanism.

Hypnotism. It had to be. He'd once seen a stage magician in Nuremberg convince a man that he was a chicken. Klaus looked up at the Welshman in mounting fury. The man—his colour had returned now—regarded him blandly. The girl beside him seemed unconcerned, leaning back on the sofa, legs crossed with one arm resting on its back, an oddly masculine pose.

"It is not hypnosis," said Jones.

Klaus slammed the magazine back into the pistol, snapped back the still-icy slide, pointed the weapon at the ceiling, and squeezed the trigger.

There was a dry click. He jerked the slide back and peered into the chamber. Empty. The mechanism had failed to feed in a round. He lowered the pistol, his anger giving way to a sense of creeping horror.

It was Welshman who quelled it. Rising, he said, "Magda, would you please fetch the brandy? I think our guest would appreciate a drink." He crossed to Klaus, who sat immobile, the useless pistol resting on the arm of his chair, nerveless fingers still curved loosely around the grip. The Welshman ground out Klaus's ash-tipped cigarette with a decisive twist, then placed his hand gently on Klaus's shoulder. "Please join us for lunch, won't you? You may wish to send your men back, you are quite safe. We have many things to discuss, Standartenführer."

And in truth, though he could not have begun to explain it, Klaus, sitting there with the frost on his useless pistol turning to fat beads of condensation in the warm air, did feel safe, in a way he hadn't for many, many years.

CHAPTER EIGHT

Magda served them a simple egg salad accompanied by bread, tomatoes, and lashings of fruit. The colonel—apparently the closest rank to Standartenführer in the regular army—had recovered from his shock. Much as he tried to remain cool and aloof, the man was obviously impressed and intrigued by Dafyd's demonstration. Power was the language his type spoke, the air they breathed.

So far the conversation had been boneless. The social niceties, small facts of island life. Of course, she let Dafyd do the talking, preferring in any case to simply study their guest.

She'd noted the way he looked at her earlier. She was used to men stripping her with their eyes, didn't give a damn—in fact, she profited, stealing energy from them every time it occurred. This fellow, though…his look carried a twist of perverted violence that would terrify an ordinary woman, and probably most men. Well. He was in for some hard lessons.

The man was a disaster. His complexion had a waxy, corpse-like aspect to it. His hand betrayed a fine tremor when he held up his fork, and the upper part of his right cheek, just below the eye, occasionally twitched in a nervous tic. When asked a direct question, he kept his eyes hooded. A pity, for their cruel, ice-blue pallor had an unearthly beauty all its own.

Extending her Sight, Magda sampled the jagged shards of his mind, tasted his wants, felt the heavy, steadying weight of the drug. He functioned, but barely, more like a machine than a man. But there was no doubt: he was their Third.

She'd only just framed the thought when Dafyd, who never missed a thing, turned to her and smiled, allowing himself just the slightest twitch of an eyebrow. She returned a tiny nod, mute reply. *Yes, he's the one. But can he be mended?*

"A fine meal, *meine Frau*," said the colonel, setting his cutlery back on the empty dish. "I thank you." He turned to Dafyd. "Now Herr Jones, tell me more about this Art of yours. I am curious."

If he expected her to clear the dishes and retire, he was going to be disappointed. Instead she picked up a ripe plum and bit into it, unconcerned at the dribble of juice that ran down her chin. His eyes flicked towards her, and she smiled, indicating that he should help himself. As the colonel's face clouded with confusion, Dafyd began talking, capturing the man's attention.

She wiped off the juice with a finger and licked at it. Once in a while it amused her to toy with men's minds, and this one needed to be reminded he wasn't the boss.

During the next hour, the colonel's mask slipped in the face of his obvious interest and hunger for knowledge. The man was no fool: damaged as he was, he had a sharp mind and a rare talent for grasping esoteric ideas. And he had needs, intense wants he'd had to give up on and bury—more reason for the addiction.

After Dafyd had expounded on the basics, the colonel sat back, lit his fourth cigarette since the meal had begun, and pondered for a few moments before speaking. Dafyd remained quiet, as did she.

"So," the colonel began. "The theory, then. Changes in the magician and the application of will are used to bring changes in the physical world." He scratched at his cheek. "What I do not understand is the larger context. You talk about controlling demons, and how this control is the power for true magic. You say these demons are the magician's teachers as in the Art he advances. But you say also that these demons protect against forces which would destroy us. And that the demons *need* us."

Jones inclined his head. "Quite. You have it all correct."

"But what *are* these demons? The..." he hesitated a moment. "The falling angels?"

Jones laughed. "Forget your bible, Colonel. Demons are entities intimately and inseparably bound to humanity. Without the one, the other could not exist. They are close to our twins, their plane of existence as close as the spaces inside the atom."

The colonel seemed to shiver slightly, but the light in his eyes told Magda that something in him immediately recognized this truth. The ancient, primal part of his being had always known it, and the knowledge comforted him. "Then each of us has a personal demon, a..." he groped for words, "...a mirror of himself?"

"Not quite. Think of it more as families, each individual in their sphere being aligned with a number of us." Dafyd thought a moment. "That's not quite correct...the reality, I believe, is less categorical, less mechanical...but it's as close as we can understand it."

"And this...realm of theirs, this demon place, what is it, really? I mean—"

"It is Hell. Don't look surprised, colonel. Despite the lack of biblical correlation it's a perfectly apt name. Hell is non-physical as we understand the term. That is, it has solidity, but outside the dimensions our senses would recognize as real; their space and time are, I believe, quite different to ours. Have you read Einstein?

"*Das Juden Physik?*" The colonel's eyes narrowed and Magda caught his flash of anger. "Be careful, Mister Jones. I have heard of it, but no more."

"Of course. In any case, Hell, the demonic realm, has its own physics, just as real as ours; and the entities there, our demons, feed off us—or rather, off our feelings. Their sustenance consists of our most acute psychic and emotional states, the most important and energy-giving being fear and suffering. Anger and sadness also, but to lesser degrees."

Disbelief. "How...?"

"I have no idea. But just as good health and positive emotions strengthen us, so suffering and negative emotions strengthen our twins in Hell. I suspect it's always been that way: complement and balance, part of the mystery of the universe—it would certainly explain humanity's propensity for conflict. So in times of war and mass suffering on Earth, Hell grows very strong. In times of peace the demons weaken, and the risk to them and us increases."

The colonel pounced on that. "The risk, you say! And these forces that threaten us, that would destroy us, what are *they?*"

Dafyd nodded. "Our existence hangs by a thread, Colonel. It always has. Outside this fragile human sphere—" he made a small yet eloquent gesture "—lies an abyssal chaos, an inconceivable hunger that would devour us all. Not out of malice or evil, you understand: those are *our* values, and the cosmos neither knows nor cares for them. No, it's simply a question of equilibrium, of balancing existence. Unfortunately, some forces are entropic. Whatever they touch is reduced, rendered disorganized."

"Killed, you mean," said the colonel, who seemed to be following.

Dafyd's lips quirked in his most ironic smile. "Oh yes. And worse. Much worse." He glanced at Magda and she experienced a chill. She shifted a little in her chair to face him as they came to the meat of it.

"When I was young," said Dafyd, "I leavened my studies with the reading of fiction. I especially enjoyed tales of imagination and hubris—Poe, Dunsany, and a young American by the name of Lovecraft. I came across his work in 1924, two years after my return to Wales. I'd already begun to suspect the truth, but my exposure to Lovecraft's work was a watershed. One line of his in particular stands out for me: *The gods of the outer hells that guard the feeble gods of Earth.*

"That one word, *guard,* that was the catalyst I needed. Though the specifics of his fiction were of course just wild invention, wonderful nonsense, this man had, with the fantastic intuition that blesses one artist in a generation, stumbled across the central truth: it is us, we humans, who are *the feeble gods of Earth.*

Klaus's eyebrows went up. "And the others? The gods of the outer hells?"

"Ah. Those would be our demons, whom our ancestors mistook for gods and devils alike."

Seeing the colonel's confusion, Dafyd went on. "The ancient Greeks, in Homeric times, understood the essentially benign nature of these entities and their protective relationship to humanity. But Plato muddies things a bit, and by the third century, the Christians had branded them as purely evil spirits, associating demons with evil and the Christian Hell. What they didn't understand, couldn't even suspect, was the existence of inconceivably powerful beings elsewhere in creation. Unopposed, these would periodically visit the Earth and scour it of life, leaving just enough to repopulate it for their next visit. Lovecraft intuited those also. He saw through the comforting myth of Christianity and its loving God, understood that the larger universe doesn't give a fig for mankind and certainly wasn't created for our comfort or convenience.

"Today it's known that in the aeons before man, the Earth suffered several great extinctions. The periods between extinctions were vast, in the order of tens and hundreds of millions of years…but who knows how many worlds are on these beings' menu, or whether a hundred million years is to them like the span between breakfast and lunch to us?"

The colonel sat stiff and erect in his chair. "But, but—*mein Gott!* Hundreds of millions of years…. How could you begin to know any of this?"

"Demons are difficult and trying to work with. They're consummate literalists and tricksters who love to bargain and win. They will trick and trap anyone who comes to them with less than complete confidence and self-control, and they twist words. But they do not actually lie, Colonel. And in the same way we have learnt the physical laws of matter, demons have access to and are able to perceive other dimensions of existence and being which we can no more than feebly intuit.

"The threat from these beings, the world-eaters, is constant, unending. Even without the cataclysmic extinctions, some sharp, unexpected, action of theirs, a breach of Hell's defenses, results in a local breakthrough, a lance-like irruption into the human sphere. When this happens, a human or a group of us might spontaneously combust, be left horribly mutilated, or simply vanish without trace. Sometimes the victims are cattle, which the enemy seems to find almost as acceptable. The attacks might leave scars on the land, or cause secondary, inexplicable phenomena. There may be strange lights in the sky, or incongruous events like rains of blood or frogs. If humanity even notices, it always manages to shrug off the event, blissfully ignorant of the fundamentally terrifying nature of the universe.

"In our dealings with demons, Magda and I have learned much about Hell, even its geography—oh yes, it has one." He chuckled. "Not remotely Dante's, but very distinct nonetheless. Most importantly, there is an Inner and an Outer Hell. And that Outer Hell is the edge, the frontier, the front line in the war."

"And I have seen it," said Magda.

The colonel turned to her in openmouthed amazement. "You have...? Impossible!"

"Not so, colonel," said Dafyd. He gestured amiably in her direction. "Miss O'Whelan is the seventh in a maternal line of seers. Her business is scrying, the parting of veils, and I've never once known her to fail. Her Sight may be unmatched in this world."

"But, but—to see *into Hell?* These are fancies, it cannot be that a woman—"

She wasn't standing for that. "Cannot be? Really, colonel? It's not much harder than reading the traces of someone's personal past." She slid into his eyes, into his mind, like a blade through water.

She dispensed with stealth. *Let him feel it, he needs a lesson.* She closed her eyes, focused. There it was, barely below the surface. Thunderflash and pressure wave from a nearby explosion, the ground shaking from the bursting shells, the endless mad crisscross of heavy armor. Men screaming in the fading echoes of the detonation. Furnace heat from armor plate smashed and heated to near incandescence. Red and black, blood and diesel, the life-essence of men and machines, all running together at his feet. Pieces of men on the ground, guts and brains plastered on pockmarked walls. Smoke and flames and the reek of shit and burning flesh.

"Blood and shit and diesel oil, colonel. Your own hell." She opened her eyes, weighed his terror. "Is that a fancy, too?"

Hot colour rose in his face and his hands curled into fists. She could hear his heart pound, feel him strangling on the breath he couldn't draw.

Dafyd raised a hand, smiling benignly. "Peace, colonel. Peace. His voice was a balm, a benediction. "We do not judge you, Sir—in fact, we welcome you. You do not know your own power, nor how much Hell loves you."

CHAPTER NINE

"So they became friends? The British couple and the SS colonel?"

"Very good friends, apparently," said Elléni. "Though she wasn't quite explicit about it, Yaya implied they had a *ménage a trois* going, or so everyone believed. And as the months went by, people began to notice an improvement in the colonel. He looked healthier, and would sometimes be seen strolling in the village or picnicking at the beach with the English couple. His soldiers also seemed more relaxed than when he first arrived, though they still kept any relationships with the locals from public sight.

"The colonel spent more and more time at the Englishman's house—*this* house—sometimes staying the entire night. All through the spring and summer of 1944, everything on the island seemed peaceful. Of course, people were hearing news of allied victories—a few people had hidden radios—and longed to be free again. But the realities of war were a world away from the everyday life of the island."

‡

47

September 28, 1943

It was three days before Klaus returned, alone this time, to the stone house.

"Well," the *zauberer* said, "it's gratifying to know you don't intend to have us shot, colonel. And nothing happens by chance. You arrived on Vóunos for a reason. Come, sit with me."

The woman entered with tea and a plate of fruit. She set the tray on the coffee table before them and poured, handing Jones and Klaus their cups before taking her place in the empty armchair. Her song-red hair fell in a long braid and she wore a simple, calf-length dress of seafoam green, belted at the waist and short in the sleeves. On her feet were plain leather sandals.

"Thank you." Klaus uncrossed his legs and reached forward for his cup, eyes down and hooded from the pair across the table from him. He took a slice of lemon and reached for the sugar bowl. "I have considered our conversation of the other evening."

"Magda didn't frighten you away then." Jones chuckled. "Good, good."

Klaus looked up at the jibe. But the *zauberer's* eyes sparkled with good humour rather than mockery. *This man is clever. Everything he does is calculated, his every action has purpose.* And the woman, this woman who'd so casually breached the ironbound door he'd built in his mind and looked into the darkest recesses of his soul when he'd challenged her, positively terrified him.

He concentrated on holding the saucer steady and getting the cup to his lips without his hands shaking. The quiet in the room was absolute, the blandness of these two deceptive. He could still turn back, And yet...

He plunged forward before his courage failed him. "As I was leaving the other evening, you said we could help one another. Please explain how."

The woman glanced at Jones, the ghost of a smile on her lips. She was beautiful, yes, but hard and cold—a beauty that held terrors for him. Icicles under moonlight in a hostile land far from home.

Jones smiled and inclined his head, all affability and easy grace. "Of course." He leaned back in his chair. "What we propose—" Klaus noted the *we*— "is simple: we need a partner, a *Third,* to use the correct term, to perform certain advanced magical operations impossible for a duo. Magda and I believe that you are that Third. We would of course train you in the basics—that is all you would need—but you should know there are risks." When Klaus didn't flinch, Jones added, "But the rewards are almost beyond imagining."

"Name them."

The *zauberer* smiled again. "First let us put our cards on the table. Magda's aims and mine are simple enough: knowledge, and the time in which to pursue our studies to the end, to a complete understanding of the cosmos and its workings. You should know that Magda," he indicated the woman with a gesture, "is in a very real way the purer of us. Her interest is solely metaphysical, her aspirations nothing less than unity with creation. Mine? Of course, knowledge for its own sake...but I admit that beyond that, I have some distinct plans, some thoughts on how I'd like to remake this world.

"But tell us of *your* dreams, Colonel. If you could have anything you wished, what would that be?"

Klaus pursed his lips. "I should like..." He closed his eyes briefly. *Of course I would. What else is there to wish for?* "I would want to right some wrongs in this world, to correct some mistakes which fools and madmen have made. I still love my country."

Jones considered this for some moments, but his look was not critical. "You would try to return Germany to the ascendant, then, if you could? To reverse the outcome of this war?"

He understands. Respects, even. Klaus let out a breath. "Yes. So long as I live and breathe. If I had the power."

Jones appeared thoughtful. "Germany leading a new world. A world," he mused, "in which all men know their place in the scheme of things, and serve willingly. Where they do not fear death in the service of that which is higher."

Klaus frowned. "I do not follow you."

The *zauberer* gave a small nod; seeming far away in thought, he sipped at his tea before going on, holding the porcelain cup as though it were an anchor to the here and now.

"I look at humanity, Colonel, and I see two types of people: herders and cattle. Perhaps one in a hundred can rightly be called herders—

those of us who, by both nature and disposition, think and care about the nature of our existence. We are the leaders. Whether magicians or priests, military men or politicians, doctors or engineers…all of us share and exhibit the distinguishing traits of intelligence and curiosity, as well as the determination to further our interests and perhaps even help direct the destiny of our species. Even if we herders are not aligned on specifics, we share these general concerns and ambitions.

"But the mass of humanity, the cattle—and I don't mean the word unkindly—what of them? What were they put here for? They don't contribute much, and generally don't look past their noses. If they care at all for anyone or anything beyond themselves, these feelings typically crumbles in the face of self-interest, or at most that of family. They lack vision, understanding. And in a universe where the survival of humanity is always in the balance and only the power of Hell and the single-minded focus of the demonic stands between us and oblivion, that is not acceptable.

"Now, the world of the Aztecs, that of the Egyptians—both were societies where men understood their place in the natural order. Societies in which sacrifice was seen as a duty, even a privilege. Of course, they imagined they were sacrificing to gods, but no matter: the sacrifices had their effect." He chuckled. "But monotheism, with its attendant perversions—Judaism, Christianity and Islam—*that* was the folly: sheer, self-serving human arrogance, positing a One God moulded in our image, our feeble species as the pinnacle of creation. The exaltation of the cattle. For centuries, we've run the world as if the herders exist to serve the cattle. But show the world the truths of existence, the metaphysical underpinnings of reality, and these childish fantasies will fade as if they'd never existed. And we aren't short of cattle to supply the motive force for Hell to remain strong."

The zauberer leaned back in his chair with his hands folded over his belly, and smiled. "So, yes, Colonel, I believe our interests may be twinned, at least for some way along the road."

Klaus could barely breathe. Hope sprang like fire in his breast. "Then you truly believe such a world is possible? A world where the social order is respected by all, and not subverted by the inferior, the ignorant?"

Jones's smile broadened. "Why not, Colonel? Why not?"

CHAPTER TEN

October 8, 1943

"You are joking, of course!" the colonel snapped.

Dafyd gave the slightest shake of his head. The colonel's eyes widened. It was eight days since he'd stopped the morphia and he seemed to be over the worst of it. But it was still touch and go. The man was severely sleep-deprived and still subject to tremors and dangerous outbursts.

"You want my *confession?* Like a priest?" Klaus tried to stare him down.

Dafyd kept his expression mild, almost disinterested. "Not a confession. I simply want to hear you talk about it." Magda, seated beside him, appeared entirely composed, but he could feel the intensity of her listening, all her senses deployed.

After a moment, the colonel slapped the arms of his chair and stood, radiating anger and frustration.

Control, Klaus, thought Dafyd, *always control. Don't let it beat you. Control the shakes.*

The struggle was evident. But after a moment, the colonel crossed to the side table and poured himself three fingers of brandy. He took a swig, then started to pace. "Where even to begin?" he muttered. He paused in mid-stride, shook his head, and began to pace again.

"It was a time...a time when everything seemed possible." His free hand moved in big, animated gestures. "Everything. We were going to be masters of the world. I was just a Sturmbannführer in the Leibstandarte SS Adolf Hitler, the Fuhrer's personal bodyguard. We led the advance into the Low Countries, tearing into them like *eine zyklon.*" He made a fist. "We almost caught the British at Dunkirk— would have done, would have crushed them, if the Lüftwaffe had done its job. It was the first catastrophe. Still, I received a promotion, and that was something.

"In 1941, the Leibstandarte came to Greece, and again the British—most of them—escaped us. The luck of the Devil. But still, it was a good time, as if we walked each day in the sunlight of the Gods." His head came up with pride, but Jones saw the shadow beneath. *Not only the memories, but the need for the morphia. Drink up, Klaus! Drink and get on with it.*

As if on command, the colonel knocked back more of the brandy, and now his face hardened.

"And then they sent us north, to join *Barbarossa*. The stupidity…" He shook his head. "At first, Russia was not so bad. We took Kiev, and cleared the Crimea. I received another promotion. Then the winter came." He stopped pacing and turned his face up, as if looking for something that wasn't there. He seemed about to speak.

"Go on, Klaus," said Jones gently.

The man ran his fingers through his hair, leaving furrows, and resumed his pacing. "We had to fall back from Rostov. The cold, it was terrible. Those fools in Berlin…our clothing and rations were ridiculously insufficient. But we fought, we survived, and in the summer of 1942, we retook the city. But the brigade was exhausted.

"They sent us to Normandy and reformed the Liebstandarte as an armored division. We licked our wounds, and enjoyed some time back in civilization. But we knew it would not last.

"In January of '43 we were sent back to Russia to defend Kharkov. Again, we were forced back, but we did not give up. In March, we retook *that* city. But the cost was terrible."

Klaus shook his head, then went on. "In June, after a rest and refit, they moved us north to Belgorod. And now it was one big falling into an endless night, the Gotterdämmerung. *Zitadelle* was the final folly." He finished the brandy and hurried on. "No matter how many we killed, the Russians kept coming. They were everywhere.

"It was after Orel. August, and the weather was suffocating. That was Russia: snow, mud, or sweating heat—there was nothing else. The bridge was blown. The rockets…their pieces shredded men like a storm of razors. Somehow we crossed the river, found a village. It was late. I…"

The colonel stopped, poured himself more brandy. *That's the way, Klaus, better than the other. Now get it out,* all *of it. Finish the story.*

He whirled back to face them. "They are animals, Jones! *Animals!* You cannot understand it, nobody can. Nobody who has not seen them. They live like pigs and die as if they did not care. It is the Dark Ages!" He drank half the glass at a swallow.

Magda had been listening with closed eyes. When the colonel remained quiet, she opened them and prompted him. "You took the men."

She'd spoken softly, but the colonel rounded on her so fast that Jones was on his feet, magic coursing and ready to stop him in an instant if he needed to.

"Yes, I took the men!" the colonel shouted, his words tumbling over each other like loose scree on a mountainside. Then, seeing Dafyd's look and posture, he seemed to collapse inwards, to yield. In a quieter tone, he went on, "I had one held down, and I…cut him, yes? I…" He closed his eyes.

Dafyd glanced at Magda in time to see her eyes close as she slipped into the colonel's mind. And to Dafyd's astonishment the world turned ghostly as the plucked images unspooled before him like film on a cinema screen. He watched in both disbelief and fascination as Klaus sawed and hacked with his big SS knife at a screaming man's bloody crotch. And like animal guts or some nightmare trophy, the limp, gory genitals dangled from his hand as Klaus, his pale, gaunt face almost unrecognizable, held them up for his cheering men to see. The lights of Hell burned in the colonel's eyes as he walked over to the chair where they'd tied the man's wife. Her sobs turned to screams as he approached. When at the last instant she tried to turn away, one of his men held her head, forcing her mouth open as Klaus stuffed the bloody ruin into her mouth before shooting her between the eyes.

The vision faded, and Dafyd, his heart pounding, was returned to this world. He turned to Magda just as she opened her eyes, and a silent understanding passed between them. Truly Hell must love the colonel.

Klaus was shaking his head, oblivious. As if to himself, he whispered, "They are not human."

When he turned to Jones, his face was the colour of ashes.

"I began on the next. And my men were with me, you understand? The Russians, these devil pigs, you know what they did to our prisoners? *Do you know?*" And now he turned to Magda, leaning forward, looming, all hard angles like a block of granite about to fall on her as she sat there, bland as butter, listening. No judgment, no fear. Just listening.

The colonel glanced at Jones. He must have seen something in his face, understood that there wouldn't be, couldn't be, any more secrets. The squareness left his shoulders and the light went from his eyes. He took a few steps to his chair and slumped into it.

"At some point another unit arrived. A young *Sturmbannführer*, new from Germany, was in command." He made a vague gesture. "He shot two of my men and his soldiers covered the others. I tried to stop him. I was arrested.

"They took me to Germany and threw me in prison. It would have been a court-martial and the firing squad, but at the last moment my old friend in the Liebstandarte, Teddy Wisch, intervened. He'd just been promoted to Oberführer, and had great influence. As a result I was sent to a sanatorium."

"And that's where they started you on the morphia," said Jones.

The colonel shook his head. "No, that started in the field. It was the only way to remain sane. Anyway, after a week it was decided to bury me in this place, to keep me out of the way for the rest of the war." He looked at them in turn. He seemed dazed as he said, "And that, it seems, was my good fortune."

‡

December 1943

In the ten weeks since his arrival, Klaus's world had been rebuilt. Instead of a broken man full of fear and bile and functioning only thanks to the morphia, he felt now as he hadn't since he was a young man. Before the war and all the rest.

He had Dafyd to thank. And, he conceded grudgingly, Magda. Dafyd had provided Klaus the motive and lent him the will to face his drug addiction. Otto had seen him through the first forty-eight hours. But after Klaus showed up at their door on that terrible third day, it was she who'd stayed with him all day and right through the next few nights. It wasn't compassion, nor a sense of duty, he thought. No, what kept her there, he realized, talking and playing cards, making sure he drank water and ate what little he could hold down, even kneading the knotted muscles in his back and legs to calm the tremors and shaking, was the conviction of her own goals; and, he understood, the fact that he, Klaus, was a necessary part in her and Dafyd attaining their own goals in their practice of the magical Art.

‡

April 1944

Magda, who always rose early, had everything ready when Dafyd came down a bit after nine. He had suggested a picnic to round off the intense work of the past weeks, and both she and Klaus had been enthusiastic. She poured coffee for them both and served it, along with bread and jam, on the patio. Klaus would join them at ten.

The day promised to be hot. The sun was well clear of the mountain behind the villa and the air buzzed with the song of cicadas. Down away beyond the harbour, the sea lay calm as oil and sapphire-blue, a striking contrast after the intense March storms. By afternoon there would perhaps be a breeze, but by then they would be roasting. It was the perfect day to spend at the beach.

"Klaus is a fast learner," she said.

Dafyd agreed. "He's intelligent and motivated. At first I wasn't sure he could be coaxed out of the pit he'd dug for himself, but his progress has been nothing short of remarkable. And of course when chickens and sheep and dogs are no longer enough, he'll be helpful in providing the needed sacrifices."

"If he survives Crane."

"Yes. That will be the real test. Two months more, I think—then he'll be ready."

In just a few months since his recovery, the German had absorbed the basics of Dafyd's esotericism and had been steady in the presence of the increasingly powerful elementals and transitionals they had summoned. With the invocation of Crane, they'd know whether he was a sound enough vessel for the work ahead.

The affinity between Dafyd and the colonel was unmistakable. She'd seen it from the beginning. Her own relationship with the colonel was more problematic, largely because of her sex. He'd been attracted to her, desired her, from the beginning, and it had taken honest words from her and a couple of strong warnings from Dafyd to blunt his instincts in that direction; even now, he sometimes looked at her with clear lust in his eyes.

Yet remarkably, this man who had both the power and the disposition to arrest and even kill them at a whim, had listened and not bridled. Despite her conviction that people acted out of free will, it seemed hard to refute that all of it—Morocco, their choice of Vóunos, Klaus's arrival—had been part of an inevitable and preordained series of events, and that she and the two men were simply actors in a play scripted long ago.

The colonel was a perfect fit. He already knew, albeit unconsciously, the forces they were dealing with and what they required of men, had unwittingly served those forces for years without any understanding of the why or how. He'd shed blood, lakes of it, and though only ritual sacrifice could actually *invoke* a demon, all blood fed the demonic. But Klaus's offerings had come at considerable personal cost; it was amazing they'd been able to walk him back from the abyss.

Predestined, all of it.

She became aware of Dafyd watching her with that boyish half-smile of his. He said, "A marriage made in Hell, some would say." And chuckled.

"You and Klaus?" she said, slightly startled.

"Your modesty becomes you, Magda. No, the three of us. A tripartite union, an occult trinity like nothing this world has known since Pharaonic times."

"You really think he's strong enough?"

Dafyd hesitated for just a beat before replying. "Yes."

She raised an eyebrow.

Dafyd chuckled. "All right: yes, I think he's strong enough to see this through to the signing of the pact and our, ah...*rapture*," he concluded with a smile. "After that, well, it doesn't really matter does it? Of course I'd be sorry to lose him—I'm rather curious to see where his vision of a Fourth Reich takes us. But either way he'll have served his purpose."

"And if he breaks before? During the last ritual?"

"There are always risks, Magda. But I think we can count on him"

The sight of Maurice, wound in flame, screaming and careening about the Lodge in Morocco. She pushed it away, replaced it with an image of still, deep water. "I hope you're right."

‡

Sitting there on the sand with his two foreign friends, caressed by warm breezes, Klaus wondered, not for the first time, at this unexpected turn his life had taken. A few months ago he'd felt it was as good as over. Now he felt alive and whole again, even optimistic, the scars and nightmares of the past years mere fading memories.

He felt no guilt at his indolence and peace while others continued to suffer and die for the Fatherland. He'd done his part, earned his peace. The responsibility and guilt had to be placed squarely on the shoulders of the führer and those who'd encouraged him in his delusions, especially the Russian adventure.

Klaus looked out to sea, admiring the sparkle of mid-afternoon sunshine on the calm blue water. No, his war was finished. The only challenge now was survival. Any intelligent man could see that Germany could no longer win, not after Russia. It might go on another two or three years, but in the end….no. And after his bout of madness and the horrors of the east, the allies would be looking for him when it was all over. He would be arrested, tried, and executed. The crimes and atrocities on the Russian side would be ignored: history was always written by the winners.

And yet, this magical work with these two, this could change things. The first power he had learned and exercised was power over himself. But though there was so much he didn't yet understand, he began to see where it was going; how by the application of this fascinating art of correspondences and unities and resonances, all manipulated by Dafyd's occult mathematics, the *zauberer* could align his mind with the universal and project his will onto the canvas of the real.

The Welshman's powers—what he had seen of them—were remarkable. That he could affect and control matter was beyond doubt. The woman's, interest and power lay—as the *zauberer* had said—wholly in the direction of divination and foresight—*scrying*, as she called it. Both seemed able to at least partially read minds, which made any pretense or falsehood impossible. It was a strangely welcome release. He'd kept so much tightly chained inside for so long. At first, the realization that these two saw into his deepest *seele* had been terrifying. But their complete lack of moral judgment had served to allay and dispel any concerns. Both of them understood and accepted him in a way no human being, with the possible exception of his faithful Otto, ever had.

They were also, in their way, fanatics, totally devoted to furthering their knowledge of the hidden world. And this commitment was something which he could both understand and admire.

He leaned forward, reaching under the cloth draped over the picnic basket for some dried figs. Dafyd, who had also been gazing out to sea, smiled. The *zauberer* had taken off his shirt and shoes but kept on his white cotton trousers. Klaus wore swimming trunks, and the woman an emerald green bathing suit with a low-scooped back. She lay on her stomach, reading a favourite book of poems. Klaus's eyes strayed along her bare back to the alluring curve of her buttocks. If she were any other woman…

"Lovely out here, isn't it?" said Dafyd.

Klaus turned to him, instantly shutting down that train of thought. The *zauberer's* eyes were bright with that trace of wry amusement which so often animated them. Klaus nodded. "It is perfect. I was just thinking of how much has changed since I met you and Magda." She smiled on hearing her name, but didn't look up.

"You've done well, Klaus," said the *zauberer*.

Klaus's lips tightened. He *had* done well. It hadn't been easy, but then what in life was? But… "Dafyd, you will forgive my impatience, but…when shall we see results?"

The *zauberer* cocked his head, eyebrows raised. Klaus, suddenly dry-mouthed, moistened his lips.

"So. Interesting as this training in the Art is—and I *am* interested—I know that you are working towards a very clear goal. And you said that I, novice as I am, could help you in this. As your *Third*, you said."

Now Magda did look up. Setting her open book face down on the sand, she turned towards them, propped up on one elbow. Dafyd clasped his hands behind his head and leaned back. He stretched out his arms, yawning hugely. Klaus heard a joint pop.

Dafyd composed himself again. "I'm sorry, the sun always makes me sleepy." He tore off a hunk of bread and slathered honey on it, chewing thoughtfully. Klaus frowned. This man didn't miss things, yet he seemed to be ignoring his question. Was this rudeness calculated? To what effect?

Dafyd swallowed, then took a long drink of water. Just when Klaus was about to repeat his question, the *zauberer*, his gaze fixed on the indigo deeps in the middle distance, spoke.

"Your recollection is quite correct, Klaus. And when you asked me what the rewards of our work would be, I, in turn, asked what you most wanted in all the world."

"I remember. And you spoke of wanting knowledge, even power, over the world."

"And you of wanting to change the course of this war, and to see Germany triumphant."

Klaus nodded. "That is so. Though I do not understand how this power would work, or how—if such were even possible—I could wield it."

Dafyd nodded. "Once or twice in a generation there rises a man like your Führer, or perhaps the mad monk Rasputin in Russia, a rare hybrid born with enormous innate power but no understanding of how to wield it. People flock to them, lured by their strength and charisma. But because they're untrained and weak, inevitably they go mad, usually causing mayhem and bringing down empires in the process. One of the goals of our Art is to train and strengthen the will and psyche so these powers may be safely contained and focused in order to further our goals."

Klaus looked at the man. He wanted with every fibre of his being to believe him, believe it was true, that he could do these things. But—

But Dafyd, as usual, understood without the need for words.

"What would you say, Klaus, if I told you that not only are these things possible, but that an even greater prize may—*may*, if we do everything correctly—lie within our grasp?"

What was he getting at? "And that would be...?"

Dafyd's reply was immediate. "Immortality."

Klaus felt his mouth fall open in sheer surprise, but no words came out.

59

Dafyd went on. "You are no doubt familiar with Goethe, colonel?"

"Of course. But Faust wanted—"

"Transcendent knowledge, not immortality. Indeed. And so do I, and so does Magda. Faust wanted it so badly he gambled his soul for a mere glimpse of it: at least Marlowe's chap got twenty years." Dafyd chuckled, shaking his head; a moment later, he was deadly serious. "What if I told you that you could have not only knowledge and power but immortality as well, Colonel? And I mean true immortality, in the flesh. Eternal life, here on this Earth." He folded his hands over his hairy belly and sat back, watching Klaus's face.

Klaus almost laughed, but checked himself. He put down his water glass, rotating it a little to seat it firmly in the sand. "I would ask you what is the price."

Dafyd barked a laugh. At his side, Magda smiled—a little sadly, Klaus thought.

"You would be wise to do so," said the *zauberer*. "The price is high. Very high. Yet no more than I think we can afford *if* we keep our goals in mind."

Klaus waited for him to go on.

"Pain, Colonel. Suffering. The fires of Hell. That is the price of immortality. And it is payable in advance."

CHAPTER ELEVEN

Elléni consulted her notes again. "In July, one of the village children went missing. Giórgos, a little boy just five years old. He'd been playing near the family's house, but when his mother went out to fetch him, he was gone. They searched everywhere, but he was never found. The policeman concluded that the child must have gone into the water and drowned, and the body been washed out to sea.

"A month later to the day, a second child disappeared, a girl of twelve. This time the villagers wouldn't be placated. When the searchers turned up nothing, they sent the policeman to the *kommandant's* house to demand that his men help in the search. But the colonel wasn't there. His aide and one of the soldiers left in the direction of the stone house, returning a short while later to say that the colonel had given permission for his men to help. But even after several days of intensive searching, the girl wasn't found and the search was abandoned."

"Your yayá has an amazing memory," said Paul.

"Yes. And of course the events of this time are burned into her mind, though it's strange she has never spoken of it before." Elléni took a drink of her wine and flipped a page. "At the end of September, another person went missing. This time it was Fotini, the girl who'd been courted by the German soldier the previous year. She'd been out walking in the hills gathering wild greens and never came home. Suspicion immediately fell on the Germans, and the policeman—who must have been terrified—was again sent to talk to Maule and demand that the colonel interrogate the soldier who'd been her lover. The colonel expressed his sympathies and said he'd hold a full investigation among his men, starting with the ex-boyfriend.

"Of course, it went nowhere. Although the policeman still had his suspicions, some of the islanders now began to look with concern at their neighbours. Rumours spread that there was a murderer among them, a madman who enjoyed killing. Others started talking about a wild beast loose in the hills, a leopard, or perhaps a bear. Of course, there never have been such animals on Vóunos, but there are bears on the mainland, so it was just possible."

Paul reached for the wine and refilled their glasses. "Nobody suspected the English couple?"

"Thanks. Apparently not. I suppose the fact that they were the colonel's friends…. Anyway, after several days Fotini was still missing, and the search was called off. And now life on Vóunos began to change. People locked their doors and kept their children close; women didn't walk alone outside the village. Everyone lived in fear. At the same time, news reached the island that Germany was losing and the war would soon be over."

‡

June 13, 1944

"Tonight," said Dafyd, "we shall summon Crane. Although one of the more benign and malleable forces of the order *Daemones,* Crane is not to be underestimated. You can expect to feel driven to speak to him, even to step outside your circle and go to him. Do neither. It will get you killed, and worse."

Klaus felt an exquisite *frisson* of pure fear. "I understand."

"Good. You will remain exactly at your place, and you will remain silent."

"And the purpose of this summoning?"

"In large part, a test of you. Magda and I are known to Crane, and probably to entities beyond his level. He is in every sense a gatekeeper."

"So. And if I pass?"

"Then we can proceed to higher work. We have gone as far as we can alone. At a certain level, the Third becomes indispensable. If our trinity proves sound, the other possibilities we discussed open up—knowledge, power, and the transcendence of mortality."

Klaus had a brief vision—these had become commonplace since he began to study with these two—of golden apples. Freyja again, the goddess whose golden apples kept the gods young. How telling that her namesake had been the touchstone of Klaus's own youth and everything that had given him joy. Perhaps it was not too late for him.

"I am ready," he said.

‡

They'd rolled up all the living room rugs again and pushed back the furniture so as to have the space they needed. Klaus fetched the lamb—he'd bound its feet and jaws tightly together with the black cord Dafyd had given him to use—and laid it on the altar. He closed the shutters while Magda lit the candles. When everything was ready, Dafyd stepped into the center of the circle.

Painted in white on the bare boards, the design was some four meters across. The Welshman worked always with utmost precision and, before each operation, filled pages of paper with calculations and equations. With the aid of a planetary ephemeris, he plotted the

presence encircling him. Magda. Turning to her, he was shocked to find her grown beyond all reason, not in size but in some transcendent way. And from her poured a current of strength and confidence so great it calmed him at once, and the dread which had been so close to breaking him instantly diminished to manageable proportions. He formed a silent *thank you* with his lips.

They turned now to the North, the last quarter to be addressed, and Dafyd began once again to chant.

The room grew vast, and the sensation was that of a silent, endless immensity. The terror of just a moment ago receded further still as Klaus's bones filled with the strength and solidity of mountains. And now, beyond the violet circle of containment, the northern end of the room overflowed with a multitude of invisible presences, so that the three of them were surrounded on all sides by a vast host of the unseen.

Dafyd made two more invocations, one each to the Earth below and the sky above, before bringing everything together in the seventh, all-inclusive pass to seal an unbreachable sphere for the operation.

Dafyd turned again to the north. He struck a match and touched it to the second small brazier, this one black, by the altar, and a low dome of blue flame formed as he began his litany.

"There is in the universe nothing which is not balanced. All is balance, and its sum is both zero, the no-thing—" Dafyd drew a circle in the air—"and the lemniscate, which is infinity or all-thing." He drew a horizontal figure-of eight. "Implicit in balance are both rest and action, harmony and chaos, creation and destruction; and the distance between opposites, the thickness of the mirror, is less than the spaces within the atom."

The quiet was intense, as if entire worlds held their breath.

Dafyd began again, voice growing in intensity, until the air in the room vibrated and rang with each syllable. Although not the first time Klaus had been surprised at the way this almost comical-looking man could don power like a mantle, the way his voice seemed now to command and shake the world was beyond belief.

"We humans," Dafyd declared, "stand on the one side: on the other are the *Daemones*. It has always been so. And both recognize that any enmity which may arise between us is dwarfed by the dangers from the enemy beyond.

"In recognition then of this mutual interest and kinship do I offer up blood to open the channel between our worlds." The *zauberer* took up a knife and, in a single, measured motion, cut the lamb's throat. The animal trembled as its life gushed over the altar, the dark blood pulsing like a living tide. The glistening pool spread, pouring over the sides to drip onto the floor.

Dafyd laid the palm of his hand flat in the creature's blood and held it up to the north. The little dome of flame in the brazier brightened and rose, turning ruby red. The ground quivered under Klaus's feet and his nostrils filled with the unmistakable odor of sulfur. In the center of the violet circle, something stirred.

The smell of brimstone intensified. Klaus watched as the stirring coalesced into a point of darkness, then quickly expanded into a hovering sphere of absolute black the width of a man's torso. The temperature in the room plummeted.

What happened next was hard to follow. The sphere reversed itself, turning inside out in mockery of any sane geometry. Though it hurt his eyes to look at it, Klaus forced himself to look as impossibly shifting curves and planes of dark light—*how could such a thing be? But it was*—clashed and sparked and melded. Waves of burning cold flowed from it. As though from a great distance, impossible tearing, grinding sounds came to his ears.

Despite the cold, the sweat ran freely down Klaus's sides. Every instinct told him to run; but the part of his mind that remembered Dafyd's warnings and instruction knew it would be his death.

And now...

The thing began to take shape, unsteadily. A bird-shape, thin and ridiculously tall. Its feathers were opalescent, its beak dull iron. Its eyes...

The room, the circle, even Dafyd to the front and left of him, faded. He tried to turn to Magda for reassurance, could not. Terror began to command him, and—*dear God! It was looking at him!*

The terrible voids of the bird-thing's eyes grew, pulling, sucking him forward. He stood on the brink of an abyss, trembling, his balance going, his will and body frozen. As all self-control ebbed, his last, desperate thought was of himself roped to Magda and Dafyd, anchored by their strength.

Blood on snow. Land and sky a seamless grey vault. The reek of diesel. Air so cold it burned. Stench and putrefaction, and the terrible silence of death. Dark carrion-birds tearing and pecking at cooling flesh, and more circling, descending.

And now fire, and the smell of burning men.

"He is better than the last, o man." The words, spoken in a high, piping tone, brought Klaus back to himself.

How long…? The smells of death and burning had gone; the undercurrent of sulfur was still there. He looked down, expecting to see lacerated, blackened flesh. Instead, he saw himself whole, unharmed, and, incredibly, still standing within his circle, with Magda to his left and Dafyd before them at his altar.

Opposite Dafyd, where the awful bird-thing had been, stood an ordinary white crane a meter or so tall. Dafyd, with all the apparent concern of a man asking the price of a basket of fruit, addressed it.

"Then we may pass?"

The crane's beak parted and simply hung open, not apparently articulating. Its unearthly, high voice trembled at the next octave and others beyond, like some mad bagpipe. "Yes. I see you are now serious. I presume you seek a pact?"

"Precisely."

"It can be done. The years-long feast nears its close, and there are those who await you in earnest."

"Oh?" Dafyd looked genuinely surprised.

"O yes." Its voice dripped with contempt. "You are…coveted…by some. You understand the price?"

"Yes. We are prepared."

And now the crane-thing did something impossible: it smiled. The effect turned Klaus's blood to ice; his skin tried to crawl off his frame.

In a sly tone that held immeasurable menace, the bird said: "You know you must abandon that silly circle upon signing?"

"We know."

The thing dipped its head as if ducking for a fish. The beak yawned again. "Very good, o man. I like not these bonds. Until the next dark of the moon, then, when you shall offer up the last sacrifice before signing."

As its words faded, the creature became tenuous, then deconstructed into those incomprehensible geometries, a perverse mathematics of non-being during which even the metallic groaning sounds that had accompanied its appearance seemed to reverse themselves. Klaus's already shocked senses staggered and he struggled to keep himself from stopping his ears. Mercifully, the process was quick: the impossibility transformed itself back into the black sphere, shrank, and winked out of existence.

Klaus was too dazed to follow Dafyd's closing words. As the numbing cold ebbed, so the room regained its ordinariness, until it was just the three of them standing quietly in their protective circles. The lamb's carcass lay on the altar. The blood—all of it—was gone. Not a speck of red was to be seen.

Magda and Dafyd left the circle. As the woman, looking even paler than her unusually fair complexion, began to extinguish candles, Dafyd came to Klaus's side and patted his shoulder reassuringly. The Welshman was flushed and cheery.

"You did very well, Klaus. Very well indeed."

"Is it gone?" His voice was a dry rasp. He could barely breathe.

Dafyd took his arm. "Quite gone. Come, it's safe to leave the circle now. I imagine we could all use a drink and perhaps some food. You have passed the worst test: I name you Third. The road to our goal is open."

‡

July 6, 1944

As the summer wound on, Magda and Dafyd spent their time in meditation, divination, and the phenomenally detailed planning that accompanied each of the rituals, while Klaus passed his days attending to the minor duties of his command and thinking about the future. Despite the triumphant tone of the broadcasts from Berlin, he could see that even his men understood that the war was going badly.

The Reich still had some strength, and there was no doubt the allies would at the least experience some harsh reverses. But it couldn't go on more than a year or two. Especially after the attempt on the

Führer's life—however Goebbels tried to frame it as the action of a few power-hungry lunatics, Klaus suspected much of the High Command would have been relieved if the plot had succeeded. Loyalty to the Fatherland, to its survival, must ultimately be greater than loyalty to one man, no matter how beloved that man. Russia had been his folly—without that, they'd would have been masters of the world for a thousand years.

And now…if everything they were doing went well—and Klaus increasingly dared to believe it would—he would have a chance to change that. He would pay the price, endure a lifetime of service and torment he could barely imagine—to acquire the *lebensraum* Germany had so long been denied and finally end the competition of the races. The Jews, the blacks, the Asiatics…seventy years from now they would be an even worse problem, a plague uncontrolled in the world. But with the type of power and charisma that Dafyd displayed now, and with Dafyd's help, he would do what the Führer had failed to.

He considered this as he bound the sacrifice—a small boy, perhaps five years old—to the altar for that night's ritual. He'd caught him playing in a secluded cove near the family house and snatched him up, aided by Dafyd's spell to prevent him being observed. The chloroform had quieted the boy in a moment. Soon, the extinction of this small life would allow Dafyd to negotiate the precise terms of the bargain they would soon be entering into.

‡

August 4, 1944

A month later, Klaus was given the singular honour of being the one to sacrifice the virgin girl whose life and mortal parts were required for the actual crafting of the agreement.

He stood before the altar, trying hard to quell the trembling inside. The weight of presences in the room was such that he felt like a conductor about to raise his baton in a packed concert hall. The candlelight caught the knife's polished blade as he picked it up and raised it to his lips precisely as Dafyd had instructed.

The girl—a child, almost—lay bound on the altar before him,

naked but for the gag across her mouth. She was tanned and strong. He marveled at the way her young breasts rose and fell with every shuddering, terrified breath. And lower, a thin down of hair on her—

He glanced up, suddenly very aware his mind had wandered. Magda stood ready at Klaus's side with a wide porcelain bowl; across the altar, Dafyd, with his characteristic half-smile, watched him attentively. Klaus wondered how obvious the erection straining at the front of his trousers was in the flickering light.

He took a breath to steady himself. The girl arched her body violently, straining every sinew in her attempts to scream through the tight gag, but all that came out was a long, muffled moan that did nothing except sharpen Klaus's mounting excitement.

A great calm descended on him. His quivering hand stilled as he lowered the knife. He admired the perfect edge he'd put on it in preparation for this moment. The blade glimmered in the light like a living thing.

A final, desperate noise escaped the girl and her eyes went impossibly wide as she turned her head, slamming her cheek to the altar. Which put the side of the neck in the perfect position.

Klaus placed a palm on the side of her head to hold it still and brought the blade down to rest the honed edge on the soft, trembling skin, tilting the tip down ready for the draw. He took a deep breath and applied pressure, just enough to part the skin and slice through to the arteries. As a line of bright blood welled up, he drew the blade in an arc like a lover's caress.

A cacophony of inhuman sounds and cries exploded from the shadows. Hot blood spurted, splashing his face and chest and running over his mouth in a warm, coppery stream. The sensation was ecstatic, shattering. He caught Dafyd's amused expression and saw Magda step forward with the bowl as he reeled under the intensity of a sudden and wholly unexpected ejaculation.

‡

Magda slept little that night. She'd never challenged Dafyd on anything, but she had to speak up. She tackled him at breakfast.

"Dafyd, I understand why the sacrifices are necessary. But I have to say that knowing why and taking pleasure in the business are two very different things."

He looked up from the book he was immersed in, a boyish grin on his face. "Klaus did get an enormous thrill out of it, didn't he?" He laughed. "Thank Hell you're not a prude."

She shook her head. "I wasn't thinking of him, Dafyd. He can't help himself."

Dafyd's eyes narrowed as his amusement faded. "I see. Well, your objection is noted, and you're certainly entitled to your scruples. Just don't expect me to share them."

His fog-grey eyes had solidified into steel. The room seemed to crackle and hum with tension. She held her breath but didn't flinch or break eye contact. He needed her as much as they both needed Klaus, and they'd not come this far to throw it all away.

After several seconds, his face relaxed, and the familiar laughter lines reappeared. He shook his head, chuckled, and returned to his book.

CHAPTER TWELVE

"Now we come to the big mystery," said Elléni. "Just days before the liberation of Athens, the German garrison on Vóunos left. Only one man saw them go—they left at dawn, picked up by a German ship off the coast—and he swore that the colonel wasn't with them. Later that day the policeman entered the kommandant's house and found it empty.

"Some days later—by now the villagers knew Greece had been liberated and were celebrating their freedom—people began to realize that the English couple hadn't been seen in the village for some time. Eventually the policeman went to the stone house to investigate. Can you guess what he found?"

Paul shrugged. "The colonel in bed with the British couple?"

Elléni burst out laughing, and he laughed with her. "In full uniform!" she added, making him really crack up. Both of them were helpless with laughter for a few moments, a relief from the fundamental horror of the story; but that knowledge made the image no less comical.

Eventually, Elléni wiped her eyes, and her face settled back into a more serious aspect. "No, what he discovered was something much darker, more evil. The English couple and the colonel all lay dead in the living room, their bodies in a state of full putrefaction. There were strange designs and numbers painted all over the floor, and three tall candlesticks covered in wax. Worst of all, the remains of a young woman—it was Fotini—with a knife buried in her chest lay on an altar in the center of the room.

The policeman ran away in sick terror. Because the affair involved foreigners he notified Thessaloniki, and they sent a detective to investigate the deaths. The detective concluded that the three had probably taken poison while performing some unknown ritual.

"But when they investigated the area around the house, they found signs of freshly-worked earth behind the orchard. They dug down and uncovered the remains of the two missing children. Of course, once the investigators had left, the policeman told the village everything, including the fact that the bodies all showed signs of violent death. The body of the little girl had apparently been further desecrated, but the policeman would not be drawn on this. But this discovery, along with the strange designs and the candles where the corpses were found, convinced everyone that the colonel and the two quiet foreigners whom everyone had rather liked had been practicing black magic and human sacrifice."

Paul stared at her. "Here? In this house?"

She inclined her head. "In this very room."

‡

September 13, 1944

Magda had retired, leaving the men downstairs to talk over their brandy. The house was quiet, with no trace of unease or errant energy loose in it. Peace reigned.

She placed a fresh log in the bedroom fireplace. The nights had already turned cold and winter would come early this year. Whether she was still here to see it was another matter: she didn't think so.

Last month's sacrifice had been the final ritual needed before the signing. She'd not much liked watching the conscious and mounting terror of the little girl on the altar as the room filled with presences, and had been glad when the climax came and Klaus, at Dafyd's signal, cut her throat and ended her ordeal. But it had all gone well. Nobody had died who'd not been meant to, and the powers had accepted the sacrifice and the terms. The remains of the little boy and girl lay now at peace in a shallow grave on the far side of the orchard.

Magda still had reservations about Klaus's stability, but after thoroughly scrying the matter she was less uneasy about the possibility of his falling apart when they most needed him. In fact, she now believed he had a vital role to play at the crucial time of their rebirth, but exactly what that was remained veiled, opaque to her Sight.

How strange it should end up here, with my going willingly to my death.

As a child she'd driven the nuns mad with her questions at school. She accepted a lot of their teachings, but even before age ten she could see all their fears and insecurities. So much of their belief was blind faith in their Good Book, reinforced by the stern looks and frowns from the Holy Father. Some of the nuns were less than brilliant, but the Holy Father, a Jesuit, was no fool. How could a man with a mind like that believe in the transparent, if epic, fictions that made up the Bible?

She left her parents and two sisters the day she turned eighteen, and went to Dublin. The big city would be a good place to start. She found work as a shopgirl and before long was spending her evenings in discussions with a group practicing Theosophy. After a year there she discovered Tarot, and before long found a teacher in the famous clairvoyant, Miss Aislyn.

After four years of intense, fulltime study—Magda had left the shop and taken a room in Miss Aislyn's house—she'd absorbed everything her teacher knew about divination and scrying. When Magda expressed an interest in furthering her knowledge through ritual and practical work, Miss Aislyn agreed. That was how she'd come to Morocco and met Dafyd. And now…

She stood undressed before her dressing-table considering her reflection in the large oval mirror. She ran her hands along her stomach, up over her breasts, down her sides to her hips. It had served well, this body, and she'd been pleased with it. Excessively fine for her needs, really, and all that virginal beauty had been wasted; but still, it made it easy to live with. How strange to think that in just a few weeks it would be given over to the worms, to decay and corruption, to crumble and return to the Earth.

‡

"What will become of our bodies," asked Klaus, "when we cross into the demonic realm?"

"They'll die," said Dafyd. "Once the soul leaves, everything stops. It'll be as if we just had heart attacks."

He sipped his brandy, watching Klaus closely. The colonel's eyes were hooded as he rubbed at his lips, lost in thought. Struggling, he was. The last doubts.

Not for the first time, Dafyd felt respect for this man who, for all his weaknesses and perversions, in turn clearly respected him. For the colonel and men like him, the world was organized like a dog pack, a strictly vertical hierarchy: if you were not below them, you were above them. It was the lens through which they saw everything. Still, Klaus had the intelligence to understand the lure of knowledge for its own sake, even if his own motives were all centered around power and control. Power came with knowledge, of course, but it had never been Dafyd and Magda's only focus. Their goal centered on penetrating the mysteries, and even the most skilled magician could only learn so much while shackled to flesh and bound by mortality.

It wouldn't be easy, the service. Seventy years as apprentices and aides to Nestor would feel like a literal eternity—there was no time in Hell. But though there weren't any records of it except, Dafyd suspected, in the deep vaults of the Vatican, he was certain they wouldn't be the first, and Crane had confirmed it. If others had succeeded and returned, they could have—almost certainly had—gone on to alter the course of history. Every culture had its stories of immortals who still walked the Earth, and secret societies that controlled man's destiny from the shadows. Would they be able to recognize those others once they returned? Dafyd thought they would, and would be able to locate them using magic.

After a few moments, Klaus nodded as though he'd come to a decision; he looked up at Dafyd and said, "What will it be like, do you think?"

"The transition?"

"No. Being there, in *their* realm. You spoke of service, and you have referred to it as mutual learning. But an existence outside the body? I cannot imagine it, except perhaps as a waking dream. Will there be speech? Night and Day? Sleep?"

"An unusually vivid dream may not be an inappropriate metaphor," said Dafyd. *Or more likely, nightmare.* "I'm not certain I can foresee the specifics better than you can, but I don't expect it will be much like this life. Certainly there'll be no day or night, no sleep, no digestive or sexual functions—those are all part of the physical. I'm not even sure there'll be differentiated consciousness. I can guarantee that the service will be grueling. And there will be pain."

Klaus nodded, but said nothing.

"Now," Dafyd went on, "Sunday is the dark of the moon, when we shall set our snare. If we do it correctly, we shall have our chance upon our return to this world."

"And the pact?"

"Three weeks later. October the eighth."

CHAPTER THIRTEEN

Paul was quiet a long time, trying to absorb it all. He had to ask the question that was bothering him. "The thing I don't get is how, if these horrific things really happened here, the whole island doesn't know about it. And especially why—" He bit off the question, frowning.

Elléni cocked her head. "Why what?"

"Well...why you didn't mention anything when you rented me the place. Didn't you know *anything* about its history?"

She stared down at the coffee table, apparently considering her reply. Her hair rippled with a slow shake of her head. "Paul, I..." Her gaze came up to meet his. "Look, when you came to me looking for a house to rent, you were just a stranger new to the island, a *xénos*. I knew the house had been empty for a very long time, and that it had a bad reputation. But I didn't know any of this."

He stared back at her. "This is an island of two thousand inhabitants! How could people forget?"

She bit back hard enough that he flinched. "These things happened seventy years ago! Most of those people are dead, or were small children at the time. " She let out a breath, composed herself. "I'd never have deceived you if I'd known the truth, even though you were a stranger. All I know is that I was contacted last autumn by a lawyer in Athens asking me to offer the house for rental." She held her hands out, palms upturned. "Yes, I knew there were some rumours and legends about it, but I don't really believe in these things, magic and ghosts. I'm not even certain about God. So I didn't pay much attention. And the old couple who look after the house are quite normal people."

He nodded. It still seemed weird that such horrific events—the disappearance and murder of three people, two of them children, not to mention their sacrifice—wouldn't be common knowledge in a place like this. But people did bury traumatic stuff.

Elléni played distractedly with a loose strand of hair. Finally, she broke the silence. "Yaya said that when the bodies had been removed for burial and the police were gone, *o Pápas* came to the house and performed an exorcism followed by a blessing. Even after it was locked up, he came every year to bless the place and the grounds."

Paul started. She had to be kidding. *"An exorcism?* Seriously?"

Elléni's brow furrowed. "Eh, yes, of course." She reached abruptly for her wine, not looking at him.

"I'm sorry, I didn't mean any offense. It's just, it's so..."

"Medieval? Paul, you're on a small island, living in a traditional community, not in San Francisco. The Devil is very real and frightening for many people."

"Right. Yes, I understand." He finished his own wine and refilled their glasses; the bottle was almost gone. His mind was racing. He didn't for a minute believe in gods, devils, ghosts, or anything he couldn't see and touch. "And yet you're sitting here, even knowing all this happened."

She gave a half-shrug. "The old priest has blessed the place, and it feels tranquil, welcoming. Fotini and the children are at peace. And I'm not very religious."

"You have a crucifix in your car," he pointed out.

"Ah. My mother, she insisted. And it does no harm. In any case, I'm sure that after so long any lingering traces of evil must have faded, even without all the exorcisms." Her face relaxed and a smile danced on her lips. "And I think you'll make this house a happy place."

He smiled back at her. He raised his glass. "To our rebirth, then—mine and the house's."

Her laugh was a chime of crystal. "Yamas!"

When they'd drained their glasses, Elléni checked her watch and leaned forward. "Well, I need to go. It's almost seven and there's still some work I need to finish at the office."

He rose with her, confused. Had he offended her? But her next words allayed his fears.

"Ah, I wanted to ask, do you have plans for Easter? I would like to invite you to spend it with us at Mikró Kástro."

"With your family? I'd love that. The only thing is my niece, Alex. She's coming to visit over Easter."

Elléni's face lit up. "Really? Wonderful! I'd love to meet her. Well, she's invited too, of course. When does she arrive?"

"She flies in to Thessaloniki on the Thursday before Easter and leaves the following Tuesday."

"All that way for such a short visit?"

"She'll have four full days. I'm already pushing it with Charly."

Elléni's brow furrowed. "Charly?"

"My sister. Alex's mother."

"Oh, of course. Well, Alex will be very welcome. How old is she?"

"Eighteen. She's in her second year of college at Cornell and has a very full academic load, so she can't miss more than a day or two."

"I understand. Well." She faced him, as if waiting.

"Thanks for stopping by. And especially for the revelations about the house—it's hard to believe these things happened here."

"I hope you'll be okay on your own," she teased. "Are you going to have nightmares, sleeping all alone?" There was mischief in her eyes, and something behind that, too. Her cheeks were definitely flushed.

He took the chance. "Do I have a choice?" And before he could second-guess himself, took her very gently by the shoulders and kissed her firmly on the lips.

Her lips parted and she slipped her arms about his shoulders. Tongues met and twined in a languid kiss. She pulled back, smoky-eyed, and whispered, "Do you want me to stay?"

"More than you can imagine."

And now she was on him, her hands on his back, in his hair, pulling him to her. His mouth found hers; reason evaporated as reactions long suppressed ignited in the swaying heat of the embrace. Her breasts strained against him in the crush, her thigh was hard against his; the suddenness of his erection surprised him.

Hiss of indrawn breath as she sought him, palmed him. Her flesh was smooth and firm as his hands slid up under her sweater, encountered lace. He eased the fabric off the plump nipple and teased. She pulled off the sweater and pushed his head down, moaning as his mouth closed over her breast. Zippers and clasps yielded, clothes were shed with mounting urgency.

Ignition became firestorm, the bedroom entirely forgotten as she sank to her knees and took him in her mouth. The world tilted and swayed.

She looked up at him, beautiful beyond belief. He said, "I want you."

She drew back, hand holding onto the object of her efforts, the other cupping him. "You will have me," she agreed.

He knelt beside her on the rug and, locked in kisses and caresses, they sank together to the horizontal. Her legs spread in irresistible invitation, one hand reaching down to guide him in. She was wet, hot. Eyes locked, they began to move, reciprocating motions shallow at first then increasing by gentle degrees as if to some unheard music. And now he was fully inside her, clasping her hands, holding them down beside her head. Her ankles crossed over his back, locking him to her. Her breaths came faster.

She cried out; he felt her shudder, and then his own climax smashed down on him and everything came to a point, the moment, the now.

After a little while, Paul attended to the stove, led her to the bedroom, and lit candles. Their second time was slower, sensual rather than desperate. This time she took charge, straddling him. He felt the delicious weight of her breasts on his chest as she leaned in to kiss him, twining her hands in his, stretching his arms over his head. Surrendering all control, he let her lead; after a while she pivoted around, facing away, and led him in an unexpectedly smooth maneuver to lie on top of her, behind her, his hips molded to her ass, never uncoupling. He set his hands on hers, forearms on forearms, pinning her down with his weight. Her moan of delight at finding herself now his captive was all the invitation he needed. Heat turned again to fire, and the world went entirely away.

CHAPTER FOURTEEN

September 14, 1944

"I've got it," said Magda. "April twentieth, 2014. Have a look."

She'd spent three days with her cards and books and the crystal sphere of Irish beryl, mind unbound and Sight loosed into the far future, scrying and taking notes and calculating charts. Their resurrection had to coincide with the waning moon; it had to take place during the hours of night; and the whole chart should be strongly aspected. But this was beyond what she'd hoped for.

"Good grief, Magda," said Dafyd, "it's perfect! Moon on the ascendant, Pluto in the first house…a cardinal grand cross, everything within a degree…"

"Remarkable, isn't it? And also a grand trine, there, in water. It's hard to imagine more dynamic tension, more sheer power, in a chart. And here's the crowning glory: April twentieth 2014 is both the Western and Orthodox Easter Sunday."

Dafyd's mouth opened. In an instant he burst out laughing.

"I thought you'd see the humour in it," she said.

He was positively shaking with mirth, his laughter filling the room. When he'd got it out, he wiped an eye and said, "So we're to be resurrected on Easter Sunday? I couldn't have wished for more if I'd tried. If I had any concerns about our alignment with the universal, this settles the issue beyond all doubt. And proves that the universe also has a sense of humour."

"And yet…it does make me wonder."

He cocked his head.

"Well, this alignment with the universal. Don't you ever worry about whether we have any true choices, any freedom of action at all? Because when you consider the symbolism of the date, the coincidence seems…. Well."

Dafyd grinned and wagged a finger at her. "You're falling into an old intellectual trap, Magda. I don't believe there need be a dichotomy. Consider your own scrying," he went on. "If the universe were wholly deterministic, what would prevent you from seeing with utmost clarity?"

"The limitations of my own skill."

"Come, Magda, you do yourself a disservice. No, we are free to act, but only in accordance with our own nature—and that, I believe, *is* determined. As Schopenhauer puts it, 'Man can do what he wills but he cannot *will* what he wills'. And there's another factor besides."

"Which is?"

"Einstein's theorems make clear the importance of the observer in any system. Since our perception of the universe is mediated by consciousness and mind, our perception of probability depends wholly on the meaning we assign to a thing or phenomenon—in this case, Easter Sunday."

She began to see what he was getting at. "You're saying that since we're part of the universe, the values…the associations that we place on a thing, like Easter Sunday…that they contribute to the outcome in some way?"

"More or less, yes. As close as language can convey. Since the fact of the most propitious planetary aspects falling on a day that has huge cultural significance in the context of what we're doing…well, I'd say the universe is tipping its hand."

She raised an eyebrow. "But is it in our favour?"

"Oh, yes. Most definitely so."

BLACK EASTER

‡

September 17, 1944

Dafyd put down the pen and rested his palms on the table. "Done," he said.

To his left, Magda watched as his elegant signature turned from bright red to a dark, ferrous brown, the blood losing its sheen as the letters became part of the parchment. Klaus, standing at Dafyd's right, appeared utterly mesmerized.

As she watched, the glamour, now complete, began to shimmer in her Sight with a power all its own, as should any true magical artifact which, by its intrinsic power, existed in more than one world simultaneously.

Glancing at her mentor, Magda was shocked to see how spent he was, what the operation had cost him. His face, normally plump and florid, was slack and pallid. There were dark circles under his eyes, and she was certain he'd lost weight. He had aged by years in these last weeks.

They had worked, together and separately, for weeks on preparing the artifact. Magda had collected a quantity of the young girl's blood at the altar as it pulsed from the artery, then consecrated and preserved it; she'd crafted the pen for Dafyd to use. Klaus had skinned the corpse and, under Dafyd's direction, flayed and soaked and stretched the membrane until it was perfect and ready for use. Dafyd had composed the formula and text: precise wording was absolutely vital, given how remarkably literal-minded demons were. Finally, he provided the unwavering hand and flawless calligraphy to copy, in the girl's blood, the words of entrammelment. They read:

In the year two thousand and fourteen, threescore years and ten from the making of this glamour, shall three people of mixed sex, two of the one and one of the other as required by Law, come together in this house during the three days of Easter; and that they not be free to leave but instead be herein constrained until, no later than sunset on Easter Sunday, we three signatories return to take possession of their physical bodies, casting their souls into Hell to serve for eternity in our stead.

Signed this seventeenth of September nineteen hundred and forty-four by

And at the end, their signatures.

Dafyd rolled the parchment into a tight tube and held it out for Magda to secure with a braid made from the sacrifice's hair. Klaus wrapped it in oiled cloth, folded the ends over, and tied it with fine wire to preserve it against damp and decay.

They went down into the cellar, where Klaus had cut a narrow, meter-deep cavity into the floor, like a miniature grave. Even if the house were destroyed, the artifact—their only remaining anchor to this plane, a beacon for their resurrection—would survive. When the time came, the artifact, like a tremendous storage battery with much of Dafyd's personal power locked into it, would supply the force needed to breach the boundary of the spheres and drive the mechanics of their rebirth.

Dafyd dropped the thing inside and Magda threw a handful of soil over it, reciting the final incantation. The men began backfilling the hole, tamping it down hard as they went, until the floor was level again.

"Very good," said Dafyd. "Now everything is ready."

PART TWO

CHAPTER FIFTEEN

Elléni lay with her head resting on his shoulder, her right hand in his left. His passion had surprised her in the best possible way. For a man who always appeared so controlled, even reserved, his lovemaking was anything but. Where she'd feared he might be cool and passive, he proved himself more than capable of taking the lead; when she'd wanted to take control, he let her. She was both sated and elated.

"Your *anástasi*," she said, squeezing his hand, "tell me about it." She'd wanted to ask him from the beginning, but the question had seemed too intimate before.

Sleepy-sounding, he said, "What do you want to know?"

"You left your job, your home, your family, to come and live here alone and make a new life. A man doesn't do this without a good reason."

He didn't answer at once. She wondered if she'd been too presumptuous in asking. She had the fleeting vision of him scratching at his throat and stalling…but that was the boy, Pétros, her last lover. She'd been feeling old, and he was there in a moment of weakness and need. What a mistake *that* turned out. It should never have got out, *would* never have got out, except that the little prick had to brag to his friends and make her look like the island slut. It was months before his pals stopped their leers and whispers every time they saw her in a taverna or in the street.

Paul shrugged. "An existential crisis, really," he said at last. "Some people would call it depression. I don't like that word."

She remained quiet, listening.

"It was ugly. I thought too much, kept to myself. Everything started to get to me. I was comfortable, doing well, but every time I looked around…I couldn't even open a paper anymore, never mind look at news on TV. We've turned the world into a hell."

She stared intensely at him, wanting to understand. "It's true there's a lot wrong with the world, but…*a hell?*"

He didn't answer, just stared at the ceiling, seemingly lost in thought. She traced a finger over his chest. "When did you start feeling that way? Did something bad happen?"

His face tightened and he bit on his lower lip. Finally, "I was dating a woman called Stacy," he said "My first marriage had ended badly, and I was single a long while. Anyway, Stacy....I really loved her. We went so far as to get engaged." He glanced at her, then turned back to the ceiling, his gaze distant again. "Steve, my business partner and I were building up our antiques business then, it was crazy. I was working all hours. Stacy couldn't take it any more, it was too much for her. She got cold feet, broke off the engagement, done, finished." He shrugged again.

"And your ex?" She had to know. "What happened with her?"

He shook his head. "She joined a cult."

"A religious cult?"

"Yes, Christian. America's full of them. Toxic little groups of delusional crazies, house churches that believe they're the only ones in the entire world that really get God's message. See, Karen couldn't have children, that was where it started. I wanted to adopt, but she wouldn't have that. After we'd given up on fertility treatments, her friend Beth told her about this preacher who could cure her, and she fell for it. After just a few weeks they had her so fucking brainwashed I couldn't even talk to her. I cut the cord right there."

"We don't have these cults in Greece. But I've read about them."

His eyes remained on the ceiling. "Faith is powerful stuff. It's destructive. And the man-made, ego-driven variety is the worst. It extends false hope, tears families apart."

"The Bible is full of warnings about false prophets," she said.

He turned to face her. "I thought you said you weren't very religious."

"I'm not. But we are all brought up in the Church here."

"Oh. Of course." He let his head sink back on the pillow. "Anyway, Karen and I split in 2002, and I got over it. But four years ago, after Stacy left, everything seemed to crash down on me. Things got really bad." He gave a little snort of what could have been disgust. "It was like she'd died, and there wasn't anyone else. I never felt so alone. Thing is, I'd never taken the time to cultivate friendships. I was trapped in my work, in the city. My sister and niece, the only family I have, were thousands of miles away.

"The fact that I had so much that others don't—a nice home, a good business, money in the bank…perversely, that only made it worse, made me feel guilty for being so fortunate instead of being happy about it. So on top of the depression I felt totally pathetic."

She shifted her grip slightly, twining her fingers in his. "You didn't get medication? For this…existential crisis?"

Shake of the head. "I believe in dealing with causes, not symptoms. I just needed a complete change of life. I needed to get away from delusional ideas, splintered minds, a sick, rage-filled, unbalanced society—and believe me, America is all that. Deeply, deeply sick. I needed a culture that hadn't entirely lost its marbles, that values family and friendship over work and money. I needed sea and woods and nature. I needed peace. Most of all, I needed to find my roots again."

"And so you came here."

"Exactly."

"And now?"

He seemed to come back fully to himself, his face settling into a tentative smile, as though trying it on to see if it would fit. "You know what? I do believe I've turned a corner. I'm starting to heal."

She propped herself up on one arm and looked down at him. "Except," she said, shaking his hand up and down on his chest in time to her words, "that now you live in a house filled with sorcery and evil and the memory of human sacrifices—and now I shall suck your blood and you'll become a vampire like me!" She made her eyes huge and frightening, opened her mouth wide, and clamped her teeth onto his neck. He burst out laughing and flipped her onto her back, once again pinning her down with both hands on hers. God, a man who didn't need to be told what she needed.

They looked at one another, grinning, excited. He bent down and teased a nipple with his tongue, making her gasp.

"What are you going to do to me?" she said, suddenly breathless.

"Whatever I want," he replied, his weight and grip holding her down. The hint of dominance surprised and electrified her, and she shuddered as he moved lower, brushing his lips along her belly, planting small kisses along the way.

Paul woke a little after sunrise. He'd slept like a dead man, more solidly than he could remember having done for years. As the memory of last night came back to him, he felt an irrepressible smile steal over his face. Life…was definitely good.

He rose quietly, careful not to disturb her, pulled on his robe, and tiptoed out of the room. The house had chilled overnight, and through the kitchen window he could see a heavy dew sparkling on the grasses at the edge of the driveway. After lighting the stove, he put on coffee and made toast. A few minutes later he took both upstairs on a tray.

She stirred as he entered. "Mmm. I smell coffee! What time is it?"

"Almost seven-thirty," he said, setting a demitasse of thick Greek coffee and her toast on the bedside table. What time do you need to be at work?"

"Eh. When I want to be." She sat up, entirely unselfconscious, and reached for the coffee. Her hair, a reddish-brown storm around her neck and shoulders, curled down to graze the upper slopes of her full breasts. God, she was beautiful.

"Although," she added, "I do have an appointment at eleven, and two new rentals to photograph and list. This is the beginning. After Easter, work will get crazy." She sipped her coffee.

He put his own cup and plate on his side, shucked off his robe, and climbed back into bed. "There's toast, too."

She set down her cup and turned to him. "After. Now hurry up and finish your coffee." Her hand settled on his thigh and moved upwards. "There's something we have to do."

‡

After she left, Paul dressed, made up the bed, and tidied the kitchen. The day was sunny and crystal-bright, with just a few rags of high cirrus far to the north. A little to the east, over dozens of miles of slow-swelling purple sea, he could just make out the peak of Mount Athos, the center of the Orthodox Church. Legend claimed that the holy mountain was an enormous rock once hurled at Zeus by an angry giant. And in this ancient land, the wellspring of western civilization, legend felt always felt close and real.

He walked along the side of the house to the orchard. The trees were well-tended, their branches healthy and open, free of water shoots and dead wood: the couple who cared for the house came every two weeks—he'd insisted on their staying on to keep the orchard and exterior tidy—and were doing a fine job. Some of the trees were in bud. He wasn't sure which were plums and which apricot, but he'd soon find out.

On the far side of the orchard was a grassy strip several feet wide, and beyond that the low stone wall which marked the end of the property. The grave site must have been somewhere along here. He glanced around, then walked to the western boundary of the orchard, towards the hill edge, vaguely expecting to find some evidence of the exact burial site. He stopped for a moment to gaze down the hillside, past pine woods and meadows and olive groves to the village and harbour beyond. There were wisps of smoke rising here and there in the village; and in the distance, far out at sea, what looked like a container ship sliding serenely along in the general direction of Turkey.

Retracing his steps with the sun full and strong on his face, he noticed what seemed to be an area of darker grass. He stopped. Could be his imagination but.... He moved back a few steps, then to the side to get a different angle against the slanting sunlight. No, it was there: a rough rectangle of ground, about the size of a narrow grave, where the grass was distinctly darker than that which surrounded it.

His heart jolted in his chest. The vision came unbidden to his mind—two village men with shovels, sweating in the hot sun under the gaze of a policeman; a few feet down, a sudden glimpse of revealed bone halts the dig. Revulsion mixed with stricken reverence as the children's decomposing bodies are first exposed, then gently removed. The grief and horror spreading plaguelike through the village.

And here, amid all this beauty…wasn't the world magical enough without buying into totally irrational beliefs? At least Karen's little cult had been relatively harmless. But when faith got out of hand—not just with delusional occultists, but also when there wasn't a body of solidly-trained academics and a priesthood to interpret and reconcile that crazy, jumbled collection of texts that comprised the Bible—nobody was safe.

An involuntary shiver ran through him. Back in the late eighties the US media had gone on a witchcraft binge, shouting that Satanic rites were taking place all over the nation—a spinoff, he supposed, of the Reaganish resurgence of the Christian Right and the born-again loonies. They'd have enjoyed burning tarot readers and yoga teachers at the stake if they could have gotten away with it. But this—assuming Elléni's yayá's story was accurate—was real. A child, a teenage girl, and a woman had all been killed in his house, in his living room, and buried right here.

And in the house…

Yaya's story had told of the colonel and the English couple lying dead among weird designs painted on the floor. The floor was covered in rugs, with little of the boards showing except around the perimeter. Would there still be traces? He took a last look at the grave before turning to walk back through the orchard.

He spent the next couple of hours unpacking the rest of his belongings and distributing them about the house. He was going to need a bookshelf, and a desk would be a good thing, too. When he was done, he stacked all the boxes along one wall and began rolling up rugs.

The boards underneath were the rich orange-brown of naturally aged pine, probably deepened by several coats of heavily-applied varnish. At first glance nothing beyond the strong grain pattern was visible, the only significant variations occurring where knots stood out among the sections of straight grain.

He got down on his knees, feeling a little silly, and began a closer examination of the surface, starting in the rough middle of the room and circling outwards. He found a couple of specks of what might have been white paint here and there, almost invisible in deeper nicks in the wood, but they could have been anything. He was about to give up when, off to the side of what he thought of as the breakfast bar, he found a few flecks of quite brilliant violet in the radial cracks of a deep brown knot. When he stood, they were just about invisible. But, examining them again close up, he was certain they were paint.

As he crouched there, he felt a sudden, extreme chill. His head came up and he snapped upright, sitting back on his heels. The back of his neck prickled. He looked around the room, heart starting to race. It wasn't the chill of fear but of frigid air, as if he'd been dropped into a cold storage locker. He suffered an instant of disorienting panic and then everything was normal, the cold gone as quickly as it had arrived.

He took a deep breath to steady himself. *Everything was normal,* nothing out of the ordinary. Suggestibility? All this business of rituals and killings had him on edge. But he'd experienced this same phenomenon just a couple of days ago, hadn't he? He remembered he'd lit the stove, even though the day had earlier been warm. He looked around again. Nothing. He shook his head and made a mental note to be alert for any recurrences of the experience.

Searching the rest of the area, he found one more trace of the same bright pigment, this time a hair-thin, inch-long streak in an irregularity on the edge of a board. Violet. Violet and white. He'd seen painted floors before, in the city, but he couldn't imagine it here; and white would be less than practical anywhere.

After a further, fruitless, search he replaced the rugs and had an early lunch. With no garbage collection, he'd have to break down all the boxes and drive them to one of the public dumpsters in town, where the villagers deposited their garbage; recycling hadn't yet reached Vóunos. He decided to keep a few, including the stout wardrobe boxes: if he had to move at some future point, they'd come in useful. He chose a half-dozen and broke them down along with the wardrobe boxes. They could go in the cellar, where he'd at some point erect some racks for wine, as Elléni had suggested.

The cellar was low-ceilinged and surprisingly cold. Not just cool, but *cold.* Perhaps because it was always closed up. He'd peeked down here just once, the day he moved in. The only illumination was a naked bulb in a wall-mounted socket at the bottom of the short stair. His shadow jerked huge and grotesque against the walls as he set first one, then another of the big wardrobe boxes at the far end. He had a bizarre, fleeting moment of pure terror as he imagined the cellar door swinging shut and somehow locking; he smiled at his own silliness.

The room was about six feet by eight, with stone walls and a hard-packed dirt floor. He was glad the bodies had been buried a distance from the house instead of down here. The house, at least, was free of remains and magical remnants.

CHAPTER SIXTEEN

October 7, 1944

In the morning they built a bonfire behind the house and burned all Dafyd and Magda's research notes and personal documents along with all the magical tools not needed during the ceremony. Dafyd had already set up a trust through his London solicitors and a legal firm in Athens for the maintenance and upkeep of the house until April of 2013—a year before their return—at which time it was to be offered for rent. These instructions would take effect once the war ended and would allow plenty of time for the artifact to attract the trio they needed. He'd also wound a simple glamour into the stones of the building to create a blind spot of sorts that would deflect too much local interest in the house in the intervening decades and ensure that the caretakers just carried out their duties, and nothing more.

In the cellar, the young girl they'd taken ten days previously for the sacrifice was bound and gagged.

Everything was ready.

‡

October 8, 1944

Watching Dafyd's motions as he worked through the now-familiar invocations to the four quarters, Klaus felt a strange calm settle on him. He should have been terrified—had been, in fact, as recently as yesterday, though he had controlled it. Even Dafyd had looked tense, and certainly quieter than usual, in the last few days. Magda, though, remained entirely composed, her outward behavior not changing in the slightest.

Powers of the fertile North,
You who rule all matter,
Home to the dark soil to which all things return…

In the course of hours, Klaus's body, *this body,* would begin its own process of returning to that same dark soil. He wished for a moment it had been in the green fields of home instead of this hot foreign land, but in the end it didn't matter, did it? Better than in Russia. Dust to dust.

He'd handed Otto an envelope with strict instructions to not open it until the morning of the ninth. Inside the envelope was a note ordering him and the soldiers to radio the Kriegsmarine for a pickup and to leave the island; telling him that Germany was finished, and that he wouldn't be returning with them.

"I am going now," he told Otto. "You shall ask no questions, and follow the instructions contained here to the letter, understood?" Otto looked stunned and pale, but did as he was told. Klaus embraced him, thanked him for his loyalty, and wished him well.

Bright crowning Sky Father above…

Seventy years. Seventy years in which to acquire the knowledge and power of these fantastical creatures that fed on human terror and did battle with unimaginable forces from beyond Earth, beyond our dimension. In just a year, he had fully mastered himself. In seventy… the prospect of returning to rule men and shape the future filled him with strength and purpose. What had Dafyd said? *We'll be reborn as demigods, Klaus. The trick I did with your pistol when we first met? That was nothing to the abilities we'll be reborn with, a superhuman power of will that can channel the raw energies of the cosmos to mold reality like clay.*

Dark shielding Earth Mother below…

He'd been shocked to learn that the glamour might attract a trinity of two women and one man, which meant there was every possibility he would be reborn into a woman's body. But Dafyd had allayed his fears. What did it matter? Reborn, they would be like demigods among mortals—physical form and strength were relatively unimportant. *Although,* Dafyd had said, *given your ambitions, I would cede you the man, if there's only one; I believe we'll have the ability to choose.* But whatever body they inhabited would, barring severe accidents, be deathless. Their greatest strength would be the visceral knowledge and intense magical power with which they would be reborn, power driven by a mind and will tempered over seventy years of service on the front lines of a cosmic war. And, in truth, now he'd healed... Klaus missed the thrill of battle and the ability to command men. His pain and suffering had been the result of a series of blunders made by a madman and his followers. But Dafyd —this was a man he could respect, a man with whom he could begin to remake the world.

And now Dafyd had completed the preliminaries and begun the invocation to Nestor, the powerful demon horse-creature whom they would serve.

As before, the room filled with presences; and as before, a hovering sphere of absolute blackness some fifty centimeters across appeared directly in front of them at the same time as the temperature of the room plummeted.

On the altar, the girl lay bound and trembling.

The difference was that this time there were no pillars, no triangle, and no violet circle of containment. There was still the circle around the three of them, but that was intended only as protection from any wayward or impulsive transitional that might appear, drawn by the gathering of elementals summoned to the four quarters.

The sphere grew, the waves of arctic cold rolling from it, intensifying until Klaus thought they would all die; but he watched, hungry and fascinated, as Dafyd slid the long blade beneath the sacrifice's breast and between her ribs precisely as Klaus had recommended, until it pierced her heart. The body jerked once, then stilled.

And now that eye-twisting transformation with its attendant metallic shrieks and groans, the vast machinery of the spheres being driven beyond the limits of tolerance. Klaus tore his eyes away, *had to,* just for an instant. And when he turned back, Nestor was there.

The creature—its eyes were so black they seemed to be holes in the world—looked very much like a horse, but with something immensely disturbing about the sleek, beautiful planes of its muzzle. Its body, too was that of a horse and yet nothing like one, in that it took up no more space than the torso and legs of a man. How that could be, Klaus had no idea, but he supposed that the thing's manifestation in our world was as much symbolic as actual, a coarse approximation of a reality the human plane could not accommodate.

"Very good. I see that you are all ready." It spoke softly, with the slightest lisp.

Dafyd and Magda replied in unison. "Yes."

Klaus licked his lips. The great head swiveled towards him. "I am ready," he rasped.

"Then let us not waste time," said the horse. "Sign."

The air shimmered, thickened, and a plain wooden lectern materialised before them. A sheet of rich, cream-coloured parchment glimmered softly on its sloping surface. There was writing on the parchment, but the curling, exquisitely-rendered characters were like no language Klaus had ever seen. But Dafyd, bent low over it, seemed able to read it. After what seemed like a long time of examining the contract, he nodded and turned to them. "It's all in order. After seventy years of service we have three days in which to supply three fresh souls to replace ours. If we succeed, we're free; if we fail, we serve for all eternity. Are we agreed?"

"Yes," said Magda. And Klaus, dry-mouthed, echoed her.

"Good." Dafyd drew a small folding knife from a pocket, nicked a fingertip, and pressed it to the parchment, leaving a small red stain. He handed the knife to Magda, who did the same before passing it to Klaus. As soon as he'd added his own blood, the lectern and contract faded from sight.

"Excellent," said the horse.

Its muzzle opened, and the blackness between those great incisors was of a piece with the blackness of its eyes—a hole in the fabric of the world, a gateway to elsewhere. In the space of a heartbeat its muzzle grew huge, the sable void of that open maw rushing toward them, surrounding them, swallowing them.

Then the pain began.

CHAPTER SEVENTEEN

Tuesday March 18, 2014

When he'd finished taking care of his US banking and bills, thinking what a nightmare this would be without the internet, Paul googled around for information on the German occupation of Greece in WWII. Though there was nothing specific about Voúnos, it seemed that the islands had been a patchwork of German and Italian occupation, with the Germans taking over the Italian garrisons after September 1943. Voúnos had been in the German-occupied zone from the beginning.

Next he did a search for Colonel Maule. The first entry was a brief one in a list of SS personnel. That one though linked to a larger and more informative Wikipedia entry. There was a good deal of information about him.

Born in 1901, Maule was a career soldier. He'd entered the army at the end of World War One and joined the recently-founded SS in 1928. Maule's history as an officer in the Leibstandarte SS Adolf Hitler read like a history of World War Two: the invasion of Poland, the Netherlands, France, Greece, and finally Operation Barbarossa, Germany's apocalyptic invasion of the Soviet union. There were allegations of atrocities committed against civilians. The entry went on,

Maule's whereabouts following the disaster at Kharkov are not known. Despite hearsay evidence that he was relieved of his command and court-martialed for assaulting another officer, Maule's name no longer appears in the Reich's official records. Though his fate remains a mystery to this day, it's probable that he was executed on his return to Germany, possibly before he was even brought to trial.

So a colonel Maule who'd served on the Russian front had existed. Although there was a possibility it was another Maule—Paul had no idea whether the name was a common one in Germany—the rank and the fact of his being relieved of his command suggested this was Yaya's man.

Paul took some notes and printed out the Wikipedia entry on SS Standartenführer Klaus Maule. He leaned back, tapping the end of his pencil against his teeth and thinking.

He could start with the lawyer in Athens. They'd be acting on behalf of the owner, and perhaps could give him some details, especially if he expressed some interest in buying the property. Or, more likely, if he greased their palms. He didn't for a moment imagine that lawyers couldn't be bought here.

But why? What was he really going to find out even if he did find who owned the property? Or, for that matter, if he could verify the truth of Yaya's story? He loved the house, loved the location, loved the views. He'd not had nightmares here, seen ghosts, felt presences or weird vibes. The place was perfect for him. So, really, what was the point? He'd stayed in thirteenth-century cottages and medieval castles and Regency homes all over Europe, and you could bet that several of them had seen ugly goings-on of one sort or another over the centuries. Beatings, torture, murder, fratricide, looting and rape at the hands of invading armies...these things happened. It was life. Only in the Western US, where the average building was less than a few decades old, was the imprint of the past missing in people's homes. Any house older than a generation or two was bound to have its ghosts.

Down the road, maybe he *would* look into the possibility of buying the place. But for now, he was happy just to live here, and the place felt nothing but welcoming.

‡

Elléni, though, *was* curious.

When she'd finished her last appointment, she called the lawyer in Athens who'd instructed her in the matter of the stone house rental and to whom she sent the remittances, minus her twelve per cent.

"*Kyrie* Galánis? It's Elléni Marinóudis from Vóunos."

Galánis was on the ball. He recognized her name immediately. After some small talk, she came to the point.

"I know you told me the house was owned by someone in England. I'm wondering if you can give me a little background on them?"

There was brief hesitation. "Is there some problem?"

"No, not at all. The renter is happy with the place and everything's fine. I'm really just curious as to its owners, and why anyone would let such a nice property remain empty for so very long."

"Ah. Truthfully, I don't know anything about the owner. We were instructed by the legal firm in England acting on their behalf."

"How long have you acted as the Greek agents for the property?" she said.

"*Kyria* Marinóudis, why all the interest?"

Damn. She took another tack, improvising. With a light laugh, she said, "Just historical, I assure you. I'm taking notes for an architectural history of Vóunos—a coffee-table book for the locals and tourists—and since the house is one of the nicer villas on the island, I'd like to document who built it, and its history of occupancy."

"Regarding the original builder and owner, the land registry would have records—"

"*Kyrie*, the land registry is two islands away, and you know how helpful they are."

Galánis chuckled. "Wait a moment, please." She heard him ask someone to bring him the file on the *Vóunos property*. There was a long pause, followed by the shuffling of paper. "I don't see anything about the original owner beyond the name, *Jones*." She made a note of it. "But I can tell you the house has been empty since... actually, since 1944," he said, a distinct note of surprise in his voice, "when we first began handling the account."

Well *that* was interesting. Empty for seventy years, but constantly tended and in good repair. Why would anyone spend so much money to keep a house empty? She pressed her luck. "How extraordinary. And the old couple here on Vóunos that takes care of the property, somebody must pay them. Do you handle that?" As she said it, it struck her as strange that she hadn't thought of it before, or just asked the couple directly who paid them to take care of the place.

"The Manólises." Galánis didn't balk at being pushed for more info; perhaps his own curiosity had been piqued. "Yes, we make monthly payments into their account. In fact, we've been doing that since—" more rusting of paper— "*heavens!* since 1958, probably when Vóunos first got a bank. The payments were made to Giannis Manólis's parents back then. I see that there were some extensive renovations that year and the next—new roof, new floors, and more. Curious. I had no idea it had always been empty."

"Very interesting." She played her last hand. "Is there any way I could contact the owner directly, or at least their lawyer in England, for—"

"I'm sorry, *Kyria*. That I can't do."

"I understand. Professional discretion." She thanked him and let him get on with his day.

So, the *Jones property*. And it had been empty all those years. Incredible. Why, then, rent it out now? It was very strange.

She wondered also about Paul. Her thoughts immediately went to the time they'd spent between the sheets. After breaking her famine of months with such a feast, she was ready for more. She almost picked up the phone to call him and ask if she could spend the night again. No, it was too soon, what would he think of her? The reflexive thought made her laugh inwardly at herself. It wasn't the 1950s, and his need had seemed at least as yawning as hers. She glowed inside as images of their passion flashed into her mind. Both of them had given and taken without reserve.

She'd been glad to hear him talk about his depression and separation. Her friend Vóula who owned the pharmacy had told her half the women on Vóunos were on antidepressants, took them like candy—although their lives were better than their grandparents or even their parents could have imagined. The fact that he'd faced down problems alone and had the courage to not only recognize his need for a rebirth of some sort but actually change his life spoke volumes. He was an introvert to be sure, but a strong and self-aware one, making a sincere effort to come out of his shell, to embrace the world and to let others in. When she'd first teased him about his anástasi, that day in the car when she took him to see the stone house, she had no idea how right she was.

CHAPTER EIGHTEEN

Klaus had always hoped for a quick death. No pain could travel as fast as, say, a bullet passing through the brain, or the shredding of the body by an artillery shell. When he'd seen Nestor's mouth yawn suddenly wide, engulfing them, he'd braced in the expectation of a rapid transition from life in the physical realm into whatever his existence was to be in the demonic, in Hell. He'd expected to just be gulped down and swiftly extinguished in the process.

The reality was nothing like that.

In the instant the velvet black of the demon's open mouth overtook him, each cell of Klaus's being exploded in molten, ineffable pain. It was as though his every nerve were being passed through a sieve and divided into a thousand smaller nerves, each capable of transmitting the same degree of sensation as the original. Incandescent screaming agony filled the universe, but he had no mouth to scream, no eyes to close; only vast, world-filling, unending agony.

‡

A lifetime later, the thought-cluster which was the irreducible core of Klaus's identity surfaced. He knew nothing but that he *was* again. For now, that seemed enough.

He became aware by degrees of things beyond his immediate selfhood. The sensation of being part of some loose-woven membrane or web, with here and there pulsing nodes of otherness, clusters he recognized as somehow akin to himself. Senses very different from but somehow analogous to sight and touch appeared to operate here. Tentatively, he reached out towards one.

<Klaus>

He stopped, went immobile, neither advancing nor withdrawing.

<Klaus> it came again. And then a sudden cascade of awareness. Of everything he'd been, felt, thought. Family, the Reich, the deadly cold, his breakdown, Vóunos, Dafyd and the woman, Magda. Pain. *Oh God, the pain!* He'd burned, buckled, melted from it, been consumed, annihilated. He wondered that anything had remained.

What *was* he?

<Klaus!>

It wasn't a voice, and he was certain he had nothing like a voice himself, this atom-thing that was Klaus. A *node*. He was a node, like the others out there. And the thing which called him in a not-voice felt, smelt, or whatever sense applied, like Dafyd.

He framed the thought, gave it form. <Dafyd?>

<Yes! We passed over together. Magda is here too>

<Dafyd, the pain, the *burning!* How long...?>

<The question has no meaning here. But the pain is finished for now. You're whole? Your memory, I mean?>

Klaus thought he was. He reached out towards the other nearby node, touched her—it *was* her, Magda, the woman—and was glad. To be alone in this place would be a quick descent to madness. <Yes. I am whole.>

<Hello, Klaus,> said Magda. The ordinariness of the words was both unsettling and grounding. He steeled himself and made the choice to embrace and return her mental touch with all its humanity, to let her simple words ground him. The alternative was to become entirely unmoored in this place-not-a-place, life-not-a-life.

<Hello, Magda.>

There was a shifting, like distances breached and their nodes coming close, coalescing. Not so much a web anymore, it seemed to Klaus that wherever they were had become more like a dense soup shot through with movement. The sense he equated to touch now made him feel as though great ponderous masses were swaying and shifting around him and the others, everything inextricably bound together in elastic, reciprocating motion. Something he interpreted as colour lanced and raked through this soup of being, altering balances and pressures. And now, something like sound, big and deep…

<Do you see it, Klaus? Do you feel it?> said Magda.

<I feel…I see…*something*. Colours and movement. Sound.>

<Our essences are reorganizing,> said Dafyd, <learning to interpret with new senses.>

Klaus remembered the last thing he'd truly seen, Nestor's vast muzzle yawning black to swallow them all. <The horse. Is it…here?>

<Certainly,> said Dafyd. <And I think we shall very soon be confronted with its true form.>

Listening to the others speak, Magda felt her own identity blur and wobble. The boundaries between their personae—if that was the correct concept—were starting to fuse and overlap. Dafyd had spoken of them being a tripartite union, a turn of phrase which could end up being more literal than he'd expected. Would they fuse into one? Would they divide again on reincarnation?

Amusement. <A bit early to think of that, Magda.>

<Dafyd? You heard me thinking?>

Dafyd—who was experiencing wild and unsettling distortions of scale, one instant having the impression that "he" was vast and the next feeling he'd shrunk to near-nothingness—assented.

And from Klaus, <I heard you, too!>

<Three into one,> said Dafyd. <Not that we had secrets from one another before, but now——>

Shock from Klaus, wonder from Magda. They'd become a single entity, a unitary being. Three in one.

In a flood of sensory impressions, the ambient darkened, thickened, swayed vertiginously, tolled like a great bell, shrieked like an ape. Smell of sulfur, taste of heated iron.

Nestor had come.

<Ah, you are here. Welcome. Now...>

A brutal cut across all thought and consciousness, the parameters of existence reset in a single, shattering jolt.

<There. Yes, you are truly one now, so much easier this way. So, let us begin your education.>

‡

Pressure—it began with *pressure*. From the one came many, from the irresistible bore of the mightiest flood, bursting and breaching and branching into an infinity of smaller and increasingly mutable capillaries of force.

Stars like campfires in the desert night. Worlds like grains of sand strewn across infinity. Where there was a sun, there were worlds; and where there were worlds, there was, more often than not, life.

Across inconceivable vastness, the universe teemed with it. The forms it took were uncountable—life swam, flew, crawled, oozed, ran, skittered, leapt, floated, and rolled. Some simply *was,* content in its immobility. And some, like man, walked on two legs.

Most of the life in the universe was local, humble, contained. Even where it developed sentience, it would not have recognized life on a neighbouring world, so many were the permutations of chemistries, forms, modalities. Those few lifeforms that transcended the local and had contact with the children of other worlds and stars existed mostly in the cores of galaxies and nebulae. None ever endured for long.

The current, the pressure, the primal motive flood, left no ecological niche unfilled. Division and mutation was its essential nature. And with so much life, there was naturally that which fed on life. In the same way that this was true on the local, so was it true on the universal.

The cut worm forgives the plow.

Everywhere, life fed on life. That which wasn't limited to planetary surfaces but could exist in the void between the stars and even the gulfs between universes perfected a nomadic existence, gorging on the life of entire worlds as it drifted past. These were the world-eaters.

But—as it cannot but be with the infinite—there were places where life developed uncommon defenses and strategies untried elsewhere.

When life evolved on Earth, random chance, responding to selective pressures, happened to provide it with a symbiote, a shadow life whose existence straddled several planes. With the coming of sentience, that symbiote co-evolved its own sentience, and with it a purpose—to defend their sphere against the incomprehensible, ravenous entities that drifted between the stars and periodically scoured worlds of living things.

The demons were that symbiote. Like all life, they required energy to sustain them, and that sustenance was the interminable, vaporous exhalation of human fear and pain that drifted like smoke, like fog, leaking from the human psyche in crisis to permeate the wider realm of Hell. Their strength waxed and waned in direct proportion to human suffering.

<But how do you resist them, the world-eaters?> asked the three-in-one.

<Like everything in creation,> Nestor replied, <it's a simple question of equilibrium, of balancing pressures and forces. Consider...>

A shell, spherical across multiple dimensions. When the demons were strong, it remained smooth, integral, unbreachable; when they weakened, it became thin, brittle, permeable. If the world-eaters—who had thrice feasted on Earth and longed to do so again—should appear in force when the shell was weak, that would be the end of both human- and demon-kind.

<And now you want to know how you will serve us.>

CHAPTER NINETEEN

Thursday March 20, 2014

Paul had spoken with the Manólises once or twice during their biweekly maintenance visits, but never in any depth. Though courteous, they weren't chatty—they spoke when spoken to, but no more. They arrived at ten, spent a couple of hours sweeping and tidying around the house and tending to the orchard, and were gone. Now the house was occupied, there was no reason for them to enter it.

But after talking to Elléni—she'd phoned the evening after they'd got together, and he'd called her last night and invited over this evening—his interest in the house's history was rekindled. It wouldn't hurt to ask the old couple a few questions.

Paul greeted the man as he was clearing the orchard of minor deadfall from the previous week's storm. After a little small talk, Paul said, "How long have you and your wife been working here?"

The man chuckled. "Since I can remember. I used to help my father."

He looked in his mid-forties. At least three decades, then. "You must have seen a few tenants in that time."

The man gathered an armful of twig and leaf litter and dumped it into the bin. "There has been nobody, only the house."

"Really? In all that time?"

The sideways nod. *Yes.*

"And your father…did you ever you stories about the house? About what happened here?"

The man's head twitched back. *No.*

Paul pressed the point. "Some people say that bad things that happened here during the war. That it has a bad history."

"I don't know anything of the war, I wasn't born," said the man. He closed the lid and began to wheel the bin away.

"How about your father? Perhaps I could—"

"Dead, many years now," the man said over his shoulder. "The house has always been empty. It has no stories."

‡

Not willing to be put off so easily, Paul fired up the motorcycle and rode to the church of Aghios Rigínos. It was a small, cupola-topped building on the main road at the edge of town, where the houses thinned into dusty green groves of olive and almond. A woman was on her knees scrubbing the front steps. Paul found *o Pápas* Tákis at the side of the church holding a shaky-looking ladder for a painter working the apex of the wall; the glare of sunlight on the freshly-whitewashed stucco might have heralded the Second Coming.

"Freshening up for Easter?" said Paul.

"As always, every year. It's hard work for all of us, especially the poor *Pápas* who must observe the strict fast." He grinned. "Apart from some of the old people, hardly anyone else does these days. But it keeps me from getting too fat," he added, patting his black-robed belly. "As the body grows fat, the soul withers away in proportion."

Paul smiled. "Can you at least enjoy a little wine?"

The *yes* head-tilt. "After the first week, but only on Saturday and Sunday. The first week is the worst. Now tell me, how are you enjoying life on Vóunos?"

"Very much. I told you I rented the stone house?"

O Pápas looked blank.

"A couple of kilometers up the hill, off the beach road."

"Oh, yes, I know the one. Yes, you did, I'd forgotten. You can see it from one of the turns."

"That's the one. I was actually wondering if you knew anything of its history."

The priest chuckled. "I'm afraid I know very little of Vóunos's history, Pávlos. I'm still a newcomer myself."

"You've been here eight years and you still consider yourself a newcomer?"

"Oh yes. It takes a generation for islanders to begin to accept you as one of them. Father Stélios, my predecessor, was here fifty-nine years."

"*Fifty-nine years?* My God. That's amazing."

"It's not so unusual."

Paul tried to get back on topic. "Father, I've been wondering… does the church keep written records on island or parish events and history?"

"Certainly. I have volumes of it in my church. And of course, some priests keep personal diaries—I do myself. What are you looking for?"

So Paul told *o Pápas* Tákis what he'd first heard in hearsay form from Elléni's friend Anna at the bar, and summarized Elléni's yayá's reminiscences of events. *O Pápas's* expression went from interested to troubled and finally to horrified.

"If these things are true, it is terrible," he said. "And you say the house was exorcised by the old priest?"

"Several times, apparently, over a period of years."

O Pápas shook his head as though to dislodge the horrors he'd just absorbed. "There would certainly be a record of that. The Church performs exorcisms to this day, but they're very rare indeed. And your house is in my parish. I'll look into it as soon as I get a chance later today. Give me your telephone number and I'll let you know if I find something."

Paul thanked him and rode off. He hadn't mentioned the evidence of disturbed earth at the supposed gravesite behind the orchard, and the paint fragments he'd found on the floorboards.

‡

Tuesday April 15, 2014

Paul woke to a gloomy light and the soft tapping of rain on the roof. Turning, he glanced at his watch on the bedside table: 7:20AM. Beside him, Elléni stirred, rolled over and draped an arm across his chest.

"What time is it?" she asked, sleepy-voiced.

The answer brought a smile, and she pulled him to her.

‡

After Elléni left, Paul went online to check his email. He surfed the web a little, then went back upstairs to shower. He'd just finished dressing when he heard a car approach. He skipped down the stairs in time to see it pull up at the front of the house. A cream-coloured VW bug from which emerged the youthful, black-clad figure of *o Pápas Tákis* with his trademark leather satchel hanging from one shoulder.

Paul had the door open by the time the priest, hurrying hunched through the rain, had reached it. "Come in. What a nice surprise."

"I hope you don't mind my coming by unannounced," said *o Pápas*. Raindrops glistened in his black beard.

"Not at all, it's a pleasure. A coffee?"

"I'd like that, thank you."

"Greek or Nescafé?" said Paul. It always amazed him that Greeks actually liked instant coffee, but Nescafé was a big deal here.

"Greek, please. Sweet."

Paul nodded and crossed to the kitchen. *O Pápas* looked around the big room and seemed to approve.

"Very nice. You keep it simple. You could have been a priest."

Paul grinned. "I like it this way. I didn't come all the way here to live like an American."

The priest chuckled. He crossed to the fireplace where a couple of logs burned happily, rested the satchel against the leg of the armchair, and held his hands out to warm them by the fire. Paul put the pot on the burner and lit the gas, then turned it to low. You had to watch Greek coffee.

O Pápas turned to face Paul, his back to the fire. "Well. I looked at the church records last night to see if there was anything about the house."

"And? Did you find anything?"

The *no* gesture. "Nothing. There's a gap in the records; the last volume ends in early 1941 and the next begins in 1947. It looks as though an entire volume is missing. Other than that, the record is complete from 1873 to the present day."

Paul frowned. "Could it just have been lost?"

The priest rubbed at his ear. "It's strange that out of twenty-five volumes, the only one missing is the one I'm interested in. Of course, your story has made me quite curious about this coincidence." He held up his index finger. "But I did find mention of exorcisms in the following volume."

Paul's back snapped straight. "You did?"

Yes gesture. He bent down and extracted from his satchel a leatherbound quarto volume; even across the room, Paul's antiquarian eye could tell from the way it flexed it was more likely to be a journal of some sort than a printed book.

"This volume covers the years from 1947 to 1956." *O Pápas* opened it to a bookmarked page. "Vasílis, the priest who was here during the war, performed the rite on October the fifteenth every year. 1956 is when *o Pápas* Vasílis retired. Stélios, his successor, continued the exorcisms, and carried them on right up until his departure in 2006. Stélios's record-keeping was meticulous throughout his tenure."

The coffee was just beginning to bubble. Paul watched the ring of foam boil up around the edge of the coffee and took it off the heat before the circle closed. "What does *o Pápas* Vasílis say about the exorcisms?"

"That's also strange. Considering how voluble he is on every matter—births, christenings, marriages, deaths, blessings of houses— his October 15th entries are remarkably minimalist, as are Stélios's after him. In fact, the wording is identical." He glanced down at the book. "*Annual blessing and seven prayers rite at the stone house,* is all he writes."

Paul brought the priest's coffee to him in a demitasse and sat in one of the chairs facing the fire. "That's it?"

"Yes. But the reference is clear." The priest closed the book and set it on the mantel. "The seven prayers are St. Basil's three prayers of exorcism and the four prayers of St. John Chrysostom. With the blessing, they can only refer to exorcism." He was quiet a moment, then, "It's strange he never told me when I came to take up my post."

"Especially after continuing the custom for five decades. Why would he hide that?"

The priest shrugged. "Perhaps he thought the house was purified, any evil long gone?"

"Right. But who would remove the wartime volume? And why?"

The priest sipped his coffee. "A good question. Nobody but the priest sees the records, and I've never heard of an instance of anything needing to be hidden from a successor. But unless the volume was stolen or destroyed—and I think both of these unlikely—my guess is that Stélios took it with him when he left."

"Is there any way of finding out?"

"That is my next intention." He drained the rest of the cup and placed it on the coffee table. Brightening up, he said, "It doesn't *feel* like an evil place, does it? And yet you say people were sacrificed here?"

"Right here, apparently, in this room." Paul glanced involuntarily at the section of floor where he'd found the traces of paint.

The priest shook his head. "Will you show me the rest of the house?"

"Delighted," said Paul. He was glad he'd made the bed.

CHAPTER TWENTY

The three-in-one swam in a bewildering ocean of forces. As it grew accustomed to its new environment, the strangeness began, slowly, to settle. Sense-analogues developed, allowing the three-in-one that was Magda, Klaus, and Dafyd to begin to interpret and interact with its new surroundings.

The ambient was a dense, turbulent sea, teeming with forces and currents. Chaotic as it was, everything seemed to have direction and purpose. In the pearl-grey brilliance, the three-in-one glimpsed what looked like concentrations of thicker material, ganglia or nodes, both near and far. The currents of energy, streaming and shot through with brighter hues, were more intense around these, propagating from them through the larger medium.

If Hell had a quality, it was metallic—brass and quicksilver, with a hot conductivity that kept the three-in-one's nerve-analogues on edge, an electric pulse cycling endlessly between discomfort and burning pain. The lack of a physical body didn't make the sensation any less unpleasant.

With the discomfort came a feeling of helpless, throbbing interaction with this strange world. The three-in-one was like a jellyfish swaying and pulsing, tossed with the tide; pulled and pushed, it might be crushed at any moment.

Dark, swirling forms of night harried them relentlessly. The assault continued, eroding their unity. Like curdling milk the three-in-one began to separate, and that would be death for each.

A face, elongated and equine, interposed itself on the chaos. <Balance! Balance and equilibrium. Hold together! Push back!>

The three-in-one responded. Unity regained, wholeness unbreached. As if taking a deep breath, the three-in-one swelled, pulling energy from the medium. Sounds like wild harps, blare of trumpets. Senses extended, it found an edge where the medium thinned, and beyond it—

Red and raw and scraping, the enemy was everywhere.

It came at them with the weight of worlds and the searing heat of suns. It burned and lacerated their lines. Each time they staggered back, Nestor and the other princes of Hell replenished their strength and marshaled the lines back into order, sending them forward again to face the searing lances of fire and soul-shredding blasts of primordial energy. Death—true oblivion—would have been a mercy, but there was no true death here, only terrible, unceasing struggle.

‡

As humans lurched and capered their blind, carefree way through the years and decades, the fight between Hell and the enemy continued unabated on the frontier of Outer Hell. Invisible tendrils snaked from the demon sphere, lacing and threading the everyday, drawing energy and sustenance from grief and nightmare, from war and famine and epidemic, from broken bone and bloody wound and every shed tear. Balance and rebalance: when humanity prospered, the three-in-one strained and suffered as—with every demon in Hell—it struggled to hold the line against the paralyzing, soul-sucking chaos beyond; when catastrophe and genocide struck humanity, the three-in-one grew vital and strong, and beat the enemy back.

By exposure and osmosis, the three-in-one learned. Learned the visceral and instinctive ways of energy, matter, and time. Meshed and melded, the three-in-one's component sentiences touched and flowed into that of Nestor and his ally demons, so that each acquired aspects of the other. The commerce was one of mutual advantage.

Within the three-in-one, each of them—Magda, Dafyd, and Klaus—was changed. *Deeply* changed. For a human consciousness, even that of a trained magician, to be exposed to forces and suffering so far beyond the normal sphere of human experience was something no human could pass through unaffected. What they eventually became was something new, with little of their original humanity remaining.

‡

After an unguessable, interminable period of endless battle and desperate defense of Outer Hell, that region on the frontier of the infinite beyond, the term of the contract drew to a close. By the agreed and universal laws of magic and the dimension-breaching power of correspondence, blood, and force of will, the artifact buried in the cellar of the stone house awoke, beacon-like. As the moon passed its full and began to wane, the artifact sent its call into Hell, and the three-in-one responded.

CHAPTER TWENTY-ONE

Wednesday April 16, 2014

"Thanks for taking care of the dishwasher installation for me," said Paul, as Elléni drove to the dock. "Why they had to pick the one day I'm going be away, I can't imagine. I'd change it, but—"

Elléni shook her head. "It's no problem. If you change it, it might be weeks before you can get the *teknítis* back, he isn't a reliable man. I'm happy to take care of it." And she was pleased that he should trust her with his keys and going into his house while he was gone.

"And help yourself to anything you want, okay?" he said.

She assured him she would.

With Easter coming, Elléni had taken a week off work. Paul was taking the overnight ferry to Thessaloniki to meet his niece, who was due to arrive at one P.M. on Thursday. They'd take the ferry back that night and arrive in Voúnos on Friday morning. That she was coming for only four days, with all the traveling and cost entailed, seemed crazy; as did the news, related by Paul, that Easter, the holiest time of the year in the Orthodox calendar, was essentially disregarded in the United States, and was more about chocolate than anything else.

She drove along the dock, stopping some twenty meters short of the small cluster of people waiting to board the ferry. It was early days, and no point in having the whole village talking about their affair. She kissed him goodbye and wished she were going with him, sharing a cozy cabin for the passage. It was a long kiss, and when they finally broke it off, she was pleased to see him looking as flustered as she was feeling.

"Go," she said, laughing and a little breathless. She made a shooing gesture.

He ran a hand through his hair and chuckled. He grabbed his bag from the back seat and opened the door. "Yes," he said, stepping out. "Take care!"

She ran a few errands in town and drove home in the waning light of day. It was a clear evening, and at every turn of the rising road she stole a glance down towards the sea, where the ferry, seemingly immobile, was just visible at the mouth of the bay. Its lights had come on, and it twinkled like a tiny toy in the indigo waters.

Elléni was a little nervous about meeting the niece, Alex. It was obvious she was the most important thing in Paul's life, more than even his sister. He'd shown her pictures—a slim, beautiful girl, quite tall; with his brown eyes and a thick mass of black curls that fell to below her shoulders, Alex looked thoroughly Greek. Elléni hoped the girl would like her. She was sure that if the girl was anything like her father, Elléni would like *her*.

And Elléni did like Paul, liked him a lot. He was the kind of man she could fall in love with. A Greek at core, but not the traditional male islander, all swagger and machismo. With the benefit of a wider frame of reference, he lacked the islander attitudes that had made Nikos such a pig, for all his good qualities. Paul wasn't afraid of strong women, and—she was certain—would never hit a woman, no matter how angry he might become.

Elléni knew she could be difficult. She was passionate, and passionate people were never easy. Men might have physical strength, but she knew that when she got angry she could—like her mother—inflict emotional damage deeper and more lasting than any blow struck by a man in a moment of anger. It was evolutionary, how the sexes had evolved. And for all that men thought they ran the world, they were nothing without a woman. Which was precisely why men feared them.

Well, this one clearly doesn't, she thought with a smile.

‡

Elléni arrived at the house at three the next day, a full hour before the man was supposed to arrive to install the dishwasher.

The house seemed to welcome her. Once inside, she lit the kitchen stove to warm the room and made herself coffee. The day had been comfortable but the nights still had a little bite, and the thick stone walls kept the house cool. Fortunately the weather forecast for the weekend was good

She noticed the fireplace was empty. It would be nice for them to have a fire ready to light when they got back. She glanced around and saw there was a small stack of firewood under the stairs, just by the cellar door, along with some kindling in a bucket and some old newspapers. Selecting some of each, she laid a fire in the grate.

As she stood back up she noticed a large, old-looking book on the mantel. The cover was plain leather, and there was no title or picture. Without thinking, she picked it up and flipped it open before it occurred to her that it might be private. But the writing was old and crabby, and the first item she saw—about the death of a village woman in childbirth—was dated December 1953. Curious, she leafed through at random. Most of the entries were brief and to do with people in the village. A journal of some sort, but whose? She turned pages, increasingly puzzled, before it struck her: it was a village priest's diary for the mid-century. She turned to the inside cover and there it was in black and white: *The records of the church of Aghios Rigínos on the island of Vóunos, 1947-1957, as recorded by o Pápas Stélios.* She shook her head, wondering what the diary was doing here, and put it back down.

She looked through Paul's CD racks, smiling at the fact that he hadn't digitized his collection. He probably didn't even have a way of playing mp3s, though of course he could plug a player into the Bose he'd set up in the armoire near the fireplace. In some ways he seemed charmingly old-fashioned, and she liked that.

He had a *lot* of music, all arranged by category. She decided to play something she didn't know: it was good to discover new things, and finding out what he liked would help her to understand what made him tick. In the end, she chose an album from the jazz section by *Pink Martini,* just because the name struck her.

Elléni listened to music and leafed through books. The *teknítis* didn't arrive at four, or at five, or even six. *One more hour then I go,* she decided. She poured herself a glass of white wine and picked another CD.

She'd just got comfortable on the sofa again and taken her first sip of wine when she heard a noise.

A high rubbing, scraping sound, it cut through the song's warm harmonies like a saw. She looked around, listening intently. Nothing.

Just as she was starting to think she'd imagined it, it came again, quieter but more sustained. The image of a rubber party balloon came to mind. As a little girl, she'd once tried to squeeze one through the metal bars of a small park in Thessaloniki, where the family had gone to visit her cousins. In the seconds before it had caught on a rough spot and popped (she'd burst into tears), it had made just such a sound.

She rose, turned down the music, and listened, but the sound had stopped again. But now there was another noise, a car approaching. *Finally!* She glanced at her watch. *Two and a half hours late. Let's hope he's quick about it.*

To her great surprise, it wasn't the *teknítis* but Father Tákis. She was very fond of him, and greeted him warmly; he was just the kindest man, and she'd known him since she was a child. For a moment she expected him to be puzzled on finding her here—she and Paul had been discreet about their affair, given how nothing remained private in Vóunos—but it turned no explanations were necessary.

"I ran into Paul on the dock yesterday," he said. "When I was up here the other day I forgot a book, a journal from one of my predecessors. Paul said you'd be here this afternoon, and wouldn't mind if I—"

"Oh yes, of course. I saw it on the mantel." She waved him in and crossed with him to the seating area. "Please. Can I get you something? A small ouzo, or—"

O Pápas retrieved the journal and dropped it in his satchel. "Thank you, but no, I still have stops to make. This close to Easter, a priest's days never seem to end. It's going to be a long evening. Anyway, I'm sure I'll—*what's that?*"

The sound was deeper this time, more of a rasp, as if someone were attacking a block of wood with a giant file. Once, twice, and it stopped.

They looked around. It was impossible to tell where it had come from; it just seemed to be in the air, as if the whole house had groaned and grumbled. The thought sent a chill through her. Where a few moments ago she'd been entirely relaxed, the history of the house rushed back at her and the cozy ambiance evaporated. She clutched her arms to her sides reflexively, a protective gesture. "It happened just before you came, too," she said.

The priest shook his head. "Strange. There's no wind, either. And we'd have *felt* an earthquake."

At her suggestion, they took a look upstairs, but there was nothing out of order and the sound didn't come again. When they came back down, *o Pápas* stopped at the foot of the stairs. "The cellar?" he said, indicating the door.

She nodded.

"Perhaps something fell over?"

Elléni shrugged. "I don't even know what's down there."

"Let's have a look," he said.

CHAPTER TWENTY-TWO

The three-in-one was spent. As it drifted away from the chaos and fray of the edge, the immediate threat diminished and the full, interminable horror of the experience settled like a mountain, obliterating everything. There was just overwhelming relief and the towering memory of fear and burning, lacerating pain.

Time passed.

Klaus and Magda, as near as ever but, like Dafyd, once again distinct essences, were still struggling to make sense of their new, unentangled, status. Together, they'd all sunk deep into some less turbulent part of the ambient to prepare for their rebirth. *The vestibule of Hell*, Dafyd thought, as he brushed against each of them, healing and soothing in an attempt to help them readjust to once again being individuals.

Magda was first to recover enough to articulate. <Where are we?> <In some kind of halfway place.>

<Limbo?> Dafyd felt an edge of humor to Magda's comment that—if he'd had a mouth with which to do so—would have made him smile.

<Or something very like it.> He continued to work on Klaus, who was coming around. Dafyd could feel fear streaming off him as Klaus became aware of their strange new surroundings. Even without any way of knowing time during the period of their servitude as the three-in-one, it had felt like an eternity to Dafyd. It would take them time to readjust to whatever this place was. Though if all went well, they would not be here long.

Although lacking a body, Dafyd noticed that with individuation he'd recovered some sense analogues. Not quite any one clear sense, more like the synaesthesia experienced during astral trances. His perception of the others blended vision with sound and touch. There was a strong emotional component, too, keenly felt as he tried to help Klaus back to full consciousness. His experience of Klaus and Magda was shifting, interactive, a subtle and complex seeing and knowing. Colours and sounds rippled, catalyzing emotions and quasi-physical sensations he had no words for, which in turn affected the metasensory impressions.

Around him, flecks and rays and shapes of all sizes, of colours known and unknown, popped into existence and just as quickly vanished, like soap bubbles. But fleeting as they were, each of these apparitions changed the tone, the feel of the place, and of his very being. Everything here was miraculously, dismayingly interdependent.

They had become astral selves. The part of his mind that was a mortal man, that was Dafyd, marveled and yet felt afraid; the part of him that was spirit accepted and welcomed the sensation.

As he worked on Klaus, Dafyd felt a tug from outside. And Magda, still so closely connected to him that their sensorium was at least partially shared, seemed also to sense it.

<Do you feel that?> he asked her.

<Yes. What is it?>

He set free that part of him not interacting with Klaus's astral being to follow the pull, trace it out and let it draw him to its source while still leaving him here. The experience was unsettling, like not moving at all while at the same time both squeezing through a tight tunnel and being exposed to the terrifying emptiness of infinite space; as though his self were duplicated, yet remained, weirdly, whole. And then he was there.

At first he couldn't identify what *there* was. *Oh.* The stone house! And beneath it, the artifact they'd buried in the cellar. It had come alive and was calling to them. But...

The him that was here thought, <We have a problem.>

<What's the matter?> said Magda.

<There's a hard shell around the house. Follow the pull, let it guide you.>

Through their residual entanglement, he felt her comply, squeezing down the tight tunnel that linked them to the artefact until she joined the part of him that was there. <A countermagic?> she said. <Is it possible?>

<I didn't think it was. But, yes, it seems to be exactly that. A *priestly* one.>

He tasted her surprise. <Exorcism?> she asked.

<Several, repeated and reinforced by someone who knew exactly what they were about. And something rather more, I'd say.>

Klaus, now more or less fully conscious, engaged with them. Aware of the discussion which had just taken place and drawn by their combined presence, he followed Magda's attention, was inadvertently sucked along the link despite his fear.

The three-in-one still obtains, thought Dafyd. He felt Klaus's bewilderment, the stirrings of fear, as Klaus saw the barrier.

<What do we do?>

<Exactly what you, as a military man, would do, Klaus: we try their defenses.>

<How?>

<First, we rejoin, tight as we can. More, closer. Yes, like that. Good. Now...>

At Dafyd's direction they released a surge of power, a current of raw, roiling energy that he shaped into a pointed wedge of force to crack the protective spell which appeared to them as a hard, iridescent membrane surrounding the indistinct image of the stone house. But the magic held, and their breaching force only rebounded from the shell. Together they tried to redirect it, but the concentration required was intense, and they were still weak; after a moment their wedge rippled and dissolved.

Dafyd called a stop. <Let's examine this a little more closely. No point wasting our energy.>

Time—even in the vestibule of Hell—was of little account, their only sense of it a vague awareness of lunar flux. Feeling Klaus's impatience, Dafyd reminded him, <Our connection with the human sphere will get stronger as the moon waxes towards the time of our rebirth. I'm sure we can find a way to smash this little cantrip.>

They waited, healing, rebuilding their strength and psychic health. After some indeterminate period, when Dafyd judged the time right, they tried again, only to have the attack scrape and skitter harmlessly off the house's protective shell; but their power was greater this time, and they hit the shell again, getting just enough purchase to set up a high-amplitude vibration before the psychic tool again lost contact.

Klaus, in a surge of anger: <so close!> And from Magda, silent agreement.

<Yes. We almost had it there.> And Dafyd was quiet a long time.

‡

<The problem, I think,> said Dafyd, <is that we're now no different to demons ourselves, and thus subject to the same rules and laws.>

<So the protection is like the magic circle we used in the rituals?> asked Klaus.

<Very much like that.>

<Then we cannot break it!>

The flavour of Dafyd's dark mirth filled the ambient. <Oh, but I think we can.>

<How?> asked Magda.

<We stored a huge amount of power in the artifact, no small part of it my own.>

<Yes,> agreed Magda. <I remember how drained you were.>

<We can't reach the artifact in the Earth sphere, the physical plane, but we're still connected to it and its power through other dimensions. We can tap some of its power to attack the priestly wards from the inside.>

<The horse of Troy?> said Klaus.

<Something not unlike it. It will cost us…but I see no other way.>

Magda remained silent.

A ripple of apprehension came from Klaus. <Cost us? How?>

<Taking power from the artifact will narrow our window of action. Remember the pact? We crafted it to those criteria, so that we had the entire three days of Easter, seventy-two hours, for our resurrection. My guess is the artifact will simply power up more slowly. At the worst, we might lose one of those days.>

<But we'll still have plenty of time?>

<Absolutely. I've no doubt of it.>

Dafyd pulled them tighter, drew them together. The others understood what was needed and joined with him, smoothing and harmonizing their essences until, individual consciousnesses submerged, they became something like the three-in-one again. The medium around them pulsed and darkened, then suddenly cleared… and they were looking out through the artifact itself into the gloom of the old cellar.

<Good,> said Dafyd. His will coursed outward like a wave, welding the three of them into a hard unity, the same pointed wedge they'd used before.

At his silent command, the artifact pulsed power. At the same instant, they drove their wedge like a thunderbolt against the tough, layered shell surrounding the house.

In a single, brief flash, the iridescent membrane of priestly protection shattered like fine crystal.

‡

O Pápas Tákis opened the door and flicked on the cellar light. A wave of cold seeped up the stair. Over his shoulder, Elléni could see a number of flattened cardboard boxes leaning against the wall, held in place by a few unopened boxes on the floor.

O Pápas took a few steps down to the landing and peered around. "It doesn't look as though anything's fallen over. The place is mostly empty."

He hesitated, then began to say something more when there was the briefest flash; a sudden pressure in Elléni's ears, like that caused by altitude, muffled his words. A second later, his groan as he buckled and pitched suddenly forward came to her all too clearly.

Elléni made a noise, an involuntary cry. She tried to reach for him, couldn't. A terror had seized her, preventing all movement. Her skin crawled with it; her muscles felt as unresponsive as wood. She watched, paralyzed, as the priest's body came to a full rest at the bottom of the short stair.

After what seemed an eternity her torpor lifted and she was in motion, down the final steps and kneeling by him. The priest's eyes were wide and staring, the pupils reduced to pinpoints. He had soiled himself. She forced an arm under his shoulders, but when she tried to raise him, his head lolled back.

"Father! *Father!*" The pounding of her heart in her ears drowned out her own voice. She let him back down, felt for a pulse; then again at his throat. Nothing.

She drew back, sitting on her heels, hand over her mouth. She could feel her chin trembling. *My God, he's dead. A stroke, or... My God!* Maybe—

She placed her palms flat on his chest and pumped, leaning forward with all her strength, rocking back and thrusting forward and down again and again in a steady, rhythmic motion. She'd only ever seen it done on television, but it was all she had. She willed him to breathe, to blink, anything. Instead he just flopped and jerked to her pumping, a pathetic, grotesque rag doll, and all the time those horrible pinpoint eyes stared upwards.

"*No!*" she shouted. "*No! Father!*" He couldn't be dead. Couldn't be. Wiping away tears, she leaned close to his face. She pinched his nose shut and pulled down on his chin to open his mouth. She blew into it, pulled away for a moment, did it again.

After a few moments she was sweating and breathing hard, and *o Pápas* was still dead. She stared at the body, dry-mouthed, numb.

She stumbled up the stairs, found her phone, and called the

emergency services. They asked her if she'd tried reviving him, and how. She heard herself answering them mechanically, as if she were listening to a stranger speak. There was some back and forth over another line, and the dispatcher assured her an ambulance was on its way. From the local, clinic, certainly—it was the only one on the island. It would be here quickly.

Elléni stood by the kitchen counter, shaking. She couldn't think. Across the room, a thin yellow radiance spilled from the open cellar door, bathing the underside of the stair in sickly light.

The police arrived within a minute or two of the ambulance. She vaguely knew the older man, Katsélis, the chief of the island's small police department. But oh Christ, why did it have to be Pétros with him? Since their five-day fling ended he entirely repulsed her, for all his twenty-three-year-old looks.

Katsélis was a big, grizzled slab of a man. "Miss Marinóudis, I am captain Katsélis." His tone was gentle; she tried to reply but only managed a small jerk of the head. What was *wrong* with her? She'd been fine talking to the dispatcher on the phone, and now she couldn't even speak.

A thought struck her. *Why hadn't she called Paul, too?* She was an idiot. But he was on a ferry, what could he do?

The captain took a close look at her and turned to Pétros. "She's in shock. Find some brandy or something and pour her a small glass."

"Please, Miss Marinóudis." Katsélis took her elbow and steered her gently to the sofa. She was glad of the support. Though the paralyzing terror she'd experienced in the cellar was gone, her legs threatened to give way at any second.

Pétros arrived with a tumbler a third full of ouzo over ice. She drank half at once. The punch and familiarity of the drink seemed to throw a switch inside her, and she felt some self-control return.

After a few moments she was able to answer Katsélis's questions and briefly recount what had happened. He listened carefully while Pétros took notes on a small pad. When she was done, the captain told Pétros to stay with her and made his way down to the cellar. She caught—and ignored—Pétros's fleeting, unpleasant smirk.

At least the arrival of other people had restored some sense of normality. She sipped at the ouzo while Pétros hovered between the sofa and the door as if she might make a run for it; she continued to ignore him.

Another policeman arrived with a case of equipment. The medics waited by the stair while the captain and the new arrival busied themselves in the cellar. Repeated flashes of light from the cellar suggested pictures were being taken.

After almost an hour, the medics carried the priest's covered body out on a stretcher. The captain removed his cap; Pétros followed. Elléni stared, numb, emotions strained past their breaking point.

The captain sat across from her on the armchair, smoking. He'd fetched a small bowl from the kitchen and placed it on the corner of the coffee table, using it for an ashtray. She wasn't sure if Paul would mind, but it seemed insignificant at the moment.

"So," Katsélis began, "the house is owned by the American, Hátzis. What were you and *o Pápas* Tákis doing here?"

Elléni filled him in briefly, explaining that Paul had asked her to be here to supervise the installation in the morning, and about Father Tákis and the forgotten journal. "*O Pápas* put it in his satchel," she said. "He had it with him when he..." She frowned. "Fell."

The captain nodded to Pétros and pointed at the satchel, which they'd evidently retrieved from the cellar and set down on the kitchen counter. Mechanically, she watched Pétros walk over to it and pick it up. When she turned back to the captain, she realized his eyes hadn't left her.

"And you and Mr. Hátzis, you are friends?"

She caught the tone. "Yes, we are. Friends." And *damn!* why hadn't she thought to call him? He needed to know what had happened.

Pétros handed the captain the priest's satchel and murmured something in the captain's ear. The captain nodded and put out his cigarette. He pulled out the journal and spent a minute or two thumbing through it. He frowned. "This is more than fifty years old. What was Hátzis doing with it?"

Elléni shrugged. "I have no idea." Which wasn't entirely true. She was beginning to have some thoughts on the subject, but she really didn't want to get into it with them.

The captain said nothing, but his eyes said he didn't believe her. He replaced the book in the satchel and set it against the side of the armchair. He lit another cigarette.

"Very good. Now, please tell me again what happened from the time *o Pápas* arrived to the accident in the cellar."

She repeated it all. The captain listened attentively, interrupting occasionally to clarify some detail.

"This sound you describe," he said, "Father Tákis heard it too?"

"Yes!" How many times did she have to repeat herself? "Yes, he heard it too. In fact, it was his suggestion that we should look in the cellar."

"And you described it as…Pétros, hand me your pad and pen, will you? Good." He looked over the boy's notes. "As 'a rasping sound, like something scraping'."

"As I told you," she said. "Exactly."

He made a note and resumed his questions. He seemed especially skeptical about *o Pápas's* returning for an old journal when she was here alone. Why had he left it here in the first place? What could it have to do with Paul? She repeated that she didn't know. The captain made more notes on his pad.

"You have Mr. Hátzis's cellphone number?"

"Yes." She took her phone and brought it up. Pétros's smile turned nasty.

"What?" she snapped. She couldn't help herself.

The smug little bastard just scratched at his throat. Katsélis—who she was beginning to think didn't miss a thing—frowned. "Go ahead please, Miss Marinóudis."

She read out the number and put away her phone.

"And you say he's coming back on Friday morning?"

Yes, on the ferry from Thessaloniki. With his niece."

The captain nodded. "Please show me," he said as he ground out his cigarette, "exactly where you and *o Pápas* were standing when he fell." She stood, and the two followed her into the cellar. They'd drawn an outline in chalk on the floor, just as they did in crime shows.

"Tell me again how it happened," said the captain, lighting a fresh cigarette. Pétros stood halfway down the stair, all ears and eyes and hotshot attitude.

More lucid now, she recounted her feelings of the moment, along with the strange terror and paralysis she'd felt. The captain stopped her.

"Wait. You didn't quite hear his words before he fell?"

"That's right," she said. "It was like—everything seemed distant, disconnected. There was a flash, like a light bulb before it dies, and for a moment I couldn't move. And then I was back, and *o Pápas* was dead on the floor there."

The captain's gaze held steady. "But you saw him fall?"

"Yes, yes. But it was as if I was outside my body, I—it was very strange." Her mouth felt dry as cotton.

The captain's eyes narrowed. "You didn't mention this before. Are you prone to these, uh, episodes?"

"No! And I could hardly think earlier. Besides, it didn't seem important."

"Kyria, everything is important!" he snapped. "A man—*a priest*— has died here. *At Easter!*" He motioned her to rise and pointed back up the stair. "Please, we'll need to take a full statement at the station."

Her mouth flapped open. She was about to protest, but then she caught Pétros's look. A nasty half-smile flicked over his lips, and he was the leering, bully-boy predator again. Screw him. She wouldn't give him the satisfaction of taking her along by force, which she could see was precisely what he was hoping for.

Elléni followed him back up the stair. She collected her coat and purse and walked right past Pétros to the kitchen, where she uncapped the ouzo bottle he'd left on the counter, poured two fingers, and— with a defiant stare at the two of them—knocked it back. Captain Katsélis raised an eyebrow, but said nothing. She slammed the glass down and walked to the door. The two men followed close behind.

CHAPTER TWENTY-THREE

Alex's plane arrived almost three hours late, and by the time she got through customs and they fought their way through the evening commute in a taxi whose driver just wanted to talk nonstop about politics and grew surly when Paul made it clear that they didn't, they boarded the ferry with less than twenty minutes to spare.

In the year since he'd last seen her, Alex had changed from a skinny teen into a young woman. Her natural jet-black hair and light complexion worked well with her goth lite style of near-black lipstick, dense eyeliner, and heavily-distressed jeans tucked into lace-up boots. Smartly hip, but none of it over the top.

When they'd settled their belongings—Paul had got them separate cabins—they made their way to the lounge. He ordered them both a glass of wine. Charly had brought her daughter up in the enlightened European tradition rather than the Puritanical American one, and from an early age sometimes let her have a drop of wine just to colour her water, rather than make drinking a taboo; at eighteen, Alex regularly drank a little wine with meals at home. *If you don't forbid it, they won't abuse it*, as Charly said.

Dinner in the ferry's cafeteria was an indifferent affair of meatballs and chunky French fries. But there was baklava, which Alex loved. By ten-thirty they'd retired to their cabins. Paul set his alarm for five and climbed into the narrow but cozy bunk.

He'd barely fallen asleep when his cellphone rang. He snatched it up thinking it might be Elléni, but the number was unknown.

"*Kyrie* Hátzis?"

"Yes. Who is this?"

"I'm Captain Katsélis of the Vóunos police. You are on the ferry returning from Thessaloniki?" Paul sat bolt upright. The question, delivered without preamble or explanation, seemed abrupt to say the least.

"Yes. Yes, I am. What makes you ask?"

"And you'll be docking at six-something, I think?"

"Yes! Look, Captain, is there something—"

"Please, Mr. Hátzis. Now: did you authorize Miss Marinóudis to be at your house?"

Paul frowned. Had the police chanced by and thought Elléni was breaking in? Given the house's distance from the road, that seemed unlikely. Besides which, that kind of thing just didn't happen on Vóunos. He had a sudden impulse to shout at the man and tell him to stop playing games. But since it rarely did any good to aggravate people, especially cops, he replied in measured, polite tones.

"Yes. I had to travel to Thessaloniki and she offered to be there when the *teknítis* arrived to install my dishwasher. Could you tell me what this is about?"

"Please, be patient a moment longer, Mr. Hátzis. What's your relationship with Miss Marinóudis?"

Paul hesitated a moment. He didn't want to lie, but he also didn't want to broadcast the fact that they were lovers. "We're friends. Good friends."

The captain didn't comment. Perhaps he was smart enough to appreciate the phrasing. "And did you have any other visitors in the last two or three days before you left?"

"No. Oh, actually, yes—*o Pápas* Tákis stopped by on Tuesday." It had been not long after Elléni left. "Look, is everything okay? Is Miss Marinóudis—"

"And what was *o Pápas* doing there?"

"He just stopped by for a visit." When the captain didn't reply, Paul added, "We'd talked the day before at the church, and he was just following up on our conversation. Also, I think he wanted to see the house."

"Was Miss Marinóudis present at the time of his visit?"

"No."

"And are you aware of any disagreement between Miss Marinóudis and *ó Pápas* Tákis?"

Paul almost laughed. "No. Should I be? Look, what—"

"Please, just a few more questions, Mr. Hátzis. Now, did *o Pápas* leave anything behind at your house?"

The question, despite its casual phrasing, sent a shiver through him. His words tumbled out as his concern mounted. "Yes. He forgot a book. A church journal. Actually, he saw me on the dock, and I told him Miss Marinóudis would be at the house this afternoon if he wanted to pick it up. Look, what's going on?"

"*O Pápas* Tákis was found dead at your house earlier this evening. Miss Marinóudis was present at the time."

At first, Paul didn't understand what he was being told, and asked the policeman to repeat it. After that, the captain had to prompt him several times before he could speak.

"I'm sorry. Yes, I'm still here. Elléni—Miss Marinóudis—is she..."

"Miss Marinóudis is quite well. She's here with us at this moment."

"May I talk to her?"

"We're still taking details of her story. But certainly in the morning."

Paul sank back in his chair. A thick glass wall seemed to have descended between him and the lounge, isolating him in an unreal, nightmare continuum. He squeezed his eyes shut, opened them again. "I.... This is terrible. How did it happen?"

Captain Katsélis told him what they knew. "It's possible he suffered a stroke or something similar, but we're considering all possibilities."

"And in…the cellar, you say?" This was all crazy. What on Earth were they doing in the cellar?

"Yes. Apparently they heard some noises and were checking the house, perhaps for intruders." He asked Paul again whether Elléni and *o Pápas* had been there together on any occasion, and was silent when Paul told him they hadn't.

"You're quite certain of that?" said the captain.

"Quite certain." Did the man suspect some kind of love triangle leading to the priest's death? *A murder?* It was unthinkable. But then so was the priest's death, in his house.

And now that his mind was working again, the fact of the priest's death in his house just after they'd been discussing its sinister past—

"And the journal," continued the captain, "do you know why *o Pápas* left it?"

"I…I don't think he meant to." Paul was about to say he'd been interested in the house's history, but decided against it. "He must have pulled it out of his satchel and forgotten it."

"All right," said the captain, with an audible sigh. "Thank you for your help, Mr. Hátzis. I'll send a car to bring you directly to the police station when you return. We'll need to take a formal statement."

Paul cursed silently. "Will it take long? Only I'll have my niece with me and…"

The captain assured him it wouldn't.

"Good. And, Captain, Miss Marinóudis…you're sure she's all right?"

"Yes. Of course she was in shock at first, but she's quite recovered. She is a strong woman. We're still talking to her, but you'll be able call her later if you like."

And though the captain didn't say so, Paul had the distinct impression that Elléni was under suspicion of murder.

‡

Paul had barely got to sleep before the alarm went off. His first impulse was to call Elléni, but there was every chance he'd wake her if she'd just got home, and sleep was probably what she most needed after the ordeal she'd been through. He'd call her later once they were home.

Half an hour later, as he and Alex sipped coffee in the ferry's neon-lit cafeteria, he explained, as gently as he could, what had happened.

Once past the initial shock Alex listened intently, occasionally asking questions. She'd inherited from her mother a big dose of solid common sense and level-headedness that made it easier for him to relate the tragedy that had occurred, and whose aftermath they'd be faced with.

"Gosh, Paul,"—she'd called him by his name for years now—"I'm so sorry about your friend. It's awful."

"I didn't know him well, but he was a very nice man. I liked him a lot. You're really okay about staying in the house?"

She shrugged. "Sure. "I mean, it sounds like he probably had an aneurysm or something. It's horrible it had to be in your house, but people have to die somewhere."

"Yeah. Actually, I thought very seriously about renting us a pair of rooms or a villa for your stay…but if you can handle it…. Well, I intend to keep the house, and I'd love you to see it." *And to meet Elléni, if she's not in jail.*

Alex nodded, and finished the pastry she'd got to go with the coffee. She seemed lost in thought for a few moments. "So do you really think the house is haunted?"

He stared at her blankly.

"Mom said you'd joked about it over the phone."

"Oh? Oh, right—yeah, I remember that." And now it was his turn to think hard. How much should he tell her about the house and its past? He didn't for a moment believe that *o Pápas's* death was anything more an accident, a horrible and tragic coincidence. But on the other hand, if she was going to stay there, he owed it to her to be absolutely honest. Deception never was his way, and Alex was both grown-up and highly intelligent. If the house's history made her uneasy about staying there, they'd find other accommodation, no problem at this time of year.

After getting a second cup of coffee—Alex was working on hers slowly, sipping rather gulping it—he began. He told her the whole story, everything, from Yaya's narrative to his discovery of the specks of paint on the living-room boards and the faintly discernible traces of the graves on the far side of the orchard. Her expression ranged from wonder to disgust to incredulity, but he never saw fear cross her features.

"Do you think I'm crazy to keep the place?" he concluded.

"Are you kidding? I mean, that's, like, serious history. Omigod! Sacrifices and black magic? I have friends who'd give body parts to stay there!"

Despite everything, he chuckled. "A nicely inappropriate metaphor in this context."

Alex, who'd just taken a sip from her cup, clamped a hand over her mouth as she realized what she'd said and managed to somehow not spray coffee across the table. When she'd recovered, she said, "On a brighter note, Mom said you had a girlfriend?"

He chuckled. "Sort of. Yeah, I guess I do. Elléni, you'll meet her."

Alex's eyes went wide. "Wait, the same woman you just told me was there when your friend had the accident? The real estate gal?"

"That's right. Hopefully, the police have released her by now."

"The police?"

"I'm sure it's just routine, but they were questioning her about Father Tákis's death. I'm afraid they're meeting us off the ferry to talk to me, but the captain assured me it would be a brief interview."

Alex shook her head and broke into a broad grin. She started to laugh.

He stared. "What?"

"I was just thinking, for someone who wanted to get away from craziness and cults, you're really doing a fine job, aren't you?"

He smiled. "The thought had crossed my mind. Now finish that coffee, we dock in a couple of minutes."

‡

127

The police were waiting when they disembarked in the grey dawn. A young officer met them and waved them into the police car parked just yards from the gangplank. The ferry had been packed with islanders and relatives returning for Easter, and everyone around gawked openly at what must for all the world have seemed like an unusually polite arrest. Paul and Alex got into the back of the car with Alex's small suitcase; the policeman got in, started the engine, and they were off.

At least they'd let him know what had happened. Not that it lessened the horror, but it had allowed him to prepare Alex. What a fucking nightmare. Paul had liked *o Pápas* Tákis, liked him a lot. Now he was dead, a friend lost before Paul even had the chance to get to know him. And even if Elléni wasn't a suspect, he couldn't imagine how traumatic it had been for her. Everything had been going so well for him and Elléni, and now—he recoiled, disgusted at himself, from that egocentric line of thinking. *The road to hell is paved with self-pity.*

As the car slid onto the cafe-lined harbor front, Paul said to Alex. "I'm so sorry about this, Alex. Hopefully it won't take too long."

She shook her head. Neither of them had slept much—she because of jet lag, he from worry. But she looked relaxed as she replied, "No worries. I have a book, and maybe they'll let me get some breakfast if it drags out. I'm just so sorry for you."

"Yeah. Well, you know the saying."

"Shit happens. Yup."

‡

Captain Katsélis looked tired and in need of a shave. But he was courteous and—presumably because he was anxious to get home himself—kept the interview brief. After taking Paul's statement, he said, "The body is being sent to Thessaloniki for an autopsy, but every sign points to some sort of stroke. There were no signs of violence on the body or at the scene."

"So you let Miss Marinóudis go?" said Paul.

"A few hours ago." The captain ran his fingers through his hair. "She was never really a suspect. But we have to rule out all possibilities. And the circumstances, an attractive young woman and a priest in someone else's house...well, you understand."

Paul inclined his head. Yes, wouldn't that have made for a spicy story to keep the local gossips happy for months. But he could see it from the captain's side. The man was just doing his job.

"And there is the question of the cellar." Katsélis raised an eyebrow at Paul. "Apparently Miss Marinóudis heard odd sounds just before the priest arrived, and they went to investigate. Have you ever heard strange sounds in the house, *Kyrie?*"

Paul shook his head. "Never. Except sometimes when it's very windy…then the house can creak a little."

"Yes, old houses will do that." The captain stood. "Well, we're finished now. Thank you for coming in."

Paul rose and picked up his coat. "Thanks. You'll let me know the outcome of the autopsy?" he said, as the captain opened the office door for him. "I liked *o Pápas* a good deal. This is a terrible thing."

"Of course." He hesitated for a moment, then said: "Mr. Hátzis, your house—you do know it has a bad reputation, don't you?"

Paul took a breath. How much did the captain know? "Yes. I do."

Captain Katsélis frowned, nodded, and waved him unceremoniously out of the door.

CHAPTER TWENTY-FOUR

Thursday April 17, 2014

O Pápas Stélios cursed. "Be still," he told Chrýsoula, "You may have all day, but I don't!" He squeezed the goat's teats rather more roughly than he'd intended and the animal bleated and stamped, almost upsetting the half-full milk bucket beneath it. Chrýsoula was a big goat, more than waist-high at the shoulders, and had the devil's own temperament.

A few minutes later he was done. He got off his knees, gave the goat's hindquarters a friendly slap, and rose stiffly. He made two fists and ground the knuckles into the muscles along his spine. God! he was getting too old for this. Had been for at least a decade, in fact. Out in the rest of the country, people more than twenty years younger than him collected their pensions. Still, the work and the magnificence of God's creation, wild and untamed in this place, kept up his spirits even when the body felt ready to fail.

But today, Stélios shouldered every one of his eighty-seven years. The vague unease he'd felt during the last few weeks had last night bloomed into nightmare. He was back on Vóunos, performing the annual exorcism at the house of the horror, when something had exploded out of thin air, tearing at his heart, shredding his soul. He awoke gasping for breath and clutching at his chest, expecting to find it clawed open. Afraid to sleep again, he lit the lamps and every candle he had and remained awake, reciting his prayers with his eyes open. Even the dawn wasn't enough to fully shake the terror.

Beyond the slice of sapphire sea which began a bare few hundred meters beyond the terraced groves, Sithonia, the middle of the three peninsulas that trailed like a God's fingers into the limpid waters of the northern Aegean, lay calm on the still waters. He could just make out the town of Sarti, over twenty kilometers away across the gulf.

The morning air sparkled and the sun felt good on his back. Here, on Athos's western slopes, the mornings were always cool. But the chill he felt today was deeper than mere sunlight could dispel.

Stélios gripped the milk pail and set off across the rocky ground towards his *kalívi*. Less bare than the hovels the ascetics of Karoulia lived in, his *kalívi* was still primitive. But unlike the true hermits, who lived on rainwater and the absolute minimum of food they got by bartering their meager handicrafts—prayer ropes, woven baskets, and the like—he enjoyed the unusual luxury of fresh milk and cheese from the half-dozen goats he and four of his near neighbours owned, as well as rough wine from their small vineyard and an endless supply of almonds, olives, and apricots. They traded produce for flour and—sometimes—coffee in Dafni, and lived well enough. This simple co-operative arrangement, a radical experiment suggested by Father Abbot and presumably approved by the bishop, brought all the benefits and more of life in a monastery, without the bother and intrusion and silly rules of living with a gaggle of dotty old men. Stélios wondered if it might be the first step in a softening of tradition with the strategic goal of reinvigorating the desperately depleted community of Athos.

When he got home, he was surprised to find he had a visitor. And not one of his neighbours, but a monk he'd never seen before.

The monk was a young man, thin and fidgety. He stuck out a hand and introduced himself as brother Rigas from the nearby Aghiou Pávlou monastery. "I came as soon as it was light," he said, producing a folded slip of paper from a pocket. "I have a message for you. From Vóunos. The priest there called the Megisti Lavra monastery, and they started checking around until they found us. Fortunately brother Dimitris, who took the call, knew of you and your whereabouts."

Stélios nodded distractedly. As he took the note, the memory of the night's terror came alive, an ugly, vivid echo of his dream. The vision was electric, unmistakable, and he knew before reading it what the message's subject matter would be.

"Please, come inside and take refreshment," he said, opening the door. "I have goat's milk, and coffee."

The young man shook his head. "Thank you. Water will be plenty. And of course if you have a return message, I will take it and see it is relayed back to Vóunos."

Stélios ushered him in and scooped a cup of water from the bucket. As the monk drank, Stélios stood by the small window, the only source of natural light in the one-room *kalívi,* and unfolded the paper. It read,

Father Tákis from Aghios Rigínos on Vóunos sends his greetings and asks after the church journal covering the years 1941 to 1946, which he believes that you may have accidentally removed. He asks that you contact him and let him know whether you are in possession of the journal, and if so, whether it might be returned.

Stélios read it again. Brother Rigas watched him, doubtless wondering what might be so important. He'd certainly read the note— who wouldn't—and noted the euphemism, *"accidentally removed"*.

What could have happened? This certainly concerned the stone house. Stélios's nightmare alone had got him thinking something had or was occurring at the place, something evil. Now he was sure of it. The message could be no coincidence. But how? He'd left the place so thoroughly cleansed and protected it almost glowed in the dark.

Between his own exorcisms and blessings and those of Father Vasílis before him, he would have sworn the place inviolable for as long as it stood.

Stélios had met Father Tákis, the new priest, when the latter arrived on Vóunos to take over the parish Stélios had guided for almost six decades. He had tarried a week for the transition, and got to know Father Tákis well enough; he showed him around the hóra and the island, introducing him to the place and its community. He'd liked the man a good deal and had no concerns over his ability to take over. But although Stélios took pains to brief the young Father extensively on parish matters, he made a point of not mentioning the stone house or the details of its history. It was time for that chapter to be closed and forgotten. Vóunos needed to heal. And to make certain it did, he had, as a precaution, also removed the journal that covered the war years and the horrific crimes committed at the stone house, which Father Vasílis had documented in great detail, and brought the volume back to Athos with him.

Which was not to say he'd done so lightly. To remove or delete any part of a church journal was to break the line of that parish's history; and recording the spiritual history of his community was a vital part of a priest's duty.

But Stélios had been born with an affinity for the hidden, the occult, and over the years his interests in that area had grown, not least because of the challenge and responsibility of continuing the exorcisms at the stone house. Father Vasílis had adhered strictly to church protocol as far as the rites were concerned—he knew evil, but only by its material signs and symptoms, and intellectually; but Stélios knew and felt evil and magic at a visceral and psychic level. And over the decades his very Christian payers and meditations had led him along strange, little-trod paths, the dark forest tracks and winding byways of the mystic and occultist. And, after dark and dangerous wanderings which came close to costing him his soul, to the gates of Hell itself.

During his long tenure on Vóunos, Stélios made a number of journeys to the holy mountain and spent time in the libraries of several monasteries. Among the thousands of books and manuscripts, God had unerringly pointed him to interesting and long-forgotten records left by practical monks attuned to the occult in times when evil and the demonic realm were taken far more seriously than today, times when even lowly parish priests might find themselves needing a sturdy magical defense against warlocks and witches, curses and spells. And so in time, through practice and prayer, fasting and meditation, he'd learned the practice of ritual magic in the service of God, and the art of scrying to reveal hidden forces and trends.

There was no question that he'd violated church doctrine in advancing his extracurricular studies and practices; but he'd repeatedly examined his heart and motives, and always found God at the centre of all. If Stélios had a gift for the occult, it was a gift from God, a gift he'd been given to fight the intrusion of evil centered on the stone house.

Without his and Vasílis's rituals, Stélios was certain that whatever dark forces the magicians had cultivated would return to the place. So as his understanding had grown, Stélios had added his own flourishes and rituals to the church's blessing and seven prayers, strengthening the sphere of protection around the stone house and driving every last shred of evil from it, until even those among the islanders who had been directly affected by the horror had begun to forget. To his lasting surprise, his annual rituals seemed to be burying the horror firmly in the past and helping the whole island to recover.

It seemed then right that his leaving Vóunos should be the final step in the island's healing. To leave the journal would risk the whole matter being reopened, brought to light; and so abyssal had been the evil there that breaking the continuity of the community's history seemed like a small infraction compared to the risk of bringing fresh attention, new psychic energy, to the events at the stone house and thus, perhaps, risking a resurgence of the evil. It was time to turn the page.

"Father Stélios?"

Stélios, who'd quite forgotten the young monk was there, turned from the window. Brother Rigas cocked his head. "Do you wish me take back a message?"

Did he? Stélios rubbed the back of his neck. The request was a simple one: did he have the journal, and would he return it. He didn't want to lie, but he also didn't want to act precipitously. Because every fiber of his being, his very soul, was screaming, *danger!* This required thought, prayer, meditation.

"No," he said finally. "I will deliver a reply before long. Thank you for your trouble. But here, look, we had an abundance of honey last year." He drew aside the curtain on the small alcove he used for a pantry and handed the monk a liter jar. "Please take this, as a gift for the brothers."

CHAPTER TWENTY-FIVE

The task accomplished, Magda was abruptly herself again, an independent consciousness.

With the protection smashed, she saw, as through a rippling layer of water, into the stone house. A man—a priest—lay on the floor: she knew at once he was dead. At his side was a woman frantically attempting to revive him. Magda recognized the room as the cellar in which they'd buried the artifact, the beacon which would recall them for their rebirth.

<That went rather well didn't it?> The thought came from Dafyd. She felt the swell of triumph emanating from Klaus as an almost physical force. Even since re-individuating, it seemed they could sense one another's every thought and feeling.

But Magda's attention was entirely on the woman kneeling by the dead man. Indistinct though she was through whatever medium connected their spheres of existence, Magda had a clear sense of her— the woman was intelligent, strong. Was she the new tenant of the house? Was hers the body Magda would inhabit on her resurrection? Magda felt a moment's pity.

<Don't.> It was Dafyd. <You've served your time, and each has their own fate.>

<And us,> said Klaus, <who are we to take?> A sudden pulse of fear came from him. <Was the priest one of the three—>

<No, I don't think so. Just an offering, an hors d'ouevre, if you like.>

Dafyd's trademark light humour more often than not contained a hard kernel of truth. As the priest's body cooled, she could taste his life force coursing up through the medium and into their three beings. It was energizing, tonic.

Klaus, with obvious relish: <Yes! I feel it too! It is as though we are feeding on his soul.>

<That is exactly what is taking place, Klaus,> replied Dafyd. <An ability, you'll be thrilled to hear, that we'll retain even after we incarnate again.> A wave of dark mirth rolled off him.

Magda's momentary burst of empathy subsided and she was herself again. A memory of the last remnant of her humanity, that feeling, a weakness she would no longer have need of and could finally shed without regret or remorse. She reminded herself what she'd sacrificed during her time on Earth, and the pain she'd endured throughout her lifetime of service in Outer Hell. Whatever power she'd accrued, the price—a seeming eternity of howling pain as the three of them suffered endless torture at the interface between Hell and the horror beyond—had been terrible. No, she'd paid in full for her resurrection and was more than ready to take whatever body their ritual had, through the power of their now-ancient artifact, summoned for her use.

Their view, though indistinct and murky, had expanded to include the whole house. The impression was peculiar, synaesthetic rather than wholly visual. But through whatever connection remained, Magda sensed movement as two fresh presences, both male, appeared on the scene. At her side—or whatever corresponded to that in this limbo—Klaus positively fizzed with excitement.

<There! They've arrived, Dafyd. These must be ours!>

<No,> said Dafyd. He was intensely focused on the blurry scene unfolding in the stone house. <It's not time yet—we have neither the power nor the channel. These two are police, just here because of the death. But the fact we're here, and able to see and act, however imperfectly, tells me we're very close. Just a day or two from our moment.>

<Of our rebirth?>

<Precisely. And with every moment that passes, we gain in strength and can see more clearly. When our three hosts are gathered together and the time is right, we'll know. And we shall strike.>

135

<But we had the power to break the protection,> said Klaus.

<Yes. But that's nothing to the power needed to incarnate, to steal a body and force out its resident soul. Like demons—which is what we now are, though of a peculiar class—we can have some effect in the world. Far more, in fact, than any demon, since we've both the power and the connection to Earth, having one foot still there, as it were. We need not be conjured, and cannot be constrained. But our resurrection is dependent on the strict terms of the pact.>

<But how will we know?> insisted Klaus. <What if the three we need don't come together?>

<They must. It's in the agreement, and no entity violates such. The mechanics of Hell are powering that pact, and will see it enforced. The three will be attracted and kept there until we possess them and eject their resident souls. Remember the terms? *That they not be free to leave but instead be herein constrained—*>

<*—until, at the midnight before Easter Sunday dawn, we three signatories return to take possession of their physical bodies, casting their souls into the demonic sphere to serve for eternity in our stead*> concluded Magda.

Dafyd laughed. <Precisely. Once our hosts are assembled in the house, they'll find they can't leave. And then, they're ours.>

‡

Friday April 18, 2014

"It doesn't *look* like a haunted house," said Alex, as Paul closed the door behind them.

He chuckled, glad of the opportunity for light relief. "They don't build gothic manses in Greece. And I cleared out the bats and cobwebs and oiled the hinges on the front door before I left."

She took a few steps into the big room. "This is where it happened? The sacrifices and ritual magic?"

"Apparently."

She turned full circle, taking it all in. "I don't get any bad vibes at all."

"I'm glad to hear it." He went ahead, and she followed him up the stairs and along the short passage.

"So this is your room," said Paul. He'd made up the back bedroom for her, and hoped the view out over the orchard and the rolling pine-covered hills beyond would make up for the lack of sea view. He'd considered giving up his own bedroom for her, but it seemed trivial. In four days here, how much time was she going to spend in her bedroom anyway?

But Alex was delighted. She threw her bag on the bed and went straight to the window. "Omigod, look at that view!"

"Do you like it?"

"It's fabulous!" She turned and hugged him. "Oh, Paul, thanks for bringing me here!"

He patted her shoulder and smiled. "I'm glad you like it. Well," he said as they disengaged, "I'm going to get some breakfast on. If you want to shower or anything…"

"Definitely. Give me half an hour. And breakfast sounds great!"

Downstairs, he hesitated just a moment before opening the cellar door. He flicked on the light and peered down the stair.

The cellar was just as he'd left it: a tidy stack of flattened cartons leaning up against the wall, held in place by those few boxes he still had to unpack. The air was still and a little musty, just as he remembered it. And cool to the point of cold.

But there, at the foot of the stairs, was the chalk outline of a body. His vision blurred and he felt his throat tighten. He forced himself down the stair and scrubbed at the marks with a rag until they were gone.

He put coffee on as he debated whether to call Elléni now or wait for her to call. It was barely eight-thirty, and she was still being questioned at eleven last night. He had no idea what time she'd got home, but there was every chance she'd probably still be asleep. But he needed to hear her voice and hear the story from her. *More to the point,* he corrected himself, *she probably needs to talk and hear your voice.*

She answered on the third ring, and he knew at once from her sleepy mumble that he'd woken her. She cut across his apology. "No, no, I left my phone on purposely. It was the middle of the night when I left the police station, and Katsélis said he'd called you, so I left it on hoping you'd call. Oh, Paul—it was so horrible!"

"Are you okay?"

"Yes. Yes, just tired. But I'm so happy to hear you. Is Alex there with you?"

"Yes. I'm just making breakfast. Want to join us?"

"No. I mean, of course…but you must take some time together just with her."

"How about lunch, then? I was going to show her around the village today and then tour the island tomorrow. One o'clock at the Argo?"

"Perfect." She sounded glad. "But let's not talk about poor Father Tákis. This is Alex's holiday, and also Easter. Another time."

He hesitated. Of course she was right, but… "I just wonder if you don't *need* to talk about it."

"After half the night telling the story over and over to the police and them questioning every detail?" A quick, harsh laugh. "No, I'm really okay. You and I will talk about it, and raise a glass to the poor man, later on."

‡

A sense of dread and impending calamity kept Father Stélios from sleep that night. His apprehension—no, it was fear, pure and simple—reached such a pitch that he lit a pair of candles to keep the profound dark at bay. The waning moon wouldn't be over the mountain before far into the night.

At dawn, he set off for the monastery at Aghiou Pávlou, stopping only at Brother Nikos's to tell him he had an errand and to ask Nikos to milk the goats in his stead that morning.

Although the distance to the monastery was just a few kilometers, the path wound over rocky hills and ravines, up escarpments and down gullies before it joined the wide dirt road from the small harbour at Arsanas for the last few hundred meters. Tired as he was from lack of sleep, the way seemed even harder than it normally would have been for his eighty-seven-year-old frame. Though he walked the paths around his *kalívi* often and worked daily at the milking, age took its inevitable toll.

There was also the guilt he felt for doing this on Good Friday. Instead of fasting and praying as he should be, he was acting on a fear, chasing down a ghost of what should have been the long-dead past.

Except it wasn't dead. He was sure of it.

He laboured up the winding, stone-paved roadway to the monastery. The climbing, many-windowed structure of white stone atop its sheer walls was larger than some villages. Behind it, a wild, deep-cleft gorge snaked up into the mountains.

Once inside the monastery there was the inevitable small talk and politeness before he could do what he'd come for. The young monk who accompanied him had looked up the number for the church of Aghios Rigínos—which was good because he'd long ago forgotten it—and written it on a slip of paper. He led Stélios to a small, gloomy room adjoining the offices, then left him to it.

The room was bare but for a wooden chair and a small table with a telephone. Stélios peered at the paper in his hand and dialed the number.

His call was answered on the second ring. "Hello?" The voice was young, male.

Stélios had to clear his throat, which had suddenly closed up. "Father Tákis?"

"Father Tákis is not here. Who's speaking?"

A chill went through him. "I am Father Stélios, calling from Athos. I received a message from Father Tákis. When can I find him?"

'One moment, please." There was some muffled conversation, the speaker placing a hand over the mouthpiece. A moment later, a new voice came on the line.

"Father Stélios, I am Captain Katsélis of the Vóunos police. Are you *the* Father Stélios? From Vóunos?"

"I am. And congratulations, Captain, on your promotion." He remembered Katsélis and knew the family. And Katsélis—who'd been a lieutenant when Stélios had left—clearly remembered him.

"Thank you. But I'm afraid I have some bad news for you. Father Tákis died last night. We're investigating the matter."

A block of ice formed around Stélios's heart. His mouth opened, but he couldn't get any words out.

"Father Stélios?"

He forced his voice to work. "Yes. I…. *Dead?* How…what happened?"

"We think it may have been a stroke."

In which case, why were the police involved? An image came to him then, and with it a new, terrible dread. "Who found him?" he croaked. "And *where?*"

"He was visiting a friend, it seems, at a house a little distance from the *hóra,* when he collapsed."

Oh dear God no! "The stone house?" he blurted. Immediately the words came out, he regretted it.

Dead silence. Then, "How did you know this, Father?" The captain's voice was a mixture of amazement and suspicion. "And what was the message you received from Father Tákis?"

Stélios recovered quickly. "A question. He was asking about some old parish records."

"I see." There was a pause. Stélios could hear the wheels turning in Katsélis's mind across a hundred kilometers of water. "And these records...would they be in the form of an old church journal?"

"I..." Stélios swallowed hard. He couldn't lie. "Yes."

There was a long pause. "Father?"

"Yes, sorry. It's just such a shock..."

"Of course. Tell me, Father, how did you know the death took place in the stone house?"

Stélios's mind raced. How did Katsélis know of the journal? He couldn't think through the ramifications of this fast enough. What he suspected about Stélios's death wasn't for public consumption, and certainly not a police matter. So—

God forgive him a small lie. "The message. Father Tákis told me he had business there. But what a tragedy! He was so young."

"Yes, very young. A tragedy indeed." The captain's tone gave nothing away. Well, Father, is there anything else I can help you with?"

"No, no. Please remember me to your family. And go with God, Captain."

CHAPTER TWENTY-SIX

Paul spent the morning showing Alex around the *hóra.* Though he was still in love with the old village, he'd grown used to it enough to experience the thrill of seeing it afresh through her eyes. She took pictures every few yards and delighted at each sudden view of the sea. Which meant she'd come back, and—he hoped, since money wasn't a problem—often.

She was also fascinated by the number of churches in the village and wanted to look in every one. "They must have one for every saint!" Alex remarked, as they paused on their way up one of the *hora's* steeper lanes.

He smiled. "There are about a hundred and fifty churches and chapels on Vóunos, and at least three monasteries. But I read the Orthodox church has close to a thousand saints."

"That figures. The Catholics have several hundred. I don't think the Orthodox Church has a formal canonization process, so they probably have way more."

"Really? How did you even know that?"

"Religious Studies. It's one of the classes I'm taking."

Paul felt his jaw clench. His irritation must have shown in his expression because Alex asked, "What?"

He shrugged. "I guess…I didn't know religion interested you so much."

Alex rubbed his shoulder. "Paul, please. I know faith is a trigger issue for you. It's not like I'm joining a cult. But I *am* interested in faith and religion, and I'm taking some units on it. And like it or not, Christianity is at the core of Western thought and culture."

He blinked. It wasn't the first time Alex had surprised him with a strongly-stated opinion and it wouldn't be the last. *Like it or not.*

"Fair enough," he said. "But interested is one thing and a believer is another. Which are you?"

She laughed. "If I said 'barely agnostic', would you disinherit me?"

Now it was his turn to laugh. "Who said anything about inheritances?"

"Humour me," she said. "Would you?"

He rubbed his ear and began to walk again. "You know my feelings about religion."

"I do," she said, taking his arm. "Which is why it's so odd that the one man you formed a friendship with was poor Father Tákis. Besides which," she added, "there's a big difference between religions and cults."

Paul didn't see it, but he let it go. Alex was smart—no, brilliant. Hopefully she'd avoid falling into the yawning traps that the eternal (and futile) human search for meaning opened up. Pushback from him wasn't going to help.

After three hours of exploring up and down the village's steep streets and narrow alleys, they were more than ready for lunch. The tavernas and cafes, somnolent just a week ago, were gearing up for Easter. All along the *paralía*—the harbourfront—tables and chairs and couches were appearing, filling the wide expanse of pavement flanking the water. As they neared the *Argo* taverna, some of the shopkeepers and waiters greeted Paul as they passed; not a few eyes settled on Alex with obvious interest.

"You're pretty well known here," said Alex.

"Well, after three months…"

"No, it's nice." She turned to him as they strolled, brown eyes searching his. "Mom was worried about you the last year or two. This place has brought you out of your shell."

He laughed. Damn, she was sharp. "Yeah, I guess it has. You can tell her I'm okay. Except for *o Pápas* having a stroke in my house, that is."

They took a table on the edge of the Argo's small terrace, right on the water. Alex sat with her face to the sun, enjoying the warm rays. "Omigod, I can't believe I'm wearing a tank in April. This feels so good after Ithaca."

"Still got snow on the ground?"

She laughed. "Only four feet or so. And it's, like, seventy degrees colder!"

They'd just ordered drinks—a beer for Paul, iced tea for Alex—when Elléni arrived. Rising to greet her, Paul saw at once that she'd been crying. Despite her broad smile, there was no hiding the puffy, red-rimmed eyes. She hugged him hard, then turned to Alex, who'd also stood. Alex's hand came up for a handshake, but Elléni—who looked ready to start crying again—was already pulling her into a close embrace. After a moment she drew back, hands resting lightly on Alex's arms, and took a good look at her. "As Paul said, you are quite beautiful," she said, in English.

Alex gave her back a brilliant smile, looking uncharacteristically at a loss for anything to say. If she was shocked at the tracks of grief in Elléni's face, she concealed it well.

"I am so happy to meet you," Elléni told Alex in English, as Paul pulled out a chair for her.

"You too," said Alex. "I've heard so much about you."

Elléni glanced at Paul, raising an eyebrow with exaggerated drama. "Eh. We will talk about this. But I must apologize for my condition." She gestured at her face as the three of them sat down. "I stopped at Aghios Rigínos to put some flowers for Father Tákis, and of course that is when everything hit me. There were many people with flowers, and much crying. It was very sad."

"People know already?" said Paul.

"Of course. It is all over the *hóra*. By tomorrow even the fish in the sea will know. Also, Katsélis was there."

"He was?" And, "The captain of police," he added, for Alex's benefit.

"Yes. He was looking through papers, I think. He has not slept; I was nearly sorry for him." She signed to the waiter, who came over, and ordered a Campari soda. The waiter inclined his head and left.

Paul put his hand on Elléni's. "So, about Father Tákis. Do you think it was a stroke?"

She frowned a little, and seemed to think hard about it. "Whatever it was, it was very quick." She gave a small shrug. "We will know in a few days."

"I'm sorry you had to be there," said Paul.

She nodded and turned out her palms. Fate, she meant. Nothing for it. Then, brightening, "Now, what shall we eat?"

They looked at their menus and made small talk until the waiter brought everyone's drinks and took their food order.

"What do you study at university?" Elléni asked Alex.

"I'm thinking of going for a double major. Psychology and Philosophy, with a side of Religious Studies."

Elléni turned a quizzical look on her. "Psychology and...? It is an unusual combination."

Alex laughed. "I know, people think the disciplines are so contradictory. But when you think about it, belief is very much a matter of psychology and culture. They're all wrapped up together. I took some units in Anthropology, too."

"Ah. And why did you choose these subjects?" Elléni asked.

Alex's lips quirked up in a smile. "Probably my mixed-up family. Jewish, Greek Orthodox, Southern Baptist…and all of them completely crazy, of course. Well, almost all," she added, with a sideways look at Paul.

He caught the look and grinned. "For the record, she's talking about her grandparents."

Alex laughed. "Yeah. And besides, Mom and Paul are godless."

"And your father?" said Elléni.

"Oh, dad's a mammonite, through and through. He went to jail for his beliefs."

Now it was Paul's turn to laugh. Elléni looked from one to the other of them, entirely confused. "This is an American religion? And he went *to prison* for it?"

Which entirely cracked them up. "You could call it that," said Paul, recovering with difficulty. "But, no, mammon as in wealth, money."

"Ahh…*mamónas,*" said Elléni. "This is a Greek word."

Alex, who'd just regained her composure, started laughing again. Elléni looked puzzled.

"No, no," said Paul, waving his hand as he tried to keep a straight face. "Don't take offense. It's true, so many words *do* have a Greek origin. It's just that since the movie, it's become a bit of a running joke."

"*My Big Fat Greek Wedding,*" said Alex.

Enlightenment spread over Elléni's features, and she relaxed. "Ah, I see. Yes, also here we thought it was very funny. But I am sorry for your father." She took a long sip of her drink.

"It's okay," said Alex. "He had it coming to him. Anyway, my parents had already divorced, and he's out now, so it's all okay."

Elléni nodded. "So, I see you already have a good philosophy. I do not think you will find your studies so difficult." She leaned forward on the table as if to get to more important business. "Now, what music do you like?"

Paul grinned. *Nice. Way to bond, girl.*

Alex gave a shrug. "All kinds of stuff. Sometimes I just listen to whatever comes on Spotify, but I do have some favourites…. Do you know Swedish House Mafia?"

"Of course," said Elléni. "The best dance music! I have many of their songs. But I like eighties metal very much, it was the music of my teens."

"Like Guns 'n' Roses? AC/DC?"

"Yes!" cried Elléni. "I *love* AC/DC! Also Guns and Roses. But the best for me was Black Sabbath! I still have everything of theirs, on CD of course."

Paul sat back, watching the girls and listening to their conversation with a mixture of amusement and concern. He was pretty fond of eighties metal himself. Laughable that the Reaganite Christians of the time associated it with Satanism. Still, the words *black sabbath*, in the context of the weird history of the stone house and Father Tákis's death, were a little jarring. He tried to laugh it off, glad to see his niece and his lover getting on so well, but the question of the house's past was becoming more urgent in his mind.

It had begun in the bar, with an innocent mention of the house having a bad history. Then came Elléni's yayá's story, at least some of which had proved all too real. The entry for the German colonel in Wikipedia and, after that, his discovery of clear evidence in the form of the grave sites and the specks of paint on his floor. Then Father Tákis, who'd confirmed there'd been exorcisms at the house. The mystery of the missing journal—probably nothing, but still an odd coincidence. And now, the priest's death.

My god. Elléni was right there with him. If he didn't die of…natural causes…she could have been—

He checked the thought. Was he making more of it than he should? He didn't think so. And what had the policeman, Katsélis, said? *The stone house—you do know it has a bad reputation, don't you?* Well, he certainly knew it now. And after the priest's death, the house's reputation would be a lot worse—Elléni had confirmed it would be all over the island by tonight. Though he didn't foresee an angry mob of villagers with pitchforks and torches storming the house, his continued residence there might not endear him to the locals. And he really wanted to be happy here.

He forced himself back to the here and now. Alex and Elléni, fully engaged with each other, had appeared not to notice his silence; they only paused now in their headlong bonding because the waiter had arrived with their food.

Well, Alex was here now, and they were stuck with the house. The next few days were about her, and he fully intended to make it fun for her. The weather was beautiful, the island was alive with excitement over the holiday, and he had the companionship—perhaps, he dared think, even more—of a beautiful, intelligent, funny woman. He couldn't remember life being so good.

So why did he feel this growing dread that something really bad was going to happen?

CHAPTER TWENTY-SEVEN

As they lingered in the timeless, shifting, astral realm, waiting for Dafyd to judge the moment right, Magda allowed her consciousness to roam, flexing her senses. Not only did her Sight still work, but it also was able to range effortlessly across whatever void or barrier separated this place from the human world.

The stone house looked so familiar, so comforting, despite its new furniture and occupants. It seemed not only ready but eager to receive them again, like an old friend.

She gave her Sight full rein, curious to see where it led.

Though the man and young girl in the house were entirely unaware of her, the emotional charge of the priest's sudden death clung to the man. Focusing more closely, she found it leading her like a scent trail to the village and the policeman who'd been in the house. And linked to him was a long trace, fine but unmistakable, tinged with suspicion and doubt, leading off across the sea to the northeast.

Magda paused. Had she a body, her jaw might have dropped.

Her Sight, always keen, had become something stronger by an order of magnitude. She saw feelings, smelt associations, tasted thoughts. Was it this place that...? No. No, it was the lifetime spent on the edge. As Dafyd had promised, her power had grown tenfold. And that of the others, too, she guessed. For Dafyd, it would be his magic and will. And Klaus? His power to compel and command others, perhaps.

She followed the trace across the dark sea, and in a short time that was really no time, she found herself looking at an old monk in a squalid, gloomy hut.

Well, now here was a thing. This priest—whose links with the island and the stone house were unmistakable—also had the Sight. Not only that, he was at this very moment preparing to exercise it, looking down at a delicately crafted scrying-bowl of the most exquisite simplicity.

As any occultist knew, there were no coincidences.

<Dafyd, you should see this. Join with me, if you will. Follow my gaze.>

At once, he did so; Klaus, lost in his own thoughts and schemes, or perhaps still recovering, appeared to have not heard.

A pulse of surprise from Dafyd. <Well, well.>

<Yes,> she agreed. <It seems we've attracted some interest. And this one has a little power, wouldn't you say?>

<Power might be stretching it, I think. But from the appearance of him and what he's about, talent, certainly. Can you tell who he is?>

She tried to probe the man's mind, sense his thoughts, and found she couldn't. <Either the medium is too thick, too distorting, or he's somehow warded. But his connection with our old home is strong.>

Dafyd was silent a while, deep in thought. Then, <Perhaps we can have a little fun with him and dissuade him from taking any further interest. We've already killed one priest today, and though this one's too far from Vóunos to be of any concern, I'd prefer to not attract more attention.> A ripple of humor, like a chuckle, came off him. <But with your Sight as a channel, let's see if he can hear me...>

‡

It was well past noon by the time Stélios was back at his *kalívi*. Every joint in his body complained, and his mind was troubled. He would have given a great deal to just stretch out on his cot and sleep, but he didn't dare do so. Not now.

Something terrible was happening on Vóunos, and he had no idea what it could be.

He fetched out a rectangular wooden box from the chest at the foot of his bed. In it, carefully wrapped in white silk, were his two simple tools: a large wooden crucifix—his *battle* crucifix, as he thought of it, which he'd made with his own hands—and the simple black porcelain bowl he used for scrying.

Of the two, the black scrying-bowl was the more dangerous, since it could as easily deceive as enlighten. If one's motives were in the slightest way impure, or the state of mind and health weakened, anything it showed could lead to evil as easily as to good, lies as easily as truth. He'd not used it in over ten years, but if ever he had need of seeing clear, it was now.

But not yet. He was too weak. A little food, a few hours' rest— without those he was afraid he might not see true. A few hours, a day, couldn't make any difference. Not that he could do anything about what might be happening in Vóunos anyway. Who was he fooling? He was just an old, tired monk who'd done his part. He should just lie down and sleep.

Listen to yourself, Stélios, you old fool! Don't you recognize the devil when you hear him?

He poured a glass of water and drank it all, then a second. He needed to work. God would sustain him.

Stélios set the bowl on his table and placed a new candle in a holder next to it. He half-closed the shutters, making the already gloomy hut darker still. Ignoring the popping and aches in his bony knees, he knelt on the stone floor and prayed.

After a long time, he rose stiffly, pulled out his chair, and lit the candle, not for light but for what the flame symbolized—truth and the presence of the Holy Spirit. He sat, cleared his mind, and gazed into the stone's polished black depths.

There was no movement for a time, long enough that he felt the beginnings of doubt steal over him. Perhaps he'd lost his abilities after so many years. Perhaps there was really nothing to see. Perhaps—

Like sunlight reflecting off a fish's scales in a murky pool, a point of golden light coalesced deep below the surface of the bowl. It trembled, dimmed, lost coherence...and then burst into pieces, fragments of light tumbling in every direction, a slow firework in the depths. The pieces sharpened, became rolling, roiling numbers and angles and algebraic symbols written with a pen of fire in the deep pool of inner vision. The sparks multiplied, rising and growing brighter as they neared they surface, until the surface of the bowl boiled with an incomprehensible array of mad mathematics. An acrid smell, like the tang of blood on hot iron, filled his head, and Stélios felt the air thicken around him. He had a powerful urge to back away, break the vision, throw a cloth over the stone before—

No! He would not.

The onslaught of brilliant symbols subsided by degrees, the fiery fragments becoming tiny bubbles that, perversely, sank back down into the bowl's depths. His eyes strained to follow them, as if the distance were very great.

And now an image formed, larger, closer. Grey and deep blue, citrine and flecks of green came together, grew in sharpness, brightened, brightened.

He stood on stony ground in full daylight. Overhead was the profoundest blue, the lapis of *Panágia,* the Holy Mother's cloak, the waters around Vóunos at certain times of day —he noted the association with the observing, rational part of his mind. There was birdsong, and the occasional bleating of sheep. The air was still and dry, the sunlight full and hot on his back.

A short distance ahead rose a low hill, and under a deep-shadowed overhang laced with the gnarled, exposed roots of the largest, oldest olive tree he'd ever seen was what looked like the mouth of a cave.

As he approached, he saw it was indeed a cave, its entrance blocked by a large boulder almost as tall as a man. He put his hands on it and pushed, trying to roll it to the side. At first it wouldn't move: how could it, it had to weigh many tons. But still he tried, putting his back into it. His legs seemed to throw taproots down into the ground, drawing strength from the depths of the earth, the steady, implacable power of tree roots, a strength that broke walls and cracked stone.

He pushed against the boulder, and the boulder pushed back. He redoubled his efforts, unsure why he was doing it but knowing he must.

Slowly, almost imperceptibly, the great stone began to move. It turned a fraction of a degree, then settled back. He pushed harder, straining muscle and tightening sinews, drawing power from the ground and channeling it through his body until he felt his bones must shatter from the effort.

The stone's motion grew by increments, its resistance lessening as Stélios overcame its inertia, aided by sheer force of will and some power he didn't begin to comprehend. The stone turned, turned; it reached a critical point, a fulcrum…and suddenly it rolled under its own weight as if that was it had intended to do all along and settled with a deep, earthy thump into the brown gloom beneath the overhanging roots by the cave entrance.

The mouth of the cave stood before him, a low, near-circular blackness tall enough to roll a barrel through, but not much more.

For all the effort it had taken to unseal the way, Stélios felt no pain, no fatigue, only a mad, burning need to forge ahead. Crouching low, he scuttled crablike into the darkness.

A faint glow followed him, clinging like a shroud and providing a little welcome light. After just a couple of meters, the space widened and grew taller so that he was able to stand. The cave walls were lost in the shadows, the rough, uneven ceiling a little above the reach of his outstretched arm. A soft-looking green lichen clung to it in places.

Before him were three stone tombs.

Stélios had a momentary, dizzying perception of being at once in his body and also outside it, watching helplessly as his vision-self was drawn, equally helpless, to the middle one of the three sarcophagi. He was cold, very cold, and his body shook from the violence of his heartbeat.

When he saw the lid was missing and the tomb stood open, he froze. He placed his hands on the shoulder-high rim and, despite his growing terror, peered inside.

The tomb was empty; the deep, smooth cavity shone in the inexplicable radiance that had followed him. When he moved to examine the adjacent tomb, some sense made him turn fully around to face the cave's mouth.

Silhouetted in the light from the entrance was the figure of a man. As he advanced into the cave, Stélios saw he was small and rather fat.

The man stopped two handsbreadths away and the light shining around Stélios fell on him, revealing his waxy features. He looked harmless enough, even jovial. He had a shock of wavy black hair and spectral, fog-grey eyes under bushy eyebrows; a smile danced on his lips. But the aura of death clung to him, and he radiated evil like a black sun.

Stélios snatched up the crucifix hanging on his breast and held it before him to ward off the evil. He willed his lips to shape the words of banishment, but his mouth was dry and his tongue stuck as if nailed to his palate, so that no sound was possible.

Two other forms materialized in the shadows, one to either side of the first, and came forward to stand beside him. One was a man, tall, with sandy hair and cold blue eyes; the other a young woman, red-haired and beautiful. Her sea-green eyes held no threat, only curiosity.

In the face of Stélios's obvious terror, the short man's smile broadened, became a wide grin. He threw his arms wide, striking a pose, and cried, in a clear voice that rang off the stone like the call to judgment, "Behold, priest! I am alive for ever and ever, and I hold the keys to death and Hades!"

CHAPTER TWENTY-EIGHT

They'd just finished with lunch when a cloudbank, driven by a sudden cold wind from the north, stole over the hills across the bay from the *hóra*.

"Oh no," said Alex. "I was loving the sunshine!"

"It is only April," said Elléni. "But the forecast is good for the weekend, it will not rain." She turned to Paul. "Well. Tonight is the Good Friday procession through the village. Usually I go to Mikró Kástro, but I thought perhaps tonight we could do this together here in Vóunos?"

Paul glanced at Alex, who was nodding enthusiastically. "We'd love that," he said, "but don't you want to spend it with your family? I wouldn't want them to be offended."

"They will not. We will be there Sunday for Easter, so they are happy. It is not the first time I remain in Vóunos with my friends on the Friday." The cloud slid between them and the sun, and the wind kicked up. She turned to Alex, who was hugging herself against the chill. "But look, you are cold. Perhaps we should go now."

Paul signaled the waiter for the check. "What time does the procession start?"

"It begins at the church of Aghios Nektários at about nine, and then stops at.... Ah, but with *O Pápas* Tákis gone…" Her face clouded over and for a moment he thought she would cry, but she recovered and went on. "I do not know what will happen at Aghios Rigínos. The coffin is already decorated with all the flowers, but without him I do not think it will be in the procession. Unless another priest says the *liturgía*."

Alex looked a little shocked. "His coffin…but without him?"

"Not Father Tákis," said Paul. "The bier. Each church decorates a bier containing an effigy of Christ, and the procession stops at each church. The priest of that church reads a liturgy before its own bier and the worshippers from that church join the procession, which then moves on to the next church."

"Exactly," said Elléni. "It goes to about midnight, so dress warmly. And after we will go for drinks."

The waiter arrived with the check. Paul put down cash, leaving a good tip. Around them, some of the other customers were starting to rise, taking plates and glasses into the restaurant's interior, out of the wind.

Paul looked at his watch. It was almost three. "I was going to drive us to Helios beach," he said to Alex, "it's a lovely walk along there, but with this wind…"

"Yeah. And I'm kind of fading a bit. It must be all the walking."

"Jet lag," said Paul. He pushed back his chair and stood. The others rose, too. "Want to go home and nap, take some down time? It's going to be a late night." He looked at Elléni, which brought a tight smile. Christ, the poor girl. She was trying to keep a brave face, but he could tell she was tired and distraught. He put a hand on her back, rubbed it comfortingly. Then, noting the gooseflesh on Alex's arms—she was wearing only shorts and a tank top—he did the same for her.

Alex nodded. "Down time would be great. Are you coming with us?" she asked Elléni, her voice hopeful.

"I…" Elléni looked uncertainly at Paul.

"Please do," he said. Alex nodded enthusiastically. "Unless you have something else…"

Elléni shook her head quickly. "No, no. Actually, I would prefer not to be alone. It has been a terrible night."

Paul glanced up at the gathering clouds; it really did look like rain. Where had this weather come from? He motioned along the street, towards where they'd left the car, inviting them to each take one of his arms; "Then let's go," he said.

‡

Alex had gone to rest in her bedroom and asked to be woken by six. In the kitchen, Paul put on some Greek coffee. Elléni was looking out of the window at the orchard, watching the steady downpour that had begun just as they arrived.

"Are you okay?" he said, reverting to Greek.

"I was thinking of Father Tákis." She turned, leaned back against the counter. "Also, I meant to ask about the church journal Father Tákis left. What was that about?"

Paul explained about the missing volume, and the discreet entries in the later one the priest had brought which pointed to annual exorcisms being performed at the house.

"Just as Yaya said," Elléni murmured.

"Father Tákis checked the later journals. The exorcisms went on right up to 2006, when Father Stélios left." The coffeepot was just beginning to bubble. He turned off the burner and took the pot off the stove.

Elléni was worrying at a strand of hair, apparently deep in thought. Paul poured their coffee, handed her one. "Speak to me, Elléni" he said.

She gave a small shake of her head, as though to clear something out. "It's…I mean, I don't believe in these things much. But the coincidences are starting to add up, don't you think?"

He motioned to the sofa. "Let's sit."

She took his suggestion and he joined her as she sank back into the pillows. He sipped at his coffee. It was rich and darkly delicious.

He put a hand on hers. "Yes, it's a coincidence that as we start finding out about these exorcisms and looking into the history, this terrible thing happens. But if you're saying there's some…*occult* force at work, black magic or something…why? How? I don't see a catalyst, a trigger." Even as the words came out, he wondered if he was trying to reassure her or himself.

"Maybe just our interest? Could we have woken something up?" She hugged herself, as if suddenly chilled.

He frowned. "By just talking about it?" He put his coffee down and slipped his arm around her shoulder, drawing her close.

Her posture relaxed as she rested her head against his chest. But a moment later, she sat suddenly upright, holding up her index finger. "Ah! and I forgot—the sounds! There were sounds, just before it happened."

"Sounds? Captain Katsélis said you'd heard a noise—"

"More than one. Just before Father Tákis arrived, and then when we were talking; it was loud, a scraping sound. Very strange. That's why we went into the cellar. He heard it too. Also..." She looked to the side, as though trying to remember. "There was something else, just as he fell. Like a flash, very quick."

"Are you certain?"

She began to say something, then stopped. Finally, "No," she said.

"It's all strange. But to say that there's the devil at work—"

A creak from the side of the room made them both suddenly turn. It was Alex, at the foot of the stairs.

"Sorry," she said, "I didn't mean to startle you. I thought I could sleep, but as soon as I lay down I was wide awake. Then I smelled coffee, and...is there some left?"

"Sure," said Paul, disengaging his arm from Elléni.

Alex was already headed for the kitchen. "Don't, I'll get it. But I couldn't help hearing you just now. You were talking about the priest, weren't you? And, *o Diávolos,* that's the devil, right?" She opened a cabinet, closed it.

Paul frowned. "The one to the left of the window, cups are in there."

"So, you understand some Greek," said Elléni. "Very good."

"Thanks." Alex found a cup and set it on the counter. She looked in the small brass pot. "Is this Greek coffee?

"Yeah, just reheat it for a moment," said Paul.

"Got it." She moved to light the gas, then stopped. She looked up at them, eyes suddenly wide. "Omigod. This house really *is* haunted, isn't it?"

Paul opened his mouth to ask what made her say that, but Elléni's suddenly fierce grip on his hand stopped him. That, and the wave of bone-chilling cold that swept over the room.

‡

<Klaus, stop!>

Dafyd's call broke his focus. Klaus's attention, which had been bent on seeing what was going on in the stone house, was suddenly pulled away from the place. He'd seen them so clearly, had felt a channel opening into the man…

<Why? They are there, three of them. I was close to slipping straight in to——>

<No! You will stop, this instant.> A bristling in Dafyd's tone that verged on anger made Klaus flinch. He'd never seen Dafyd flustered. And it wasn't just the words: Klaus felt himself compelled in a way no human being had ever been able to command him. It wasn't simply a question of being ordered by a superior; the *zauberer* controlled Klaus's very will. Had he always done that?

<Good,> said Dafyd. <And no, of course I haven't!> He concentrated for a few moments on the house in its shimmering vision-bubble, trickling soothing energies into it to calm the three occupants.

<What happened?> said Klaus.

<You startled them. They felt you begin to open the way, through the artifact.>

<Felt me? How——>

<Look at them, they're freezing! The temperature in the house probably just dropped fifty degrees.>

Incomprehension from Klaus.

<Do you remember every time we conducted a ritual in the house, how it got cold? Hell is endothermic, it absorbs energy every way it possibly can, not just from humans. When a channel is opened, Hell takes everything it can.>

Klaus would have shrugged if he'd had a body. <What does it matter? If the artifact is working, they cannot leave.>

Dafyd continued to dribble in power, reassuring the three in the stone house. When the moment was right—and it would be soon, he could already feel the forces, like components of some giant celestial machine, moving inexorably into alignment—it would make taking possession of their bodies so much easier.

When he was done, he addressed Klaus again. <Remember we borrowed power, Klaus. Be patient. We have one chance to do this right, just one. And it will take the three of us working in concert, applying the right force at the right time and at my direction. Waste your energy now, and you won't have another chance.>

<And when is this 'right time'?> said Klaus. <This damned place knows no time. How will we know without clocks?>

Dafyd felt a surge of anger. <Because I shall tell you!> he snapped. Damn, the man was impatient. Had the lifetime of struggle and pain they'd endured at the edge been too much for him? Was this the old Klaus they'd first met, the hollow wreck from the Russian front, all the healing undone? Dafyd shoved that thought aside. <Have you forgotten everything you've learned? Klaus, it will be obvious when the moment has come. Look at the scene, at those three in the house. Right now, it's like looking through the bottom of a glass full of treacle, isn't it? Try to get through that and you won't have the strength left to take and keep a form. Do you want to risk that?>

Klaus was suddenly full of doubt. Had the Welshman misled them? <You never said it was going to be so difficult.>

The answer came quick and sharp. <It's not difficult unless you make it that way by going off half-cocked! Disobey me, Klaus, and you're on your own. Do you understand? Or perhaps you really want to go back to the struggle, to Outer Hell, for all eternity?>

To the endless, searing agony they'd just broken free of. A conflict that made his time in the East seem brief and benign.

He didn't like it, but for now he had to accept it. <I understand. I shall do as you say.>

Magda not only remembered the lifetime of hell, she could still feel it. She might lack nerves and tissue in this form, but whatever nerve-analogues her soul possessed were every bit as sensitive. How any of them had retained their sanity after a lifetime—it had seemed a thousand of them—of resisting the assault from *out there* seemed miraculous to her. She wasn't sure that Klaus, who was wobbly enough to start with, *had* retained his.

She again felt sympathy for the woman—but which one?—whose soul she'd be condemning to serve in her stead. She forced the feeling down. She'd worked all her life towards this single goal. Once reborn, she'd have an open-ended lifespan in which to study, practice, and master her knowledge. To understand the hidden forces of the universe, to plumb its infinite complexities and meanings, to be at one with it and take part in its shape, its evolution…that was the only thing she cared about, the only thing she'd *ever* cared about.

And nothing was going to take it away from her.

She briefly considered the two women in the house; one of them was so very young, just a girl. Ordinary people, with no expectation that they would soon die and suffer endless pain in the afterlife. How long would it take them, with no foreknowledge and no hope of salvation, to entirely lose their sanity when they found themselves on that terrible frontier? No time at all, she imagined. And better perhaps to go mad than to know what it really was that your soul faced for all time.

But even if a thousand people had to suffer the torments of eternal damnation for her to succeed, a minor sense of guilt for the soul she damned to Hell was a price well worth paying.

And the guilt would soon pass, she was certain.

CHAPTER TWENTY-NINE

Father Stélios sank back against the chair, gasping for breath. He'd thrown a towel over the scrying bowl and pushed it away, along with the horrors it contained.

He stumbled to the door and threw it open, desperate for light and air. Outside his hut, he gazed up at the brilliant sky, gulping in great lungfuls of the spicy-warm mountain air. Still he suddenly doubled over and began to retch. After a few moments on his knees, with nothing left to expel, he forced himself upright.

Blasphemy. Blasphemy and sacrilege! His visions didn't lie. That the Satanist from the stone house—there could be no doubt it was him—should appear in the form of the Christ surrounded with the imagery of the Resurrection to address him, and do so on Good Friday...what could it mean?

It meant, for one thing, that the magician wasn't truly dead and gone. In trance (the church preferred the phrase, *holy rapture*) or out, Stélios still knew the difference between dream and reality. And these three had been wholly real, even if the other content of the vision was symbolic.

He took a few steps and lowered himself to the grass, sitting with his back against a boulder.

When, a lifetime ago, the bodies had been discovered in the stone house, they were found at the center of a ritual circle of complex and unusual design. Father Vasílis, his predecessor on Vóunos, was called to the house just hours after the discovery, when everything was still in place.

The assumption—it was all in the journal, and Father Vasílis had told him the same in conversation—was that the magician, along with the woman and the SS colonel, had died in the backlash of forces from a ritual gone wrong, their souls taken by demons. Between that and the decades of prayer and exorcism at the stone house, that should have been the end of the matter. Stélios had been in the house himself on a number of occasions, and had never sensed anything lingering.

But the fact of Father Tákis's sudden death, combined with the vision Stélios had just endured, was impossible to ignore, however much he might wish to. What if their conclusion had been wrong all along, and the magician and his companions had not died by accident in a ritual gone terribly wrong—what if their deaths had been intentional?

That thought opened a Pandora's box of possibilities, all of them terrifying. Why would a Satanist do such a thing? No matter how dark the brand of magic a man practiced, anyone who understood the workings of the unseen wouldn't lightly imperil his soul. An amateur like the legendary Faust, someone mad for knowledge or the pleasures of the flesh, might be tempted by a trade or bargain; but to an initiate, nothing imaginable could ever be worth the tortures of eternity in the demonic realm. And that was surely where the three souls in the ritual circle had gone.

It didn't make any sense.

And why *now?* After, what…? He did a quick calculation. After a full seventy years had passed, why was whatever had taken place in the stone house making itself felt again?

Seventy years. The biblical threescore and ten.

The days of our age are threescore years and ten.

A lifetime.

As with all evil news, the truth came like a hammer-blow. The ritual, the deaths, Good Friday, the magician's cheery words from *Revelations* in Stélios's vision, the symbolism of rebirth from the tombs in a cave—

"Behold, priest! I am alive for ever and ever, and I hold the keys to death and Hades!"

It *had* been a trade, a bargain. The three had traded away their souls, offering a lifetime of service in return for physical resurrection.

And—if such a thing were even possible—immortality.

‡

It took Stélios less than five minutes to pack his battle crucifix, a little food and water, and his travel cloak into his satchel and leave the hut. Fatigue and creaky joints were forgotten in the urgency of the moment. There was no time to lose.

The day was warm, and Stélios was glad of the light breeze that stirred the hardy little pines and dense shrubs crowding the narrow trail. By long habit of taking small steps and many, he maintained his modest pace even up the steepest inclines and ravines.

As he walked, he reviewed all the occult knowledge and techniques for dealing with evil he'd acquired over the decades. He had his prayers, he could ward and exorcise. His battle crucifix had seen real spiritual combat a handful of times when, in the course of his researches, he'd touched the borders of the infernal and had to defend himself. You couldn't fight evil without knowing evil, and sometimes that meant straying far from the well-trodden ways of church doctrine. With every victory, he'd gained power. That he could call down the fires of heaven, he had no doubt. Whether he was a strong enough vessel to contain the power needed to fight a sorcerer who could return from Hell…that was another question.

By midafternoon—perhaps half-past three, by his reckoning, for he owned no watch—Stélios was back at the Aghiou Pávlou monastery. His arrival during ninth hour services was not appreciated; but after a good deal of grumbling, his insistence was rewarded and he was shown into a large, sparsely furnished audience chamber to wait.

The abbot was a big man, and solid. Piercing blue eyes set over a big nose that showed every sign of having been broken and reset perhaps more than once suggested this was not a man to trifle with. Not that Stélios cared a great deal, for he himself was in no mood to brook opposition; but to Stélios's relief, the abbot's manner was, as always, easy and open. It would make the business of Stélios's request easier.

When they'd dispensed with the preliminary courtesies, Stélios came straight to the point. "Father, I must travel at once to Vóunos. A matter of the greatest urgency. I shall have to hire a *kaïki* in Dafni to take me, and I need your help. I have no money and no idea of the cost."

The abbot nodded. "Vóunos. I know you spent many years there." He tilted his head slightly. "And the nature of this emergency?"

The question, a reasonable one which Stélios had anticipated, was still one he'd hoped to avoid. One didn't lightly raise matters so far outside the normal orbit of church business with a superior; and while *o Diávolos* was a topic of common discussion and concern for the church, ritual magic, pacts with the devil, and knowledge obtained through visions were subjects raised only—if at all—in hushed tones with one's closest brethren. But where the fight against evil was concerned, God had no love for the timid.

"Evil, Father Abbot. Purest evil. There's an old house there in which a magician, a devil-worshipper, performed a number of rites and sacrifices—*human* sacrifices. It was during the war. I, and Father Vasílis before me, recited the seven prayers and the blessing there every year. When I left the island, the house had been utterly cleansed."

The abbot's mouth hung slightly open. After a moment of stunned silence, he prompted Stélios to go on. "And?"

"And my replacement at Aghios Rigínos, Father Tákis, a young, healthy man, died in the house last night of unexplained causes."

The abbot's eyes grew very wide. He'd gone quite pale. "And you know this...how?"

"Brother Rigas brought me a message from Father Tákis this morning. Tákis telephoned here yesterday, looking for me. The message was about the house. When I called back this morning, the police told me of his death." He took a deep breath and added, "I have *looked* into the matter, Father. And I am sure the date has not escaped you. If I do not go to Voúnos at once, the consequences…" He shook his head.

To his great credit, the abbot took Stélios at his word. Not for the first time, Stélios wondered if the abbot might be more than a common churchman himself. You never knew on Athos.

"The money is not a problem," said the abbot. "What else do you need?"

"Father Abbot is too kind. Perhaps if there is someone who knows Dafni and is used to making arrangements for travel…"

"Brother Athanasios can help you. He knows everyone. I'm only sorry that none of my monks has…*specialized* knowledge and experience in the area of this difficulty you face." The abbot moistened his lips. "You will permit me to say that your errand seems…." He made an indecisive gesture with his hands.

"Too much for an old man?" Stélios allowed himself a grim smile. "Whoever—or whatever—broke that protection may be too much for any of us, Father, specialized or otherwise. Assistance in simply getting to the island will be more than sufficient."

CHAPTER THIRTY

Elléni had just long enough to feel a shock of real fear before the cold dissipated almost as quickly as it had arrived.

Paul, who'd let go her hand and risen, moving instinctively towards his daughter, now stood uncertainly, looking around. "It's gone," he said. "Christ! You both felt that, right?"

Alex's eyes were quite round. "Are you kidding?" She stepped around the counter and moved to the middle of the room. She looked this way and that, as though trying to feel where it had come from.

Elléni stood too. The windows were all closed. But the cold had been intense, like something from the North Pole. Turning to Paul, she saw that his face was almost white.

"Are you all right?" she said, placing a hand on his arm. Alex joined them, and the three of them stood close together, an instinct for protection, by the end of the sofa.

He nodded. He was looking towards the front door, as though expecting someone..

"What?" she said.

He shook his head, like someone trying to shake off a dream. "I felt…" he turned to Alex, then to her. "Weird. Like being outside my body and in it for a moment, like double vision."

"Paul," she said. She wanted to say that she was frightened, that they should leave. But the sensation had entirely passed now. The house was warm and cozy.

He rubbed her back, trying to comfort her. "Whatever that was, it's gone now," he said. "I wonder if we're not just spooking ourselves."

"You are serious?" said Elléni. "You think we all just imagined that?"

Paul rubbed the back of his neck. He went back to the sofa and sat, though his posture remained tense. "No, no. But maybe we just felt a cold draught, and…"

"Suggestion can be very powerful," said Alex. "Like with bone-pointing among the Australian aboriginals. People regularly die because they think the shaman's cursed them. It's quite possible they simply die of fright. Also," she added, "even if you do have a ghost, it's not a given that it's evil. It could just be lost."

Elléni nodded. The strange thing was that the house didn't *feel* evil. For all the bad things that had happened here, and even with poor Father Tákis last night…now she really thought about it, she felt comfortable, welcome. Perhaps she was worrying over nothing.

Still, she was rattled. So when Paul went to take care of Alex's coffee and offered Elléni an ouzo, she was more than a little grateful.

"Thank you," she said, as she took the cold drink. "And then in a few hours, we shall go down to the *hóra* for some food, and then the procession."

‡

By evening, the rain had died away. They went out around seven-thirty, had cocktails and *mezés* at a bar, and made their way to Aghios Rigínos, Father Tákis's church.

The crowd was large and solemn. Guided by Elléni, Paul and Alex made their way inside and joined the line in front of the flower-bedecked bier containing its Christ-effigy. Following Elléni's example, Paul dipped his head and kissed the brow of the painted figure, feeling not a little selfconscious. Alex did the same; her cheeks were flushed, and for a second she looked strangely moved, almost as though she might cry. The olive-skinned Christ's wide eyes stared unseeing.

They stood a long while outside, watching the crowd grow. A steady stream of people came up to Elléni to commiserate over the tragic events of the previous day; some, Paul suspected, were just curious and eager for gossipworthy tidbits. Several cast dubious glances at him and Alex. The sun set and stars began to appear.

Eventually, the procession arrived and the bier was brought out, led by the priest standing in for Father Tákis. Elléni handed Paul and Alex candles, and lit them. There was a brief, moving eulogy for father Tákis, and many people cried openly. Paul felt his throat tighten, and Elléni, her face running with tears, gripped his arm.

Finally, after a lengthy liturgy, the crowd started off, threading its way along the narrow village streets, candles flickering like souls in the night.

Two churches, two more flower-laden biers, and several liturgies later, the procession reached its end at the small church just behind the harbor. It was around midnight, and the crowd—which was certainly just about the entire population of the village—dispersed to relax and mingle in the bars and cafés along the strand. They sat at one of the outdoor tables and ordered drinks. The night air was crisp and cold.

When Elléni's friends Anna and Stávros stopped by, Paul's heart sank. Anna had been the first one to express her fears about the house. He really didn't need to hear more.

But they hugged Elléni warmly and seemed delighted to meet Alex. To his surprise, nothing about the house or Father Tákis was mentioned: they genuinely just seemed to want to hang out and celebrate. And the fact that both spoke English, and could talk to Alex, was a bonus.

More drinks were ordered, and rounds of *mezés*. The three girls were talking up a storm, and Stávros turned out to be very knowledgeable in the area of Greek antiquity and archaeology, both things which interested Paul a good deal.

Nikos from the hardware store showed up with his younger brother, Spyros, who was at university in Athens. They pulled up chairs and joined the group. With his near-perfect English and ridiculously good looks, Spyros took an immediate interest in Alex, who responded with brilliant smiles and lively engagement. Watching them with quiet amusement, Paul caught Elléni's glance. He gave her a wink and she took his hand. Even the policeman, Katsélis, accompanied by his wife and teenage daughter stopped by to exchange greetings.

Paul relaxed. After the tragedy and stress of the last twenty-four hours, the evening was turning out wonderful. He hadn't enjoyed being around a large group of people in a long time, longer than he could remember. They ordered food and then more drinks, and laughed and talked deep into the night.

It was dawn by the time they returned to the stone house, exhausted but happy. The house was chill, the stove long cooled. Alex hugged him and Elléni and went off to her room.

He held Elléni close under the covers, her naked skin warm on his, her curves molding to his own body and encircling arms. Closeness led to arousal, then lovemaking, after which they both fell quickly into a deep sleep.

CHAPTER THIRTY-ONE

Stélios stood by the window of the monastery's main office in his rumpled cassock, fidgeting and twisting his fingers together.

It was almost six, and the water below had taken on that ambiguous hue it always did as the sun edged close to the western horizon. He was already tired from having not slept the entire previous night, and certainly in no condition to face what he feared was developing at the stone house.

It was a little over a hundred kilometers to Vóunos, about seven hours by *kaïki* if the waters were calm. He imagined that he'd at least be able to rest on the passage. If they could just find a boat to take him.

The Athos peninsula, an autonomous zone administered by the church and quite separate from the rest of Greece, was undeveloped to the point of primitive. Roads across the mountainous, forested terrain were rough, and the monasteries and tiny settlements scattered either on the coasts or just a little inland were most easily accessible by sea.

Brother Athanasios had been on the telephone for almost an hour. The tiny port—really just a jetty and small breakwater—at Arsanas, just a kilometer down the hill from the monastery, was empty. Athanasios had been trying to find them a boat in Dafni, the port village some ten kilometers to the north, so far without luck. The handful of fishermen who owned boats were either out on the sea or else spending Easter with family on the mainland.

Stélios was vaguely aware that the tone of the monk's voice had turned suddenly optimistic. Wrapped in his own grim thoughts, Stélios hadn't really been listening to the one-sided conversations for a while; now he turned back towards the desk at which Athanasiou sat, and paid attention.

"…good, good," the monk was saying, "thank you. Yes, it will have to do. At least from there we can probably find something. But I implore you to hurry—the sooner you can get here, the better." A brief pause, then, "All right. We will be waiting."

When the monk had hung up, Stélios said, "Well?"

Athanasiou shook his head. "I managed to find one, but he won't take you to Vóunos."

Stélios frowned. "So what good…?"

"He's willing to take you to Ouranópoli, where his relatives are. He was planning to leave in the early morning, and I was able to persuade him to make the detour to pick you up and go tonight instead. He'll be here in an hour and a half, at half-past seven"

What in God's name was the man thinking? Ouranópoli was a small port town just across the Athos border, on the narrow, sea-strangled neck of Chalkidiki in the province of Macedonia to the north. It was probably two hours' sailing—in the wrong direction.

His dismay must have shown, because the monk was quick to add, "I know it's out of your way, but the man assures me you'll be able to find someone there to take you. Father Abbot has instructed me to cover all your needs. I will give you two hundred euros, that should be more than enough to hire a boat."

Stélios stared. The notion was optimistic, to say the least. "At ten o'clock on Good Friday, in the middle of the processions? Really?" He ran his hands over his bald pate. He wanted to curse, but managed to restrain himself. It wasn't Athanasios's fault. The man was doing his best.

The monk hesitated a moment before saying, "Forgive me, Father, but when did you last eat?"

"I—" But it was a good question. Though he'd packed some dried figs, a small block of cheese, and a large piece of bread in his satchel, all he'd had since rising was a glass of water. Sleep or food, a man could go for a time without one or the other; to ignore both was never a good idea.

"You have ample time to take a meal and a glass of wine with us before setting out, Father. With a long night ahead…"

"Yes, yes. Thank you, brother. Please, lead the way."

‡

The boatman—Giórgos was his name—showed up closer to nine than eight. The night was black, the waning moon still below the horizon. Stélios, wrapped in his travel cloak and lulled by the steady lap of the sea against the jetty, had been dozing on the ground with his back to a carob tree while Athanasios, who had come to wait with him, paced and grumbled.

The monk complained to the boatman and began berating him as soon as he cut the engine to coast in. "We agreed thirty Euros for you to arrive on time!"

It didn't wash. Stélios could see the man's frown by the sudden flare of the boat's lanterns, the only illumination other than the flashlight the monk had brought for the walk back up to the monastery. Giórgos tossed the monk a rope, leaving the engine idling. Athanasios looped it around a rusted iron ring and pulled the boat in to the jetty.

Stélios took his leave of the monk, thanking him again for his trouble. The boatman took Athanasios's thirty Euros with a grunt and thrust out a hand to help Stélios aboard.

The *kaïki* was narrow, the canvas awning threadbare, with a patched tin chimney rising from the engine cowling and poking through the centre of the fabric. One aisle was crowded with two small plastic barrels—olives, Stélios guessed—and containers that probably held oil. Under the planking that served as seating along the *kaïki's* sides were stored nets, fuel containers, and various types of gear.

He sat himself by the gunwale near the wooden engine cover. His breath smoked in the lurid glare of the lanterns.

They cast off with little ceremony. Giórgos adjusted the cowls on the lamps so they only shone light forwards and put the engine in gear. When they were a few minutes out to sea, Stélios looked back. Black on black, the land was barely discernible against the water; he saw the glimmer cast by Athanasios's torch as the monk picked his way back up the hill to the monastery where a handful of the innumerable windows showed a light. The monumental building that once housed a community of hundreds was now home to just thirty or forty of the faithful.

The boatman hugged the coast, ignoring the bulbous, illuminated compass mounted on the side of the engine cover and keeping a few hundred meters from the shore, far enough to be well clear of any coastal rocks. He reached below his seat and slid out what looked like an old wooden toolbox—it had rough handles made of rope—and lifted the lid. Inside, atop a few odd tools and tins and what looked like much-folded sea-charts, were a couple of bottles. He extracted one, uncorked it, and took a long pull before offering it to Stélios, who refused with a raised palm and a word. The man grunted and set the bottle aside, pushing the toolbox back under the seat with his heel.

Stélios exchanged a handful of words with the boatman, more out of politeness than anything. Silhouetted in starlight, Giórgos showed little interest in conversation, preferring to chain-smoke cigarettes and take frequent drinks from the bottle resting against the pile of rags by the tiller. At least he kept his eyes on the water ahead.

Stélios drew his cloak tighter around himself and fell into an uneasy sleep.

He woke to the faint sounds of bouzouki music and a dazzle of lights. After not seeing a settlement larger than Dafni with its few score inhabitants in almost a decade, the small town of Ouranópoli just a short distance across the choppy water looked like a metropolis.

The sea, he noticed, was rather rougher than when they'd set out.

What had he done to deserve this? He'd served his time in the world and tended his flock, even when that had meant guarding against the horror of the stone house, an evil whose nature the average citizen of Vóunos couldn't begin to conceive of. But he'd felt that evil firsthand, felt its unholy taint, and had some inkling of what the English magician and the other two had been dealing with. *O Diávolos* of legend, the goat-footed bogeyman of the common man, the simple, easily understood counterpart to *o Théos*, to God, was a matter for levity compared to the reality of the demonic entities whose realm was never more than the lifting of a veil from ours. The three in the stone house had done business with that realm; and though Stélios could never get to the bottom of it, discover the true nature of the transaction that had cost three innocent lives in successive sacrifices at the warlock's unholy altar, Stélios had always feared that the business wasn't over. Now he knew it; though what he was going to be able to do about it, even if he could get to Vóunos, was debatable.

He pushed aside his doubts. God would help, or he would not.

The quayside was deserted, but the tavernas just across the narrow street appeared crowded and noisy. The procession had finished, then, which was to the good.

The boatman cut the throttle and let the kaïki glide in to the quay, engaging reverse and bringing it smoothly around until the old tyres hanging off the gunwales kissed the cement of the dock.

The sounds of music and laughter rode out on a smell of grilled fish and calamari. Stélios's joints complained as he rose, but at least he'd slept a bit. He leaned over the side, holding fast to one of the iron rings while Giórgos stepped ashore and tied up.

"Do you know any of these people?" said Stélios, gesturing at the crowded cafés and tavernas. "Anyone who might be willing to take me on to Vóunos?"

The man's head flicked back in the "no" gesture ."It's my sister's town, not mine," he answered in his rude, offhand way. "I don't know anybody here."

Stélios paid the man, thanked him for his help, and took his leave.

He walked into the nearest taverna—the nights were still cool enough that they'd not yet set tables outdoors—and sought out the owner. The man was small, fat, his face sheened with sweat from trying to keep up with orders. At least he was polite. But his eyes widened as he listened to Stélios's request.

"*Tonight?* It will be very hard to find anyone to go anywhere before Monday or Tuesday, Father. Especially that far. And the sea is forecast to get bad tonight. But I can try. Perhaps old Apostólis, or Níkos…" He rubbed his chin, looking out at the crowd. "I saw him just earlier on, but now…. Wait here," he said, pulling out a chair for Stélios. "I'll see if I can find them."

CHAPTER THIRTY-TWO

Saturday April 19, 2014

Captain Katsélis sat at Father Tákis's battered desk in the little room which served as an office at the back of Aghios Rigínos, put out his cigarette, and drummed his fingers on the table.

They'd found nothing unusual or of obvious interest during their visit to the church and the adjacent residence yesterday, but something had made Katsélis return this afternoon, some gut feeling this was no natural death and that somewhere under all this lacklustre normality must be a clue as to Father Tákis's sudden death.

The only thing that had seemed out of place was Father Stélios's extraordinary assumption about the death having taken place at the stone house, and his subsequent—and very obvious—lie about the message he'd received. What was it the old priest—God, he must be ninety!—had said? *He was asking about some old parish records,* that was it.

And here, at Katsélis's elbow, was the volume of old parish records which the dead priest had left at the stone house.

One entire wall of the small office was lined with bookshelves, and among them were a couple of dozen similar volumes. He'd glanced over their spines earlier, but only enough to ascertain that they were records of a similar sort to this one. Each was labeled with dates; some covered as many as ten years, others just seven or eight.

He looked again at the volume beside him and read its spine, though he already knew the dates: 1947 to 1956. He had read a few pages then glanced through the rest: it was just a dry record of minor events and milestones in the parish. He would put it back.

Turning to the shelves now, he ran his finger along the books' dry spines, noting their years as he did so. Several, annoyingly, were out of sequence: as he came to these, he replaced them in the proper order. Katsélis prided himself on his sense of order and his attention to detail.

Once he had them back in order, he realized there was a volume missing. It was the one before the volume he held in his hand.

The last shelved volume before it was labelled 1934-1941; so the one missing would have covered the years 1942-1946. Just four years, far less than the average. The captain's pulse began to race. And it was the war years, when whatever evil had really taken place in the stone house was said to have occurred.

He'd heard about the place, of course, even as a child, but somehow conversation about it had always been discouraged. They said a devil worshipper had lived there during the war, and that young people had disappeared, and even been sacrificed to *o Diávolos*. Though the captain was a religious man, he didn't really believe in the traditional *o Diávolos*—but he did believe in evil, and evil people.

What was the priest trying to hide?

He lit another cigarette, opened the book in his hands, and began to go through it slowly, methodically, this time.

After two more cigarettes and page upon page of mostly dull, if occasionally historically interesting detail on the daily life of the parish in the immediate postwar years, he found what he was looking for. The entry, dated October 15, read, *Annual blessing and seven prayers rite at the stone house.*

Well, well. *Annual* blessing. He flicked forward into 1948, and there it was again. October fifteenth. What was the seven prayers rite? And what was the significance of that date? Had something dire occurred in the stone house on that day? He leafed through the book, found the same entry for that date on each year. He picked up the next volume in the sequence and found the identical entry on that same date every year.

The captain slid the book into place on the shelves and lit another cigarette. And then it struck him.

Priests weren't the only ones who kept records.

‡

Elléni woke suddenly. The room was light, but in an oddly muted way. Either it was still early, or it was very gloomy out.

Next to her, Paul was sleeping solidly. She was terribly thirsty. That, and the lancing pain in her head as she swung her legs off the bed and hauled herself upright, let her know she'd had too much—no, make that *far* too much—to drink last night. God, tequila shots! What had she been thinking?

She slipped on her jeans and shirt. The smell of coffee greeted her as, a little unsteadily, she negotiated the old stair with its narrower-than-usual treads.

"Good morning!" said Alex, brightly. She was sitting on the sofa in a robe, earbuds on and a book open in her lap. She turned down her mp3 player. "How are you?"

Elléni scrunched her eyes against the light in the living-room window. "It is possible I will die," she said, "but thank you for making coffee. That, perhaps, will save me."

Alex laughed. She popped her earbuds out and came over to join Elléni at the kitchen counter. "Too many drinks? But what a great night! I had so much fun. And the procession was very beautiful."

Elléni, who'd been looking around the kitchen, squinted at her. "You were not bored, just sitting at a bar with strangers?"

"Coffee's in the thermos," said Alex, pointing. "I used the drip cone, hope I made it right. No, I wasn't bored for a minute." She grinned. "And Spyros? Omigod!"

Elléni grinned. "He is very good-looking, eh?"

"Are you kidding? So that's what they mean by Greek Gods." Alex reached into a cabinet, handed her a cup.

"Thank you. I hope I shall feel better."

"Is Paul still asleep?"

"Yes." Elléni looked around, saw the time on the microwave. Five minutes past noon. "No! We have slept all morning?"

"I think I only woke up because of the jet lag. She went to the kitchen window. "I was hoping we'd get to visit some of the monasteries this afternoon, but it looks like rain. It's been getting darker for the last hour."

Elléni frowned. "Really? They said it would be nice, even hot." She joined Alex at the window. There was a heavy overcast, and the sea had that look of iron it got during stormy weather.

‡

With every hour (of course there was no such thing in Hell or this inbetween place, but even after a lifetime in Outer Hell Dafyd's psyche must have retained some connection with time on the physical plane), Dafyd felt the power gather. He also found his reach broadening, making him feel more aligned with the world they were soon to re-enter. And more able to influence it, as though he were connected to it by invisible tendrils.

If he pulled on them, would it have some effect in the human sphere? *As above, so below.* It had always been the rule in magic—change effected in the finer, higher spheres determined that which took place in the physical, coarsest of all worlds. Spirit shaped thought shaped matter. That was all there was to it.

But at the moment there was no need for him to exert himself. Quite the opposite, in fact: the best thing was for him and the others to conserve their energy. The artifact would take care of the rest. They would still have plenty of time. All they had to do was be ready.

PART THREE

CHAPTER THIRTY-THREE

Paul came downstairs to find his two girls, as he'd begun to think of them, deep in conversation on the sofa. He kissed Alex on the cheek and Elléni on the lips. "How's your head today?" he asked, grinning.

"It is not so good. But you look full of life."

"I'm okay," he agreed. He walked over to get coffee. "So what's the plan for tomorrow with your family?"

"We will go there at about ten in the morning. By then the men will be grilling the lamb, and most of the food will be prepared. Of course, we must hope for the weather, otherwise the lamb will be a problem; but if it rains and it is not too bad, they can make a cover for the grilling. Easter is an all-day celebration for us, you know." She looked at her watch. "But it is almost one. I will go there now to help my mother and my aunts for a few hours. Also I think you and Alex will enjoy some time for just the two of you."

Alex shook her head "Nah-uh. I *love* hanging out with you."

That brought a big smile from Elléni. A warm glow spread in Paul's chest. When Alex was younger, she'd gone through a phase where she desperately wanted a big sister. Maybe she'd found her.

Elléni reached over to give Alex a hug. "Thank you, Alex. I think we will be good friends." She turned to Paul. "So, I will call you later and perhaps we shall have dinner all together?"

"Sounds great." He took her in his arms and kissed her. "I'm glad my haunted house hasn't totally scared you off."

As they disengaged, he was surprised to see her face had turned serious again. *Of course it has, idiot. She saw a man die here a few hours ago, and she was alone.*

She looked at him, eyes grave, and said, "Well. We must hope the deaths and tragedies shall be completely finished now."

‡

Friday April 18, 2014

When the taverna owner returned, he was apologetic. Old Apostólis was helplessly drunk, and Nikos's sister from Hamburg was in town for the holiday, so he wasn't going anywhere for several days. Stélios thanked him and moved on to the next taverna to see if he might have better luck there.

He stopped at every table, asking the men if they had a boat, and if they did, if they'd be willing to take him out to Vóunos. There was a band playing, and Stélios had to raise his voice, almost shout, to be heard. Most of the replies were polite and respectful; some of the patrons clearly thought him half-mad, and from the corner of his eye he caught one man making circling-around-the-temple gestures with his index finger once Stélios's back was turned, which brought guffaws from his companions at the table.

A fat man with an unkempt mat of oily black hair and wine on his breath, came up to him. "What can I do for you, Father?" he said.

"You're the owner?"

"I'm Yíannis, Father. This is my place."

"I need to someone to take me to Vóunos," said Stélios. After the years of quiet solitude, the music and general noise in the place was oppressive. His head was starting to pound and his already strained nerves were fraying.

"Tonight?"

There was an explosion of laughter at a nearby table, so that Stélios had to shout to be heard. "Tonight. Now!"

The man put an arm around Stélios's shoulders and guided him to the side of the taverna, away from the worst of the noise. "Father, forgive me, but what's the hurry? If you wait until Monday, there's the ferry from—"

"Monday is too late."

"Why?"

Stélios hesitated. What could he say? "A critical ecclesiastical matter. A priest has died there."

The man grimaced. "I'm sorry to hear that, Father. But still, you can't expect people to drop everything and take you. It's Easter."

Stélios's every effort at self-control suddenly failed. "You think I

174

don't know?" he snapped back. "If you can't help me that's fine, but at least let me try."

Yíannis made a placating gesture. "All right, all right. Wait."

Turning to the crowd, he clapped his hands for quiet. The customers at the nearest tables looked up, but the band and the rest of the crowd didn't even hear him. He got up on a chair and tried again, banging a spoon against a bottle and finally roaring for quiet at the top of his voice until first the crowd, and finally the musicians, went quiet.

"The Father here," said the man, indicating Stélios, "has to get to Vóunos. Tonight. Says it's very urgent. Can anyone take him?"

"I can pay," said Stélios.

"He says he'll pay!" added the owner.

There was a ripple of quiet words, but nobody volunteered..

"Well?" said the owner.

A very large man at an end table stood. Spreading his hands, he said, "Father, it's Good Friday. Easter is for families. Nobody is going to go out."

Which brought a buzz of agreement.

"There's a ferry on Monday," called another man.

Widespread approval. Stélios caught the words, "crazy monk" more than once.

"And besides, the sea is getting bad!" called another man.

That got even more agreement, and in an instant the whole place was alive again.

"Nonsense!" shouted Stélios. "My father was a fisherman. When I was a child, he used to take me out in weather twice as bad!"

But nobody was paying attention. People turned back to their friends and resumed their conversations. Yíannis looked down at him from the chair, spread his hands in a helpless gesture. At the back of the taverna, the band started up again.

Yíannis got down off his chair. "I'm sorry, Father. I told you, it's useless," he said.

Stélios made his way along the strand to the next taverna. A cold wind had come up, and he pulled his cloak tight about himself. He was tired—he never stayed up this late—and his bones ached. This shouldn't be so hard.

Fifty years ago, or even just a generation, nobody would have refused to take a priest at his word. They'd have dropped everything to help, holiday or not. The mere fact that a priest was in need during the holiest days of the year would have been the deciding factor in helping him, bad seas notwithstanding. But people's faith, as well as the public standing of the Athos community, had been in decline for years. And the incident of last summer, when the rebel monks at the Esphigmenou monastery had—quite justifiably, he thought—thrown petrol bombs at police and bailiffs, had only served to further tarnish the church's image in the eyes of the laity.

But the world was what it was, and God had never promised him an easy path. He took a deep breath and entered the taverna.

Half an hour later, he was back on the street. It was almost two in the morning, and the north wind cut like a knife.

Well, God, I'm out of ideas. Any suggestions?

CHAPTER THIRTY-FOUR

Saturday night/Sunday Morning April 19-20, 2014

Despite the threat of rain, Paul and Alex spent the afternoon driving around a few of the island's monasteries and taking in some of the more spectacular views from high up on the island's rocky spine. It remained mostly dry, and though the skies were lead-dark, the clouds stayed above of the hills, so that the vistas of the island and the surrounding waters were clear.

They got back to the house at dusk, changed, and met Elléni at Olympos, the nicest of the island's restaurants, where she'd managed to get a table despite the place being booked solid. It was early by Greek standards—nine-thirty—and there were still a few tables empty, but the band, a violin, bouzóuki, and mandolin trio backing a young woman with a haunting voice, was already cooking.

The food was plentiful and good, and the place was loud with song and laughter. A few people came over to hug Elléni and meet

Paul and Alex. He was grateful that the noise levels precluded too much conversation, which could quickly have turned to Father Tákis.

The drizzle in the village had intensified into a steady rain by the time they returned home, a little after midnight. Although the party at Olympos was just getting started, Elléni, still fragile from the previous evening and, before that, the tragedy at the house, looked all in. When Paul suggested leaving, she didn't argue.

"Anyone for a nightcap?" said Paul, after hanging up his jacket.

"Just a big glass of water," said Alex.

"Do you have some liqueur?" said Elléni.

"Limoncello. Will that work?"

Elléni nodded. Yes, it is not Greek, but I like it very much. Ah! But I forgot." She reached into her bag and pulled out her phone. "My father asked me to get a bottle of Metaxas for them, and to tell him if I did. Now he will think I have forgotten."

Alex stared. "Won't they be in bed?"

Paul laughed. "This is Greece. Nobody goes to bed before two even during the week, never mind on a holiday weekend."

"Yes, this is correct," said Elléni.

While she dialed, Alex rose to give her some space and joined Paul at the counter. After a moment, Elléni stood, looking at the phone in her hand, and walked over to the window. She looked perplexed.

"Problem?" said Paul.

"I have no signal."

"That's weird. It's usually so good here." He pulled out his own phone. She was right: he had no bars either, zero, and a red "x" over the antenna icon. "That's the first time this has happened to me." He tried it anyway, speed-dialing Elléni's cell. Nothing.

"I guess you don't have a landline?" said Alex.

"No."

Elléni shrugged. She dropped her phone back in her purse and came over to them. "Eh, perhaps the system is down. Anyway, it is not so important."

"Try outside," said Paul, crossing to the front door. "You might get a signal there. He opened the door for her, making a sweeping, exaggerated gesture of invitation. But Elléni and Alex had frozen midstride. Both were staring, slack-jawed, through the doorway. *What the hell?*

177

Paul turned to look for himself.

What he saw was precisely nothing. On the other side of the doorway was only a softly-glowing-grey wall of dense, shifting fog.

‡

"What the hell…?"

Paul couldn't believe what he was seeing. He looked back at Alex and Elléni, whose open-mouthed expressions mirrored his own feelings. Elléni had gone very pale.

Where there should have been a stone walk along the side of the house and their two cars parked by the olive tree, there was nothing. A depthless, impenetrable miasma filled his vision. The only thing like it he'd ever seen was on a ski trip at Tahoe when he'd been caught in a whiteout, land and sky merging so seamlessly that he lost all depth perception.

The uniform grey facing him was utterly undefined. It looked neither solid nor gaseous, and would probably have been black but for the waning moon overhead that they'd seen rising on the drive back from the restaurant. That must be lighting it, making it look as if it were glowing. He looked up; the others followed his gaze.

"It's everywhere," whispered Alex.

She was right: the fog or whatever it was had enveloped the house like a shroud, blocking out any view of the night sky. It didn't seem to quite close above them; Paul caught glints of ruddy light above and had an impression of something like a narrowing vortex or funnel, though in the dark it was hard to be sure. He forced himself to breathe.

Stepping forward, he carefully extended a hand, palm half-raised, fingertips outstretched. Alex said, "Paul…", and he caught a quick hiss of indrawn breath from Elléni.

There was nothing there. And yet there was. The tips of his fingers were veiled by the medium, but without any appearance of movement or flow. Fear coiled and shifted in his gut at the strangeness of what they were facing. It was as though his hand was simply less *there*. The sensation was of a semi-solid, like a gel. There was no sense of warm or cold, and not really of touch, but whatever it was resisted his movement.

"What *is* it?" said Alex.

Paul shook his head. Heart pounding, he withdrew his hand, examined it. It was fine.

He took another step forward and, cautiously, pushed further into the opaque mass, until his hand and forearm became barely visible, like a drawing that had almost been erased. There was definite resistance, soft but firm. He pushed a little harder. For all its softness, whatever was beyond there was unyielding, like foam-wrapped iron.

He pulled back. His arm, thank heaven, seemed normal; the dark, shifting wall showed no sign of having been breached.

"Whatever it is, it's solid. It gives, but just to a point." He shook his head. "Weirdest thing I've ever seen."

"Let me check the other side," said Alex, and hurried into the house. Paul took Elléni's hand and led her back up to the doorway.

Alex had crossed the living room to the window and thrown it wide. "Exactly the same on this side," she said, and started up the stairs at a run.

"And still no phone," said Elléni, in a strained voice.

"At least the power's okay," said Paul. He looked back out at the flat grey, suddenly aware of the preternatural quiet.

"Same upstairs," called Alex, as she hurried back down. "In every direction, just...nothing."

"My God..." said Elléni. Her face was putty.

Alex joined them. "It's like the rest of the world no longer exists," she whispered, staring out the wide-open door.

"We're cut off," he said. And immediately felt like a fool for stating something so obvious. "But *how?*"

Elléni turned quickly, as if to say something, then closed her mouth. Finally, "We should have left here. There is something terrible. I—"

As if to underscore her words, a shockwave of cold, just as they'd felt yesterday, rolled over them, coming from *inside* the house. From a cool spring night, they suddenly felt themselves transported into the depths of winter. At the same time, the power went out.

"Oh, shit," said Paul. "Hold on, got a flashlight." He found the kitchen drawer where he kept it and a moment later they had light. He shone it towards the girls, who were standing near the still-open door. The cold was so intense that he felt himself already starting to shiver.

"Christ!" said Alex. "Th-this is so not good!"

"We have to get out!" cried Elléni. Before Paul could react, she was over the threshold. She paused a bare instant then stepped forwards into the nothingness.

"Elléni, *don't!*" Overcoming his paralysis, Paul leapt forward. In the few strides it took him to reach her, she'd become almost entirely shrouded in fog, only her back and a portion of her trailing arm and leg visible. Behind him, Alex cried out. He took another step and grabbed Elléni's forearm just before the mist fully claimed her.

He didn't have to pull. She yielded back into him, and with his other hand now on her shoulder, they did an awkward backstep, like drunks on a dance floor, until she was completely clear of it and they'd crossed the threshold, back into the house.

"*Íne éna teíchos,*" she said. *It's a wall.* She turned to face him.

"I know," he said. His knees felt as if they might suddenly give. He hugged her to him a moment, the flashlight beam playing across the wall of fog, then reached out with his foot and swung the door shut. Holding onto her hand, he led her back to the kitchen.

Alex turned to the stove and began to crumple newspaper. "We have to do something to get warm," she said, through a fog of exhaled breath.

"Good thinking. Go for it. Elléni, stay here with Alex, I'm just getting us more lights." He crossed to the dining room credenza where he kept a pair of battery-powered LED lanterns and a box of candles for emergencies. In a moment he had the lanterns powered up. He put one on the fireplace mantel and the other on the kitchen counter, lighting up each area with hard white light so that the dark was driven to the corners of the living space.

Elléni, holding onto him tightly, was shivering. "I am af-afraid," she stammered.

Paul nodded and gave her a reassuring squeeze. "At least we have propane," he said. He twisted the knobs on the stovetop, lighting all four burners. He held his hands over them for warmth, motioning her to do the same.

Alex was laying a little teepee of kindling around the crumpled paper core in the open stove. Without turning, she said, "This is more than gh-ghosts, right?"

His niece had taken the most practical course of action, without anyone telling her to. Despite the fact that she was trembling with cold, she worked methodically. *Just what Charly would be doing.* He felt a wave of love and gratitude for her.

"I think so. There's *something*…at work here." He'd been avoiding saying it. And now that he thought about it, that was weird in itself— it was so fucking *obvious.* "Exactly what it is, I don't know. But it's something, some magic. And I don't think it's good."

"The sacrifices," said Elléni.

He nodded. Their every word turned to steam as the temperature continued to drop. He took a deep breath to smooth the words which, like his body, wanted to shake like leaves in the wind. He didn't believe in this, in *any* of it—but it was happening. "The old priest, before Father Tákis…he came here every year to perform an exorcism and bless the place. It was in the book."

Alex placed a second log against the kindling and reached for the matches with a shaking hand. "So the b-blessing ran out?"

"Maybe." His hands, over the burners, were warm enough, but the cold on his back was like the embrace of death. Alex struck a match, held it to the newspaper. As the paper caught, hungry yellow flames licked up through the cone of dry kindling. She dropped the match inside and swung shut the stove door.

"Good job," he said. "There are coats upstairs in the wardrobes. Let me see what I can dig up."

He picked up the flashlight and they followed him up the stairs, unwilling to stay alone, he supposed.

"Whoa!" said Alex, halfway up the stairs.

"It's warmer," he said. And it was, by maybe twenty or thirty degrees. "Still cold, but not subzero. The cold is mostly radiating from the downstairs."

When they reached the top, Elléni turned and stared back down the stairs, biting her lip. Paul touched her arm, and she grabbed his hand in both of hers.

"Job number one, warm clothes," he said. Then we'll work out what to do."

"What to do? We have to get out!"

"I know," he said, leading her into the bedroom, where Alex was already searching through the wardrobe.

Paul handed Elléni a bulky sweater and the woolen pea coat he'd had for an age. "The cold is the immediate danger. Nothing for it."

"We could stay up here," said Alex.

"It…" he shook his head. "I'd rather be near the door, even though we can't get out. Up here…"

"Feels like a trap?"

He glanced at her and nodded. He hadn't wanted to say it.

He gave her his winter jacket, the one with the fur-trimmed hood, and put on an old Arran, with his ancient country tweed jacket and a scarf over that.

Alex looked at the two of them. And, bless her, laughed. "Omigod, look at us!"

"Come to sunny Greece," he said, and now he and Elléni were laughing too, though Elléni's mirth was clearly strained.

"Grab a blanket off each bed. I've got a couple more in this closet, and let's get back to the stove while we figure out what to do." Even if the air temperature continued to drop, the radiant heat from the stove would still warm them if they stood around it. But what the hell else they could do, he had no idea. The situation was unknown and, when he looked at it, terrifying. The immediate need to fight the cold had kept them occupied, but he was afraid of what might happen as the reality of their situation sank in.

Because something told him this was only the beginning. And that really scared him.

"It's a good thing you brought heavy clothes," said Alex.

"I was thinking I might do some traveling once I got settled," he said, buttoning up the front of the jacket. "So, yeah."

As they reached the bottom of the stairs, something hit him. It came from nowhere, rushed him, took his mind like a hawk plucking a mouse from a field. One instant he was himself, the next he was retreating into a primal place of shelter and protectiveness, some cave of the psyche, away from the ravening, crazed thing that had burst into his mind. Elléni's scream came to him across a still distance, barely reaching him through the dark billows of whatever had replaced his sanity. The thing had filled his being like an inflating balloon, crowding him out and taking possession of everything except this tiny, hard core of selfhood. He was distantly aware of crumpling, falling to the ground. *Is this what happened to Father Tákis?* He thought fleetingly of Alex, wanted to reach out, couldn't—his limbs had slackened, all control gone. And now even the option of thought and the distant connection it offered to her, to the world, to any world, faded, and he sank into the warm, still black.

CHAPTER THIRTY-FIVE

Friday April 18, 2014

The kaïki bobbed in the small waves which slapped against the quayside. Stélios looked around. Everyone was in the tavernas, and the dock was entirely empty.

He hesitated. He'd never, ever in his life, even as a child, taken a thing which didn't belong to him. It went against his every instinct. And yet here he was, back in front of Giórgos's untidy kaïki, the very one which had brought him here. And in plain sight under the seats along one side were two twenty-litre containers of fuel.

I don't believe this, God. Are you serious?

No reply came, only stillness. Stélios looked around again, hoping to see someone. He would just move on, find someone else to ask. But still, there was nobody.

He took a deep breath, let it out. Bending over, he pulled on the boat's mooring-rope, bringing it tight up against the quay; he extended a sandaled foot and stepped inside. The boat wobbled and his ancient knees protested as he struggled to retain his balance.

He eased himself along the boat to the stern, resting a hand on the engine cowling for balance. Lowering himself with a grunt onto his knees, he pulled out the old toolbox where Giórgos kept his drink and opened the lid.

His heart leapt. They *were* sea-charts, two of them; though the relevant one was torn along two folds, it was usable and clearly showed Vóunos, almost dead south-southwest of here. Good. Once he was out of the harbour and in the clear, he'd light the lanterns and examine it more carefully. He had charts, he had fuel, and he had a compass. And although it was over sixty years since he'd taken the tiller of his father's kaïki, the boats had hardly changed. All he had to worry about was the weather, and keeping a straight course. If nothing went wrong, he could be on Vóunos by mid-morning.

Stélios pushed himself stiffly up—God, his knees!—to his feet. He unslung his satchel and placed it on the seat by the tiller. Although he'd not seen Giórgos start the engine—the boatman had left it running when he stopped to pick him up—Stélios hadn't seen him turn a key to shut it off. His father's kaïki had had a starting switch under the engine cowling, but this one didn't open at the top. Stélios soon found the panel on the left side of the engine housing and, not wanting to strike a light, crouched painfully and felt around in the deep shadows inside. There was nothing that felt like any kind of a switch or button, just the hard, cold contours of the engine, and some sort of pipes or manifold.

He extricated himself from the narrow space and sat his old frame back down by the tiller. His breath huffed out, a release of tiredness and frustration. *What was he thinking?* He couldn't even work out how to start the thing, never mind crossing unaided over a hundred kilometers of rough seas at night and actually landing where he intended. He slapped in annoyance at the knob on the useless gearstick in front of him.

And there it was. There, on a small raised panel under the compass, a large button, visibly green even in the dim light, next to another, black, button. He shook his head and chuckled.

He was just reaching forward to push the button when a voice interrupted him.

"What are you doing, old priest?"

Stélios looked up, startled, arm still extended, to see Giórgos the boatman, owner of the kaïki he'd been about to steal, glowering down at him. The man pulled a cellphone from his pocket and began to dial.

‡

184

Saturday April 19, 2014

There was nothing in the police computer about the stone house, but the paper files yielded a wealth of information, none of it easy reading. By the time Katsélis finished the last page, it was almost eight P.M. His wife had called three times; last time, she'd read him the riot act. His mouth was foul from coffee and cigarettes and he had a pounding headache.

He took three aspirin, washed them down with the watery remains of his iced frappé, and went to the window. The dark sea was restless, throwing tall showers of spray over the breakwater at the harbour mouth. Low, iron-grey clouds that must be kilometers thick promised to unleash torrents of water at any time. He felt a moment's sorrow for his people, for the island families who would be denied the simple pleasure of celebrating outside and grilling meat in the open. This was not going to be an ordinary Easter.

How could he not have known about the stone house and its horrors? There were places on Vóunos where less dramatic things had occurred which every child knew about. The rock crazy Maria had tried to jump off with her baby, and the bakery which had burnt down, taking two adjacent houses with it; the last was in the eighteen hundreds, and it was still talked about. How could an entire community have forgotten about black magic and human sacrifice, and especially when it had occurred during the evil days of the Nazi occupation?

Perhaps because it was too terrible.

Perhaps.

Or—and he knew the thought for a product of his Byzantine mind, which always looked for plots and complications—because something had willed them all to forget it. Some spell cast over them all by the magician before they all died in there.

But why? What were they trying to do when they died?

He stood there, puzzled and tired, allowing his mind room to work, his thoughts to skip and play over the facts, looking for connections and nodes.

The telephone rang, startling him. Not his cell, but the one on his desk.

"Katsélis," he said.

Kalispéra, Captain." The voice was a man's, old, and coarse as broken stone. "Ouranópoli police, Major Antonides."

Ouranópoli. What the hell did anyone in Ouranópoli, all the way up there, want with him on Easter eve? "Yes, Major. How can I help you?"

"We have a priest here who insists he knows you. One Father Stélios."

Katsélis's scattered thoughts snapped into sudden focus, a searchlight beam punching through the fog in his head. "Yes. Yes, I know him. But…he's *there?* In Ouranópoli?"

A chuckle of tumbling gravel. "He's here. Actually, he's been in our cells since last night, but I have him sitting outside my office. My sergeant is making him a coffee."

"In your cells, you say? For what? I spoke to him just—"

"Yes, he told me. The father was caught trying to steal a *kaïki* in the early hours of this morning. At first he wouldn't talk; when he did, my men thought he was raving. I've been in Xanthi for two days, just got back. They kept him locked up, waiting for me to return. Anyway, I spoke to him as soon as I heard what happened. He has a very curious story. I don't even think he expected me to believe any of it. The man is tired and frustrated beyond caring what anyone thinks."

Katsélis held his breath.

"Are you there, Captain?" Antonides sounded amused.

"Yes. Sorry, I…did he mention a stone house?"

"Yes. It seems he wants very much to get to Vóunos. So, do I send him for psychiatric evaluation, charge him with attempted robbery, or just return him to Athos?"

Katsélis shook out a cigarette from the pack and lit it. The man was going to think he was crazy too, but…. "I think, sir, it may be very important that he get to Vóunos."

"So there is something to his story, then."

"Yes. I don't know how much he told you…"

"Quite a bit. One doesn't hear talk of black magic often outside of books and films. But we're close to Athos here, Captain, and not all of us have become secularized. I have seen many strange things in my life, and I don't think this is a crazy man sitting outside my office." He was silent a moment. "You really believe this is life and death, then?"

"A priest died in the stone house last night," said Katsélis.

"So he told me. All right. There's a medical helicopter at Iérissos, just north of here across the isthmus. I can use it for emergencies, although there'll probably be hell to pay if I do—but perhaps also if I don't, eh?" He barked a laugh. "Well, I've been thinking of retiring anyway. Expect your priest within the next few hours, I'll call when he's on his way."

CHAPTER THIRTY-SIX

When the moment came, the ineffable machinery that linked the worlds functioned like clockwork. As Dafyd watched, the scene "below" (it was impossible to think of it otherwise) became suddenly clear and distinct. Where previously they'd only been able to see inside the stone house, now they could hear its occupants as well. Dafyd had the feeling of being at the mouth of a funnel, almost as though gravity were working on him, pulling him down towards Earth, towards the house, towards his new body.

Klaus, evidently, was more than ready. He was already on the move, flowing like a wave to the world below, to life, to corporeality. Dafyd saw the man's body flail and collapse under the shock of Klaus's entry. The women screamed.

Entering the man's mind was like nothing so much as a shell-burst, an explosion of sound and light, but dazzling, joyous, triumphant. Klaus felt the man's self retreat before him, running like a rabbit before the hounds. Sensations Klaus had forgotten—arms, legs, the sense of a physical body—were everywhere, filling him with the huge, forgotten, delicious weight of the material, the meat-body. He reached for it all at once, like a driver seizing the controls of a vehicle careening off the road. The body spasmed and then he had it, was pulling it together. He fended off the hands reaching for him, got his feet under him and his palms on the ground.

Too much at once! At the same time as the motor parts of his mind automatically went to work righting the capsized body, so his thinking self merged with the man's mind. The sensation was overwhelming and he felt himself freeze. Even though he could feel the personality draining, fleeing, the man's entire life, a whole being, broke over him like a flood. In a single, chaotic instant, Klaus was drowning, going under, fighting for breath.

Dafyd held back, watching the struggle. The terror radiating from the scene was palpable, life-giving. Dafyd felt it suffuse him, an inhalation of raw strength and vitality; he was aware of Magda at his side, doing the same. The man's grip was breaking, his psyche reeling under the impact of Klaus's entry. Pain and fear poured from him in great waves, and they soaked it up like sunlight. Dafyd delayed his own entry into the woman's body, delighting in the furious, energizing glow of the man's psychic obliteration.

‡

Sunday April 20, 2014

Alex watched, paralyzed, as Paul collapsed to the ground by the front door. Elléni's scream broke her paralysis, and she shouted, *"Paul!"* She dropped to her knees and reached for him where he lay on his back. But his eyes—oh, God! his eyeballs were *vibrating!*—had snapped open and his hands came up, hitting at hers and fending her off.

Elléni's hands grabbed her shoulders, pulling her back. Paul had his hands on the ground and looked ready to push himself up off the floor. But there was a string of drool trailing from his mouth and his chest heaved like a bellows stoking the flames of some mad hell.

She let Elléni pull her back upright. Black spots swam before her eyes, and she could barely breathe. Paul's mouth opened, but the strangled, inarticulate sound that came out of it, a soaring moan that cut suddenly off, made them both scramble back. Elléni's hands tightened like clamps on her shoulders. Alex's every muscle went rigid as her skin tried to crawl off her.

Paul's eyes had steadied; now they turned up to the ceiling and rolled entirely up into his head. His head lolled sideways on his neck.

Alex, trembling now, turned to Elléni, who was still clutching painfully at her shoulders. In a voice Alex barely recognized as her own, she whispered, "What's happening to him?" But Elléni, white and drained of blood, didn't—or couldn't—reply.

Paul's attempt to rise faltered. One leg kicked out and his arms went slack again, dropping his shoulders back to the ground.

"It is not him," Elléni said, in a voice flat with disbelief. Then, loudly, as if finding a residue of strength somewhere, she cried, "We must do something!"

The idea that he was having some kind of seizure ghosted through Alex's mind, and she moved instinctively to help him, but Elléni held her back. And she was right to do so—it was like he was possessed. This wasn't like any kind of a seizure Alex had ever heard of. Epileptics didn't try to get up in mid-seizure, and their eyeballs sure didn't vibrate! *I'm living a horror movie.*

As she struggled to think of anything useful, Paul's body arched. His fists beat on the ground and his mouth writhed. His head snapped back and he shouted, "Nine!"

Alex flinched and Elléni, recoiling in shock, suddenly let go of her shoulders. *Nine,* just the one word. And now again, quieter, *"Nine!",* as he squirmed around on the floor.

"Elléni!" she shouted, grabbing the woman's arm. "Come on, the kitchen!"

Elléni stared—the white was showing all around her eyes—but let herself be dragged along.

Alex flung open a cabinet door. "I remembered something I read," she said, reaching for the first pot she found. She handed it and its lid to Elléni and grabbed a large frying-pan. From the kitchen drawer she took a metal ladle and started banging on the pan in her hand. Beyond the counter, Paul was still squirming and twisting around.

"Bang on the pans," shouted Alex, "hard! Make all the noise you can. We have to drive it out!" She scrambled back into the living room, smashing away at the heavy pan and yelling, "Go! Get out! Get away!!" at the top of her voice. Behind her, Elléni did the same, and in a moment the room was ringing with a crazy cacophony of noise.

Paul was writhing on the floor, hands over his ears. Ignoring her instincts—*it's not him, not him, not him*—Alex approached, bending over and beating away at the pot just inches from his head. Elléni joined her, clanging away on the other side of him and shouting, *"Exo! Exo!"*

189

Caught between them, Paul's body rocked and shuddered feebly, as if the fight were going out of him. And then with a last, sudden convulsion, he sprawled limp and lifeless as a puppet with its strings sliced through.

‡

The hot flow of emotion dwindled abruptly, as if cut through by a knife. Uncertainty, hesitation…and now the fear came from not only the man, but from Klaus also.

<He's in trouble>, said Magda, as they watched the stolen body thrash and flail. <What's happening?>

It was the question in Dafyd's mind, too. Had Klaus gone in too fast? Should they hold back, go easier? The shock alone should have been enough to sever the man's soul from his body and send it tumbling into the void. But Klaus was having a hard struggle to gain control.

Dafyd let himself flow into the scene, homing in on Klaus. But easy, careful! He needed to calm him, make sure Klaus stayed in control before Dafyd took the woman.

With a conscious effort, Magda resisted the pull to join them. Although she was vibrating with strength and need, her every instinct told her to hold off. *This isn't the moment!* The vague doubt she'd more than once felt over Klaus, her inability to clearly see outcomes with him, was a caution and warning against haste. The moment was too uncertain, too dangerous—*just look at him*. No, in spite of the way being open and her very physical instinct to dive in, join them, take the young girl's body—how she longed to feel those youthful limbs as hers, to breathe in the sweet air of the world again—caution held her back. After a lifetime of training her intuition, she knew better than to ignore it.

‡

A cold wave of revulsion had drenched Klaus as the man's life opened to him—the man was a Jew. *A Jew!* That he should have chosen one of them…but he hadn't had a choice, had he? And in the shock of discovery he'd lost control, and the man—Paul—was fighting back. He'd dislodged him, sent him running, but not followed through hard, and now the pig was counterattacking, fighting him. Klaus was vaguely aware of his-their body thrashing around on the ground. He shouted—couldn't help himself—*"Nein! Nein!"*, and the women backed away.

Klaus turned there in the man's mind to face the other with a curse, ready to destroy him, send him fleeing from the body and straight to Hell. There was a sense of Dafyd somewhere at Klaus's back, perhaps to support him, but the man Paul was the problem. Though he couldn't see him, Klaus felt him with strange senses—a frightened, angry, desperate presence, a looming blazing darkness in this cavern of the psyche. Something inside Klaus snapped, all control abandoned, and he dove forward at the other with a savagery and will he'd thought lost back in the billowing flames of the east. Now—

The world turned to chaos under an assault of noise and screaming. The shock of it cut across his attack, and as Klaus's attention swung this way and that between the madwomen beating their pots in his ears, the other, Paul, smashed into his consciousness, knocking him down, obliterating thought, driving him back and up and out....

Darkness.

<Klaus?>

He came back by degrees. To the limbo-place, abstraction of existence. The newfound weight and presence of the physical, of a body, of *life*, lost, gone.

<No. You weren't prepared, and the girl, she was cunning. But you almost had him, Klaus. Why did you hesitate?>

<A Jew. The man is a Jew!>

<A body is a body.>

<Dafyd, let him recover,> said Magda. The violence with which Klaus had been expelled made her glad she'd not gone in.

Assent from Dafyd. <We have time. The trick with the banging and shouting was startling, it confused me too. But it won't work twice. The next time we take them together and break them all at the same time.>

Klaus cursed himself. The return of corporeality, the weight and fullness of being in a body, had been a moment of supreme triumph.

<It's all right,> said Magda. <Next time you'll have him.>

<Would you prefer the woman?> asked Dafyd. The question came tinged with humour. <I'll take either, your choice.>

A Jew. Could he stand it? But Dafyd was right: a body was a body, and it was the body he wanted. Driving out the soul would kill the Jew. <No. The man. Next time I shall have him.>

CHAPTER THIRTY-SEVEN

"It happened so fast," said Paul. He was hunched in the armchair, wrapped in a blanket and nursing the ouzo Elléni had poured him. She was propped up on the arm of the chair, her arm around him, chestnut curls tumbling over the woolen pea coat. Alex, bulky in Paul's winter jacket, sat crosslegged on the floor by his feet. "It—*he*—came out of nowhere. The hatred…" He shook his head.

"It was the colonel?" said Elléni. "You're sure?"

He nodded. The man had hit him with the force of a locomotive bursting full speed from the black mouth of a tunnel. In an instant Paul lost control of his body, felt himself shrunken to a point inside his own mind. He glimpsed an abyss, hung over it in the full and terrible knowledge that if he should fall into that darkness there was no coming back. He'd teetered, hadn't he, on the very edge, felt himself about to fall under the relentless assault of that other, desperate mind, until at the very last possible instant the pressure had relented with the girls' ruse, allowing Paul to regain his balance. He'd fought back then, fought like he never had in his life. Fought *for* his life.

"Thank you," he said, looking from one to the other of them. "Without you…" He shook his head.

"Thank Alex," said Elléni, "it was her idea to make all that noise."

"How did you know to do that?" said Paul, his breath curling smoke in the frosty air which—small mercy—at least hadn't got any colder.

"Anthropology studies. Making noise to drive out demons. It's something common to cultures all over the world."

"But that was not a demon," said Elléni. "If I understand what is happening here…it was the spirit of a dead man."

Alex shrugged. "It worked, right?" She gestured to the window. "But we're still trapped. We need to figure out what the heck is going on here."

Elléni rubbed her cheeks in a tired, protective gesture. "I am afraid that was only the beginning."

"You think he'll come back for another try?" said Alex. Both women turned to look at him.

Paul sipped at his ouzo. "The question is, what's he after?"

Elléni frowned. "After? He wants to kill you."

"I don't think so. I mean, yes, I did feel that I almost…died. But I don't think that was his intention. It felt—" a forceful shudder ran through him— "like he wanted to take over my body. *I* was just in the way."

Alex stared at him. "God."

"Exactly."

"But why the colonel?" said Elléni. "If the story is true, he was just a friend of the others, the real magicians."

"I can't imagine why," he said. "But yeah, they're here, too."

"You know that?" said Alex.

He nodded. "I sensed it in his mind. Like they were right there, close. There are three of them."

Alex's lips parted, but it was Elléni who spoke.

"And three of us," she said.

"Right." He hadn't wanted to go there, but it was out.

"But they are dead!" said Elléni. Her face was bleached bone. "They found them all dead, here, in this room!"

"It makes me wonder what the priests knew, the ones who did all those exorcisms. And what really killed Father Tákis."

Alex jumped up. "We have to get out of here!" she said. For the first time, she looked really afraid. Until now, she'd taken it in her stride, an adventure, a scary game. Now it had become real.

Paul put down his glass and stood, shucking off his blanket. He put his arms around Alex—she was trembling now—and she set her head against his chest, holding tightly onto him.

"It's going to be okay," he told her.

Close by, Elléni caught his look and joined them, placing a reassuring palm on Alex's back. "Paul is right," she said. "If we work together, it will be okay." But her gaze when she glanced at him betrayed her doubts.

Alex squeezed him and pulled back. "Thanks," she said, nodding. Her chin trembled, but she forced a smile. "I'm okay."

He crossed to the front door, opened it. An arm's reach away, in the narrow space between the house and the darkly glowing mist, a steady snow was falling.

He shook his head and called back over his shoulder. "Come and see this."

"How...?" said Alex.

He looked up. Between the darkness and the fat snowflakes sifting down on them, it was hard to gauge where the mist began, but it seemed to pretty closely follow the outline of the house. "It's raining out there," he said. "But when the rain hits our weird little envelope of cold here..."

"Hauntings are often associated with sudden waves of cold. The phenomenon is well-documented." Alex rubbed at her arms. "But this is taking it to extremes."

Elléni frowned and went back inside. The others followed her.

"The fog appeared after we got back," said Paul, moving to stand by the stove. Alex and Elléni joined him as he warmed his hands in the stove's radiance. "I think it's a good bet it's here to prevent us leaving, isolate us."

He looked at his watch. It was a quarter to one. "Maybe it'll dissipate with the sunrise. That's almost six hours, give or take. I've got spare batteries for the lamps." He opened the stove door and added a cut log. "And at least oxygen doesn't seem to be a problem."

"He...*they*...will try again," said Elléni. It wasn't a question.

Paul turned to Alex. "Do you have any other tricks? The noise worked, might work again. My fear is if they hit all of us at once."

Alex shook her head. "Nothing. Not that I remember, anyway."

Elléni reached into the coat and fumbled around at her neck until she drew out the small gold crucifix she always wore on the end of its fine chain. "Perhaps this." She turned to Paul. "Do you have a larger one?"

"Uh-uh. And in any case, I'm afraid it wouldn't even work for nonbelievers like us." He racked his brain for ideas, but all that came to mind were cheesy formulas from old Vincent Price movies, like wreaths of garlic and silver bullets. Still.

"Do we have the luxury of not believing anymore?" asked Elléni.

He frowned. "One thing I do know is that we can't risk falling asleep."

"I will make coffee. We should eat something, too."

"Protein. Not too much, though, don't want to get sleepy." An idea struck him. "A circle! For protection. Would that help?" He turned to Alex.

"Ummm…" Her brows knotted in thought. "I've got it! Holy water! We trace a circle on the floor with holy water."

Elléni looked at Paul, then back to Alex. "But we do not have holy water."

"It's just salt water that's been blessed," said Alex. "I can do that."

Elléni stared. "You know the correct prayers?"

"Not exactly. I did research exorcism rituals for a paper but I don't remember it all. But I think spirit and intention counts for as much as words in these things."

"It can't hurt," said Paul. "Go for it."

"Do you have spring water?"

"Sure, a whole case of it."

Minutes later, Paul and Elléni stood by the woodstove, watching in fascination as Alex held her palm over a small dish of salt. "Creature of salt," she began, "I bless you in the name of the Father. Let all evil be gone from you, leaving you purified and filled with good for this holy purpose."

Creature of salt? The Father? Paul bit his lip as warring emotions clashed inside him. He was proud of his niece's courage and cleverness. But the ease—and sincerity!—with which she intoned the words triggered all kinds of alarms. Was she turning into a Christian?

Alex added the salt to the jug of spring water she'd prepared, swished it around, and held both hands over it.

"Creature of water, I exorcise you in the name of the Father and cast out all evils, filling you with good and purity, that you may bless this place and grant us protection from evil."

The blessing completed, she walked around the kitchen counter and began to dribble the consecrated water in a wide circle around the entire living area. "Help me even it up, join up the drops and splashes," she told them, "so the circle is unbroken."

Paul, feeling a bit silly, got on his knees and followed her, drawing his fingertips though the little puddles and globs on the hardwood floor, connecting them up so as to not leave gaps. The wet flooring shone softly in the light from the lanterns.

Elléni looked on, her face a battleground of wonder and doubt. "What now?"

"Now we get inside," said Alex. She turned to Paul. "Hey, what about some music, too? They don't like noise, so maybe—"

"Brilliant! That's my girl." He gave her a high five. If nothing else, it would help keep their spirits up. Anything to get them through this.

"But we have no electricity for your stereo," said Elléni.

"No problem. Boombox has fresh batteries." He opened the lower doors of the armoire and placed it on the upper shelf next to the Bose. He turned to Alex. "What do you think, heavy metal?" He grinned broadly at the irony of using a music genre the popular press usually associated with black magic as a defense against it. But it was the loudest, most aggressive music he owned. And it *felt* somehow right.

Alex laughed. "Way to go, Unc! What've you got?"

Paul was sorting through his hundreds of CDs. He chuckled. "Quite a lot. Let's start with Ylectröde, see how the undead handle that. Got three albums of theirs. Then there's Blue Öyster Cult, Zeppelin, Kromeskull, AC/DC, Motörhead.... And it's all downhill from there."

‡

Saturday, near midnight

Captain Katsélis sat in the police SUV, watching the helicopter wobble to the ground in the gusting winds. The rain was coming in sheets now, strafing the concrete apron and drumming like furies on the roof of the vehicle. As the machine touched down, he turned up the collar of his raincoat, tugged down on the brim of his hat, and got out. His umbrella would be useless under the idling rotors, and downright dangerous. He started off towards the chopper, hunched over against the wind and noise. The door opened as he reached it, and there was Father Stélios, even older and more wizened than he remembered him, framed in the doorway. He looked haggard, either from fatigue or from the flight, which must have been trying in these conditions. Next to him, the pilot with his crowning headset held up a hand in silent greeting.

Katsélis touched the priest's arm and leaned in, shouting to the pilot, "Can you make it back in this weather or do you need to stay?"

"It's not so bad over the sea," he said. "You have the worst of it."

Katsélis waved to him. "Fly safely, then, and thank you." He took the priest's hand. "Come, Father."

The old priest scrambled out, and, they scuttled through the downpour to the car. Once inside, Father Stélios thanked the captain. "Without you, I would be spending Easter in a cell in Ouranópoli."

"At least you were safe there," said Katsélis, as they turned back onto the road. In the rearview, he could see the helicopter's running lights rise and tilt as the machine took to the air again. "There's a clean hand towel in the door pocket if you want to dry your face."

"Thank you. Tell me about Father Tákis."

Katsélis gave him the facts of the case according to the woman's statement. "We're still waiting for the autopsy report," he added, with a glance at the priest.

"Is there anyone at the stone house?"

"A foreigner who is renting it. His young niece is also with him."

The priest's mouth was a tight line.

"Why did you take the wartime journal?" said the captain.

The priest sighed audibly. "At the time, I told myself that the village needed to forget what took place there. But in truth, I think I was the one who wanted to forget that such things could happen, denying the truth by concealing the book." He shook his head. "Every year, when I carried out the exorcism and prayers, I left the place fearing that something lingered there, some residue of evil no prayer could cleanse."

They rounded a curve and neared a pair of new rental villas on a small promontory of land with a view. Both villas were brightly lit, illuminating the rain bouncing off the car roofs so that it looked like sparklers. But just as they drove past, the lights flickered and died, and the villas vanished in the murk.

"The storm," said Katsélis. "I wonder if the power to the whole island's gone?" He almost swore, then remembered he had a priest in the car. Below and to their left, where the lights of the *hóra* should have been visible even through the rain, there was only night.

He turned off to the right, up towards the stone house.

"What are we facing, Father? What is happening at the stone house? And why now, on the holiest of days?"

The priest dug around in his satchel, pulling out a large wooden crucifix inlaid with silver, its end threaded through with a leather cord. The silver shone in the faint backwash of light from the headlamps.

"A resurrection, Captain, but not one to celebrate. An obscene parody of the return of our Saviour—and probably not just one resurrection, either."

Fear prickled at Katsélis's scalp. "A resurrection? You mean—"

"I mean the dead back coming to life, Captain. The three who died in that house. The magicians. The Nazi."

Katsélis felt cold fingers clutch at his heart. "Resurrected? But, *how?*"

"I suspect a pact with Hell. This Satanist, his power was..." He shook his head. "Anyone in that house is in the most terrible danger, Captain. Do you understand? As the rest of us will be if we don't stop this." He pulled the leather cord over his head and patted the crucifix into place on his chest.

The pallor of the priest's face in the dim light only served to heighten the captain's fear. "Can we?" he whispered.

Father Stélios gave no answer.

They reached the fork where the main road veered off to the left. Katsélis bore right, turning onto the dirt road to the stone house. Slowing, he reached into his pocket for his cellphone and punched in Pétros's number.

Pétros answered on the second ring; there was conversation and raucous laughter in the background.

"Petro, get in your car and meet me at the stone house. I need you."

There was a moment's silence; then, "Now?"

"Yes, now. At once."

"Captain, the power's out and—"

"I *know* the power's out!" he shouted. The priest glanced at him. "And I don't care! Do you want to keep your job?" God, he didn't need this.

"All right, all right. Sorry, Captain. Yes, I'll leave now."

The road was quickly turning to a river of mud in the downpour. He hoped Pétros would be able to get his battered little Fiat up to the house without getting the thing stuck. Not that the idiot would probably be any help, but he'd feel better with some backup, even if it was just Pétros. *Backup against what, though? Against a black magician returned from the dead?*

He realized with a shock that he didn't even have have his pistol. He wasn't in the habit of carrying it when he wasn't in uniform, and he'd left both at the station.

He slowed the vehicle to a crawl to negotiate the last hairpin turn, and a moment later they topped the small rise and reached the stone house.

The SUV slowed and stopped where the muddy track dead-ended onto the grassy area in front of the house. Katsélis hadn't even realized his foot had relaxed and backed off the accelerator. From the corner of his eye, he noticed that the old priest was, like himself, staring openmouthed at the incomprehensible sight before them.

Where the house should be—*had been,* just yesterday—was instead a whirling vortex of darkness, a coal-black fog shot through with evanescent sparks of deepest blood-red. The base of the vortex occupied the space where the house should have stood, and rose, narrowing like an inverted, swaying funnel, disappearing into the black sky from which it seemed the entire Aegean Sea was pouring down onto the world.

CHAPTER THIRTY-EIGHT

Dafyd watched the three in the stone house with growing amusement. They'd swaddled themselves in bulky clothes and blankets against the cold leaking through the interface. And they were *dancing,* or something like it. Their movements looked vaguely tribal and primitive, the sort of ritual dances savages practiced. Obviously the three in the house had resorted to this laughable expedient in the hope of frightening them away. And they'd drawn a wobbly circle around the living room with hastily-consecrated water—he could see its faint golden glow from here. Well, well. The child was imaginative, if nothing else.

Of course, neither ruse would do them the slightest good: in a few moments their immortal souls would be driven screaming from those strong young bodies into the torment of Outer Hell.

<Klaus?> he said.

<Yes. Yes, I am ready now.>

Dafyd examined the colonel as best he could. The man appeared fully recovered now, solid to all Dafyd's extended senses. He'd not expected Klaus to be so brittle when the moment came, to be so easily driven off. But he'd gone in early, alone. This time would be very different. And he'd at the very least provide Dafyd some cover while he gained control over his own host body.

<Good,> said Dafyd. <Magda?>

As he turned his attention to her, Dafyd thought he caught the barest edge of something he didn't understand, something wholly unfamiliar—doubt? regret? But it was gone before he could even grasp its shape, replaced by her usual dependable calm and willingness to follow where he led.

<Ready,> she said.

He tried to see into her. Had he imagined it?

And of course she saw his scrutiny, caught his intent. <I was just considering the girl. So young, so innocent.> Then, <Yes, I'm ready.>

So that was it. Commendable. She was young enough that she could afford to entertain scruples, but he knew from watching her during the sacrifices that she could be depended on to keep the prize in sight. She'd been rock-steady when she collected the blood from the girl dying on the altar, holding the bowl as blood splashed and overflowed hot onto her bare hands and wrists. She also knew the unendurable, mind-melting agony which awaited her—awaited them all—if they should fail. No, she would not flinch at taking this girl's body and damning the girl's soul to that terrible edge in her place.

<Very good. Then let us be about it. Strike hard, strike fast, and don't let anything come between you and the prize. In a few moments we'll clench hands in the flesh and make the stone house ring with our laughter. Ready?> The others signaled that they were. <All right. Together then, three, two, one...*now!*"

‡

Sunday, smallest hours

"They held their heads with laughs of paiiiin..."

Elléni had never heard the band, Ylectröde, before. Like the best metal, it carried an element of humour, of conscious self-parody, that somehow reinforced and validated the wild, uplifting deluge of pounding percussion and breathless screaming guitar riffs. The sound made her grin, made her want to throw off this stupid coat and dance and do crazy things. Except for the terrible danger they were all in.

"Furies tearing 'cross the skyyyyyy..."

But Alex was ahead of her. She turned up the volume on the boom box, threw off the winter jacket, and started to dance in the middle of the living room. In a moment, Paul and Elléni joined her, dancing in the confused light cast by the few candles and the battery-powered LED lantern on the kitchen counter, laughter turning to wreaths of mist in the freezing air. It was crazy, unthinkable. It felt so good!

"Hell behind their eyeeees..."

"This is fucking awesome!" shouted Alex. Her hands waved snakelike in the air, describing arcs and circles while her feet pattered and skipped on the floor. Paul's dance was more grounded, more disco; his feet moved but remained on the ground as his shoulders jerked back and forth to the beat. In a moment, all three of them were smiling. Elléni let out a yell as she threw off her own coat and surrendered to the moment. Alex danced towards her, and in a moment the two were gyrating around one other like orbiting moons.

"All around the cities burnnnn..."

Now Paul shimmied in close, his solid presence drawing the three of them together to turn and spin like a small solar system. Caught by the infectious madness that seemed to have possessed them all, he unwound his scarf and pulled the bulky Arran sweater over his head, throwing it over his shoulder to land on the other side of the couch.

In the background, he thought he heard thunder. It seemed appropriate.

"As rats writhe on electric rails
Swallowing up the nighttttt… "

‡

Once he'd ushered his friends out the door—it was pouring out there—Pétros made his way to the bathroom, holding the flashlight and weaving a bit as he went. He splashed cold water on his head and neck, cursing. Foggy from alcohol and hashish, he really didn't want to face the captain. But how to get out of it? You didn't argue with the captain when he was in that kind of mood. And although it could get boring, a job in the police on this small island was as comfortable and secure a position as you could have in these ugly times. Even with the reforms and the austerity, the civil service was still as good as it got in Greece. And whatever cuts other sectors might see, the police would be last to suffer. When the old man retired, Pétros would have a good crack at his job and all the benefits and respect that came with the position. He wasn't about to risk *that*.

He toweled himself dry, brushed his teeth, and ran a comb through his hair before taking a close look at his face in the mirror. His eyes were bloodshot, but not too bad. It was gone one in the morning and the chief probably wouldn't notice in the dark; besides, Katsélis's sense of smell was blunt enough from all the cigarettes he smoked that he was unlikely to pick up any lingering traces of hash smoke on Pétros's clothes. Good enough.

Should he get into uniform? The captain hadn't said. But he wanted him there now, *at once*. Well, that settled it.

Pétros pulled on a jacket and his baseball cap. He retrieved his pistol from the dresser, just in case, along with a second clip ready-loaded with nine rounds. He didn't know what this was about, but from the captain's tone it had to be urgent. Since it concerned the stone house, he imagined the slut Elléni was involved. She'd made a beeline for the rich foreigner from the moment he'd arrived, and of

202

course she was fucking him. What had happened to Father Tákis, he didn't know, but he'd known from the first moment at the scene that she was guilty as hell. He'd have arrested her and charged her with murder on the spot, and no doubt he could have made her talk. But the captain was slow and played by the rules. Still, they'd find out the truth in the end.

In the time it took him to cross the street and unlock his car, his trainers were soaked through and a runnel of rain had found its way down his neck. *Screw this shit,* he thought, as he turned the key in the ignition. And he'd promised his parents he'd be there by eight in the morning to help with the lamb, which they'd have to find a way to cook under cover now, probably in the shed with all the doors and windows open. That meant moving a ton of crap out of the way.

Somebody was going to pay for this.

‡

Stélios stared through the blurry windshield—the wipers were still going, but they barely helped—at the scene before them.

The light from the SUV's headlamps, splintered and refracted by the downpour, didn't touch the slowly whirling, swaying, spangled black *thing* that rose before them, just a dozen meters away across the grass. The scene ahead looked like a scaled-up evil manifestation from the darkest reaches of the imagination, something out of *Revelations*—fitting, given his vision of…God! was it only yesterday? He heard, with a sense beyond hearing, the susurrating groans of a million damned souls.

The captain's voice was powder-dry. "What *is* that?"

Opening up his inner vision, Stélios felt the darkness stretching out towards them with ravening tendrils of pollution and decay. He fought back the urge to scream. "It is Hell," he whispered. The words came out without his willing them.

Stélios closed his eyes. Clutching the crucifix at his breast in a trembling hand, he visualized the cloak of protection, weaving it around the two of them, around the car, as he silently intoned the formula that went with it. Depleted as he already was, the effort cost him: he felt the already bone-deep fatigue grow, dulling his mind. But as he worked, the sensation of imminent menace seemed to dull and recede, until he could once again think and breathe.

Reaching into his satchel, Stélios grasped his battle crucifix. He worked the handle and opened the car door a crack. A cold gust sliced into the car and the rain sluiced down over his hand. "Stay here," he told the captain.

"Wait," said Katsélis, "My sergeant is on his way."

Stélios attempted a wry smile. "And what will you do when he arrives? Shoot your way in?" He pulled the *skóuphos* tight down on his head, gave the door a shove, and stepped out into the storm.

The light fabric of his cassock and inner garments gave little protection against the downpour, and his face was running wet and his shoes soaked through before he'd gone five paces. The wind whipped at him and the rain was sheeting now, making it hard to see; water lay centimeters deep on the already-saturated grass.

A car door slammed, and a moment later the policeman was at his side. He'd not bothered with the umbrella, and his hair was plastered to his dripping face. "What can we do?" he shouted over the noise of the storm.

As they drew closer, what had appeared as a solid black vortex now looked less substantial, a spiraling web of crackling dark through which Stélios thought he glimpsed the lines of the stone house. A feeble glow came from what might be the ground floor windows. The air was pungent with ozone.

"Stay here." Stélios put out a hand to stop the captain. He took a deep breath, silently began the prayer, and stepped forward.

A few short strides took him into the edges of the disturbance. Something very like lightning flashed—though there was no thunder—lending the vortex a bizarre quality, defining its every particle and billow of force so that it seemed almost a solid. Still reciting the prayer, Stélios held out his crucifix. The sky pulsed with white fire and now the thunder came, shaking the ground beneath him.

A chaos seized him. Visions doubled and tripled in his mind, blotting out the scene with a crazy kaleidoscope of fragmentary half-formed visions: the precise and ponderous meshing of the vast machinery of the spheres, the infinite, unfeeling gears of the cosmos; something, or several somethings, rushing earthward from the other side of the dimensional rift or funnel into which he'd stepped; a distant boundary, an edge, a terrible frontier of heart-stopping horror from which every sense recoiled—

Stélios faltered. An apocalypse of thunder burst directly overhead and he reeled, the prayer frozen on his lips. The hand clutching the crucifix was suddenly on the ground, steadying him; he'd fallen to his knees under what had felt like a giant's blow. Cold water ran over his wrists and bathed his legs. Though wind and rain tore at him, they were nothing to the force of the magic that had created this.

He realized he was rocking in place, moaning. He was too old, too weak. He'd been a fool to think he could fight something like this, could stand alone against the forces of Hell.

Give up and die, old man—it's finished.

Something—someone—had hold of him. Strong hands grasped under his arms, pulling him up. Upright again, and somehow he'd got his legs under him, and they were holding, if barely. A hand pressed his fingers tightly around the crucifix he'd almost lost.

He turned to look into the water-ruined face of the captain.

"The house, Father. The people inside."

Stélios understood. The captain's other arm was still around his waist, steadying him. Stélios held up a hand and nodded. "Yes. Yes. I'm all right."

He straightened, and the captain let go. The lightning and thunder came almost continuously now. From the strobing, rain-lashed darkness, a young man appeared.

"Pétros!" said Katsélis. "Good man."

The newcomer looked terrified. Under his cap, bloodshot eyes showed circles of pinkish-white around the dark irises. His face was chalk. He shook his head at the captain in a parody of speechless incomprehension.

Stélios turned back towards the house. In the brilliant flashes, its outline became visible beyond the vortex; but Stélios knew that its existence in this world, this sphere, had been somehow suspended, truncated. To reach it…

He widened his stance, bracing himself against the storm, against the chaos, against his terror. He drew on the deep roots of the Earth and the vastness of space, channeling stillness and strength into his being until he felt himself growing, growing, until he was filled to bursting with the force of God's word. It reverberated through him as if he were a mighty bell in the instant of the hammer's strike, and if he held the force in any longer he would crack. He thrust out the battle crucifix and shouted a word of power.

CHAPTER THIRTY-NINE

They committed.

Dafyd and Klaus rushed out and away, pouring into the Earth sphere as finally as any diver ever sprang from a high board. Magda saw them, sensed them go, and so strong was the sensation that she was almost sucked down herself. But something made her resist, hold back.

What was she doing? Part of her being strained to follow them, explode back into the material and into the waiting girl's body, sending the hapless soul tumbling away into Outer Hell like chaff while she, Magda, drew her first new breath of Earth's sweet air. Was she making the most terrible mistake? To not follow could doom her, doom them all.

Except…

Except that the part of her which saw shadows cast through time and space, the part she'd spent her life training, the part which scried…as before, when Klaus had jumped the gun and got himself into trouble…that part told her to hold back.

And yet the pull was so hard to resist. What if she missed the moment, the one chance? Besides which was her loyalty to Dafyd. He'd never let her down, never let her set a foot wrong. He was her teacher, her benefactor, her friend. Everything they'd been through together— Maurice's death, the flight from Morocco, the rituals, the blood, the physical death and the eternity of suffering and transcendent horror at the boundary—to let him down now was to risk everything.

Always look after yourself first, dear.

He'd told her that, told her himself, hadn't he? And more than once. It was one of his cardinal rules. Loyalty and friendship, human values which had once seemed so right and noble…belonged to another world, another life so long abandoned that she wondered at the persistence of these feelings. Like love and hate, these things had begun to burn away even during her apprenticeship. What were mere human values and sentiments to the ultimate goal? What were they to someone who'd felt the hot gush of a sacrifice's life wash crimson over her hands? What meaning had they after the agonies of Outer Hell?

She braced herself against the pull of the material. *Wait,* she told herself. *Wait.*

‡

Alex felt the shock in the room when it happened. Elléni, dancing right next to her, screamed, *"Alex!"* just as a pulse of intense cold knifed through the air. The hard glare of the LED lanterns threw huge, writhing shadows of them on the far wall.

Alex turned to her just in time to see Elléni stop dancing in mid-step, hands flying to the crown of her head as if to stop it exploding. Alex reached instinctively for her, stopped herself, then lunged for the boombox in the open armoire. They'd agreed this might be their only defence, and she wasn't going to let them down—they might not get another chance. She cranked the knob all the way—*to eleven,* Mom would have said—and smacked the big red "Turbo Bass" button for good measure, feeling the black plastic of the player literally pound under her hand with the sudden, deafening increase in volume. The effect was immediate and painful. Recoiling from the shrieking wall of noise, she turned back to the room.

Elléni was on all fours, shaking uncontrollably, face hidden behind a swinging billow of hair, hands clawing at her cheeks. A few feet away, Paul lay sprawled against the back of the couch, hands pressed hard on his ears and his mouth open in what might have been a scream—except with the apocalypse of noise in the room, how would she know? His eyes were wide and mad, fixed on some random point.

Alex leapt forwards. She had to help him, *do something,* help him drive out the thing trying to possess him. She could be hit herself any moment, wasn't sure why she hadn't been. All she knew was they couldn't give up. If they could just keep fighting, make it to the dawn, perhaps—

She'd reached the couch and was about to grasp Paul's shoulders when his eyes turned towards her.

Alex screamed. The tsunami of screaming guitar and vocals receded as though a glass wall had descended around her. Time turned to sludge.

The face was Paul's. The eyes were Paul's. But the look...

If one sucked the soul out a body, this is what you'd be left with. *Lights on, nobody home,* the silly saying came to her. But this wasn't an absence of intelligence but instead of warmth, of light, of humanity. The look in those eyes, the set of that face, that mouth close enough to touch—*to kiss,* came the perverse thought—was empty, void, inhuman.

A few months ago she'd seen a YouTube video on the latest breakthrough in robotics, a Japanese robot designed for counseling over a video link. In trials, volunteers had consistently scored the robot significantly better in videolinked counseling sessions than the human counselors used as controls. The robot's face—that of a young man—was flawless in every detail, its expression one of gentle, encouraging compassion, perfectly rendered and coordinated from chin to brow, from the slightest flick of the lips and flare of the nostrils to the minutest crinkling of the eyes and cant of the brows. It would have passed for human anywhere, and Alex would have told it her life story without a moment's hesitation.

Until someone turned it off. In that flicker of transition from powered-up to standby mode, when its facial "muscles" relaxed the synthetic tissue into an agreeable, neutral state, there was a fraction of a second in which all the humanity left the features, as if the soul had been sucked out of it quicker than an eyeblink. She'd been so shocked she'd spilt the cup of iced tea she was sipping all over her laptop, sending her scrambling to pull out the battery before worse damage happened. When she told her friends, they'd laughed at her. But she'd never seen an expression like that on a human face and never wanted to again.

Now it was on Paul's face, right here, facing her. She hovered, frozen, incapable of any movement or thought. Somewhere was muted sound, and in the corner of her vision, Elléni staggering to her feet, trying to stand.

Paul reached out a hand towards Alex.

Something in her snapped. She yelled, *"NO!"* and reflexively, faster than thought, slapped his arm away with one hand while the other lashed out snakelike to land a hard, open-palmed blow against the side of his head. She felt the heel of her hand smack full against his ear and gasped as his head spun half around from the unintended force of the blow, sending him sprawling back.

"Oh, shit!" she muttered, backing away without thinking. The world released its breath; the music, screeching lunacy, was back. Time resumed.

Her hand stung and throbbed. The fuck had she *done?* In her terror, she'd slapped her uncle, hit him hard enough to knock him unconscious. God! Was he even breathing?

Motion on her left caught her eye. Elléni stood, her shadow looming sinister behind her. Her hair was a mess and blood welled slowly from several long red gashes where she must have clawed open her cheeks during the seizure or whatever the hell it was.

Her lips moved. Alex couldn't hear a thing over the blare of music, but at least Elléni was okay. Even in her obvious disarray, she seemed to have recovered some control. She smiled, radiating calm and sanity. Score! The loud music had worked—they'd driven one of them back and she'd at least temporarily put the other out of action.

She turned back to Paul, saw his chest was rising and falling, so he was at least breathing. But what to do with him? She turned back to Elléni to ask for help.

Elléni pointed at her ears, then at the boombox, shaking her head. She was saying, *turn it down, turn it down!*

Alex ran a hand through her hair and let out a breath she didn't even know she'd been holding. And Elléni was right, she couldn't think with the damned noise, and her nerves were fried. She nodded to Elléni and turned to the boombox.

‡

Elléni fled down an ever-shrinking tunnel of darkness. With sudden and devastating finality, *he* had exploded into her head like a thunderbolt, sending her running. It wasn't only fear, she hadn't even time to feel that—there just wasn't room for the two of them.

In the instant he entered, she knew him. His mind, his soul, everything that was Dafyd Jones had raked and gouged and interpenetrated everything that was—had been—her. In a heartbeat, if she still had one, it had happened, game over, done. There'd been no fight, no chance for one. She'd tried to resist, but the magician's psyche had simply overpowered her, leaving her no place in which to hide or shelter from the suffocating force of his presence. He'd given no quarter, none, and everything that was Elléni, every particle of her, had been squeezed and compressed to a tiny, naked thing and blasted away like a sparrow in a hurricane.

She rattled and tumbled between narrowing walls. No sight, no sound, only the sense of terrible speed and finality. In the instant of collision, she'd known the magician, known him in the round, all that he was and had been, all he aspired to. And as she sped towards— what? death?—his laughter and obscene sense of triumph followed her.

As her momentum and pressure approached the unbearable, her fragmenting thought touched upon Paul and Alex. They'd been caught, all of them, in the magician's snare, and how could any human resist so powerful an evil? She wished she'd taken Paul away, never shown him the house. Now he and Alex would die, too, and it was her fault, all of it.

There hadn't even been time to talk about love.

How was it possible to feel pain without a body? But pain was exactly what she felt, pain that built and built in intensity, the pressure and abrasion from the mad rush growing until it was all she knew. Just as she reached the point of madness, she felt a sudden release, a bursting out into a void, expanding in all directions like blood gushing and spraying from a severed artery.

Stillness.

She was alone.

Alone in somewhere not a place so much as a state, a condition of being. Wild, unsettling distortions of scale assaulted her. She couldn't see, hear, touch in any way she understood—something other than ordinary senses operated here. She felt as though she were in a thick soup, had a sense of what might be other thoughts, other consciousnesses, pulsing in the dark, intuited but removed from any sensory contact. There was something like but unlike sound, a great, deep tolling as of distant bells the size of houses.

Vague shapes and colours moved and melded here, as if she were adrift in some dense medium. She felt pressure one instant, lightness the next. She tasted distant ringing sounds, heard the bitter tang of red-hot iron. She was going mad.

And now she felt something close, close. She had the impression of eyes large and liquid, more curious than hostile, and the unmistakable sensation of warm vapour, like great, soft breaths playing over her. It felt good, almost a caress, wonderful after the terrible cold.

In her mind a shape began to form. The dark eyes grew solid, and around them features, soft fur, a...muzzle?

She was looking at the enormous face of a horse.

Stélios felt as though he were pushing against a mountain. In a very real way, he was—the evil here in this storm-lashed hell was palpable, its edge just a few meters away. He heard one of the policemen cry out as if struck as he released the power he'd summoned into his body. A blaze of light roared away from him, piercing the whirling wall of darkness like a burning lance. Stélios felt his body shake and shudder with the discharge and knew that this assault would cost him, cost him perhaps more than he could pay in his current condition.

The funnel of blackness seemed to sway, and the area closest to the strike's focus ceased abruptly to sparkle. The dead zone grew outward, until the entire lower part of the black funnel greyed, taking on the look of ashes. The thing began to lose some of its solidity and he saw, through the swirling particles and the windblown rain, and—*snow?*—the ghostly outline of the stone house.

"My God," someone said. Blinking hard against the water streaming down his face, Stélios turned. The young policeman—Pétros—stood ashen-faced. White showed all around his eyes, and he looked ready to piss himself.. "My God," he repeated.

The Captain looked barely more composed, but his face had the set of a man struggling with and finding his courage, conquering his instinct to bolt.

The lightning flashed again, less vivid this time, and the thunder came a couple of seconds later.

Stélios tugged at the strap of his satchel, repositioning it on his shoulder. *Damn the years!* He'd never felt so weary. Dazed with fatigue and soaked through, all he wanted to do was lie down—right here, anywhere—and go to sleep. It would be easy. It would be quick.

The captain moved to his side. "What can we expect in there, Father?"

The priest shook his head, sending fat droplets flying.

"In there?" said Pétros. "You—we're going *in there?*"

"People are in danger!" snapped the captain. "Mortal danger."

"Worse than mortal," said Stélios, stepping towards the gyre of ashes.

The slow-turning black seemed to thin as they neared it. There was soft yellow light in the two lower windows of the house nearest the front door, though all other detail was lost to the storm and the dark, whirling wall, and to the softly falling snow on the other side of the gyre.

Stélios held out his crucifix and braced as they entered ashen part of the funnel. His hand and arm grew faint and indistinct, and then he was inside it. To his surprise there was no resistance or sense of anything at all except a sudden, biting cold. The drop in temperature was so sharp that he gasped despite himself.

"What..." began Katsélis. He pulled his jacket tight around himself and looked up in astonishment at the falling snow. From the house came a cacophony of discordant, screeching music, clearly audible even through closed windows. In the house it had to be deafening.

Behind them, Pétros made a sound partway between a sob and a whimper, abruptly cut off when the captain glanced sharply back at him.

The frozen grass crunched underfoot as they crossed the few meters to the house. Pétros's teeth were chattering as he said, "My G-God, the *cold!*" Moving through a fog of his own breath, Stélios felt it too and wondered he wasn't shivering himself. With every cell crying out to him to stop, he supposed it was just simple conservation of energy.

Forms moved indistinctly in the dim light behind the net curtains. "At least someone is still alive in there," said the captain.

They had reached the door. Stélios turned to the two policemen.

Between their drowned appearance, pallor, and visible shivering, they looked almost comical. He imagined all three of them looked in serious need of rescue themselves.

All at once, it was quiet. There was no sound from the house, the screaming din had cut off. Then a woman's voice, too muted to make out words., though the tome was urgent

"Stay close to me," whispered Stélios, forcing himself forwards, "both of you, and trust nothing once we enter."

Pétros reached into his jacket pocket and pulled out a pistol. He pulled at it, hands trembling, and something metallic snapped into place with a loud *click*. Katsélis frowned.

"Put it away, Pétros," hissed the priest. "You can do nothing here."

Pétros shot a look at the captain. "Then why—"

Stélios cut him short. "Keep your voice down! The people in there may not be who they seem to be. If they've been…taken, only I can save them. I think *you* understand, Captain?"

"You believe the magicians may have…possessed them? The American and Miss Marinóudis?"

"Exactly. They've chosen this time, this place, these bodies, for their rebirth. If I'm overpowered, then it's too late, there's nothing anyone can do. At that point, use your judgment."

Katsélis nodded. He turned to Pétros. "Give me—"

Inside, a woman screamed something. It sounded like English.

Stélios took a deep breath. *God, let me have the strength.* He set his hand on the freezing cold dooknob and turned it.

CHAPTER FORTY

Entering the woman was like stepping through a door from an airy, open landscape into the confines of a cozy cottage. For a second, Dafyd was entirely disoriented. All perception abruptly cut off, he was reduced to a point of consciousness bounded on every side by something other, which, despite a delicious familiarity, pressed hard from every side on the nugget of his being.

The instinct to panic flared: had he got it wrong? What if you couldn't simply enter another human and shove their consciousness aside, taking over their body as a soldier might commandeer a vehicle from a civilian? What if the resident owner, rather than resisting and offering a fight which Dafyd would win, just absorbed the intrusion, making room for him and simply allowing him to settle into some tiny niche of her being from which he could not access the senses or nerves, seize the controls as it were…what then? How long until the binding power of the contract recalled him, and Nestor snatched him back from the earthly to serve out infinity in the nightmare of Outer Hell?

Calm. Extend senses. Feel.

In the extraordinary silence of absolute sensory deprivation, he imagined taking a deep breath. He gently extended his awareness, like gas flowing through a membrane, or water trickling under a door into an adjoining room. His consciousness crept stealthily outward, feeling, feeling in the quiet dark like a blind man lightly tapping a cane before him.

And *there* was something: an edge, the merest shadow of thought…

An explosion of noise and movement and chaos broke over him like an ocean wave. In an instant Dafyd went from being an isolated mote of thought surrounded by stillness to suffering a sensory assault like nothing he'd ever known. He flailed, fought to orient, balance—

She knew him in the moment he knew her. The woman, Elléni, recognized the violation, had been expecting it, or something like it. Dafyd experienced the most startling disorientation as his identity and hers cycled and alternated, pulsing back and forth like current in a circuit. The woman broke her wild dance, cried out once to the girl nearby….

The action broke the loop, giving Dafyd his opportunity. The contact had been enough. In an instant he righted himself and struck. He reached out with the sureness acquired in the mad moments in which their selves had blended and smoothly wrested control of the body. As he did so, he lashed out at the woman's self with every ounce of force at his disposal. A swift, brutal kill, no room for error here.

The woman was no weakling; powerful as his attack had been, she fought back, rounding on him in turn with catlike ferocity. She attacked him inside and out, clawing at his psyche, tearing at his-her face with her hands, raking nails deep into the soft flesh of their cheeks in a frenzied struggle for control. They stumbled, knees struck ground in a jarring impact. Breath came ragged and short, and for a long, awful heartbeat, it was in the balance.

Then he had her.

Her scream was internal, the anguished, primeval howl of every living creature in the moment of knowing its death has come. It filled the fleshly house Dafyd had stolen, energizing him even as it shook him. It was the same scream he'd loosed when, a lifetime ago, Nestor first took him and the others and they'd plummeted into the symphony of nerve-flensing suffering at that appalling, chaotic frontier.

He felt her presence slip from her skull, heard the scream linger and echo as her soul tumbled from this plane into the void. Then he was alone.

Dafyd stood. Despite his swelling sense of triumph, he felt oddly dissociated, an outsider. It would take a little time to get used to this, to feel the body as his own. Only he didn't have that time: until they were all three certain they'd consolidated their hold and irreversibly expelled the three whose bodies they'd stolen, they were in danger.

The renewal of sensory perception almost took his breath away: the hard flare of the lantern making weird play of shadows against the walls; the waxy smell of just-extinguished candles; his weight on his feet pushing against the wood floor; cold, cold air; the burning pain where the woman had raked her—his—cheeks as they struggled; the stale taste of coffee in his mouth; and over it all, the screaming wall of discordant noise coming from the machine on the floor in the corner of the room, making all thought and reason difficult.

From behind his new eyes he looked out on a room at once familiar yet strange. The younger girl looking expectantly at him, half-relieved, as if waiting for him to speak. So Magda had made it, too. Not only made it, but she was apparently in full control. Excellent. He smiled. Not for the first time, he experienced a tingle of surprise on finding he cared strangely for her.

But Klaus…the man's body was collapsed on the floor by the sofa, inert.

The noise in the room was unbearable. Had to stop it. He pointed to his ears, then called to Magda. "Turn it down!" he shouted, pointing to the radio-thing or whatever it was. "Turn it down!" He doubted she could hear him, but she seemed to understand. She bent to the device and punched a button. In an instant, blessed quiet.

"We need to help him!" cried Magda, pointing to the unconscious form on the floor. "I was frightened. I panicked and hit him, and he just went down."

Dafyd nodded, amused to hear the American accent on her—they would all need a while to accustom themselves to this. Himself perhaps most of all, what with this gender transformation. But then he'd always welcomed new experiences.

Magda knelt and took the man's hand. As Dafyd looked down at him, a doubt seized him. *Had* Klaus made it? The moment he'd entered the woman, Dafyd had lost all direct connection with the others. There was no knowing.

He reached down and shook the unconscious man by the shoulder. "Klaus," he said, "Wake up. Wake up! We made it."

‡

Alex froze. *Klaus?* What…? And Elléni's voice was…weird. And English-accented.

She knew at once what it meant, and her bones turned to ice.

The magician. Not Elléni, but a body-thief, an intruder, an evil, undead thing.

Releasing Paul's hand she recoiled instinctively, hands rising to her mouth, but too slow to prevent a scream escaping. Time continued to crawl as her mind boiled in a crescendo of revulsion. She was going to throw up. But still some small part of her seemed almost detached, as though watching the scene.

The Elléni-thing turned, her overly calm expression giving way to one of surprise. "Magda, what—" she began, and stopped, open-mouthed. Understanding flooded her features.

Oh holy shit—

She sensed a movement to her right, whirled. Paul's eyes had opened. His lips writhed and he seemed to be struggling to speak, but that soulless robot expression had left his face. He rose onto one knee, reached out and gripped the intruder's, Elléni's, proffered hand.

"Paul!" screamed Alex, "They're here! *It's not Elléni!*"

The Elléni-thing also turned to look at Paul. His words, when he spoke, tumbled out in a confused rush. Of German.

What the fuck…. Alex's head went light as steam. Ridiculously, she thought, *so this is what they mean by "getting the vapours".*

English. German. The whole story was true, and….

The world went to nightmare. For an instant she was able to believe she was asleep, that it *was* just a nightmare, but she knew all too well it was real, all of it. Something—the black magician, the leader—had taken over Elléni. And Paul….

Omigod. The Nazi colonel.

Time trembled, stopped.

It was all over. In an instant, time would resume and *something* would invade her, some evil soul-sucking entity—*the woman in the story? The Elléni-thing* had *just called her Magda*—would invade her head, and it would all be finished.

A choked sob escaped her. Magic, vampires, ghosts, zombies… it had all seemed so much fun. Late night horror movies. Ouija and Tarot. She'd been so into the stuff.

Now it was going to kill her.

A leaden cloak of grief and loss enveloped her, crushing, suffocating. She closed her eyes.

She'd been so happy, looked forward to so much. Graduation, a career, a love. Now…Mom, Paul, all her friends, her hopes and dreams, all lost, and for what? So some soul-sucking Satanist fuckups from the dead past could be reborn.

No.

The tiny part of her that had seemed outside it all roared back, gripping her. The world snapped back into focus.

No!

Like a thrown switch, freezing fear turned to incandescent fury. She wouldn't go down, not without a fight. Not gonna happen. Fuck this shit.

She gulped a huge breath, felt her body tense, and opened her eyes.

Bring it on, motherfuckers!

‡

Paul struggled to regroup. Something had shattered him like porcelain. Some core of him—mind, soul, whatever—persisted, but barely. He felt like a spectator in his own head. No sense, no control. He could barely think.

No, there was slight perception. Impressions came, but remote, fragments borrowed or reflected through a series of dim mirrors in a tunnel. Two faces framed as in a cracked lens. One face had blood running down both cheeks.

Understanding slowly surfaced.

Elléni. Elléni, hurt, bloodied. And Alex, arms stretched towards him, imploring. Screaming something. Screaming something at *him*.

And now he felt it, the presence, the other in his own head. Maule. And in that instant everything snapped together.

The colonel was saying something, using Paul's own mouth. Without even thinking, Paul attacked. He had no hands, no mouth, but his hatred and his will were force enough in here. He felt the colonel's mind reel as he struck, felt him lose control over the mouth and body. Paul hacked and slashed at the intruder, wielding his hatred like a machete, like an axe.

The other was fast. After a moment of shocked confusion, he met Paul head-on in what felt like a physical impact. The man's cruelty and madness were like nothing Paul had known before, and he staggered back under the sheer brutality of the other's counterattack.

Without limbs, they punched, wrestled, kicked; without nerves, pain lanced, seared, transfixed. The intimacy of the conflict heightened the desperate horror of it. He *couldn't* lose, couldn't. If the other won....

He fought for Alex, for Elléni. But for every blow he delivered, the German seemed to land two.

Little by little, Paul felt himself shrink, diminish, grow weaker. His strikes grew feeble while each of the madman's blows fell heavier than the last. Despair lacerated Paul's soul. He felt the core of whatever he had become shrink and compress until there was nowhere left to go.

I could have loved you, Elléni.

There came a last, shattering blow, an explosion of pain, and he felt himself hurled from his own skull, rushing towards the widening mouth of a tunnel of utter darkness.

CHAPTER FORTY-ONE

Stélios threw the door open.

The room was as much shadow as light, lit only by the white flare from a pair of small lanterns on opposite sides of the room. Directly in front of him, in the wide living area, were three people, all frozen in attitudes of surprise.

A man, sprawled against the couch; a woman, her face and hands bloodied, standing next to him; and behind her, a terrified-looking girl of perhaps twenty. Coats and winter clothing were strewn around, and several half-burned candles stood on the fireplace mantel.

Stélios almost fell back. He'd felt the demonic before, but never like this. The room was saturated with an aura of evil so strong it seemed to pulse and throb.

He was only fractionally aware of the policemen behind him. All his attention was focused on the room's occupants, and especially the woman with the bloody face. She'd recovered immediately from the surprise of their arrival and turned to face him squarely, feet planted, palms open at her sides, a wholly masculine pose. And now Stélios understood, as the woman's face transformed in his sight to a man's, round and apple-cheeked, with a shock of black hair and fog-grey eyes.

So this was him. The magician, the Beast of Vóunos. The one who sacrificed women and children, who made deals with the devil. After a lifetime, here he was, resurrected on this holiest of days in blasphemous parody of Christ's own resurrection. Although Stélios had suspected—no, he'd *known*—this would happen, the reality shook his faith to the core. How could Christ and all the saints permit this? Why did God suffer good men like Father Tákis to die and allow men like this to breathe His good air? And leave him, an old, tired fool, to face such evil alone.

He trembled, and not only with the cold.

The man by the sofa was starting to rise. The young girl was edging away, looking wildly about, as if she might shatter into naked hysterics at any moment.

Stélios's hand shook as he raised his battle crucifix and began to intone the prayer reserved for these extremes. His voice began small, wanted to crack; he forced it to grow and resonate.

As the words of the prayer poured from him, the woman—the Beast—laughed. He turned to the man on the sofa and helped him up. He said something in English, of which Stélios understood little. Something, from his glance, about the girl, who was now backed up against the window.

The man by the couch moved quickly. In three long steps he was in front of the girl, grasping for her arm. With a curse, Katsélis appeared on Stélios's left, moving to help her.

The magician raised his arms and made a sudden gesture with both palms towards Stélios, as if bouncing a large ball towards him. A shock of air, a concussion—

Stélios was on his back in the doorway. His head rang. His body felt like lead. He raised his head, placed his hands—he'd lost the crucifix—on the floor to push himself up.

With an angry shout, the young girl lashed out, kicking and punching at the man trying to grab her. He dodged the kick, but she stepped forward and caught him a punch square in the face, knocking him back. She ran forward, stooping to the ground near where the captain was getting to his feet.

Stélios resumed the prayer, louder. The girl thrust his crucifix back into his hand and reached under his arm to help him up.

Stélios kept chanting, his attention on the magician, the crucifix raised before him like a flaming brand as he struggled to rise. In the wall of hurt that his back had become he felt a tickle of power, like a lick of flame at the very base of his old spine. It warmed instead of burning, brought strength instead of pain.

The man from the sofa had recovered now and stood close by the bloody-faced magician, glaring at them. The magician simply watched as Stélios and the policemen—they'd been knocked down too—got to their feet. A smile played on the Beast's blood-crusted face.

"Very creditable." The words, spoken in clearest Athenian Greek, came strangely deep from the woman's lips. "You have courage, Father. But there's nothing you can do here, and your prayers have no power."

Though the words were for Stélios, the magician—his-her face was beaded with sweat, as if his possession of the body and perhaps even his defense against Stélios were costing him some effort—kept glancing at the girl. The young policeman, Pétros, had moved protectively in front of her, the pistol in his hand pointing in the direction of the magician.

Stélios finished the prayer and launched directly into his own invocation, playing his last, strongest card. If it failed, the backlash of forces would kill him; and even if he succeeded, the effort might cost his old life. No matter.

With his first words the magician seemed to waver before him, but then steadied. He said something to the man from the sofa, who nodded and moved towards them.

Katsélis was on his feet now. He stepped forward to stop the man, but the other was quick. Stepping inside the captain's guard, he delivered a rapid punch to the abdomen, then another; the captain doubled up with a cry of pain and fell to one knee.

"You're too late, Father", said the magician. "These three are mine. Let the girl go and take your policemen—we mean no harm to you or anyone else. In a few hours we'll be gone and will never trouble this island again."

"Monster!" shouted Pétros. The pistol came up to aim directly at the Beast just three meters away. "No harm? You take people's bodies and—"

Stélios turned to stop him, but the man from the sofa was faster. He leapt forward, shoving the priest aside to reach Pétros. Pétros caught the movement and swung the gun around.

The shot, deafening in the closed space, drowned out Stélios's desperate cry.

‡

Elléni stared disbelievingly at the horse's head taking shape in front of her. Not a horse, not really…though it looked very much like one, there was something she couldn't put her finger on which made it quite something…else. The horse's head seemed impossibly large, large enough to blot out its body if it had one, and yet it didn't feel close enough to do that. And the contours of that muzzle, the geometry, were all wrong. There was some trick, some strange distortion that made it impossible to see the rest of its body or anything else, if there even was anything to see in this horrible place-not-a-place. She shrank inside herself in a paralysis of fear.

She'd died. Of that she was certain. The undead magician had exploded like a bomb in her head, driving her—or whatever was left of her—into that terrible dark tunnel. She'd read about near-death experiences, in which people spoke of hurtling down a tunnel into the white light; though she'd found the idea comforting, she never for a moment believed it. No, death was something final, a clean break, the end of self, mind, consciousness. She didn't believe in a soul or spirit of any kind. If there was energy that left the body, it simply dissipated back into the air or dirt. From being to nonbeing, that was all.

So what was *this?*

CHAPTER FORTY-TWO

Alex hadn't understood a word that had been spoken, didn't care.

She saw the gun swing their way, saw the brief flash from the muzzle. The ear-shredding *crack* of the shot made her deaf to her own scream as Paul crumpled forward onto the ground at the priest's feet, almost close enough to touch. Blood, thick and bright, began to ooze from under him, pooling and steaming on the wood floor, precisely outlining each new board it crossed as it spread.

Shouting, *"No!"* she dropped to her knees, everything else forgotten. She slid an arm under his shoulders, vaguely aware of the old priest's chant resonating above them, and tugged at Paul's belt with her other hand. Somehow she got him onto his back. Icy fingers raked her heart as his eyes stayed shut and his head lolled, flopping on his neck. *Pale as a fucking ghost.*

But he was breathing! Heavy, ragged breaths—but breaths!

Now she had him on his back, she could see where he'd been hit. It was hard to tell with all the blood, but the bullet appeared to have caught him in the left side, low down on the ribcage.

"Paul!" she yelled. "Paul! Talk to me, dammit!" Forcing herself to breathe, to *think*, she tried to remember what little she knew of first aid. She put her hand on the area—*oh God, the blood was so hot!*—and applied pressure, looking around for something with which to better staunch the flow.

Someone was shouting in Greek. The older guy, the one who'd taken the punch in the stomach, was kneeling beside her. He stripped off his jacket, quickly folded and handed it to her, indicating she should press down.

The shouting was coming from the younger man. He had the gun pointed at Elléni or the magician or whoever the fuck it was, but with his pistol arm shaking like that he was likely to miss at any range.

He didn't get time. The jacket guy, now on his feet, grabbed the young guy's wrist and bent his arm up, yelling something. He reached for the pistol with his other hand, and the other let him take it without a struggle, all the fight suddenly gone from him.

The old priest's chant was rising. He'd stepped back a few inches to give her room, but still Alex and her wounded uncle were literally at his feet, directly between him and the Elléni-magician, just a few feet away. She was right in the firing line of whatever was being invoked.

The magician spread his feet, planting them like trees. Helpless to do anything but watch, Alex felt the strong urge to break into laughter, give way to hysteria, descend into the absurdist madness which her world had become. Just give in, let go, whatever. It would be so easy. But with her uncle unconscious, maybe dying, in front of her and her hands covered in his warm, sticky blood, she had to keep a grip.

Without taking her eyes off the magician, she bent close to Paul's ear and whispered, breath steaming in the icy air, "Paul! Don't give up! Come back, now! *Come back!*"

And now the magician was nothing like Elléni at all, and the urge to laugh evaporated entirely. It was still Elléni's body, but Alex found herself looking at someone—some*thing*—quite different. One moment he was a chubby man with red-apple cheeks and a mat of black hair; the next, a slowly twisting pillar of darkness whose space-black mouth tilted and wobbled menacingly towards them.

The magician's hands came up. Open palms curled in an obscene, coaxing gesture of invitation. She had a weird, fleeting vision of algebraic symbols and equations floating in the air, popping in and out of existence quicker than the mind could grasp. He spoke words, but the language was none she'd ever heard. His voice was a rich, ringing tenor, unctuous and deadly.

The two men who'd arrived with the priest stood spellbound, watching. The older one still had the gun, but it hung loosely at his side. Directly above her, the old priest's voice was rising in tone and power. The air in the room was suddenly thick and ropy, and she couldn't see clearly. The floor beneath them began to tremble, and she felt the magical explosion coming with the certainty of someone about to be struck by lightning. She closed her eyes as her skin tried to crawl off her.

Oh Jesus, no!

‡

As he tumbled toward the gaping mouth of that terrible blackness, Paul felt something pull at him, slowing his momentum. The pinpoint of self he'd become rocked and shook. A moment of wild disorientation and—

He was back in his head, in his skull, with the madman. Not that the madman saw him: the German was shouting and yelling, his essence ricocheting off the invisible walls with such unhinged energy that Paul had to fight to retain any kind of integrity or sanity himself and not just give himself over to total psychic collapse, which was what he most wanted in that instant. Every iota of his remaining self-awareness begged to let go, to be freed from bounds and limits and constraints, from thought and pain and responsibility, to careen howling with the madman, tearing through eternity like a comet blazing towards the sun. *Let go.* It would be so easy. *Just let go.*

As if from a lifetime ago, something whispered to him. It was vanishingly faint, a slender silken thread cast across hurricane-wracked seas, already almost out of reach—

He reached.

His body—his earthly body—lay in a small puddle of bright blood. Alex was on the ground, holding him, pleading with him. There were others, and strange forces; weird currents of colour and force wove and lashed around her, but she ignored them.

I love you, Alex. To even frame that was all he could do. It took all his focus, everything he had. Above and below, everything had gone to madness and ruin. He was tired. Hell, he was *dead.*

The thought was liberating. Finally, he could just let go.

Something slammed into him and he was back in his skull. The madman tore and screamed at him like a force of nature. But even as Paul fell back, something deep within, something long guarded and walled, snapped. He watched powerless, selfhood and id diving out of the way barely in time to avoid annihilation as an elemental fury long held inside exploded out of him and hit his enemy like an express train.

The madman's howl of rage filled Paul's world. As quick as it came, it died, swept away by the force of Paul's reflex attack. A wave of vertigo as Alex, himself, and that awful gaping blackness swallowing the speck that was Maule all occupied the same space, pulsing maxima-minima and strobing onoffheavenhellblackwhiteyesnolifedeath—

Paul gasped.

Cold air rushed into his lungs and pain throbbed hot in his side. His body was enormously heavy, yet a soft arm supported his neck and head without trembling or apparent effort.

He opened his eyes.

Alex was looking down at him, tears streaming from her eyes. There was a voice, chanting, and something was wrong with the air. It had substance, was somehow twisting, braided. The floor trembled and vibrated beneath them.

He smiled at her. "Hello Alex."

Her eyes widened. "*Paul!* Oh, God! I thought—"

Then the house shook, and everything went to hell.

‡

Dafyd was in full control now. The woman had been a good choice. The body was young, strong, capable of handling the power he would wield. Was wielding, even now.

The old priest had power, but not nearly enough. His nose had begun to bleed from the effort, and if the strain didn't kill him first, Dafyd would. He should have accepted Dafyd's offer to let him go free. It had been generous. Instead, the old fool had doomed himself and the two with him also.

The priest had ceased his prayers and launched into some unknown invocation or cantrip, his own perhaps. It didn't matter. The rules here were Dafyd's, the workspace bounded and constrained by the pact, the artifact still buried in the cellar. He could feel it from here, radiating power, linking this place to Hell. And though he could feel the operational window starting to close, it was long enough. They were operating in Dafyd's house, and now he would end it.

He'd lost Klaus, of that he was certain. Unfortunate but unimportant—the colonel had served his purpose. The shock of the gunshot had been too much for him, and between adjusting to the body and dealing with the priest, Dafyd had had his hands too full to prevent it. More puzzling was where Magda had got to. A mistake, perhaps, or last-moment fears. She was a real loss, would have been of great use to him as he resumed his work in the world. Together they could have accomplished so much. She might still turn up, but no matter. And Hell needed all the help it could get.

He called it to him, the mouth of Hell, the same that Nestor had used a lifetime ago to gobble them up and take them into service. In an instant the room was charged, the air heavy and cording with magic. The stone house trembled and shook.

Strange—that hadn't happened before. As quick as he framed the thought, he understood that the effect was a product of the warring forces he and his opponent had unleashed.

Dafyd squared his shoulders. With a spoken word of power he visualized the key in his mind and reinforced it with every ounce of his will.

So let it be written…

‡

It was now or never.

Magda saw that Dafyd had the priest—and what a formidable old man *he* was—fully engaged, and the power vibrating in the stone house was enough to make any transition effortless, a matter of the slightest will…for as long as it endured.

And it wouldn't endure long. The window was closing, the machinery of the spheres cycling. Whether Dafyd prevailed or not, in a few moments the way would be closed, the spheres sundered, and she'd be sucked back into Outer Hell.

Magda focused her attention on the girl, Alex. It was time.

In the moment she willed herself down and in, Magda understood, and froze. It wasn't possible, *couldn't* be—but it was. It was real, and it would be the end of her.

The girl was too close to the priest, almost touching him, protected by and even part of the enormous power that he was in this very instant channeling and preparing to wield, swordlike, against Dafyd. Magda might get in, but even if she did there was every chance she'd be bounced out, either by the sheer power or by conscious attack from one or both of them. She knew her own limits. She was a seer, not a fighter, and with the forces the priest was drawing down, Magda didn't rate her chances.

But right beside them, a few steps away...

The younger man was barely there, slack-jawed and staring, utterly overwhelmed by what he was witnessing. His defenses were down, his will at zero.

In the instant Magda made the decision, she acted. She slipped down and in, stealing into the man's body like slipping into a fresh-made bed with the covers turned down.

The man was fuddled, his thinking loose from drugs and drink and his complete inability to comprehend what he was seeing. But his body was young and strong.

The moment was perfect. With everyone nearby intent on the drama playing itself out between Dafyd and the old priest, she coiled herself around the young man's psyche, gathered all her strength, and squeezed.

It took no time at all. By the time he realized what was happening it was too late, and she was in full control. Even as she assimilated all he was and felt the ground solid beneath her, he was beyond hope of recovery. She saw him recede in her inner vision, tumbling away into darkness with a silent scream, well on his way to meeting Nestor.

How sweet and fresh was the taste of air.

CHAPTER FORTY-THREE

Despite the terrible cold in the room, Stélios felt the sweat trickling down his sides and the sticky blood from his nose flowing over his mouth. The air in the room had become thick and acquired a ropy, twisting quality.

The Beast before him—Stélios no longer saw the woman's body now but the true figure of the undead blasphemer who'd stolen her form—struck a pose and made a gesture of power. The room rang as if with the tolling of a giant bell. A sinister whorl of darkness began to materialize behind the Beast, filling the space from floor to ceiling and limning the magician in an impossible dark light.

The mouth of Hell.

It thickened and grew, the darkness becoming more solid. Sparks and points of light of no colour known on Earth flickered within its slow-turning depths, and Stélios could feel the pull from it. It was slight at first, a child's fingers plucking at his robe, but growing. Stélios strengthened his chant, blinking against the sweat dripping from his forehead. He wiped the blood from his mouth and chin with the back of his left hand, keeping the crucifix as steady as he could in his right.

The pull of the mouth grew stronger, so that Stélios had to place one foot forward and brace his body, pulling his spine taut, leaning slightly back against the rising force. He was aware of the wounded man at his feet rising, aided by the girl. Didn't they *feel* it? Or was it just he that was going to be sucked away into Hell?

He couldn't resist this for long. The crucifix thrust out before him felt tiny and useless against the power of this monster who could call forth the mouth of Hell. Stélios had always believed God to be the greater force, the one against which no evil could stand. Why then was he so powerless now?

O God, give me strength to banish this monstrosity! Take my life, but spare these others.

A sudden movement, and unseen forces snatched the crucifix from his hand. Even as he heard it clatter to the ground, the pull from the mouth doubled and Stélios felt himself sucked violently forwards. He stumbled, almost fell. And then the young girl—seemingly immune to the pull of the mouth—was in front of him, palms against his chest, steadying him against the deadly suction.

Over her shoulder he saw the wounded man take two quick steps forward and thrust a crucifix—his battle crucifix—hard against the Beast's breast.

A shriek curdled the already roiling air. A primal, visceral expression of horror, fear, and madness, the cry went on and on, reverberating in the room, turning his guts to ice. But the young girl was strong, and held him firm against the draw of that hungry blackness. And now, even before the Beast's cry faded, Stélios felt the pull begin to diminish, as if the sucking power of that dark mouth were wholly occupied with the imploding power of the magician.

‡

The horse's muzzle opened, revealing darkness so black it was a hole in the universe. Elléni's every sense broadcast terror, but she had no body, no nerves, to act on the fear. The black void grew, filling all her vision. She couldn't move, couldn't cry out, couldn't do anything but stare into the yawning void which she knew was about to swallow her whole. And then? She was already dead, and in any case was powerless to resist. She steeled herself for whatever was coming.

This place that wasn't a place, this place that was all *wrong*, seemed to eddy and pulse. The darkness receded a bit, and now she could see around the horse's head again, where lancing colours tore and pushed at the shifting, opalescent soup of the non-place.

She felt more than heard something she interpreted as a scream, and sensed something falling toward her through the dense medium. A human shape, a man—

Him! Jones, the magician, the one who'd cast her out. He tumbled past her, clawing and grasping at the soupy non-air, mouth wide in a scream that seemed as far as the stars yet close as skin. In the instant his eyes met hers, she saw the terror in them.

Then he was gone.

She felt herself pulled again, but this time the horse grew smaller, smaller, and she was rushing headlong though a dizzying void, faster and faster until—

She stopped.

Something had stopped her. There'd been no impact, no deceleration, she'd just…stopped.

She felt suddenly warm, heavy, and terribly tired. She opened her eyes.

‡

Dafyd's scream followed him as he streaked along a narrow, suffocating bore of strangeness. Just as the friction and pressure became unbearable and he felt himself about to be extinguished, the monad of selfhood which he had become burst free. The pressure was gone, and all sense of movement ceased.

He'd been here before. The swaying, shifting nature of the medium, the impression of ponderous, reciprocating masses, the sparks and lances of colour…

The ambient darkened, thickened. Somewhere a great bell tolled. Somewhere, something shrieked like an ape. A burning radiance and the grainy, searing touch of heated iron flooded his consciousness, though he had no senses, no body.

And before him, filling his world, were the impossible, immeasurable planes of Nestor's dark muzzle, lips curled back to reveal powerful incisors.

The horse's coal–black eyes burned into his soul. <Well. The contract is filled. And here you are.>

Fear like shards of frozen glass pierced Dafyd's being. He reached out for Magda, for Klaus—but the three-in-one was long gone. He was alone.

<This is wrong! It's *her* you want, the woman, Elléni. I had her—>

<You had her, but you failed.> Something close to amusement, even laughter, but tinged with infinite malice, radiated from the horse-thing. <You lost, little man. You underestimated.>

The horse's muzzle drew closer, and now Dafyd felt the pull from the gaping pool of blackness between those great, flat teeth.

<*No!*> he implored. <*No! The pact said*—>

<Arrogant little human! You presume to command me? The pact said three for three. The conditions are met.>

The muzzle opened wide, and before Dafyd could frame another thought he was sucked into the void. The darkness didn't last. With the sense of parting of a curtain, he found himself again surrounded by the red, raw chaos of Outer Hell.

Blast-furnace heat seared, serrated blades ripped. A force like molten mountains bore down on him, crushing and smearing the irreducible atom of being he'd become. All around him, the host of the demonic and their minions, demi-demons like himself, souls damned for one or other reason to hold the line for all eternity, buckled and rippled before the onslaught of the enemy. And underscoring his agony was the knowledge that there would be no death, no welcome oblivion, no hope of delivery at the end. Only this mind-shredding, white-hot pain until the collapse of the universe.

‡

"Thank God," said Paul. "I thought…I thought we'd lost you."

He was kneeling beside her, one hand holding hers, the other holding her head off the floor. Even pale as she was, with her hair wild and cheeks torn and bloody from where she'd clawed them open, she was the most beautiful thing in the world.

Alex and the captain had helped the priest over to the sofa, where he'd more or less collapsed, utterly spent. The captain had called the ambulance, and the young policeman who'd arrived with Katsélis had torn up a fresh sheet and bound Paul's wound, working with a quick efficiency which surprised him. The boy stood close by now, looking down at Elléni and smiling benignly. He seemed strangely calm and unaffected by it all, almost serene.

Elléni smiled up at Paul and squeezed his hand. Her other hand went to her cheek, and she winced, her whole body tensing "Ah! What—"

"It's okay. You hurt yourself trying to resist him. It'll heal."

She frowned, but seemed to accept it. "Is it over?"

"Yes. They're gone. It's over."

As she took in his bare chest, a puzzled look crossed her face. Then she noticed the linen wrapped around him and the spotting of blood on the pad. She struggled to sit up. "Paul! Are you—"

"Sh, shh." He put a hand on her shoulder to try to keep her calm, but she wasn't having it. She half sat up on one arm, gently touching the pad on his side with the fingers of the other. He winced, and she pulled her hand away.

Oh, God, Paul—"

"I'm okay, really. The bullet just ripped my side, don't think it hit anything major." He'd been lying on the floor, his body collapsed, when Maule had exited, probably thrown out by the shock of being shot. But once Paul was back and understood what was happening, he was able to get up and act. The wound burned like hell now, but he hardly felt it at the time.

Her eyes brimmed with tears. She sank back down and he felt her relax, letting her head sink back against his hand. "And it's warm again."

"Yes. The cold went the instant you came back." He smiled down at her.

She held his eyes, and the shadow of a smile began to form on her lips.

"Paul?" she said.

"Yes?"

"Kiss me, will you? And don't let me go again."

CHAPTER FORTY-FOUR

It was almost five by the time they got back from the island's little clinic, where they'd dressed and stitched up Paul's wound and taken care of Elléni's torn cheeks. They wanted to keep Paul in bed for a day or two but he wasn't having it. The weather had cleared and the predawn sky was brilliant with stars and a high-riding waning moon.

"Omigod," said Alex, "what a sky!"

Paul, more than a bit stupid from the morphine they'd given him, chuckled. The resilience of youth. But his niece was one in a million. So much strength and spirit. "Next thing you'll say all the horror was worth it just to stay up and see this."

She laughed. "I wouldn't go that far. And I'm sooo ready for bed." She turned to Elléni, whose bandaged cheeks made her look like a hamster. "What time do we need to be at your folks' house?"

"I shall be there early," but you can come at about eleven, even twelve?"

"That'll work," said Paul.

"And of course you will bring *o Pápas Stélios,* yes?"

"*Sígouros,*" said Paul. Certainly. Alex had been adamant on giving the old priest—who was close to complete collapse from fatigue—her bed, insisting she'd sleep just fine on the couch. "Goodnight, sweetheart," said Paul, as he hugged her. "Thanks for all you did. You were just incredible."

Elléni took her turn, holding onto Alex for a long while before she let go and followed Paul upstairs.

‡

The Easter celebration at Mikró Kástro was an eye-opener for Alex. All the stories she'd heard and movies she'd seen about how Greek families partied were true to the last detail.

There were probably forty people there under the warm sun. Several folding tables had been pushed together to make one long table covered in bright-patterned tablecloths. Everything was wonderfully rustic and informal, from wine served in the plain small tumblers the tavernas used to the mismatched chairs and plates. Aromas of woodsmoke and herbed lamb filled the air—the smells were making Alex's stomach rumble and putting a razor edge on her appetite—and there was laughter all around. Wizened old women in black sat next to apple-cheeked children while the men smoked cigarettes and tended to a pair of spitted lambs. Most of the younger women were busying themselves in the kitchen, where bowls and platters of vegetables, rice, olives, salads, cheese, breads, sweets, and fruit covered every surface and spilled over onto the dining room table.

Elléni's parents welcomed Alex and Paul warmly, making a particular fuss over Alex. They'd all agreed the previous evening, before even the cops left the house, to keep the entire episode a secret and bury the stone house's past once and for all.

Alex could see Paul was moving carefully, but at least his injury wasn't visible; poor Elléni, cheerful and spirited despite her bandaged cheeks, had concocted a story about being attacked by one of the island's hundreds of feral cats when she'd dropped a bag of trash into a bin outside her house and accidentally surprised it: the story seemed to fly.

Father Stélios was the star of the day. For the first half-hour after they arrived he was surrounded by Elléni's relatives and friends, and there was much laughter and more than a few tears of joy at seeing him back. Paul handed Alex a glass of wine, and they clinked glasses together, watching as the old priest chatted with a small group of older people.

"You were just amazing," he said. "We'd never have got through this without you." He put an arm around her and pulled her close. "Just promise me you're not going to join a cult."

Alex took a sip from her glass. The wine was lightly chilled, fruity, and wonderfully refreshing. "Actually, I was thinking I might start one." She laughed. "But seriously, Paul, I don't know. It's hard to dive into this stuff…religion, faith…without wondering. One thing I believe is that there's real good, and real evil. But whether it's confined to human beings or comes from something beyond us…." She shook her head.

His expression had turned inward. "Real evil." He wet his lips. "I certainly felt it."

And now she asked the question that had been on her mind since she woke up. "Last night…" she began.

He shot her a quick look over the rim of his glass, suddenly very present.

"No, I don't want to open it all up again. But one thing's been nagging at me."

He took a drink of wine and raised an eyebrow. "What's that, sweetheart?"

"Well, when you told me the story on the ferry, I know there was a woman with the magician, right? But she didn't show up did she?"

He frowned. "That's been bothering me too. The colonel attacked me, and Elléni got the big guy, but…" He gave her a searching look. "You didn't feel anything at all?"

"Uh-uh. Not a shadow."

"Hell, who knows?" He shook his head. "The main thing is they're gone. Father Stélios re-exorcised and blessed every bit of the house again this morning, including the cellar. It's over and done, *finis*." He drank the rest of his wine in one gulp and looked over at the old priest. Paul seemed to listen a moment to the conversation, then broke into a grin. "Everyone thinks he's coming back to replace poor Father Tákis and run Aghios Rigínos."

"Seriously, at his age? He's got to be ninety years old!"

Paul chuckled. "Yeah, But I think he's considering it. Look at that twinkle in his eyes."

And looking at Father Stélios as he drank and chatted as though nothing had ever been wrong in the world, just a few hours after he'd faced down an undead black magician and a revenant Nazi colonel, Alex thought her uncle might just be right.

‡

Captain Katsélis kissed his wife and thanked her as she brought him a cold beer. He sat in the warm sunlight of his garden turning the spitted lamb over the coals and savouring the simple joy of being alive.

The boy Pétros's declaration—delivered in the car last night immediately after he left the stone house—that he was going to leave the police force immediately had taken Katsélis completely by surprise. Though after what had happened it was probably for the best. The boy had acted irresponsibly, and it was a miracle the American hadn't been killed. As it was, Katsélis was going to have make up some story—God alone knew what *that* was going to look like—which didn't involve the supernatural. In any larger department he'd have already had to write up and submit a detailed report, but with it being Easter and with no superior here on Vóunos he had a small window of time in which to get creative. He'd work out something to keep the truth hidden. Fortunately the American was of the same mind, and had agreed to just tell the clinic staff it had been an unfortunate accident.

‡

Magda woke to a strange beat, like eerie music. For a brief instant she was entirely disoriented…then she remembered, and understood. She pushed back the bedcovers and answered the cellphone.

It was the boy Pétros's mother, boiling over with energy as she greeted him with the traditional Easter formula, *Xrístos Anésti*. Christ is risen.

"Alithos anésti, Mama," she replied without hesitation, fully in command of the departed boy's voice. *Truly he is risen.* She smiled as she spoke the words.

"Eh. For once you sound awake. Are you coming soon?"

"Of course, Mama. I'm just going to shower and dress, and I'll be there by ten."

"All right. And Pétros…" The woman hesitated.

"Mama?"

"I was just remembering last year. Please try not to argue with your father this year. I know he can be difficult, but he means well."

Magda laughed. "I promise, Mama. You can count on me to behave."

The woman sounded relieved. They said their goodbyes, and Magda hung up.

Well, well. The boy was no great loss to the world.

She turned on the shower and stepped inside.

The hot water felt incredible on her skin. There was so much to clean off.

What a remarkable world she'd been reborn into. With all the boy Pétros's memories accessible to her, she'd be able to keep up appearances and function well enough. Adjusting emotionally to this new, changed world would take longer of course, but she was intelligent and adaptable. She'd survived a lifetime in Outer Hell without going mad, so the technological and societal change here on Earth in the last seventy years, however far-reaching and dramatic, shouldn't present any special problems.

She'd have to be careful and correct while she worked off her week's notice with the police, didn't want to arouse suspicions. As with the family, it would mean acting strictly in character with the boy. Still, she didn't have to be the obnoxious pig he'd been. By now he'd have met Nestor and been pressganged into service, and good riddance.

Once the dust settled, she'd announce her desire to move and leave the island, perhaps even Greece. Time, perhaps, to return to Ireland. She could already feel the edges of the new power that came with her rebirth, and it wouldn't be difficult to acquire the necessary funds to set herself up for a good long while. A new identity—given the nature of today's world—that would be a little more trouble, but nothing a little ritual work couldn't fix. She'd buy a modest property somewhere on the west coast, County Cork, perhaps, and settle back into a life of study.

Rinsing the shampoo from her hair, she thought of Dafyd. It was unfortunate that he hadn't made it. Would he have had a better chance if she'd not delayed and then acted on her own? There was no way of knowing

Klaus, she didn't give a damn about. The time spent in Outer Hell had undone all the healing that had taken place in their time with him, and his thoughtless action in trying to prematurely possess a body had almost ruined their planning. And unlike her and Dafyd's goals, the colonel's obsession on conquest and world domination had been worthless.

But Dafyd…really, she'd deceived him, and now he was burning in Hell along with Klaus and the boy. Still, she felt no real remorse. He'd told her to take care of herself and she'd done exactly that, just as she thought he would have if their fates had been reversed. Three for three, the iron conditions of the pact had been met. And there'd been no other option but to hold back and steal into the boy's body while the others were distracted by the main event between Dafyd and the old priest.

Her intuition had saved her soul.

She turned off the water and stepped out of the shower. She reached for a towel and started to dry herself off, basking in a shaft of warm sunlight pouring through the open window.

Sunlight. Now there was a thing.

There was so much to understand about this magnificent cosmos. She couldn't wait to get started.

∞

AFTERWORD

To be kept informed of Dario's new book releases, please sign up at http://eepurl.com/6VSMr for automatic notification. We take your privacy very seriously: you will only be contacted when a new book or story is released; your personal details will remain 100% confidential; and you can unsubscribe at any time.

Reader support and word-of-mouth are absolutely vital for independent authors. If you enjoyed this book, please consider posting a brief review online, mentioning it on social media, and, of course, telling friends. Thank you so much.

ABOUT THE AUTHOR

Like most writers, Dario has lived several lives in one and enjoyed an eccentric career trajectory. He's worked in a warehouse, driven trucks, drag raced motorcycles, had a small import business, enjoyed a twenty-five year career as a decorative painter, and currently divides his time between writing and publishing.

Dario is also the author of *Aegean Dream,* the bittersweet true story of a year spent with his wife on the real "Mamma Mia!" island of Skópelos, and *Sutherland's Rules,* a caper-thriller novel about two lifetime friends who take off on a seriously dangerous last hurrah. His other works include *Free Verse and Other Stories,* a collection of six Science Fiction short stories, and several short fiction pieces. In addition, Dario is also the editor and publisher of three Science Fiction novella anthologies, The *Panverse* series.

To see a full list of his work with detailed descriptions, please visit the Panverse Publishing website at www.panversepublishing.com/books) or Dario's Amazon author page at http://tinyurl.com/qh4tb8r.

ADDITIONAL NOTES

1. In Greek, male names lose their final *s* when the person is directly addressed; so if I were asking someone called Stávros to join me, I would say, "Stávro, come and join me."

2. Since it's very difficult for an indie publisher to have separate editions for each territory, I made a conscious decision to use English rather than American spellings throughout this book. I hope my US readers will understand.

3. Although Vóunos, my fictional island, gets off lightly, the Greek nation suffered multiple horrors during the Nazi occupation. Not least of these was the fate of the Greek Jews, a larger percentage of whom were murdered in Nazi death camps than was the case with any other Jewish community. Between 60,000 and 70,000 Greek Jews, over 85% of the total, died in the Holocaust, most of them at Auschwitz-Birkenau.

IF YOU ENJOYED THIS BOOK...

...read on for an excerpt from Dario Ciriello's exciting 2013 novel, *Sutherland's Rules*.

What reviewers say about *Sutherland's Rules:*

"Sutherland's Rules is a fast mover, a real page turner"
"After just a few pages, this novel was impossible to put down"
"Sensational debut novel"
"An excellent read that left me wanting more"
"I found myself deeply involved with the characters"

Turn the page to read the opening scene of *Sutherland's Rules...*

DARIO CIRIELLO

SUTHERLAND'S RULES

Dario Ciriello

ONE

THE HELICOPTER was still circling, *woppa-woppa-woppa*, when Christian arrived. Peggy had told him about it when he phoned in.

It was Christian's habit as owner to arrive at work around nine-thirty, a small luxury he'd earned, damn right he had. Not that he even needed to call, which he did every morning at eight-thirty, because Peggy could perfectly well run things without him and after four years he trusted her implicitly. His morning check-in with her was a kind of guilty reflex, more to let her know *he* was on the ball than anything else.

Woppa-woppa-WOPPA as he opened the car door. God, the thing was loud, banking low over the water just a couple of hundred yards away, downdraft messing up the satiny, grey-misted sheen of the Sound. A boat out there, too: a Coast Guard launch holding position below the chopper, and was that black shape a diver? They'd found something, or were trying to. A whale, a body, bales of contraband—anything was possible. How could they stand it in the boat, the noise had to be deafening. Not to mention going into that water, dry suit or not, and the wind from the rotors beating at you and whipping up an icy chop. With early March frost still sparkling on the north side of the roofs, better they than he. He'd never been a fan of cold water.

Woppa-woppa-woppa. Christian was glad to close the door on it, first the outer, then the inner, which cut the racket down to a tolerable level. He had enough shit to deal with without that as well. He hated noise, and thank God for the double-paned windows and heavy insulation he'd installed. It had cost a fortune, but if you wanted to store perishable herbs, roots, powders and dried flowers thirty feet from the waters of Long Island Sound, good insulation and climate control equipment were mandatory.

Walking into the office always made him happy. The scent coming in off the street was like being transported into an exotic eastern fantasy land, and that was only the glassed-in office. The storeroom was something else altogether, a heady atmosphere of sensual, exotic, pungent, and mysterious aromas that caused visitors' eyes to widen in wonder when they entered.

He greeted Peggy and hung his coat and scarf next to hers. In the storeroom where Estefan packed and shipped all the internet orders, the bulk of their business, the kid caught sight of him through the clear partition and waved. Christian smiled and returned the greeting.

Jerking a thumb towards the door as he crossed to Peggy's desk, he said "So do we know what all that's about? It's like being in a bloody war zone!"

"Not a clue." She handed him a slim sheaf of papers as he walked up to her desk. "You got a letter. From England."

"A letter?" He did, right on top of the pile. It had British stamps on it. Christian never received any letters these days, just fliers and junk, and the statements and bills that some utilities and credit card companies still insisted on sending despite having talked him into electronic billing on the pretext this would help them save the planet. Receiving a letter was like traveling back in time.

He recognized the writing on the envelope at once. Billy, his best friend ever since his late teens. Only Billy would use the postal service for a communication in this day and age. Odd that he should send it to his work address, though.

"Did you hear the news last night?" said Peggy.

Christian's mood, which had momentarily rebounded, went back to its cellar. "Don't get me started." It wasn't the first time; there'd been previous calls for the FDA to regulate the twenty billion-dollar supplement industry, but they'd crashed and burned in the face of strong industry and public opposition. This time the pill barons had brought out the heavy artillery and come after his hide.

"It could have been worse," said Peggy. "I mean, even if it passes we have two years before the regs kick in, plenty of time to find new lines. And you can bet there are going to be appeals."

"I hope so. But it's a witch hunt, nothing less. We're just trying to make a bloody living, and the bastards want to close us down with their scare tactics and bullshit studies."

"It's a witch hunt all right," she said. And, straight-faced, "Be sure you hide the cat or they'll accuse you of having a familiar."

Peggy could always make him smile. He mock-swatted her with his unread *Times* and told her to get back to work.

In his own small office, Christian slit open the envelope with an antique, stiletto-style opener and fished out the letter.

There were four sheets, folded one inside the other. The outer three were blank; inside those was a single page, unencumbered by letterhead or even address or date lines. The hand was unmistakably Billy's, textbook British cursive from the mid-century, with a slight rightward lean and Billy's uniquely-formed cursive e: ε. Like the envelope, the note was written in plain blue ballpoint. It read:

Chris,

Remember that IOU I told you about years ago? It's come to life. Contacts are refreshed and it's time to collect. Can you come to London? I need your help. Don't delay.

Always,
Bill

He read the letter again just to be sure. Jesus. After all these years. He'd forgotten all about the IOU and the hash, but of course Billy hadn't. And Billy wanted his help? He shook his head in amazement.

Outside, the helicopter was still circling; he could just hear Estefan's music playing in the stock room.

No wonder Billy had chosen snail mail over email. It was the one means of communication not subject to electronic surveillance. Christian had read somewhere that even the best intelligence services had the greatest difficulty in ungluing and invisibly resealing an envelope, you often couldn't just steam them open; and the three blank pages, he guessed, were there to foil optical systems. Not that anyone would be interested in Christian's mail. He'd been a model citizen for almost forty years.

Billy was no Luddite, but his insistence on maintaining a low profile was an article of faith. When Christian last saw him, Billy had a loaded, gamer-quality desktop computer which he never hooked up to the internet; the connected one was a cheap laptop which he only used for email and basic web surfing—safe, vanilla stuff. Anything he considered at all sensitive he did on a library computer rerouted through one or more anonymous proxies, or from an internet café.

And, yeah: though the note would have meant nothing to a stranger, it was definitely sensitive. Which might be added reason for sending it to the office.

I need your help. Okay, but for what? How could he help?

In the small office kitchen, Christian took out a mug, then replaced it in favor of a cup and saucer. Simply receiving a letter from England had made him nostalgic for Things Prim and Proper. He reached for the coffee pot, decided on tea instead. Hell, go the whole way.

Peggy had bought a large tin of Walker's shortbread Petticoat Tails, his favorite. He took a couple, then two more, accurately arranging them on the saucer's edge two on each side, like fletching on an arrow shaft.

Back in his office, he closed the door, set the tea beside him on his desk, unfolded his *Times*, and let his eyes flick over the headlines. More US deaths in Afghanistan.

Afghanistan.

Well, no coincidence, the country had been in the news just about daily for an entire decade. But his eye wouldn't leave the word, and in the blaze of neurons, a circuit closed.

Contacts are refreshed and it's time to collect.

Oh, fuck.

Billy had to be out of his mind.

But he'd also been clear: *I need your help,* he'd written, and Billy never asked for help. He wanted Christian in London, now, and forget about discussing this other than in person: Billy didn't trust the phone any more than he did email and would just change the subject or play dumb.

Billy was his best and oldest friend, and Christian owed him, owed him big-time. He couldn't—wouldn't—refuse. He'd do anything for Billy.

Anything, except maybe something that would get them both killed.

No, this needed face time, and reason. Get some clarity and try to talk him out of it. He re-read the letter. *Contacts are refreshed*, that was the key item. Something had brought the past, almost forty years dead, to fresh—and, at least in Billy's mind, urgent— life.

But this was huge. Trying to talk Billy out of it would be like trying to stop the sun rising.

Christian sipped at his tea, ate all four shortbread fingers in rapid succession, and drained the cup. He navigated to the British Airways website and began checking boxes. Today was Tuesday. Carol was away till Sunday. The office was under control. He needed a break, and Peggy and Estefan could run things just fine without him.

He suddenly realized it was quiet outside. He turned to the window. Sure enough, the chopper had gone, replaced by the wheeling and crying of gulls. Far off to the left, a barge was just emerging from the grim, erector-set span of the Williamsburg bridge; further out, the mist-veiled, bar-graph bulk of Manhattan, which could have been the far shore of the Thames on any similar morning, triggered a visitation of images from almost a half century ago, a time so different to the present that it seemed another world.

SUTHERLAND'S RULES

"A smart, sexy, high-tech thriller"

Available in print and all digital formats
Also available as an audiobook from Audible

Panverse Publishing
www.panversepublishing.com

CPSIA information can be obtained
at www.ICGtesting.com
Printed in the USA
LVOW04s1605011215

464892LV00021B/1364/P